Death of a Riverkeeper

Arnold Gingrich

1903–1976

Faithful flyfisher and many-sided man of letters who loved books and fine writing, honored the lessons of Walton and Halford and Skues, worshipped music and its sister arts, fished with a mixture of skill and elegance and love, savored literature and the humanities and fine cuisine, committed himself totally to preserving our bright rivers tumbling swiftly toward the salt, heard the magic in their music, gloried in the quicksilver poetry of the fish themselves, and happily collected many things over many years—fishing tackle, paintings and sporting prints, books, antique motor cars, toys and miniature artillery pieces, elegant split-cane rods, exquisite vintages and rare violins, and a richly varied and celebrated circle of friends.

OTHER BOOKS BY ERNEST SCHWIEBERT

Matching the Hatch
Salmon of the World
Remembrances of Rivers Past
Nymphs
Trout

Death of

ERNEST SCHWIEBERT

Illustrations by the Author

a Riverkeeper

Introduction by Geoffrey Norman

Donald S. Ellis, Publisher, San Francisco

Creative Arts Book Company

1984

Grateful acknowledgement is made to the following for permission to reprint published material: "Oklahoma Sunshine" by Bud Reneau and Hal Bynum, Copyright © 1973 by Chess Music, Inc. & Buckhorn Music Publishers, Inc., BMI, P.O. Box 120547, Nashville, Tennessee 37212.

Published by Donald S. Ellis, San Francisco, and distributed by Creative Arts Book Company, 833 Bancroft Way, Berkeley, California 94710. This edition is published by arrangement with E.P. Dutton, 2 Park Avenue, New York, N.Y. 10016.

ISBN: 0-916870-72-3
Library of Congress Catalog Card No. 80-10824

CONTENTS

INTRODUCTION

On the banks of the Henry's Fork of the Snake River, just upstream from the Railroad Ranch, three men stand watching the water and eating lunch from a Styrofoam cooler—roast chicken, uncooked broccoli, carrots, bread and cheese, some white wine poured into paper cups. Four anglers are fishing this stretch of the river, all of them close against the far bank waiting to see a big rainbow take an ant from the water's surface. No one's catching fish.

One of the anglers finally makes his way back across the river, turning upstream so that he faces into the strong current. In five minutes or so he is across. He climbs the bank and walks past the three men eating lunch, then stops. He looks at one of the men and cocks his head a little, as though to verify his original sighting from another angle. He has a young face, very eager.

"Say," he says to the man he had been studying, "aren't you Ernest Schwiebert?"

"Yes, I am."

"No kidding."

"Nope."

The kid's waders are still dripping, and his floppy hat is pulled down over his eyes, giving him the shipwrecked appearance that trout fishermen have when they are out of the water. He examines Schwiebert for a minute. "You know," he says at last, "I just can't believe it. I really can't. I've been reading your stuff all my life. I mean it's like you're my *hero*."

Ernest Schwiebert, to his credit, laughs.

Every subculture produces its private stars, people who are

unknown to the rest of us but who are giants to the the aficionados. Pool shooters have theirs, no doubt; likewise bridge players and mountain climbers. Arnold Schwarzenegger was a god among body builders long before he became known to the rest of us. Among fly-fishermen, the best-known figure is almost certainly Ernest Schwiebert.

Schwiebert was still an undergraduate at Ohio State when he sold his first book some thirty years ago. It was called *Matching the Hatch*, a phrase that has entered the vocabulary of fishermen so solidly that some of them must assume that its origins are biblical, or at least go back to Izaac Walton. First editions of the book now sell for seventy-five dollars and more. Its publication led Schwiebert, who was studying architecture, into a second career. He has since traveled the world and fished its finest rivers, from the Test to the Rogue. He has fished and dined with all manner of celebrated people and has been written about in magazines as diverse as *Fly Fisherman* and *Town & Country.*

But Schwiebert is more than a man who fishes well and writes about it—though his admirers, like the kid in the floppy hat, can't understand why any man would want to be more. In the early Sixties, he took two doctorates from Princeton—one in architectural design and planning, the other in art history. By then he had published a second fishing book, called, to the dismay of some, *Remembrances of Rivers Past.* (He has no apologies for the title: "Hemingway said, 'If you're going to steal, then steal good.' Anyway, that is not the best English translation for Proust's title.") Schwiebert has written for the architectural journals and published a book called *Architecture in Search of Criticism* with Princeton University Press. For several years he was with a large New York architectural firm; now he has his own consulting operation.

One does not have to probe very deep to see two themes in Schwiebert's life: angling and learning. They are not antithetical or even exclusive; virtually anyone who has ever fished for trout seriously has begun to think of it as a form of inquiry. Trout fishermen collect insects and preserve specimens, identifying them by their Latin names. They take water and soil samples, keep logs and records, publish their findings, and engage in feuds over where credit should go for advances in learning. It is safe to say that no angler in history has ever taken all this more seriously or cultivated it with more dedication than Ernest Schwiebert.

"I've been here all morning," the kid says. "Fishing a renegade. Nothing."

"Well, that's a good searching fly, but searching flies don't work so well on this river. You need to find a feeding fish and figure out *exactly* what he's rising to. These are probably the most selective trout in the world." This is the central tenet of hatch matching—trout feed on specific insects at specific times, and to be successful, an angler's flies must imitate them as closely as possible.

"What's likely to work this time of year?" the kid asks.

"The green drakes are starting to come off," Schwiebert says. "But sometimes the big fish don't go for them. They mask a smaller hatch. Inermis, especially. In a week or two, we should be seeing flavilinea. That's a very good hatch."

When Schwiebert and others began to study mayflies intensively, they had to use Latin names, which strikes many fishermen as unnecessary and snobbish. "There simply weren't any popular names for the species we were coming up with," Schwiebert explains. "The Linnaean nomenclature was the only thing available."

After two hours, the kid is impatient, ready to use all that he has been told. "Listen," he says, "all this time you've been here and you haven't even rigged a rod. Aren't you going to fish?"

Schwiebert smiles. He has a wide, durable face, the face of an athlete, even a boxer—a strong chin, a thick ridge of bone above his eyes, and a broad smile. "Maybe later," he says. He opens another bottle of wine, pours, and says, "You've got to remember what Gingrich always said: 'The least important part of fishing is fishing.'"

Arnold Gingrich, whose interests were as varied as those of the magazines that he founded, managed to cherish fishing and to keep it in perspective at the same time. Schwiebert dedicated his most recent book, *Death of a Riverkeeper*, to Gingrich:

> Faithful flyfisher and many sided man of letters who loved books and fine writing, honored the lessons of Walton and Halford and Skues, worshipped music and its sister arts, fished with a mixture of skill and elegance and love, savored literature and the humanities and fine cuisine, committed himself totally to preserving our bright rivers tumbling swiftly toward the salt, heard the magic in their music, gloried in the quicksilver poetry of the fish themselves, and happily collected many things over many years—fishing tackle, paintings and sporting prints, books, antique motor cars, toys and miniature artillery pieces, elegant split cane rods, exquisite vintages and rare violins, and a richly varied and celebrated circle of friends.

Although he swore a blue streak when he was on the water, Arnold Gingrich was amiable and offhand when he wrote about fishing. It was a pastime; he made that clear. He and his type were gifted amateurs in the best sense.

Sometime after the Second World War, the Gingrich-like figures began to be replaced by a new kind of angler. Call them mechanics—they were interested in equations and not aesthetics. For them, catching fish was the whole point. They were aided by technological innovations. Glass and graphite replaced bamboo in rods. Nylon replaced silk in lines and leaders. The new equipment was both less expensive than the traditional and easier to understand and maintain. But it changed the spirit of the enterprise ever so subtly. The ancestry of bamboo rods is traceable to violin making. Graphite is a spin-off of the space program.

A new kind of fishing book also began to appear about this time, one that was completely uncluttered by anecdote or by description of woods and stream. No flesh-and-blood fishermen moved through these books. They were all technique and—following the example of *Matching the Hatch*—full of descriptions of insects.

But while Schwiebert could hold his own with the best of the mechanics and in some ways anticipated them, he was after something more. I remember reading an article he wrote for Esquire in the early Sixties called "Legend and the Letort," which detailed the innovations of a few Pennsylvanians who fished one of the limestone streams of that state and had come up with some new tactics and flies. I had never fished for trout when I read that story, but it made me want to. The story was typical of the gift that Schwiebert was cultivating in those days—an ability to synthesize the style of the old fly-fishermen like Gingrich and the best of what the mechanics were doing.

Schwiebert's efforts resulted, some twenty years later, in the publication of *Trout*, clearly his masterpiece, in ambition if nothing else. The book is almost eighteen hundred pages long, published in two slipcased volumes, and priced at seventy-five dollars. All the drawings and the colorplates are by the author. Everything that Schwiebert has learned about trout is there, and it is impossible not to be awed by the sheer encyclopedic accomplishment of the book. The writing is discursive and anecdotal and, for some tastes, far too rich. But, to Schwiebert's credit, he seeks to create a mood.

Increasingly, this exasperates the mechanics. His worst reviews have been in the most specialized fishing publications. An *Audubon* editor writing in *Field & Stream* and the reviewer for *The Washington Post* praised *Trout* just about without reservation. The review in *The Flyfisher*, though favorable, was not a rave. The same reviewer was downright hostile to *Death of a Riverkeeper*, while *The New York Times*'s Red Smith found the book a delight. One editor of a fishing magazine, a genuine admirer of Schwiebert's, says, "I think he ought to write fiction. He'd have a better vehicle for all that he knows."

The kid, much as he savors the presence of his idol, moves on and goes fishing. Schwiebert and his companions sit and talk and watch the river. Above them there is a screeching battle between an osprey and a bald eagle. It lasts for half an hour, both birds riding the high western thermals until the eagle gains a five-hundred-foot advantage in altitude. He folds his wings and begins to dive. The osprey breaks and runs before the sound of the eagle's shriek reaches the men's ears. The episode recalls all sorts of things for Schwiebert and his companions, and there is an hour of talk about birds of prey.

Finally, when the sun is beginning to settle and the sandhill cranes are coming over the river with their otherworldly ratchetting sound, the trout begin rising and Schwiebert decides it is time to get in the water and fish. He begins to work the large rainbows with the sort of concentration that you find among, say, great baseball hitters. For an hour he fishes and catches fish, some of them very nice fish, the kind many anglers will never catch in their lives. Still, he follows each cast intently and makes every pickup and new cast carefully and positively.

The sun falls below the mountains and the air is colder almost by the minute. The stars are the only light whiter than the snow that covers the peaks of the distant Tetons. It is almost full dark when Schwiebert quits. He has caught and released some ten fish. Out of the stream he notices the cold for the first time. He shudders, shucks his waders, and says, "Little whiskey will go just fine now."

He and his friends compare results. He has outfished everyone: "I had one real nice one. Twenty inches. Took that little sooty sedge. Used a number eighteen."

There is talk of dinner that night, the last on this trip. Tomorrow, Schwiebert leaves for home. He'll have a week before he is off to Iceland, where he will fish for salmon with the actor Richard Crenna in a segment of ABC's *The American Sportsman.* After that, Alaska. He may travel to Chile in the winter; he is a consultant on a park project there that is, he says, "twice the size of Yellowstone." And there are two long writing projects, as well as the business of his consulting group and some speaking engagements. Ernest Schwiebert is never idle—except when he stands on the bank of a stream, watching for signs of feeding fish.

Death of a Riverkeeper

THOUGHTS IN COLTSFOOT TIME

It is still raining softly this morning, after several days of false spring that started the coltsfoot blooming in the sheltered places. Deer are browsing through the oaks and beeches behind the house, their coats still the somber color of winter leaves, although the snow is finally gone. Grouse are drumming in the overgrown orchard, and it is almost time for fishing.

Coltsfoot is a spare, dandelionlike flower, and as with many other wild flowers, history tells us that the coltsfoot is an alien species. It traveled across the Atlantic with our colonial forefathers, since its tiny hoof-shaped leaves were dried and burned like incense to treat asthma and colds. Coltsfoot is found on the sheltered slopes and ravines that capture the late-winter sun, although only its bright blossoms are visible above the carpet of winter leaves this morning. Its flowers signal the weakening of winter, in spite of the bitter April weather, and in my library in these Appalachian foothills my thoughts are filled with boyhood summers in Michigan.

My first memories of fishing are there, in a simple cedar-shingle cottage among the hardwoods and pines, fifty yards above a lake that shimmered in the August sun.

Lily pads filled its shallows, turning over lazily and drifting in the hot wind that smelled of orchards and cornfields farther south. Red-winged blackbirds called restlessly in the marsh. The lily pads were like the rowboats moored at the rotting dock, shifting and swinging in the wind until their stems stretched and pulled them back like anchor lines. The hot wind rose and stirred each morning, offering no relief from the weather.

The boats were poorly maintained, with peeling paint and rusting oarlocks and eyebolts. Their wrinkled seams desperately needed caulking. Moss-colored water surrounded a half-drowned bailing can in the boat that went with the cottage. The other rowboat was filled with water. Its wainscoat bottom rested on the mud in the planking shadows of the pier. Its middle seat sheltered a small colony of tadpoles hiding in its anchor cord.

The hot wind dropped and died. Locusts started their harshly strident cadenzas in the trees, and the little lake was a tepid mirror at midday, its still surface marred only by the restless hunting of its clear-winged dragonflies.

My mother was sleeping in the bedroom upstairs. Our family had rented the cottage for the month, and my father planned to complete a textbook he was writing, but the fishing interrupted his daily schedule. The staccato of his typewriter on the screened porch filled our afternoon silences, and I dozed fitfully in the summer grass, thinking about the ice cream the farmer's wife made across the lake.

One morning when we went for eggs and milk, I watched the farmer's wife working with her tubs and cracked ice and salt in the springhouse. While she stopped to wipe her face, she let me wrestle with the crank of her ice-cream maker.

It was a summer of sweet corn and ripe watermelon and cherries, mixed with fishing for bluegills and yellow perch and bass. But it was also a summer of poverty and poor crops, when the wheat farmers were driven from their homesteads in the high-plains states, and the duststorms soon followed. During those tragic years, my father and other college teachers were still employed. Small businessmen and major corporations and banks failed, and many factories and mills stood ominously silent. Many families in southern Michigan lost their orchards and house mortgages and farms, but that boyhood summer beside a lily-pad lake was strangely filled with riches.

It was perhaps the simple rhythms of our lives that sustained us through those Depression years, and the bass fishing was a critical part of our family rituals that summer.

My father usually awakened just before daylight, while mother still lay sleeping under the quilts, and climbed stealthily down the narrow stairs to the kitchen. Cooking smells of scrambled eggs and crumb-batter perch and sausages drifted through the cottage, and in spite of his efforts to let us sleep, there were always the grating scrape of the skillet on the wood-burning stove, mixed with the muffled clatter of cups and plates. The rich aroma of coffee lingered in the cottage long after his breakfast was finished.

Sometimes the lake was covered with fog, and I heard him collect the oars and fishing tackle from the porch. Sometimes he simply disappeared into the mist, carrying his equipment down toward the dock. It was delicious to lie there, only partially awake under the patchwork quilting, listening to the familiar sounds and rituals of his embarkation. Planking creaked when he reached the pier, the lures in his tackle box rattled when he placed it into the boat, its padlock chain rattled across the eyebolts and pilings and the oarlock rhythms marked his passage through the lily pads.

His fishing was a liturgy that I was still too young to share that summer, although sometimes he took me along to sample its secrets, and on those mornings I waited restlessly through breakfast with delicious shivers of anticipation.

We caught nothing those mornings, but I clearly remember the flashing handles of his reel, surrendering line as his lure arched out toward sheltering pockets in the tules and pickerelweed and lilies. Once there was a wild splash that engulfed his red-and-white plug, but the largemouth was not hooked, and when the summer ended it had been our only strike together. It was usually getting hot when we rowed back across the lake, and I sat happily in the boat, trailing my fingers in the water and listening to his strokes.

Textbook manuscript occupied the hours after lunch, and the rattle of his typewriter echoed across the lake. His work progressed well that summer, except for the brief disaster on the screened porch when a sudden storm scattered his pages across the wet floor. Late in the afternoons, his interest in history waned and his preoccupations ebbed, and we knew that he was thinking about the evening's sport when he started to sort through his tackle.

It was time to clean and lubricate his prized Pfleuger reel, its components lovingly collected in a saucer and sorted on the oilcloth-covered table. The weedless spoons and tiny spinner blades and wobble plates on his lures were carefully polished. Pork frogs and fresh pork-rind strips were cut with his fishing knife on a cheese board, and he patiently sharpened the nickel-plated trebles.

Supper was always early that summer, and when the shadows lengthened across the boat-pier shallows, it was time for fishing. My father gathered his equipment and loaded his boat, rowed out through the lily-pad channel, and began casting along the weedy shoreline. His fishing had its mixture of rhythms and rituals, and he seldom returned before nightfall. Sometimes it was completely dark when we heard his rowing, and I usually met him at the dock, waiting in the darkness while he secured its padlock. It was always exciting when he reached down to lift a dripping stringer of fish. There were usually two or three bass, and once we returned proudly along the path to the cottage while I held the flashlight on a six-pound largemouth.

It remains a special summer in my mind, rich with memories of swimming and bass fishing and sleeping on the porch, with the crickets and whippoorwills filling the night. It was a bucolic summer when my parents were still young, and mixed with such memories is a brief episode that took place on a grocery trip to Baldwin.

Our route into town crossed a trout stream, and my mother stopped the Oldsmobile just beyond the bridge when a solitary fisherman caught my eye. The little river flowed swiftly, tumbling past the timbers of the bridge, and there were mayflies dancing in the sunlight. Its riffles seemed alive over its pale bottom, where the cedar sweepers and deadfalls intercepted its glittering currents. The counterpoint of its river music filled the morning, its lyric images as sharply focused as yesterday after forty years.

The trout stream was utterly unlike the lukewarm shallows of the lake, tumbling clear and cold from the springheads in its cedar-swamp headwaters. Watercress thrived in the seepage places below the bridge, and the passage of the river only briefly touched the sunlight. Its ephemeral moments in the sun were quickly lost again in its sheltering cedars and willows. Its bright currents seemed startlingly alive there, collecting its rich palette of foliage and sunlight in its swiftly changing prisms, until their lyric threnodies seemed to promise a world of half-understood secrets.

The most pervasive memory of that summer remains the solitary fisherman working patiently upstream, the swift shallows tumbling between his legs, while the silk fly line worked its lazy rhythms in the brightness of that August morning.

It was the genesis of a lifelong odyssey in search of trout and salmon, a pilgrimage that started in Michigan, and has since carried me into the remote corners of the world. There are many happy echoes of those travels, memories embracing rivers and river people and the richly colored fish themselves, and with a cold rain misting through the black-trunked trees, thoughts of fishing and the butter-colored coltsfoot in the sheltered places help pass this season of discontent.

A TALE OF TWO HEMINGWAYS

The eagle circled lazily in the early thermals, where the river bottoms grow steadily more arid in the patchwork basin below Sun Valley. There are still a few irrigated ranches along the river, lying hidden in cottonwoods against the pale, wind-polished hills. Cattle and sheep forage on the sagebrush slopes. The cottonwoods are already sparse at Bellvue, and before the country road reaches Picabo, the valley is almost a desert between its sheltering hills.

It was still cool after our leisurely breakfast in Ketchum, and the morning light was soft on the mountains. There is little wind on such Idaho mornings, and the trees are turning yellow along the rivers after the first hard-frost nights.

Late summer is perhaps the best season for fishing Silver Creek, the famous trout stream thirty miles from Sun Valley, in a brief time of chill nights filled with glittering stars and warm shirt-sleeve mornings when the currents are covered with tiny mayflies. The wind stirs lazily through the mornings, gathering in the barley fields and scattering a bright confetti of leaves into the current.

Another melancholy morning in southern Idaho! Jack Hemingway waved his muscular arm jokingly at the cloudless skies. *Sometimes I think it's forgotten how to rain around here!*

Suits me fine! I said.

The basin opens gradually below Hailey, where the chalk-colored bluffs rise above the cottonwoods behind the town. There are potatoes and stubble fields and pastures farther down the valley, where intricately rigged irrigation sprinklers travel the bottoms like water sculptures, partially concealed in their changing rainbows of delicately misting spray.

The smooth sagebrush hills are straw-colored beyond their barley-field bottoms, where the narrow Gannett road reaches for miles across the table-flat floor of the valley. The basin is completely arid except for the irrigation channels that lie straight as a surveyor's line across the fields. When we left the county road, the pasture dust billowed out behind the station wagon, and was chokingly bitter in the nostrils.

It doesn't look like trout country, I said.

Hemingway stopped at a cattle gate. *It's trout country all right!* he observed while I unhooked the chains. *Wait until you see the* Tricorythodes *hatches on the water!*

Sounds pretty good, I said happily.

Ernest Hemingway was a trout fisherman all his life, and there are family albums that include a fading photograph taken along Horton Creek in Michigan when the writer was only five, and fished in a floppy straw hat with an immense split-willow creel suspended around his neck.

Still limping from the mortar wounds suffered at Fossalta di Piave, on the bitterly contested Italian front in the First World War, Hemingway spent an entire summer fishing in Michigan. Those experiences were later woven into his famous story "Big Two-Hearted River," and family history tells us that Hemingway was almost late for his wedding because he was trout fishing on the Sturgeon.

When he returned from the Spanish Civil War to work on his celebrated book *For Whom the Bell Tolls* in 1939, Hemingway chose to live and write at Sun Valley. It was not long before he discovered the shooting and fishing there along Silver Creek.

With friends like Gary Cooper, Ingrid Bergman, and Clark Gable, Hemingway soon came to love the fine bird-shooting in its valley. They floated its watercress sloughs for pintails and mallards, and hunted pheasants in its barley fields. Fishing was excellent too, and its fat free-rising rainbows soon made Silver Creek their favorite trout stream. The family tradition of fly-fishing still lives.

Jack Hemingway is his oldest son, and is such a dedicated trout fisherman that he sometimes fishes as much as 200 days a year. Hemingway still lives at Sun Valley, and since his boyhood summers there, he has considered Silver Creek his favorite too.

His writing went well here and Papa really loved it! Hemingway explained that morning along its headwaters. *It was full of big trout and its fishing was terrific!*

You mean the fishing went sour later?

Silver went downhill sharply after the Second World War, Hemingway continued. *People just fished it too hard.*

How did they fish it out? I asked.

They fished most of the season then, Hemingway explained. *Silver is too weedy to fish hardware and bait in the summer, but in the early spring before the weeds are growing, the fish are easily caught—they spawn much later in its headwaters and the spawned-out kelts are ravenously hungry and easy to catch. It's a pity to take them!*

Spawned-out and thin and foolish? I asked.

They're ridiculously easy then, Hemingway agreed, *but our fly-only regulations have turned everything around.*

It's unusual to find something getting better.

That's right, Hemingway nodded.

His father is buried at Sun Valley, but in a sense that Ernest Hemingway might have liked, his spirit still thrives there in his oldest son. Jack Hemingway is fifty-three, with the boisterous moods and insular silences found in some of his father's characters, and is unmistakably his father's son in his sport and philosophy and style of life. His resemblance to his father is quite striking, and remarkable enough that some Sun Valley regulars tell the story of the old Hemingway crony who encountered Jack Hemingway in the street, and stumbled pale and shaken into the Christiania bar, thinking that he had actually seen a ghost.

Jack Hemingway was the cherubic towheaded boy whom his father nicknamed Bumby, and who lived with his young parents in a cramped Paris flat above the courtyard sawmill in the Notre-Dame-des-Champs. Bumby and a baby-sitting cat christened for Scott Fitzgerald both passed into literary history in his father's posthumous collection of stories *A Moveable Feast,* which described their friends and their Paris world after the First World War.

During the Second World War, Jack Hemingway became an

infantry officer, and participated in the bitter fighting that engulfed southern France. His military career started in command of a military-police detachment that was guarding a compound under tight security, and when his troops reported a parade of military trucks arriving at his checkpoints, loaded with excellent French cheeses and freshly baked pastries and vintage wines, Hemingway became wildly curious.

Finally he confronted the training officer in command. *I'm not sure what you're doing in here,* Hemingway challenged in his excellent French, *but I've seen what you're eating and drinking—and I've decided I should be part of your operation!*

Hemingway was promptly recruited into an intelligence unit trained to maintain liaison with the French underground. He later parachuted into enemy territory with a fishing rod strapped tightly along the barrel of his machine pistol, and was finally wounded and captured on a mission behind German lines during the Battle of the Colmar Pocket. Hemingway spent the remaining months of the conflict in German prison camps, attempted several abortive escapes and actually reached Switzerland during one ill-fated adventure. His freedom in neutral territory was comically short-lived when an enterprising Swiss literally sold him back to his German captors.

Taught me something about profit, Hemingway laughed, *and it taught me something about people too!*

Hemingway literally explodes with his enthusiasms, and even his solitary moods along the river can dissolve into spirited cadenzas of whistling, echoing happily through the meadows.

His cycles of high spirits are probably checkreined with a modicum of self-control combined with his wife's good sense. Puck Hemingway is an Idaho girl whose father rejected Hemingway until he stopped fishing and tried steady work. He had worked sporadically before with the Winston rod-making company in San Francisco, but soon found it impossible to make a living selling tackle and went back into the army.

Puck wouldn't marry me unless I was really working, Hemingway explained, *and since I was always fishing with Winston rods instead of trying to sell them—the military seemed more sensible, and soldiering was really the only trade I knew!*

Hemingway later tried working as a stockbroker in Portland and San Francisco after leaving the military again, and finally returned with his family to Sun Valley in 1967. He has settled down enough to serve as elder in the church and teach languages in the local private school, and was appointed to the Idaho Fish & Game Commission. Between these duties, mixed with tennis and morning jogging and writing a book about his adventures in wartime France, it is increasingly difficult to get those 200 days on the stream.

The foothills are filled with partridges, pheasants, chukar, quail and sharp-tailed grouse. There are still plenty of ducks and geese. The high Sawtooth country still holds elk, bighorn sheep and deer, and this season Hemingway traveled north to hunt antelope with his half-brother Patrick in Montana. The shooting is less important than his fishing, and Hemingway counts his love of trout and fine tackle and flies as perhaps his best legacy from his father.

Papa primed me with a mixture of strategy and cunning, Hemingway explained. *He loved trout fishing, but he seldom took me along with his fishing friends—he waited a whole summer without letting me go, and then he gave me an old Hardy bamboo just when it was time to send me back to New York to school!*

Better than pushing a boy too hard, I said. *Sometimes a thing that is withheld becomes sweeter.*

Papa transformed fishing into something mystical and secret! Hemingway finished rigging his tackle. *Although I'm past fifty, I still can't get enough of it!*

Silver Creek is unique among our American trout streams. While there are many spring creeks in our western mountains, none of the others can match its character and volume of flow. Silver is perhaps less dramatic than the Firehole at Yellowstone, with its spectacular hot springs and geysers, but Silver has its own secrets.

The Firehole exists in a relatively high alpine basin, like the Henry's Fork of the Snake, in its lodgepole country fifty miles farther west. The Firehole is one of many exceptional fisheries that are born in the Yellowstone and Teton country.

Silver Creek is startling in less obvious terms. Its ecology parallels the storied British chalkstreams of Hampshire and Wiltshire, where fly-fishing blossomed five centuries ago. Silver is startling because its swift-flowing springheads rise without prelude or warning from a flat valley floor that would literally remain an alkaline desert without its remarkable life-giving springs.

Hydrologists believe that these giant springheads are echoes of ancient river channels, and are still fed by seepages from the Big Wood, which drains the basin below Sun Valley. Its primordial drainages once flowed southeast, between the barren mountains and the volcanic Timmerman hills, draining toward the Snake across the deserts below the Craters of the Moon. Its Pleistocene channels were subsequently erased in gargantuan eruptions of lava, filling the ancient riverbed between Bellvue and Gannett and forcing the Big Wood into fresh fault-block channels and fissures farther west. These eruptions were relatively recent, measured in terms of geological time, and completely transformed the character of the region.

Some zoogeographers argue that aquatic life was probably eradicated during these flowages of molten lava, and that extensive reaches of ancient river were reduced to boiling water and steam. Such theories are corroborated by the oral histories suggesting that Silver Creek held no trout or whitefish in frontier times. Since the distribution of fish species largely occurred in the glacier-melt of the late Pleistocene period, it is possible that these seismic and volcanic eruptions did erase the aquatic life in the ancient watershed, and that they were empty of fish when the waters cooled again.

The basin is a remarkable aquifer in our time. Its immense deposits of alluvial basin-fill lie over a bedrock structure of fractured lava and fertile sedimentary geology. Whatever the subterranean roots of these remarkable springs, and their startling volumes of flow, it is still the soils chemistry and Stygian character of the entire valley that combine to create Silver and its unique ecology.

Soils chemistry in its headwaters is so alkaline that it reaches the threshold of toxicity for some agricultural use. Well-meaning fishermen have continually attempted to introduce trees along its grassy banks over the years, and have been baffled when the soils chemistry killed them, while the ambient stands of aspens and cottonwoods continue to thrive. Freshly tilled acreages on adjacent ranches are permitted to lie fallow for a season or two, simply working and reworking the earth without planting, while precipitation and exposure to the atmosphere leach out the toxic alkalinity. Such agricultural practices have greatly multiplied the erosion there, and both wind- and water-transported sediments in the drainages are perhaps the most critical problem affecting Silver Creek today.

The subsurface hydrology is fertile too. The bedrock underlying its drainage systems combines sedimentary limestones and phosphates with porous lava and river aggregates. Other hidden sources of rich alkalinity are possible, such as hydrothermal fissures in the river bottoms below Sun Valley itself, and other subterranean factors like marl deposits. Each of these factors ultimately affects the water chemistry of Silver Creek and its springheads, leaching their alkalinity from twenty-odd miles of subterranean geology.

The combination of such latent fertility with relatively stable volumes of flow is remarkable. Its echoes are obvious in the rich growth of elodea, watercress, stoneworts, ranunculus, cattails, tules, water lilies, veronica, potamogeton, and chara that distinguish Silver Creek from a typical western trout fishery, with its slightly acid currents tumbling steeply from snowfields above the timberline. Such fertility is also obvious in its dense populations of fish life, both its trout and its coarse-fish species.

Since the springheads are relatively constant in both temperature and volume of discharge, the watershed is a sanctuary for wading birds and waterfowl during both late-summer drought and winter ice. Its fly life and fish both thrive and enjoy rather stable rates of growth, because water temperatures that remain close to their optimal range of metabolic temperatures sustain aquatic life perfectly, and shelter its populations from the sixty-percent factors of winterkill that decimate both fish and fly hatches in most streams.

Bird life and trout are both supported by the exceptionally diverse population of food-chain organisms. Fish-eating birds and predatory trout both thrive on a surprising abundance of frogs and baitfish, and virtually each of the aquatic species is sustained by the incredible numbers of aquatic insects and tiny crustaceans. Other birds congregate along the stream, competing with its predatory swarms of dragonflies for hatching clouds of mayflies and sedges. These exceptional fly-hatch populations are sustained by fertile densities of zooplankton and phytoplankton, and sheltered in the fertile growths of aquatic vegetation that undulate in its gentle flow.

Yet each of these factors is only a symptom in itself, echoing the fertile soils and water quality in the drainages, and the rich bottom sediments that collect in its depths.

Silver is really amazing in the spring! Jack Hemingway observed on its headwaters that morning. *There are red-winged blackbirds quarreling in the cattail marshes with our yellow-headed species, geese clamoring for nesting sites, cattle and sheep in the pastures with young calves and lambs, bees gathering pollen in the wild flowers, trout rising everywhere, all mixed with the sounds of the stream—it's the unique music of Silver Creek!*

Since the stream remains relatively open in winter, at least above the irrigation hatches and impoundments, the old Sun Valley property is a refuge for extensive population of wintering ducks and geese. The big marshes in its Stalker Creek headwaters have been extensively drained since the Second World War, and their vast populations of wintering birds have been forced to use the remaining habitat downstream. When the rivers and reservoirs in southern Idaho freeze tight, these springhead flowages are sometimes the only ice-free refuge in hundreds and hundreds of miles.

Summers on Silver Creek provide optimal nesting conditions for several avifauna, and both ducks and geese particularly love its marshy banks and sloughs. Plover and sandhill cranes and curlew are plentiful too. There are gyrfalcons and red-tailed hawks and terns. Golden eagles are plentiful, and surprising numbers of bald eagles arrive in the winter months. Ospreys and kingfishers thrive too, with populations of marsh hawks and kestrels and prairie falcons. California gulls share the watershed with goshawks and burrowing prairie owls. Sandpipers and yellowlegs and kildeers are migratory visitors, along with substantial numbers of snipe. Wilson's phalarope loves these Idaho bottoms before its autumn odysseys into the pampas of Argentina.

But perhaps the most remarkable example of its thriving bird life lies in a stand of aspens in its headwaters, which shelters a thirty-nest heron rookery at Sullivan Slough. Some fishermen resent these gracefully solemn birds, but their diet consists more of frogs and meadow voles and mice than of fish life, and field studies suggest that the trout in their present diet consist more of foolish hatchery fish than of the surviving wild strains.

Herons eat some trout, Hemingway admits ruefully, *but the herons are so beautiful that even a hardcase trout fisherman like me has to grant them the rainbows they get!*

Suckers and whitefish are easier to catch, I agreed.

That's probably true, Hemingway agreed. *Any trout they catch was a foolish fish that probably deserved culling.*

Silver Creek has received extensive plantings of hatchery rainbows over the past fifty years, and these stocks are principally hybrid mixtures of several landlocked and anadromous strains, artificially created through modern fish culture. The fishery is restricted to the headwaters by the desert heat downstream on the Little Wood. Unfavorable summer temperatures there prevent the downstream migrations typical of hatchery rainbows.

Other problems have evolved with the breeding of these hatchery hybrids. Fish culturists have shaped them like poultry, attempting to attain the most growth in the shortest possible time and at the lowest cost. Such criteria are wholly admirable in poultry production, and perhaps for trout intended as restaurant and supermarket fare, but they have resulted in fish poorly suited to survive after they have been planted in a wild habitat.

Early selection for spawning and hatchery production schedules has created another nightmare, since it has created an artificial strain of rainbow that attempts spawning in the fall. Such behavior is puzzling in a species that nature conditioned to spawn in the spring, and is hardly useful for survival in the wild.

Still other echoes of such hybrid selection are troubling. There are startlingly reduced numbers of eggs in mature hatchery females, and their percentages of fertility are reduced too. Perhaps the most unhappy effect of these fish-culture practices is the truncation of their average life spans. Wild rainbow strains enjoy life spans averaging six to eight years, but these hatchery rainbows have lost such longevity, and three-year-old specimens are rare.

Crossbreeding between existing populations of wild fish with the survivors of hatchery plantings only dilute the genetic integrity of their offspring. Such denigration of our fisheries has been a tragic echo of modern trout management everywhere.

Yet the resident populations of the Silver Creek headwaters, and the surviving stocks on several private ranches, still bear strong traces of their origins in the fine McCloud strain native to northern California. These superb nonmigratory rainbows, originally found only in the McCloud watershed, were perhaps our most valuable subspecies, although hatchery mixing with migratory steelhead strains occurred surprisingly early in our hatchery programs. The first stockings in Silver Creek took place late in the nineteenth century, before the wholesale dilution of our hatchery strains took place, and the echoes of these beautiful wild fish still persist.

You can always tell the old Silver Creek rainbows, Hemingway insists firmly. *Their spotting patterns and configuration and coloring are completely different—and they're much stronger!*

Without future introductions of inferior hatchery strains, these older stocks are probably more durable in genetic terms, and could probably dominate the hybrids. The surviving native stocks are increasingly rare, and should perhaps be isolated from future genetic denigration, along with a program designed to restore the wild rainbow stocks.

Although their diet may simply result from the abundance of mayfly hatches in Silver Creek, its rainbows seemingly rise more freely to aquatic insects than their cousins elsewhere.

Silver has nothing but rainbows until it gets out into the rattlesnake flats beyond Picabo, Hemingway continued wryly. *Out there in the sagebrush we've got some brown trout too.*

You serious about rattlesnakes? I asked warily.

I'm always serious about rattlesnakes, Hemingway grinned. *Rattlesnakes are a fine tool in trout management these days, because even a rumor about rattlesnakes will discourage most people!*

Let's look for fish instead, I said drily.

We spent two hours fishing the upper shallows on the Sun Valley acreages, watching a hatch of tiny *Tricorythodes* flies emerge and gather above the riffles in an immense mating swarm. The morning sunlight was quickly filled with thousands and thousands of mating spinners, their chalk-colored wings like minute snowflakes. The river flowed still and smooth, its currents empty of rises.

They're waiting for those spinners to complete their egg laying! Hemingway pointed. *It's really a big swarm of flies—just watch the fish take them when they're finally on the water!*

I can't wait! I yelled back.

When their mating dance was finished, the spent flies drifted downstream in the surface film. Big rainbows cruised the shallow flats, dimpling softly between their heart-stopping wakes, and circling back to gorge themselves on the tiny mayflies.

Our tiny white-winged imitations were dressed with delicate gray tails and black dubbed bodies, and in spite of their delicate twenty-four hooks, we took and released a dozen good fish. *How about some lunch?* Hemingway called downstream when the spinner fall was finished. *The fish have stopped and it's our turn!*

Sounds perfect! I waded ashore.

Hemingway retrieved his bottle of Sancerre from its icy seepages in the watercress, its label slipping down the glass after its baptism in the spring. We sat happily in the meadows across from the heron rookery, talking about his boyhood and his father.

When did your father stop fishing? I asked.

Papa lost most of his equipment when a steamer trunk failed to arrive from Paris, Hemingway replied. *So many Hardy rods and reels he bought with the royalties from* The Sun Also Rises *were lost that his heart just wasn't in it—he'd been just like a little kid when he got those things from Hardy's in Pall Mall!*

But you kept fishing, I said.

That's right, Hemingway said thoughtfully. *Maybe I was looking for something I could do as well as Papa did it—and trout fishing on Silver was the first thing I found.*

Papa was a tough act to follow, I agreed.

After lunch we drove downstream to fish the Point of Rocks water, and sat watching a red-tailed hawk skillfully working the thermals on the wind-polished hills. There was a fine hatch of pale yellow-bodied mayflies and the fish took them greedily. We both took several trout while the activity lasted, and during the lull that followed, mating swarms of *Pseudocloeon* spinners triggered another fine rise of fish. We sat in the warm grass and finished the wine and watched, knowing we could catch them but letting them work.

When the heat of afternoon had passed, we explored the lower river in the lava outcroppings below Picabo. It was perfect grasshopper weather there, with a hot wind that kept the red-legged *Orthoptera* active, and dropped them into the current. We caught and released a number of fine browns and rainbows.

Working back upstream to the Purdy stretch, Hemingway found a fine three-pound rainbow taking grasshoppers. It was a difficult cast into the warm wind that eddied downstream, with the fish lying in a small backwater behind a hummock of grass, but the trout took immediately. Hemingway played it skillfully through six leapfrogging jumps. It finally surrendered while he fussed with a folding British trout net, its meshes hopelessly tangled with its collapsing frame, until it was safely netted and released.

It took so long to get that fish, Hemingway laughed infectiously, *that he's lying here like an old friend!*

Hemingway had decided to spend the twilight hour on the Sun Valley tract upstream, and we found hundreds of tiny *Pseudocloeon* flies along its channels in the elodea. The trout started porpoising softly to the spent spinners pinioned in the surface film, and I took a brace of fish on a minute bright-green imitation. The last fish of the day took my tiny fly with an almost imperceptible dimple, bolted upstream into a labyrinth of roots and cartwheeled in a brief series of jumps that stitched my leader through the willows.

That was a pretty good fish! Hemingway observed while I retrieved the broken nylon. *Sure did you in a hurry!*

Let's quit while we've still got some dignity! I said.

Dignity is a little thin around here!

The twilight sky grew lavender and yellow on the horizon, etching the soft serrations of the foothills, and we drove back into the gathering darkness toward Sun Valley.

Several years earlier, the stretches and sloughs in the headwaters of Silver Creek had been offered for sale, threatening public access to the property there. *It's the finest piece of Silver,* Hemingway explained thoughtfully, *but there was nothing to ensure that its new owners would continue to permit public fishing.*

Philanthropy is rare, I agreed.

Hemingway conceived a strategy for protecting public access to the Silver Creek headwaters. It involved the Nature Conservancy, a private foundation created to preserve endangered or ecologically unique properties through outright acquisition. Its unique posture enables the Conservancy to move quickly in crisis situations for which government agencies, both state and federal, lack the time, funding and political stomach.

The Nature Conservancy agreed to become involved in purchasing the Sun Valley Ranch at a price of more than $500,000, with the stated intent of transferring the property to the State of Idaho. Hemingway requested matching funds from the Bureau of Outdoor Recreation in Washington, and received a verbal commitment from Secretary Nathaniel Pryor Reed at the Department of the Interior.

Spencer Beebe of the Nature Conservancy arrived at Sun Valley to meet with the owners of the property, and the selling price was reduced because the Conservancy was a nonprofit buyer and Beebe committed the organization to the project that week. Beebe requisitioned both Hemingway and me along Silver Creek that same afternoon for a series of meetings and fund-raising luncheons and banquets in several cities, and we started on a year of such travels.

Our early efforts proved so successful that the owners agreed to reduce the price still more if the Nature Conservancy could raise half the funds in only four months, and with more than $300,000 already donated for the project, we doubled our efforts.

Trouble came without warning at this point, when the State of Idaho balked at accepting the property and its four miles of prime fishery if the deed contained such restrictions as fly-only or no-kill management. Our acquisition committee was stunned, since the public access to the property had historically been tied to fly-only regulations in the past.

It should have been no surprise, Hemingway suggested wryly. *It's a perfect yardstick of political stomach!*

Our fund-raising schedule had already secured sufficient capital that only the matching federal funding remained, but those funds were contingent upon deeding the property to the State of Idaho. Unless the state officials changed their position, our entire strategy for saving public access to Silver Creek was threatened.

Beebe and Hemingway were elated about raising more than $300,000, and argued that we were already committed to our donors. It seemed like an astronomical sum, but the Conservancy quickly decided to raise the entire price of the property.

These problems had also forced the Conservancy into a curious position. Its past role had been limited to the acquisition of properties and their subsequent transfer to local political jurisdiction. With the purchase of the Sun Valley acreages, the Conservancy would become both owner and landlord, but it chose to proceed.

The second phase of fund-raising was started, and the owners of the property agreed to another reduction in price if the remaining money were paid before the end of the year. The committee returned to its strategies of buttonholing foundations and major corporations and people at fly-fishing banquets. Several magazines and television programs were enlisted in the campaign. Both foundations and corporate leaders responded generously, along with fishing clubs and large conservation groups and many fishermen themselves.

Perhaps the most memorable contribution was a single coin taped to a letter from a little girl in Boise. *My daddy loves Silver Creek and I love my daddy,* she wrote. *I hope this money helps!*

Boise Cascade contributed $100,000 to the Silver Creek project, which was the largest single cash donation in the history of the Nature Conservancy at that point, and its young president John Fery played a major role throughout the campaign. The Union Pacific railroad was also a major contributor, and with its gift a few weeks before Christmas, the Nature Conservancy became the owner of the Silver Creek Preserve late in 1977. More than 1,000 individuals contributed too, in gifts ranging from pennies to $50,000, and public access to the headwaters of Silver Creek was protected in perpetuity.

Its restrictions of fly-fishing only were continued, and a no-kill policy was started during a period of extensive ecological studies. The Conservancy appointed a resident manager, and a management study group was recruited. Its rosters include experts in fisheries management, aquatic entomology, limnology, forestry, ecology, icthyology, botany, agriculture and livestock operations, agronomy, reptiles, avifauna, and fly-fishing itself. Studies were launched in soils chemistry, plant cover, fly hatches, reptiles, hydrology, aquatic vegetation, water quality, fish populations, wind erosion, water-transported silts, limnology, and its large heron rookery.

It was decided that waterfowl shooting on the Silver Creek Preserve should be closed, not because the management committee was opposed to hunting, but because it wanted to complete its studies of other bird life and their migratory use of the property before reaching a final policy on bird shooting. Both eagles and herons use its ice-free waters extensively in the winter months, and the first herons return to inspect their rookery during duck season. During the research and the shooting restrictions, the waterfowl population exploded so dramatically in the Silver Creek Preserve that more than 10,000 ducks and geese were often observed on its waters. Their abundance triggered a fresh political problem. Duck hunters placed immense pressures on the Nature Conservancy to open its property to shooting, and tried to force the Idaho Fish & Game Commission to withdraw support for its preserve status. Waterfowl experts were hired to explore the role of the refuge in the duck populations throughout the watershed, and their conclusions surprised everyone involved, from antihunting agitators to the most rabid hunters.

The excellent shooting in the drainage basin before the Second World War, when Ernest Hemingway and his celebrity friends hunted its waterfowl sloughs, was firmly rooted in the huge springhead marshes on its tributary flowages. Those spring-fed marshes were largely drained in the years at midcentury, and their capacity to sustain vast flocks of nesting and migratory waterfowl was lost. The decline in shooting quality throughout the basin could be traced directly to the drainage of these wetlands, but the restrictions on shooting in the Silver Creek Preserve had worked to create another primary zone of first-rate duck habitat. It was not as extensive as the marshes that had been drained, but it was pulling and holding vast flocks of waterfowl, and the duck shooting on its periphery was getting better and better each season.

The fishery displayed some remarkable changes too. Both fishermen and oldtimers agree that the past few seasons have witnessed an explosive change. Fly hatches have been better than ever, particularly in the populations of the primary *Baetis* and *Ephemerella* and *Callibaetis* species. The spinner swarms of tiny *Tricorythodes* and *Pseudocloeon* flies have been immense, lasting from summer into late October. Both more trout and fish of increasing average size have been reported in census studies and electrofishing work by biologists. Field research conducted by both state and private teams confirm that the only sizeable populations of rainbows more than two years old are found in the Silver Creek Preserve, and in the Purdy irrigation lagoon immediately downstream, where no hatchery fish are planted. Such data suggest that genetic pollution is serious in the middle and lower mileage, where hatchery strains are continually mixed with the wild populations. It is obviously tempting to credit these changes to the restrictive regulations and no-kill policy alone, but the dramatic improvement of the fishery involves other factors too.

The field studies suggest that both fish and fly-life communities have enjoyed a peak cycle in population. Weather patterns and reductions in agriculture have resulted in less erosion. Aquatic vegetation has flourished too, particularly in the most desirable gravel-rooting plant communities, perhaps reflecting another aspect of peaking cycles. The discharge flowages from the springheads have also increased, exposing larger acreages of clean bottom gravel, with a corresponding abundance of the diet forms that thrive in silt-free habitat. Such habitat improvement also suggests that a significant population of postspawning adults simply chose to remain on the Silver Creek Preserve instead of migrating farther downstream after their egg laying.

However, there are some clouds on the horizon. Commercial hatchery interests, with strong political influence in the legislature at Boise, have applied for permission to extract sufficient volumes of flow from Silver Creek to operate two major trout hatcheries on its lower mileage. Few people seem to realize that fish hatcheries are serious pollution sources, and a state hatchery is already in operation on a major Silver Creek tributary.

The prospects of currents warmed in a labyrinth of rearing ponds and concrete raceways, the eutrophication triggered by fish wastes and partially eaten food pellets farther downstream, the interference with spawning migrations by the hatchery diversion structures and the inevitable escape of inferior hatchery-fish genetic strains into the wild-trout fishery are disturbing.

It was getting dark when we reached Sun Valley and stopped for dinner at the Ore House. *You spent the day fishing Silver with Hemingway?* another fisherman asked. *How were the fly hatches?*

Hemingway's pretty good at finding hatches.

He understands Silver all right, the bartender agreed, *but did you ever hear about his technique fishing maggots?*

Maggots? I gasped in disbelief.

Hemingway is pretty strong about his fly-fishing. The bartender skillfully rinsed a half-dozen glasses. *But this spring he went up to Pend O'Reille with the other fish commissioners—and was observed fishing kokanees with maggots!*

Nothing strange about that! Hemingway exploded in laughter. *What is the maggot—except a premature fly?*

THE TROUT OF THE SHAMROCKS

Mary Colgan stared down from her feather-littered workbench when the horse carriage clattered through the Parliament Street. Its fittings and polished-leather coachwork and tack gleamed in the weak spring sunlight, and its high wheels creaked and rattled against the harsh counterpoint of horseshoes on the paving stones. The hansom cab disappeared into the gray steep-walled street, and the startled pigeons rose among the chimneypots of Dublin.

The shopgirls were out walking along the Liffey, where the college boys from Trinity were counting salmon from the stonework bridges, but young Mary Colgan was behind in her fly dressing. Her nimble fingers had been working with delicate spentwing drakes for the coming mayfly season on lakes like Sheelin and Corrib.

It was almost warm in the cobblestone streets at midday, but the spare fly-making loft high above Garnett's & Keegan's tackle shop still held the chill damp of the Irish winter.

The young girl apprentices at the fly vises were rubbing their cold fingers, and kept their feet on the tin warming boxes filled with coals from the potbellied stove. Their teakettle was kept on the hot plate under bins of gamecock hackles and exotic bird skins, and the girls were heavily bundled against the wintry chill of the loft like seamstresses in the stories of Dickens.

What's that sedge pattern you're dressing? I asked.

Welshman's Button, Mary Colgan smiled.

John Hanlon is the proprietor of Garnett's & Keegan's, the finest tackle shop in Ireland, its shelves and glass-topped vitrines filled with exquisite flies and intricately made Wheatley fly boxes and gleaming British reels. Split-cane rods still dominate the racks behind the counters, in a time when most rods are glass or graphite, and another alcove is filled with stag rifles and the graceful straight-stocked double guns made famous by British artisans in the eighteenth century. The principal tackle salesman is perhaps the most famous trout-fishing writer in Ireland. J. R. Harris also monitors the young fly dressers at Garnett's & Keegan's, while his book *An Angler's Entomology* has been the bible on fly hatches in the British Isles. The richly stocked mahogany fly drawers surpass the selections available in the tackle stores of London and New York and Paris.

Clare de Bergh is among the finest fly-fishers in Europe, and we had first met over lunch in Oslo, after she had spent a highly successful week of salmon fishing. Our paths crossed later on another salmon river in Scandinavia, the swift little Nordurá in western Iceland. We had corresponded about the trout and salmon fishing in her native Ireland, and when the Aer Lingus flight from New York landed at Dublin, I sought her advice about the fishing at Limerick.

Where can we find some flies? I asked.

Garnett's & Keegan's is the best place, she replied without hesitation. *Dick Harris will be there this morning, and he's fished everywhere in Ireland—he knows the hatches on the Maigue.*

We took an antique, high-ceilinged taxi from the airport into the center of the city, and walked across the Liffey into the Parliament Street shop, where Harris was sorting a fresh consignment of flies. Harris is a short, ruddy-faced man in a suit of burlap-colored Irish tweed, and he greeted us with curiosity.

You've taken several day's fishing on the Maigue? Harris asked. *You're really quite fortunate.*

I'm looking forward to fishing it, I said.

It's exceptionally beautiful water, Harris explained, *particularly in the meadows around the castle and the ruined abbey—and it has some of our best fly hatches.*

It's quite a fertile fishery, De Bergh agreed.

What hatches are coming now? I asked.

Harris rummaged through the fly chests, passing their trays of brightly colored salmon patterns. *You'll find quite a mixed palette of flies hatching now.* He selected a drawer filled with delicate little sedges and mayfly duns and spinners. *Sometimes you'll have to observe each fish and its feeding behavior to discover what it's taking—and it might be everything from our little Silverhorns to Cinnamon Sedges or the Knotted Midge.*

What's a knotted midge? I asked.

Harris brightened with an embarrassed flush. *It's just a name we use to describe our midges,* he stammered awkwardly and laughed, *when the males and females are joined in mating.*

It's two flies dressed on a single hook? I asked.

That's right, Clare de Bergh smiled.

What about the mayfly season here? I said.

Our best sport when the mayfly is hatching, Harris continued with a faint smile, *is usually found when the fly is up on loughs like Sheelin and Corrib and Mask—but we have river hatches too.*

What about the Maigue water?

You should find a few coming now, Harris said, *and the fish should be coming to them soon.*

What about your famous Bluewinged Olives?

Too early, Harris replied quickly, *but you might see excellent hatches of our Iron Blues in rainy weather.*

Let's have what I'll need, I suggested.

Harris selected a beautiful Wheatley box from the cabinet behind his counters, and sorted a series of elegant dry-fly imitations into its intricately lidded compartments. We talked briefly about the fishing at Limerick and farther south on the Ring of Kerry, and agreed to a tentative fishing date on the Rye water.

We walked back through the narrow streets, and stopped for a lunch of perfectly boiled salmon and small potatoes and salad at the charming Buttery in the Royal Hibernian hotel. The taxi carried me through the rainy streets after lunch, and I caught the afternoon train to Limerick. Its polished mahogany and velvet-covered seats and gleaming brass fittings echoed the trains in the Hitchcock films, and the thatchwork villages and whitewashed farms flashed past our carriage in the pastoral Irish countryside.

There was a driver waiting at Limerick, and when I reached the little country hotel at Adare, the young riverkeeper was waiting in its public house. *Roger Foster!* he introduced himself warmly. *We've been expecting you all afternoon!*

I'm really excited about fishing your beats!

We can still fish this evening if you wish, Foster interjected. *The beat just above the castle is free.*

It's possible to hold your supper, the porter said.

Let's go fishing! I agreed.

It was already evening when we reached the Footbridge beats above the castle, swiftly put up our equipment and walked downstream through the water meadows. The river was about seventy-five feet across, flowing deceptively swift and still between undercut banks of waist-deep grass. The surface was like a mirror, its currents undulating in beds of trailing weeds, and the trout were starting to rise downstream.

There were several species of mating mayflies over the water, in dancing swarms that rose and fell in the lengthening shadows. Foster pointed to several big *Ephemera* drakes, their chalky bodies readily visible in the evening light, and the sedges swarming along the grassy banks. The rises were mostly delicate bulges and swirls, with an occasional splash against the banks.

When they come like that, they're usually on the sedges, Foster suggested quietly. *Try that fish along the grass.*

The brown-hackled sedge settled into the current and flirted with the trailing grass. The trout came out from its hiding place and almost took the fly, but it balked and refused in the last moment, half-drowning its hackles with its splashy swirl.

Well, I shook my head, *he looked!*

Seems he found something wrong, Foster nodded. *Let's see if we've got a smaller Cinnamon Sedge in my boxes.*

The keeper rummaged through his shooting coat and found a sparse little sedge imitation, its dark-olive silk and mottled woodcock wings and hackles dressed on a fine sixteen upeye.

It's beautifully tied, I said.

Our trout are really quite shy, Foster explained. *Sometimes they take an imitation dressed a bit smaller than the naturals.*

Foster replaced my larger pattern and I dropped the fly just above the feeding trout. It took splashily and was gone.

That got him going, I laughed, *but I missed him!*

I'm not certain he took it, Foster said.

The trout were erratic that evening, porpoising steadily in the surface film and showing with occasional splashy rises. We took two or three fish on dry-fly imitations of the egg-laying sedges, until I watched a bold rise occur where no insect had been fluttering, and saw a second splash that almost drowned an escaping sedge that had obviously just hatched. *They're on the hatching flies!* I shouted downstream to the riverkeeper. *They're not on the sedges themselves!*

You're probably right, he responded.

I took a good trout on a sedge fished wet, confirming those observations, before it started to rain and the fish stopped feeding. The soft rain glistened in the meadows when we walked back to the station wagon. We drove back to the Dunraven Arms, and Foster stopped with me in its public house for a glass of Guinness, and we talked briefly with a couple who had traveled from São Paulo in southern Brazil to fish the castle beats of the Maigue.

It's just as beautiful as my father told us! Richard Dolan ordered another round. *It's worth the trip from Brazil!*

Where did you fish today? I asked.

Dolan turned to the riverkeeper. *Roger had us fishing the meadows above the castle grounds,* he replied.

They were fishing the upper beats, Foster explained, *and we also took them to try the Camogue.*

What's its fishing like? I asked.

It's a limestone tributary with excellent fly life, the young riverkeeper explained. *It's the little Camogue that transforms the Maigue into such a fine fishery—the Maigue rises in peat bogs and its waters are quite barren until they mix with the Camogue.*

Where are the principal spawning grounds?

The Camogue is quite fertile and has fine pea-gravel riffles, Foster replied. *Our fish largely spawn there.*

Do you stock any trout? Dolan asked.

We raise pheasants for drive-shoots on the castle grounds, Foster smiled and drained his glass, *but our fish are wild.*

How was your fishing this evening? Dolan questioned.

We took a few good fish, I replied.

We're on better water tomorrow, Foster added, and we shook hands. *I'll meet you all in the morning.*

Well, I asked, *what do you think of the river?*

It's really pleasant fishing, Dolan said.

Dolan, his wife chided him drily, *it's simply the most beautiful trout stream in the world!*

We went into the dining room, where the proprietor was holding our dinner, and returned to the public house for cognac later. When it closed its doors and I returned to my quarters in the garden, the gentle Irish rain was drumming on my windows.

The village street is lined with simple, whitewashed, thatched-roof cottages, and the following morning it was filled with foxhounds and hunters in scarlet coats. The horses stood and circled restlessly, waiting for the Master of Fox Hounds to start the hunt. It was still raining gently, and the foxhounds shook themselves while the horsemen sat their sleekly groomed hunters, watching the pewter-gray clouds anxiously. Several riders finally disappeared into the hotel for stirrup cups of Irish whisky, while we stood with our fishing gear in the foyer with the old porter.

It's a little early for whisky, I smiled.

Begging your pardon, the old porter laughed when the foxhunters went back outside, *it's never too early!*

Perhaps you're right, I nodded.

The old man brushed some mud from his uniform. *It's a soft morning we're having today.* His lyric brogue richly filled the foyer. *It's better for fishing than for chasing after foxes!*

Much softer and we'll need an ark! I laughed.

The young riverkeeper arrived just as the foxhunters clattered off toward Limerick, their scarlet coats gathering to cross the stonework bridge that arches the river above the village. Dolan drove off to fish the lower meadows, where the ruins of a twelfth-century Cistercian abbey lies along the river, while we drove in through the castle grounds to fish its beat.

Dunraven Castle is a formidable structure of limestone ramparts and intricately crenellated battlements, but like several famous Irish castles, it was built largely in the last century. Its terraces and sloping lawns and gardens reach down to some of the finest pools on the Maigue. Peacocks and spotted deer and pheasants wander its gardens. Its single Victorian tower dominates the village and castle grounds and meadows, and that morning the roads and roof slates glistened in the rain, although it was clearing.

We crossed the stile above the ruined abbey, where a single masonrywork arch spanned the weirs. The trout were working steadily in the rain. There were several flies on the water, and merely matching the hatch was unworkable. Some aquatic insects are more common on some types of water than others, and a particular fish can find one species concentrated in its feeding currents. Its response is predictable, and such trout focus their attention on that specific diet form until they will accept nothing else. Such selectivity is the secret of catching trout on difficult waters, and dressing flies to imitate specific insects dates to the *Treatyse on Fysshynge Wyth an Angle,* which was written at Sopewell nunnery in the fifteenth century.

The fish were typical that morning on the Maigue. The trout lying under the swift-water weirs were concentrating on the sedges hatching from their currents. Fish in the smooth flats were taking the somber Iron Blue mayflies that emerge there, particularly on such rainy spring mornings. The trout lying in the deeper pools of the Maigue, like the weedy half-mile lagoon below the castle itself, are often tempted to focus on the *Ephemera vulgata* drakes that hatch from its silty bottom. The sedges along both banks were swarming with caddisflies, and the riverkeeper and his ghillies spend much of their time studying the rising trout to discover what each fish is taking.

Roger Foster is quite knowledgeable about the Maigue and its fly hatches. His early years where spent fishing and working as a ghillie in northern England at Driffield, with its famous trout-fishing club, and this young riverkeeper from Yorkshire is a skilled fly dresser. His knowledge of aquatic hatches throughout the British Isles is formidable, rooted in a tradition that ranges from the early nineteenth-century writings of Alfred Ronalds to the recent books of writers like Harris and Goddard. During our week's fishing together, I learned to admire his knowledge and skills, both as the gamekeeper for Lord Dunraven and the manager of his fishery.

The alders and water grasses were alive with somber slate-colored caddisflies, and in the quiet pool above the castle, the little Cinnamon sedges were emerging. The trout were starting to work greedily, and the soft rain had almost stopped when we walked upstream from the stile at the old Abbey Bridge.

Look there! I pointed to the run under the alders. *Look at the Iron Blues on the water—think they're taking them?*

The rises we could see were splashy and bold. *Perhaps,* Foster studied the water doubtfully, *but I'm not sure.*

Several good trout were rising in the smooth currents above the weir. Tiny fluttering Iron Blues were coming down there, along with a few fluttering sedges. Some large *Ephemera* drakes were also emerging, but the fish drifted back with them cautiously, and finally refused to take them. The first cast covered them with an Iron Blue.

Refused it! I thought in surprise.

The fish rejected several decent floats, although they drifted down its feeding current, riding perfectly and seemingly drag free. The trout finally did not bother to inspect my fly.

They're pretty particular, I sighed. *It's definitely not the Iron Blue this morning—what are they taking?*

Most of the rises are pretty strong swirls, Foster said.

Perhaps they're still on hatching sedges?

It's quite possible, the young Yorkshireman nodded, *but I don't believe they're taking anything on the surface.*

Downstream from the stonework bridge there was a splashy swirl in the quiet water, and a sedge escaped clumsily from the rise. The fish tried a second time at the fluttering insect and missed, scattering water clumsily in the shallows.

See that fish? I said eagerly. *It tried for a hatching sedge—and it missed the adult too!*

Exactly! Foster agreed.

The young riverkeeper is typical of the British fishermen on the border rivers of Yorkshire, and his leather fly books are filled with soft, partridge-hackled wet flies. *Have you a Partridge and Olive in your coat?* I asked suddenly. *Or perhaps a sparse Woodcock Spider with a dubbing of dark hare's mask?*

Those are Yorkshire dressings! he frowned.

That's right, I smiled, *but do you have them along?*

I've got both, he said.

Foster searched his fly books for a pair of sparse little Woodcock Spiders, and I quickly knotted one to the tippet. The line darted back and forth in the misting rain that drifted along the river, and I dropped the fly above the fish. It settled and drifted under the surface and started into its swing. I followed the fly-swing with the rod, feeling the line bellying the little wet fly past the fish, and I teased it with the tip. The trout responded with an eager swirl, and I tightened into a strong fifteen-inch fish that telegraphed its struggles back into the throbbing cane.

That's the secret! I thought happily.

The episode is typical of the chess-playing overtones that exist on hard-fished trout waters. The soft-hackled fly was the solution on that particular morning, but as more time passed, the clouds darkened and surrendered a misting series of showers.

The tiny slate-colored *Baetis* flies that had been hatching sporadically were coming steadily now, and the character of the rise forms changed too. The splashy swirls were replaced with confident bulges and dimples in the smooth run above the weir, and the trout picked the Iron Blues from the surface like berries.

They've switched, I suggested.

I believe you're right, Foster nodded and filled his pipe. *Try the Iron Blue on that trout along the tules.*

The tiny slate-gray pattern worked perfectly. We both took good fish for almost an hour, until the hatch passed its apogee and started to wane. Some trout continued to take the little Iron Blues, but there were some refusals to our flies too. Finally the fish were still working steadily, and rejected our imitations completely.

What's happened out there? I asked.

I'm not quite sure, Foster replied. *Let's observe them a while until we discover what they're doing.*

It makes more sense than just casting!

The rises were coming in a surprisingly steady rhythm now, and the trout hovered just under the surface, pushing their noses into the film when they took something. There were too many rises for the few insects still visible on the currents. The rise forms were clearly to something on the surface, their bulging rings filled with tiny bubbles in the flow. The feeding rhythms increased almost imperceptibly, until the rises were a series of interlocking circles, bulging and drifting downstream in the smooth current.

It looks like they're on spent spinners, I suggested.

It's quite possible, Foster agreed thoughtfully. *I've observed a few swarms of mating mayflies—and if their egg laying is finished we might have their spent spinners on the water.*

It could explain the steady feeding, I said.

That's right. Foster nodded and tapped the ashes from his pipe. *The rise forms rule out gnats and reed smuts.*

Perhaps its the Iron Blue spinners?

Try one, Foster suggested.

We had worked out the puzzle again, and we both took fish consistently until the spinner fall was finished. It was time to leave for our afternoon beat, and we walked back toward the abbey bridge. Coming downstream past the weirs, Foster spotted a large fish working boldly under the alders across the river. It was a relatively long cast, perhaps seventy-five feet into the shade of the trees, and the rises were utterly different from the soft spinner feeding.

What the hell is that fish doing? I asked.

It's certain that he's not on the Iron Blue spinners. Foster cupped his hands to shelter his pipe from the weather. *Not making strong rises like those!*

The rises were both splashy and sporadic. There were still a few large *Ephemera* drakes coming off, hopscotching and fluttering along the current like diminutive crippled sailboats. The erratic intervals between the rises suggested that the big trout might be taking them. The size of its rises also suggested it might be feeding on something relatively large, and perhaps capable of swimming.

You think he might be taking the drakes? I asked.

It's quite possible, Foster replied. *There are good marl deposits in the still water above that trout—but I've been watching him, and he still hasn't taken any of the adults coming down.*

Their nymphs can swim, I suggested.

That's right, Foster agreed excitedly. *They're burrowing nymphs that can swim like minnows when they're hatching—and that fish could be seeing a lot of them in his line of drift!*

You're the chess master, I laughed. *What do you think?*

Foster searched through his leather fly books and passed me two large imitations. *Try one of these nymphs,* he said.

Two large mayflies came fluttering clumsily over the trout and floated through safely. The fish had ignored them, but just as they were past, there was a dull flash as the fish took something and turned along the bottom.

He's definitely nymphing! I said.

I believe you're right! Foster nodded. *He's not taken a single one of the drakes coming over him!*

I dropped the nymph well above the trout, let it settle back into its line of drift and fished it teasingly like a minnow when it passed the alder where the fish was lying. There was a bold flash deep in the current as the big trout took it hard, and I left the keeper's nymph in its jaws when my tippet parted.

Rotten piece of luck! Foster shook his head sympathetically. *The fish was at least four pounds!*

Luck nothing! I said sheepishly. *Owe you a fly!*

We had lunch under the huge twisted beeches at the footbridge, and sat in the grass, talking lazily when the weather turned warm and bright. Foster predicted a better fly hatch that evening, but just when the flies began coming and the trout started to rise, a sudden downpour ended our fishing well before twilight.

It was still raining hard when we reached the car. *Well,* Foster laughed as he stowed my wading brogues, *we can always stop off at the public house for a pint and trade a few lies—more trout are caught in Irish pubs than anywhere else in the world!*

Fishing is always good in pubs! I agreed.

The following morning I drew the footbridge water with my roll of the dice cup, and the young keeper wandered ahead on the footpath to look for rising fish. Pheasants cackled in the water meadows, and we had seen peacocks in the deer park. Pigeons flew back and forth over the roof slates of the castle, and the rain had stopped, with weak sunlight filtering through the overcast.

Foster was hopeful of a hatch of drakes, the classic mayfly on the rivers and loughs of Ireland, but it was still a little early for such big *Ephemera* flies in large numbers. *The mayfly is already up on Lough Derg,* the young keeper explained, *and the flies are probably ripe on Lough Sheelin and Lough Corrib too.*

Clare de Bergh has already gone to Oughterard, I nodded. *She has a cottage there on Corrib.*

She knows her fishing, Foster said.

There's a big drake on the water now! I pointed to the mayfly under the trees. *But the trout are still refusing them.*

They're not on anything yet!

There were stands of huge conifers along the Maigue, and I stopped to study the rough, reddish bark on the trunks which soared a hundred feet into the afternoon sun. Other species of tall conifers stood deeper in the groves.

These big trees look like sequoias! I shook my head in disbelief. *And those others look like Douglas fir and Englemann spruce—what are they doing on the grounds of an Irish castle?*

You're right about those trees, Foster grinned. *Lord Dunraven has a collection of trees from all over the world.*

What about monkeypuzzles from Patagonia?

His araucarias are over there. Foster pointed downstream toward the castle. *Beyond the deer park.*

It's strange to find them here, I said.

Downstream past the exotic monkeypuzzles, the Maigue wound out through its beeches and sycamores and alders to the footbridge meadow. The afternoon was alive with hatching and mating flies.

Thousands of tiny mayfly spinners were mixed with occasional hatching *Ephemera* flies, and there were clouds of swarming sedges. The bank grasses were crawling with these caddisflies, and I collected them like picking berries until my specimen bottles were filled with slate-colored Silverhorns and mottled *Sericostoma* flies and Cinnamon sedges. The river was soon alive too, with trout rising everywhere.

They're probably on sedges, Foster observed drily.

Clouds of caddisflies rose out over the current as we passed on the footpath. *It's likely with blizzards of caddisflies on both banks,* I laughed and almost choked on a fluttering sedge.

Leave a few for the fish! Foster grinned.

We've got five or six species out there. I tried to cough and clear my throat. *How do we tell which flies are hatching?*

Silverhorns hatch mostly at night, Foster explained, *and our season for the Welshman's Button is about finished.*

What about the Cinnamon sedges? I asked.

Try one, Foster suggested.

The young riverkeeper passed me an elegant sedge imitation, and we walked the footpath, casting to every fish in reach. There were several bulges and swirls of refusing fish under my fly, mixed with one splashy hit that drowned its hackles without actually touching it. Foster was fishing downstream, and I watched him hook and release a fine trout. The young keeper promptly rose and hooked another just above the weir. Two other fish bulged under my fly, and when a third fish refused it splashily, I walked downstream for his advice.

Dry flies aren't working, I complained.

Foster was preening his sedge carefully. *I'm fishing the dry fly,* he explained, *but I'm fishing it with our induced-rise method—sometimes it teases them into taking.*

How does your method work? I asked.

It's not particularly new, Foster explained. *It's been used in England to imitate our Caperer for more than a century—but it really works when the fish are on egg-laying caddisflies.*

What's a Caperer? I asked.

Our Caperer is a little sedge that scuttles and flutters about on the surface, the keeper replied. *It excites the trout!*

Like the other egg-laying caddisflies!

That's right, Foster nodded.

The young Yorkshireman demonstrated his secret over another

rising fish. His gentle false-casting worked out line gracefully, until his fly settled softly over its line of drift, about twenty inches above the trout. The little cinnamon-dark dry fly had scarcely started into its drift when Foster gave it a subtle twitch, let it float freely another six inches and then teased it again with his rod.

It was simply too tempting, and the fish took the twitching sedge hard. *So that's the induced-rise method!* I laughed. *You tickled that trout until it went crazy!*

Sometimes it works quite well, Foster admitted.

Breaks the dry-fly rules a little.

You mean the dry-fly religion of fishing upstream, Foster laughed, *and its dogma of the drag-free float?*

Rules are made to be broken, I agreed.

His induced-rise method worked miracles that morning. We took almost fifty trout between us, averaging perhaps twelve to thirteen inches, and our best fish was a richly spotted Irish fish of three pounds. Our twitching flies were so effective that we finally stopped fishing, and walked back to explore the split-willow lunch basket and the bottle of Chateau Beychevelle.

Later that afternoon, the weather darkened again and a soft rain drifted along the river, triggering a fine hatch of Iron Blues in the treeless moors of the upper beats. There were a dozen fine trout rising above the meadow weirs, and the currents were covered with a regatta of tiny mayflies.

With trembling fingers, in spite of the trout-filled morning below the footbridge, I selected a tiny slate-hackled Iron Blue from the selection purchased at Garnett's & Keegan's. *It's quite strange,* Foster laughed. *No matter how many fish we catch, it's always exciting to see trout rising to a hatch of flies!*

You're right, I agreed.

We took several fish before the hatch ebbed into late afternoon and the weather grew stormy and cold. The chill wind blew across the gentle hedgerow country from Ballinskelligs and Killarney, and it was raining hard after dinner at the Dunraven Arms.

The night lamps flickered in the thatched-roof cottages of Adare, and the dark wind rose in the mountains along the Ring of Kerry. The cruel seas stormed and seethed against the rocky headlands. Rain rattled down my windows through the entire night, and the storm sighed along the roof slates of the castle. The weather did not pass until daylight, with a faint moon showing through the ragged clouds, and after breakfast the Dublin radio promised good fishing weather throughout Ireland.

It was still when I reached the river meadows, cool and slightly overcast, and the Maigue flowed quietly past the Abbey Bridge. Foster was stringing his old Hardy rod when I reached the stile. *It's a fine morning for fishing,* the riverkeeper smiled, *and we'll find another hatch of Iron Blues below the castle.*

Let's fish them! I suggested happily, and we walked upstream as the trout were starting to rise along the beautiful little Maigue, in a meadow alive with shamrocks.

THE FLY BOOK

It is late summer in Princeton, and walking down through the campus toward the railroad station, we can sense the coming fall. Fishing is almost finished on the Beaverkill and the gentle Brodheads for another year. Sycamores are turning yellow on the streets where the old Princeton families built their mansions a half century ago, near the houses of Grover Cleveland and Woodrow Wilson.

There are only a few weeks before the football crowds will gather on the playing fields beyond the station, their split-willow baskets filled with cheese and cold chicken and wine in the rich tradition of Scott Fitzgerald.

It is the season of change, with a faint perfume of burning leaves drifting on the wind, mixed with a cackle of pheasants from the cornfields. There are a few shooting friends who ride my commuter train, and there are scraps of talk about shotguns and bird dogs. It is difficult to hide our disappointment in the morning papers, because we are deskbound in the first days of woodcock hunting.

But this particular morning was not without its compensations for a fisherman. The train appeared through the autumn haze, its cyclops eye staring toward Pennsylvania Station. Its regular passengers came aboard, and the daily bridge games and sports-page dialogues started. Once the train had left the station, a commuter whom I had met a few times walked back to my seat.

Understand you fish salmon, he said.

That's right. I folded my paper and smiled. *Probably more than I can afford with the rod fees today.*

Salmon fishing's getting expensive? he asked.

That's right, I said.

Well, the commuter explained, *my uncle used to fish salmon and he left me his old fly book—don't fish salmon myself and I wondered if you'd take a look at his collection.*

Where did your uncle fish? I asked.

Don't really know. The man shook his head absently. *Quebec and New Brunswick and maybe a little in Europe.*

Let's take a look at his flies, I said finally.

The commuter returned to his seat and rummaged through a thick pile of memorandums in his attaché case. *Here's the fly book,* he said. *Thought you could tell me something about them.*

We'll see, I smiled.

The fly book was surprisingly thick, a vintage Hardy found in the catalogues that followed the First World War. Its leather glowed with the patina of many summers, its thick felt pages surprisingly fat and secured with a thin strap and small, leather-covered buckle. There were several hundred flies, carefully sorted and aligned.

They're beautiful, I thought.

Some of the heavily dressed traditionals were quite old, with loop eyes of fine cable and silkworm gut. There were several strip-wings from the Dee in Scotland, including two thickly dubbed Ack-royds and a single Jock o'Dee, dressed on huge 8/0 irons. The same felt held a half-dozen beautifully slim dressings from the Spey farther north, using 5/0 and 6/0 hooks, with darkly mottled wings of brown mallard and trailing hackles of palmer-tied heron. Although I have never fished the Spey in late winter, somber Scottish patterns like the Grey Heron and Lady Caroline and Green King were familiar enough.

It was possible to imagine the old man in some past season, working these big winter irons in the swelling snowmelt at Gran-town-on-Spey or switch-casting patiently down the rocky pools be-tween Invercauld and Balmoral Castle.

Perhaps he fished the Punt and Wash-House and Brig o'Dee! I studied the flies thoughtfully, lost in memories of salmon rivers. *Perhaps he even took a fish at Queen's Favorite!*

There were many classic fly-patterns too, richly conceived flies like the Durham Ranger and the Thunder and Lightning and Jock Scott. Green Highlanders and Silver Greys also held places of honor. Bright-feathered flies like the Childers and Dusty Miller and Black Ranger were mixed with darker dressings like Sir Richard and Black Doctor and Black Dose. There were a few silvery flies too, with several Night Hawks and Lady Amhersts mixed among a rich palette of exotic patterns, like the Benchill and Candlestick Maker and Gordon.

These treasures were old and authentic dressings with married wings of florican, swan, bustard, blue chatterer, macaw, toucan, and jungle cock. Golden pheasant veiled bodies of slightly tarnished silver and fading, bright-colored silks. There were tiny tips of tinsel, and ribbings that combined flat tinsels edged with a delicate strand of oval silver wire, and these gleaming embellishments were faintly oxidized with the passing years. Such patterns were tied in the storied tradition of old masters like George Milward Kelson and T. E. Pryce-Tannatt.

Can't tell where he fished these flies, I thought. *Perhaps he was after springers on the Tweed or the Torridge or the Wye, although he might have fished the Restigouche or the York too.*

The felt leaf that followed held similar traditional flies, mixed with several big Waddingtons tied in standard dressings, like the Thunder and Lightning, Black Doctor and Jock Scott. Several tube flies in simplified dressings of the Blue Charm, Thunder and Lightning, and Garry Dog were hooked there too. These tubes had delicate, nickel-plated trebles pushed inside their hollow cores. With these modern patterns were a dozen huge Scottish flies, mostly gargantuan variations of the Torrish and a pair of gaudy Helmsdale Doctors.

These Waddingtons and tube flies look like the workmanship at Dickson's in Edinburgh, I mumbled half aloud, drawing a startled look from a stockbroker in the adjacent seat. *But those big Torrish irons must be the work of Megan Boyd!*

Megan Boyd is the premier fly dresser of salmon patterns in the United Kingdom, her feather-littered cottage located along the Brora in Sutherlandshire. She was recently awarded the British Empire Medal, when the royal honors list from Buckingham Palace cited her singular magic with fur, feathers and steel, and called attention to her unique contributions to foreign exchange through a thriving trade in salmon flies. Her versions of the Torrish, which is called the Scalscraggie in the Strath of Kildonan, are immensely popular during the late-winter spates that drain Sutherland and Caithness.

Look at that! I admired a huge Torrish.

Its bright hackles gleamed in the sunlight that filtered in through the grimy windows, and its silvery body was veiled in tiny feathers of the rare Indian crow. The train shuddered and braked clumsily into the station at New Brunswick, while I studied the richly mixed feathers in the antique pattern's wings.

The opposite felt was covered with big hair wings dressed on 1/0 to 3/0 hooks. There were several sparsely winged Orange Blossoms, the hair-wing variation on the Dusty Miller that evolved in Quebec, mixed with a dozen Abbeys, their bodies shaped from a dark, wine-colored crewel. The collection of hair-wing patterns included a full compliment of Black and Silver and Rusty Rats, with a brace of green-bodied Cossebooms providing a counterpoint of bold color.

These flies smell like the Restigouche! I thought excitedly. *But they liked the Abbey on the Alta too!*

Admiral William Read loved to fish similar patterns on the Alta twenty-five years ago, and favored its upper beats above Jøraholmen. His giant, fifty-nine-pound cockfish was killed there with a 5/0 Abbey on the Steinfossnakken, the sprawling pool that lies under sheltering escarpments at the wild Gabofoss waterfall. His trophy salmon was traced on the wainscoating at Sautso, in the sitting room of the fishing house built for the Duke of Roxburghe.

Turning the felt leaf slowly, I discovered several gaudy patterns dressed with startlingly bright feathers. These large flies were mixed with smaller dressings, although most were shaped on gleaming 4/0 and 5/0 irons. *These flies look like the work of Olav Olsen,* I thought. *Perhaps the old man fished with him at Hunderi, and walked the casting platforms there when the glacier-melt was coming.*

The smaller flies included a few somber versions that looked like the workmanship of Erling Sand, who comes from a family of Norwegian fly makers farther south in Engerdal. His flies are fully dressed in the typical Norwegian style, but his feathers are prepared in a more subtle mixture of chroma. Several of these flies were tied on graceful low-water hooks. There is good late-summer fishing on several rivers in the Sognefjord country, like the Aurland and Naerøy and the pastoral little Flåm, but the best of these summer salmon fisheries is unquestionably the swift-flowing Laerdal.

Maybe these Dusty Miller irons were tried on the Årøy! I thought happily. *And he probably fished the Tonjüm in low water.*

Beyond the soiled windows of the train, the storage tanks and refinery towers and piping systems reached toward Staten Island, but my thoughts were several thousand miles farther east in the steep-walled valley at Laerdalsøyri, where the herring gulls fill the mornings with their cries above the ferry slips.

The old man must have loved the casting platform above Moldebu. I remembered its gentle planking structure and the current tumbling through its pilings. *And perhaps he enjoyed a twilight supper on the scrollwork porch at the Lindström.*

There were almost six dozen exquisite low-waters too, with sparse throat hackles and slender feather-wing style. Such flies had their roots in the philosophy of Arthur H. E. Wood, who developed a unique method of fishing Atlantic salmon on the lower Dee in Scotland. The classic Wood low-water patterns were all there. Most of these flies were delicate Blue Charms, mixed with a few Silver Blues and March Browns. The others were a colorful assortment of other William Brown dressings like the Jeannie, Jockie, and Logie, plus a few slender Lady Carolines tied on the exquisite Wilson low-water hooks.

It seemed possible that the old man had actually fished them on the lower Dee, where Wood had perfected his theories on the shallow pools a few miles above Banchory. His water is still beautiful, and I fished it with a mixture of wonder and reverence a few seasons ago. There were also a dozen sparsely tied hairwings mixed with these low-water standards, their bodies scarcely thicker than the hooks that their floss concealed, and their slim style unmistakably the work of John Smith, a famous flymaker at Ballater.

The old man must have fished there! I stared at the brackish channels below a refinery trestle, where a gull sat watching the oil-covered water. *Wonder how he liked Canary and Malt Steep?*

The train gathered speed slowly again, sliding out under the trusswork structure of the Newark station, and the sunlight reflected dully on the current that eddied through the bridge pilings.

The fly book concealed some familiar artifacts, as well as patterns from the fly shops of Europe, and I fingered happily through a collection of Miramichi patterns. Several looked like the craftsmanship of tiers like Ira Gruber and Wallace Doak, and included dressings like the Oriole. There were the flies that John Atherton loved too, and painted in his book *The Fly and the Fish,* beautiful patterns like the Squirreltail and Minktail. The pair of delicate little Blackvilles seemed to suggest that they had been born at the fly-dressing bench of Bert Miner. Frayed nylon that remained in a brittle half hitch behind the head of a solitary Green Butt seemed to indicate that its owner had fished a riffling hitch in Newfoundland.

Jack Russell's old camp on the Miramichi is possible. I studied the frayed silk wrappings and dull tinsel. *But the old man might have hitched on the Serpentine or the River of Ponds too.*

Several other patterns were clustered together in the felt, and these flies were puzzling, although I discovered that they included a small assortment of pale Crosfields and Blue Sapphires and somber black-winged Sweeps. These were old favorites of mine.

Iceland! I thought. *He fished there too!*

These patterns are immensely popular among the knowledgeable men who regularly fish the rivers of Iceland. The fishing logs on those subarctic rivers from the Laxá in Pingeyjarsysla, to the tumbling waterfalls of the little Straumfjardará under the Snaefjellsnes volcano, are ample testimony of their effectiveness. The single purplish-hackled Blue Vulture confirmed my conviction that the old man had traveled to Iceland, since the unusual guinea-fowl dressing had its beginnings on the rivers above Reykjavik.

It seemed certain that the old man had fished the lingering twilights there, perhaps the gathering ledge shallows in the wildflower meadows of the Laxá at Husavik. Perhaps he worked his greased-line tactics at the Holakvorn on the lower Vatnsdalsá, where storied salmon fishermen like Charles Ritz and John Ashley-Cooper and Roderick Haig-Brown have plied their craft. It was also possible that he fished Stekkur on the Nordurá, and Dyrafljot on the pastoral little Langá.

Maybe he even fished the Grimsá, I whispered to myself, *and learned to love Strengir and Skardshylur and Laxabakki like I have.*

But the other patterns were still puzzling in spite of familiar dressings like the Peter Ross and Watson's Fancy. Mixed with these Scottish loch flies were several darker dressings aligned in the felt, flies like the Bibio and Sooty Olive. But it was a frayed Connemara Black that tipped the scales, and I wondered when the old man had traveled to Irish rivers like the Blackwater and Ballynahinch.

But the Bibio and Watson's Fancy are sea-trout flies, I thought. *Perhaps he fished at Cashla or Lough Currane instead.*

It was pleasant to speculate about the old man in his twilight years, journeying through the lovely countryside of Ireland, and I remembered the time I spent at Ashford Castle, and the swans in the gardens that reach down toward Lough Corrib. Such memories drift like a fishing boat on Lough Mask during its mayfly season, and I thought that the fly book had also journeyed with its owner through Limerick to explore the sea-trout lakes along the Ring of Kerry.

Its owner probably enjoyed the fine dinners in the high-ceilinged dining room at Ballynahinch, lingering over a subtle Pauillac before taking coffee in the castle library. It even seemed possible that the old man had walked upstream through the trees to fish from the masonry casting platforms below Ballynahinch, worked the pondlike holding water that Paul Hyde Bonner loved in the moors downstream and enjoyed the swiftly gathering currents at Derryclare Butts upstream.

It's beautiful there, I thought, remembering the painting of its lake over the mantelpiece at Ballynahinch. *He must have loved it.*

Six final flies were baffling. Five were relatively dark dressings with gold bodies and a thorax dubbing of olive seal fur. Claret hackles were faced with speckled guinea. The fully dressed wings were intricately married, mixing golden pheasant with a multicolored veil of swan, all sheathed in teal and brown mallard. The topping was a shining layer of golden-pheasant crest, and the wing was completed with jungle cock and blue chatterer. Paired horns of bright macaw were gracefully arched above the curving feathers that formed the wings.

What are these? I puzzled.

The last dressing was silver-bodied and equally unfamiliar. It had a delicate butt of scarlet crewel, its throat hackles a pale green and faced with speckled guinea. The wing was shaped over a pair of large jungle-cock feathers sheathed with golden-pheasant tippets. There were accents of multicolored swan dyed a delicate blue. The entire wing was partially veiled in barred mallard from the flanks of a mature drake, and completed with jungle cock and kingfisher. There were horns of blue macaw and a topping of pheasant crest, its golden fibers exquisitely curved above the wing feathers.

Finally I remembered where I had seen such patterns, thinking about the half-dozen flies from the feather-littered shop of Belarmino Martinez in the collection of William Ropner in Yorkshire. His dressings are created in Pravia, where the swift Nalon joins the Narcea in their tumbling descent from the forests of Cantabrica in northern Spain. My head was quickly filled with thoughts of the Navia and Eo, where the late General Francisco Franco often fished with his dark-haired little granddaughter, and of the ruined Roman bridge that vaults gracefully over the Deva-Cares.

It was possible to imagine the old fisherman there, enjoying a tureen of richly mixed seafoods and rice in some riverbank *hosteria* with a bottle of simple Spanish wine. Perhaps that dark Rioja would last through his supper to the platter of Galician cheeses and coffee, and later he might finish with a cognac glass of Fundador.

Such Spanish villages along that northern coastline are a peaceful refuge in this cacophonic century. There would not be many salmon in a week's fishing rights, perhaps no fish taken anywhere along the entire river, but it would not matter. Spain is the only place in the salmon angler's world where camellias and orange blossoms are blooming when the coin-bright fish are coming.

That's what these flies are. I was thinking about the Spanish flies in my own collection. *They're the Martinez patterns!*

When our train crossed the brackish marshes below Hackensack and plunged into the Stygian depths of the railroad tunnel under the Hudson, these pleasant reveries were shattered. The train roared through the darkness, its rumbling multiplied to such earsplitting crescendoes that all thoughts and conversations were completely erased.

We finally escaped the tunnel, clattering in through the intricate network of switches and spiderweb wires, until the train shuddered and slowed itself jerkily into Pennsylvania Station. It was time to join the milling crowds that fill its labyrinth of stairs and escalators and corridors. Reluctantly I closed the leather fly book and secured its strap, and returned it on the platform.

They're beautiful flies, I said.

We started toward the stairs through clouds of steam. *Are they worth anything?* my friend asked eagerly. *Should we try to sell them or should we keep them in the family?*

But they're a whole fly-fisher's life, I protested.

So we should keep them. He nodded thoughtfully. *You mean you could figure out where my uncle fished just from his flies?*

Something like that, I said.

That's pretty exciting! The man slipped the fly book into his raincoat. *Anything else you can tell me?*

Nothing, I said. *Except that I wish I'd known him.*

THE RIVER OF HUMILITY

It was after two o'clock when the bartender closed the pool tables at the Stagecoach, switching off the lights over their faded playing surfaces. The waitress collected the empty bottles and cocktail glasses and ashtrays from the tables and windowsills. The pool cues were carefully racked and the young bartender left the yellowing cue ball sitting on the worn felt. Two fishermen and their bearded guide had been shooting nine-ball after a long day's float on the spate-swollen Madison downstream from Varney Bridge.

The young bartender quickly washed and rinsed his glasses, and stacked them skillfully against the mirrors, where they caught and echoed the flickering lights of the beer signs. The local patrons sat nursing their last-call drinks. The waitress finished clearing her tables and sat talking with her friends, other young waitresses who had the night off or had stopped in for a nightcap after closing earlier. There was an old sheepherder sleeping with his head in his arms, his darkly stained hat covering his face, and his shabby cowboy boots hooked in the bar stool.

Fishing tomorrow? the bartender asked.

We fished the Firehole today. I grudgingly surrendered a half-finished drink. *We're on the Henry's Fork tomorrow.*

Those rainbows over there are tough, he said.

The bartender let his local customers out the street door and carefully closed the blinds. The waitress switched off the jukebox and pinball machines and beer signs, and the bartender wiped down his bar before trying to wake the old sheepherder.

André Puyans was already starting a second platter of fried eggs when we met for breakfast at Huck's Diner. There were ragged layers of mist hanging in the lodgepoles when we left West Yellowstone and climbed toward Targhee Pass. The surface of Henry's Lake was pale and still beyond its summit, and the bottoms were alive with grazing antelope and nesting sandhill cranes. We crossed the headwaters of the Henry's Fork at Mack's Inn, several miles below the gargantuan springs that give birth to the river, and stopped for licenses at Last Chance.

We left the fishing van at the upper fence line of the Harriman Ranch, crossed the irrigation canal on the split rails and walked downstream carrying our waders. Two hundred yards downriver, several fishermen were waiting for a mating swarm of tiny *Tricorythodes* flies to finish their egg laying. The morning sunlight was filled with the fluttering of their tiny white-winged swarms.

When their egg laying was completed, and the little mayflies were drifting in the surface film, the trout started to rise. Their rise forms were typical of spinner-fall feeding on those late summer mornings. While the little spent-winged flies were still drifting in the surface film, the trout took them with a methodical sipping rhythm, bulging and dimpling steadily while it lasted.

Look at all those fish! I said excitedly.

Such spinner falls last only a few minutes, and the fishermen who had waited for the egg laying to finish were casting frantically to the rising fish. One fisherman was surrounded by working trout, and his casting rhythms grew more and more desperate as the bulging rainbows refused his flies. The minute spent-wing flies were almost impossible to see in the current, but the feeding rhythms of the fish grew faster and faster, until suddenly they stopped. The morning rise to the *Tricorythodes* swarms was over.

The fisherman cursed angrily and threw his bamboo rod like a javelin, and its silver fittings flashed in the morning light. It traveled its brief trajectory and splashed into the river. The smooth current flowed quietly again, its tongues undulating in the rich beds of chara and potamogeton and bright-green fountain mosses.

Ever see anything like that? Puyans asked.

We watched the unhappy fisherman cross the river, angrily leaving a wake that scattered trout in all directions. *You mean so many fish rising in one place?* I finished stringing the double taper and added a tippet. *Or a fisherman throw away his rod?*

Both! Puyans laughed.

The fisherman reached the grassy bank and stared back grimly at the river. *Remember where it sank?* I asked.

Don't really give a damn! the fisherman growled.

What happened? Puyans asked.

Been fishing over these goddamned fish since breakfast! the fisherman explained bitterly. *I've never seen so many trout rising, and I haven't caught a thing all morning!*

What were you using? Puyans asked.

Everything that usually works! The man shook his head. *Renegades, Humpies, Grasshoppers, Muddlers, and Royal Wulffs!*

Those flies work everywhere but here, I said.

What's so special about this river? the fisherman protested in surprise. *Those are great patterns everywhere!*

These fish don't seem to know that.

You could make a living on the Henry's Fork! Puyans clapped the unhappy fisherman on the shoulder. *Betting people that their favorite fly-patterns won't catch these fish!*

He's right! I agreed unhappily.

The Henry's Fork is perhaps the finest trout stream in the United States, its headwaters a marriage of the outlet at Henry's Lake and the remarkable aquifers that rise at Big Springs. Their flowages are virtually constant, measuring almost 90,000 gallons per minute at a uniform fifty-two degrees.

Its drainage basin between Henry's Lake and Ashton includes more than a thousand square miles of forests and bunchgrass flats and sagebrush country. Other springheads and tributaries like the still-flowing Buffalo multiply its volumes of flow to more than 250,000 gallons per minute in the Box Canyon below the Island Park Reservoir. The fertile little Warm River joins the Henry's Fork a few miles below Mesa Falls, and the river discharges more than 500,000 gallons per minute through the reservoir at Ashton.

The watershed of the upper Henry's Fork is largely managed by the Forest Service. Its timber and plant cover and grazing are mostly intact, and its geology is remarkably permeable and stable.

The river is relatively shallow, and its profile is surprisingly gentle in its headwaters, measuring less than a thousand feet in its first thirty miles. Its winding flowages are 200 to 350 feet wide, except in its braided meadow channels, and its surface drainages are relatively minimal. The ecology of the watershed results in a remarkably stable and fertile aquatic habitat.

Knowledgeable anglers familiar with the river argue that its fertility and fly life make the Henry's Fork of the Snake the finest dry-fly stream in the world. Its prolific hatches emerge steadily throughout the season, sometimes in such profusion that a dozen species might be emerging or egg laying simultaneously.

Such extensive hatches and spinner falls can trigger spectacular rises of fish, although its trout are extremely selective and shy. Its currents are often encrusted with spent and emerging aquatic insects, and there are so many flies on the water that success is less a problem of matching a specific fly hatch, than a more difficult problem of finding which species the fish are taking.

These rainbows are really difficult, Puyans explained. *Just when you finally work out what they're taking—everything changes again and they're on something else!*

The river is almost 300 feet wide at the boundaries of the Harriman Ranch, and its free-rising rainbows are a challenge that attracts skilled anglers from everywhere. During the better fly hatches it has become a shrine for expert fishermen, and unlike most rivers in our time, the beautiful Henry's Fork is fishing better than it was in my boyhood years. The quality of its sport comes from the happy cornucopia of its character and its natural fertility, and the impact of its recent fly-only regulations.

Its 200-mile valley produces grain and fat potatoes and trout of remarkable quality, and the fertility of the river and its surrounding ranches and farmsteads is rooted in the unique ecology of the entire watershed.

Below the irrigation reservoir at Ashton, the river is multiplied by the flowages of the Fall and the Bechler, which rises in the southwestern highlands of the Yellowstone. The ill-fated Teton is flowing free again, following the tragic collapse of its controversial Teton reservoir, and it joins the Henry's Fork below Rexburg. Fishing is good throughout its entire river system, but the most productive habitat is found above the Mesa Falls, particularly on the Harriman property—a unique stretch of river willed to the State of

Idaho with the stipulation that its ecology be protected, and that fishing access be limited to fly-only regulations.

The special fly-only regulations proved so successful that some form of special regulations now applies from Lower Mesa Falls to the Big Springs, and the twenty-eight-mile stretch between the falls and the Island Park Reservoir is managed as a wild-trout fishery without the stocking of hatchery strains.

Between the south boundary of the Harriman Ranch and the Lower Mesa Falls, artificial flies and single-hook, barbless lures are required. From the Harriman property to the Island Park Reservoir, the same fly-fishing and single-hook-lure regulations apply, but there are no special regulations on the headwaters or the reservoir itself. The brief mileage below Big Springs is closed to fishing. Except for the closed water, and the stretch from Island Park Reservoir to Lower Mesa Falls, the river upstream from Ashton has a limit of six fish daily, with only two trout over sixteen inches. Between the reservoir and the waterfalls, three fish under twelve inches and a single trophy trout above twenty inches are permitted. The Harriman property itself is included in these daily catch limits and is fly-only water.

The philosophy behind these regulations argues that the primary brood stocks should be protected, in terms of both the quantity and the quality of their spawning. Earlier regulations on the Harriman water permitted no fish over fourteen inches in the daily creel limit, and a superb population of big rainbows soon resulted without costly programs of stocking hatchery fish. Some biologists firmly believe that the vitality and configuration and wariness that permit a fish to thrive and grow large are genetically transmitted. Protecting the large brood fish, while culling out the gullible trout below spawning sizes, bore remarkable fruit in recent years, and knowledgeable critics believe the new trophy-fish limit is a mistake.

It was politics again! Jack Hemingway explained recently in Sun Valley. *Some people just can't catch a big fish without wanting to kill it—yet these same people don't manage their cattle by butchering their best bulls and cows each year!*

André Puyans and I met with René Harrop along the river at Last Chance, and we sat in the warm meadows waiting for another hatch of flies. Harrop is a remarkably skilled fly dresser from Saint Anthony, a small potato-farm community on the lower river, and he understands its moods and fly hatches and fish almost better than anyone in the Henry's Fork country. Harrop has proved those skills many times on the river in recent years.

You know, Puyans studied the current thoughtfully, *that poor guy who threw away his rod had a point about wondering what makes the Henry's Fork so unique.*

You're right, I nodded.

It's really a combination of factors, Harrop agreed. *Starting with the giant springs at its source.*

It's the biggest chalkstream in the world, I suggested.

Don't forget Henry's Lake, Puyans added.

The first trapper to explore the Henry's Fork country was John Colter, the scout who left the Lewis and Clark expedition before it returned to Saint Louis in 1806. Colter helped a second party of fur traders to establish a stockade on the lower Yellowstone, and then disappeared south into the Absarokas to explore future trapping grounds. His solitary explorations carried him into Jackson Hole, where he crossed the Tetons to the Henry's Fork in 1807.

The river itself was later christened for Colonel Andrew Henry, who had formed the Rocky Mountain Fur Company with William Henry Ashley in 1822. It was later that Colonel Henry organized the first trapper's rendezvous on the Green River in Wyoming in 1826, but his first party had wintered on the Henry's Fork sixteen years earlier.

Alexander MacDonald described these early years in his charming book *On Becoming a Fly Fisherman,* which was published at Boston in 1959. It was illustrated with a delicate frontispiece of watercolors by the late Leslie Thompson, and his work depicted several important Henry's Fork hatches and their imitations.

Henry Stamp was an early homesteader in the valley, but its angling traditions probably begin with Alfred Trude, a wealthy Chicago attorney who acquired a large cattle ranch on the river in 1889. Trude became famous four years later when he successfully prosecuted the man who had killed Carter Harrison, the colorful mayor of Chicago who sponsored the World Columbian Exposition. Harrison's son subsequently served five terms as mayor, and was a serious angler who often fished the Trude property. The younger Harrison is credited with the first hair-wing trout flies, which were dressed on the Henry's Fork, and named for his host after a successful baptism.

Fishermen were also traveling to fish the Stamp property before the close of the nineteenth century, and several wealthy Californians founded the North Fork Club there in 1902. Four years later, another group purchased the remaining acreage from Stamp to build their Flat Rock Club. The famous Coffee Pot Club was founded about 1911, and its members consisted of fishermen and their families who wanted something more comfortable than the spartan quarters and cuisine customary at the North Fork and Flat Rock memberships. The stories of their sport, and the market fishermen who supplied the Union Pacific trains and Yellowstone hotels, are a remarkable testimony to the fertility of the river and its fishery before the First World War.

Some of the mileage they fished lies submerged under the Island Park Reservoir, and both the oral history of the valley and the memoirs of Carter Harrison tell us that they struggled back from the river with catches they found difficult to carry.

However, such reservoirs are not invariably fatal to their watersheds and fisheries. Both Henry's Lake and the Island Park Reservoir function as giant stilling basins in the spring, collecting the spates and spring snowmelt, and settling out the river's murkiness when its sister rivers are high and discolored. The sediments that precipitate out in the depths of the reservoir are a source of fertility too, since the silt beds are composed largely of richly alkaline soils chemistry, collected across the past half century. Such silts have apparently magnified the ambient fertility of the river.

The remarkable fertility of the river can pose some unusual trout-fishing problems. Perhaps the most striking are the riddles of multiple and masking fly hatches. Multiple hatches can come in many forms. Sometimes there are several species emerging at once, and a mixture of careful observation and trial-and-error tactics is needed to find which hatch the fish are taking. Trout often concentrate on species that are readily available, or are more easily captured with a minimal expenditure of energy, but such logic does not always apply.

The masking hatch is another puzzle. It occurs when the trout are working steadily during a major hatch, yet refuse effective imitations of that species. Such selectivity is invariably focused upon less obvious aquatic-diet forms, either because they are more easily captured or the fish have grown accustomed to them. There was a remarkable example of masking-hatch behavior two seasons ago, when I was fishing with Jack Hemingway and Dan Callaghan.

The big drakes are coming, Hemingway explained when we reached the river and rigged our tackle.

We were fishing the Harriman mileage during its early-summer hatch of lead-winged drakes, and the first of these large olive-bodied flies were already fluttering down the current when we arrived. Big fish had started working, and it was difficult to rig our tackle because of the steady blup-blup of their feeding.

The big mayflies were still hatching in the early afternoon, and were mixed with a regatta of tiny yellow-bodied duns. Since there were more of the drakes hatching, and the olive-bodied flies were twice the size of the yellowish species on the water, we decided to fish imitations of the larger species. Its flies were everywhere on the smooth current below the ranch and its outbuildings.

We promptly caught several trout. Although the fish were only ten to twelve inches, our success tempted us into staying with the big dry-fly imitations, and I took several more fish before I found a really large rainbow porpoising against the bank. Its leisurely feeding exposed a heavily spotted dorsal, and a huge tail that sent waves along the trailing grass. It was working in a steady rhythm, and I dropped my fly cautiously into its line of drift, but the big rainbow simply inspected the float and rejected it.

That's strange, I thought. *The others wanted it.*

The big trout was still working steadily, but it ignored a series of drag-free floats. Several times it took something I failed to see, just before my fly reached its feeding station, and twice it took something just after the fly drifted past.

What's he taking? It was an intriguing puzzle.

Finally I stopped fishing and watched the trout. It was obvious that the fish was not taking the lead-winged drakes, although the big flies were coming down its line of drift. Several times it dropped back under a big drake that was hopscotching down its current tongue and rejected it too, drifting back to its feeding station to inhale something smaller in the film. It was puzzling behavior for a large trout and I was fascinated.

Another lead-winged olive came down tight against the grass, and the big rainbow drifted back lazily to inspect its passage. The big mayfly struggled clumsily in the current. The fish pushed its spotted nose against the fluttering drake, drifted with it in the current for a heart-stopping moment, and slipped back upstream. The big drake finished drying its wings and flew off.

That's amazing! I thought.

The big trout rose again and took something. The fish tipped back again under a fluttering drake, refused it after a brief moment of indecision, and dimpled lazily to take something smaller.

But this time I spotted the pale sailboat-shaped wings of its prey half-pinioned in the surface film. Another pale little dun drifted in its feeding lane and was taken without hesitation.

It's been on the nymphs of those pale flies!

The big rainbow settled into a steady rhythm of surface feeding now that the pale little duns were emerging. Their nymphs had been in the surface film all along, mixed with the somber nymphs and lead-winged drakes that were hatching from them, but the pale-yellowish hatch was the species they wanted. The big drakes had been hatching for only two or three days, but the yellowish *Ephemerella* flies had been a staple diet form for several weeks. The big trout was obviously suspicious of the bigger drakes, since they were much darker and larger than the fly hatches of the preceding days. Such behavior is typical of large trout that have been caught and released, and I rummaged through my flies for an imitation of the pale-bodied duns.

The fish drifted back under the first drag-free float, intercepted it tight against the trailing grass, and took the tiny fly softly. It shook itself angrily when I tightened, and exploded upstream. *Finally he took it!* I thought happily.

The big rainbow stopped its first wild run, and jumped three times in graceful pirouettes that flashed silver in the morning light. Suddenly the reel was protesting again, and the fly line sliced past me in the current. The tippet raked briefly against the fountain moss and elodea, and the leader knots throbbed with their tufts of pale-green vegetation. Finally the trout jumped again and shook it free, stripping the reel deep into its backing. There were other half jumps and wild threshings on the surface downstream, and I was waiting for the fragile tippet to shear against the current drag or the tiny fly to pull free, but the fish was still there.

It's a miracle! I whispered.

The fight settled into a patient struggle against the straining nylon, with the big fish circling stubbornly and threatening to root into the weeds. It burrowed under a trailing bed of potamogeton late in the fight, but lacked the strength to break the delicate tippet, and I worked it free.

It's almost finished! I thought excitedly.

The big rainbow finally surrendered and measured better than twenty-two inches, and I gently worked the tiny fly from its mouth. It held restlessly in the net meshes, regaining its strength while I waited, and suddenly it was gone. It was a perfect example of masking-hatch behavior, in which selective fish reject an obvious fly hatch to concentrate on some other diet form.

The river sustains a remarkable spectrum of fly hatches, ranging from the huge *Pteronarcys* stoneflies in its swifter currents to the incredible populations of white-winged *Tricorythodes* and *Pseudocloeon* flies in hook sizes as small as twenty-eight. Some of the finest fly hatches on the Henry's Fork occur in the early summer, starting with the salmonflies in its Box Canyon stretch, and the big lead-winged *Ephemerella* hatches that follow. There are pale morning hatches in the first weeks of fishing too, and a superb hatch of smaller slate-winged olives comes off at twilight in July. Some knowledgeable big-trout fishermen like the brown-mottled *Ephemera* drakes found in the slow-flowing stretches of the Harriman property. Several other species display heavy mating swarms, and the spinner falls of the *Tricorythodes* and *Callibaetis* and *Pseudocloeon* mayflies can trigger some beautiful rises of fish on the Henry's Fork. Mixed with these hatches throughout the season are swarms of slate-colored sedges, and a rich palette of ants and grasshoppers and beetles. Perhaps the easiest fishing occurs in its grasshopper years.

But it's never really easy! André Puyans argues.

You'll find that its bank-feeders are less picky than the small trout at midstream, René Harrop explained further. *They're always on terrestrials along with their aquatic hatches.*

Those smaller fish are usually more selective, Puyans agreed, *because they're almost entirely on mayflies and caddis.*

And our hatches are pretty tiny flies! Harrop added.

Obvious surface feeding to a visible hatch of flies is common on the Henry's Fork, but both men agree that the most spectacular rises of trout usually are found there after a mating swarm of mayflies, when their spent adults drift flush in the surface film. During those spinner falls, the fish lie just under the water, and porpoise and dimple gently in a steady feeding rhythm. Strong swirls and surging boils usually point to *Trichoptera* feeding, and the fish are either taking the emerging sedges before they can escape into the atmosphere, or rising splashily to egg-laying caddisflies.

Bold rises at midday are sometimes to grasshoppers and beetles.

Sometimes important pieces of the Henry's Fork puzzle are found in a knowledge of the river and its microhabitat. Its watercourse is almost entirely of moderate depth, and its subtle flows echo its relatively gentle profile. Yet it does display some variations in its character, and its fly-hatch activity is directly related to such subtle relationships. Weather can also play a major role in hatch matching on the Henry's Fork.

Microhabitat is an intriguing factor in fly hatches. Major flies like the big lead-wing drakes, and the slate-winged *Ephemerella flavilinea* and the several pale morning duns, are all gravel-loving species that hatch from the flowing channels between the weeds. Mayfly hatches like *Siphlonurus* and the speckle-winged *Callibaetis* and the tiny *Pseudocloeon* flies hatch from the weeds themselves. *Tricorythodes* nymphs are particularly fond of cover along the banks, and the round handful of many-brooded *Baetis* flies that thrive on the Henry's Fork are swimming nymphs that prefer the moderate currents there. The brown-mottled *Ephemera* drakes have silt-burrowing nymphs, and their hatching is concentrated in the slow-flowing stretches. Such knowledge of the relationships between nymph behavior and microhabitat can help determine what the fish are doing in a particular feeding-lie.

The egg-laying behavior of mayflies is another intriguing factor in fishing the Henry's Fork. The spinner falls of species with nymphs that prefer flowing currents are invariably found downstream from the riffles and oxygen-rich currents where their eggs are laid. Slow-water flies like *Ephemera* and *Pseudocloeon* and *Tricorythodes* usually mate and oviposit over quieter currents. Since the spent adults of any spinner fall are difficult to see on the water because their wings and bodies are trapped in the surface film, the character of the current immediately upstream from a sudden flurry of spinner-fall feeding is a primary clue in matching the hatch.

Weather and wind are often critical factors too. Blustery winds can sailboat the hatching flies off their principal lines of drift, until the trout are forced to concentrate on the hatching nymphs, which are not affected by the wind. Misting drizzles with little wind are particularly good dry-fly weather, because a gentle rain can slow the drying of the freshly hatched wings and keep the flies floating on the current longer. Steady winds can often drive so many hatching flies against a downwind bank that the fish migrate there to feed, and particularly high winds will sometimes concentrate feeding activity in the shelter of the upwind shores.

Storms are sometimes a factor in changing the normal patterns controlled by factors of microhabitat. Two seasons ago, during an unusually heavy period of brown *Ephemera* hatches, a twilight squall scattered the emerging duns upstream. So many flies were carried off on the wind that there were strange mating swarms the following nights, and a spinner fall of these big brown-mottled drakes on a stretch of the Henry's Fork where they are seldom observed.

What about leader design? I asked.

Some people fish as much as twenty-five feet, Harrop replied. *Hemingway likes his leaders that long, and most fishermen use tippets as delicate as 5X and 6X.*

Some fishermen fish still finer tippets?

That's right, Puyans laughed, *but I usually fish about fifteen feet with a thirty-six-inch tippet.*

Three-foot tippets? I said.

Gives you a better drag-free float, Puyans continued, *and we usually fish downstream to these fish.*

They're that tippet shy? I protested.

False-casting can scare them too, Harrop nodded in agreement. *Casting upstream usually spooks these trout no matter how well you cast, or no matter what tippet you use!*

That's really shy! I admitted.

We walked downstream and reached the islands on the Harriman property, and the fish in their back channels were already rising greedily to a hatch of tiny *Pseudocloeon* flies. I took a dozen rainbows on a little Gray-winged Olive dressed on a twenty-six hook. The pattern worked wonders during the emergence of these tiny green-bodied duns, but suddenly the fish started refusing it.

They've switched! I yelled.

René Harrop was fishing a hundred yards upstream, where the still currents riffled down from the islands and shelved off deep against the grassy banks. When I looked upstream to see how he was doing, Harrop was studying the water intently and not fishing. It was obvious that his fish had turned fickle too.

What are they doing? I shouted.

I'm not really sure! Harrop shouted back. *These fish have stopped and I've got a big swarm of tiny spinners here!*

Think it's the spinners?

It might be, Harrop answered. *These little spinners are the green-bodied species that just hatched.*

You think these fish are really that picky?

Sometimes they are! he laughed.

Harrop is perhaps the most knowledgeable fisherman on the Henry's Fork, and his ability to observe subtle changes in selectivity and feeding patterns is widely acknowledged along the river. The minute spinners of these twilight *Pseudocloeon* hatches are exactly the same color and size as the freshly hatched duns that emerge an hour before their mating swarms. There is no difference in these two stages of their life cycle, except that the duns drift on the current with upright wings and the tiny spinners come down spent, their pale wings pinioned in the surface film. Their imitations are tied on twenty-six and twenty-eight hooks, and it seemed highly unlikely that only the silhouette of their spent wings lying in the film could prove critical with such tiny flies.

You think a little polywing pattern would work? I yelled upstream. *These fish won't touch the upright anymore!*

Try it and see! Harrop shouted back.

There were several spent polywings in my Wheatley, and I changed flies looking up against the sky. Several large fish were dimpling softly in the smooth currents downstream, where I was looking into the waning light. There was a delicate sucking swirl on my first cast, and a fat sixteen-inch rainbow exploded when it felt the hook. Three more took the little polywing before it refused to float, and I tied a fresh pattern to the tippet in the failing light. The first drift with the fresh pattern hooked an acrobatic four-pound rainbow that stripped the shrill Hardy into its backing.

They seem to like the spinners! Harrop observed wryly.

We found Puyans in the water meadows upstream, muttering to himself about the huge rainbow that he had hooked in the shallows and had lost when it bolted downstream through a submerged fence. *Well,* Puyans grinned happily, *what about these fish?*

They don't make too many mistakes, I admitted.

They're really pretty fair about it too! Puyans laughed. *These Henry's Fork rainbows make fools of everybody!*

It's a river that really tests you, I agreed.

It's the toughest river anywhere, Harrop smiled. *It's the difference between checkers and playing chess!*

FAREWELL MY LOVELY

There was early frost in the river bottoms in late August, and the flight ducks migrated upstream in the mornings, their crisp wing-beats whistling above the swift channels. Whiteface cattle grazed stolidly in the pastures. The mowing crews had finished their work in the hayfields, and their carefully stacked bales echoed the desert ruins farther south at Acoma and Chaco Canyon and Taos.

Gunnison mornings were like that thirty-odd years ago, when it was a favorite boyhood river. We sometimes stayed at the old Cooper guest ranch, and beyond its corrals and outbuildings, the river flowed swift and low through its channels in the coyote willows and alders.

Across the tractor-bridge trestle, where the Tomichi bottoms reach thirty miles back toward the Cochetopa Pass, the irrigation ditches lie in intricate lacework patterns across the hayfields. The river itself was a labyrinth of channels riffling across the valley floor. Its old cottonwoods moved restlessly in the August wind, and the first cold nights were already changing their color.

Breakfast sizzled in our cabin on the Cooper place. Our tackle hung on the porch nails, and we rigged our equipment there, stringing rods and wrestling with our waders.

The morning hatches were particularly good, and sometimes we fished the evening spinner falls. There were other trips too, when we tried floating the river farther downstream, almost to the threshold of the storied Black Canyon of the Gunnison. There was one spring when we found the river running clear during its willow-fly hatches, and I remember a six-pound brown at Sapinero.

Those were happy summers in western Colorado, which I described in the book *Remembrances of Rivers Past,* and later we watched angrily when the famous Gunnison mileage between the Cooper property and Sapinero was drowned in the huge reservoir completed at Blue Mesa in 1965. It was a time of mourning among Colorado fishermen.

Well, we thought in resignation, *there's always the Black Canyon itself—they can't ruin that too!*

The somber Black Canyon of the Gunnison was still farther downstream, its 2,000-foot precipices and cathedral walls still a primeval echo of frontier times, and seemingly impenetrable.

Our sanctuary was also violated in the next five years with the completion of the ferroconcrete dam at Morrow Point, and a full twenty miles of the upper Black Canyon were submerged in more than 400 feet of water. The unblemished canyon and its river had been maimed. Fishing groups sought desperately to block a second project at the threshold of the Black Canyon National Monument itself, only fifteen miles downstream from Morrow Point.

Their coalition eventually lost a series of court fights, and the Bureau of Reclamation broke ground for its Crystal reservoir project in 1972. The Crystal impoundment is completed now, and its steep-walled gorge is still filling, forever dooming the last fishable stretch of the Black Canyon of the Gunnison.

Pete Van Gytenbeek and I had often talked about the old days on the Gunnison watershed, in places as varied as the Purdy meadows along Silver Creek to the venerable Brown Palace in Denver. When he proposed a farewell expedition through the gorge, I happily accepted his invitation to join their float.

It sounds exciting! I agreed over lunch in Manhattan. *But something between a weekend lark and a wake!*

We received permission from the Bureau of Reclamation to travel the entire canyon between Morrow Point and its Crystal site, and were assigned three days in late September. Our party was quickly mobilized, with a breakfast rendezvous in Montrose.

David Crandall is the director of the Upper Colorado watershed for the Bureau of Reclamation, and he joined us over breakfast that morning, offering us a helicopter ride to give us a bird's-eye perspective of the entire Gunnison river system.

It's the only way to understand it, Crandall insisted.

We boarded the helicopter in Montrose, while the remainder of our party embarked with its boats and trailer rigs and vans for the river. We agreed to meet for lunch at Morrow Point.

The helicopter engine whined and caught, and we lifted off from its pad hanging nose down into the wind, climbing south toward the San Juan mountains. The farms and small ranches along the Uncompahgre lay ahead, its silty channels winding sluggishly through a checkerboard of orchards and sugar beets and melons. The rich patchwork of irrigation sprawled toward Utah, which lies a hundred miles farther west on the horizon, its mountains lost in the haze.

It was nothing but desert here a century ago. Crandall pointed beyond the river. *The Uncompahgre was always moody—it was silty and unpredictable even in frontier times.*

Our helicopter flew west along the river, its tadpole shadows ghosting across the villages and truck farms and ranches, and the network of canals and irrigation ditches that glittered in the September morning. Crandall explained that the early homesteaders found the irrigation potential of the Uncompahgre relatively limited, and that its discharges had been augmented with transfusions through the Gunnison diversion tunnel completed in 1909.

The Uncompahgre diversion tunnel was one of the first projects completed by the fledgling Bureau of Reclamation, and it was so politically important to the Republican party that President William Howard Taft traveled to Colorado for its dedication.

Politics are important out here, I thought wryly.

The Gunnison itself was ahead, beyond the tree-lined streets of Delta, and our pilot circled back upstream toward the scrub-oak rim that conceals the Black Canyon itself. The river wound against its spare dove-gray foothills, its channel lined with cottonwoods and willows. *It's pretty silty down here,* I pointed.

It's been silty below the canyon since I was a kid, Crandall nodded, *but our Crystal project will change that too—it's got discharge chambers that will eliminate those sediments.*

Sounds pretty good, I admitted grudgingly.

Its tailwaters should flow absolutely clear, Crandall predicted, *and they should stay cold enough to extend the trout habitat as much as twenty or thirty miles farther west.*

What about the Uncompahgre? I asked.

Its water will run clear too, Crandall answered, *and cold down to its junction with the Gunnison.*

The helicopter sliced low across an arid mesa of piñon and scrub-oak thickets, and then flared suddenly to hover over the mesa rim. The yawning gorge completely dwarfed its river, tumbling like a necklace 2,500 feet under our whirring rotors.

There are places where its somber walls are scarcely fifty feet apart, and the spring spates leave an angry scour line where they rage high along the cliffs. There are winter months when the sunlight never reaches the river and impenetrable twilight fills the gorge, giving the Black Canyon its somber name. Its Painted Wall rises almost straight from the tumbling currents, its precipices more than twice the depth of the Royal Gorge on the Arkansas.

The pilot dropped ahead into the gorge itself, and our shadow slipped and leaped along its steep north wall. Our helicopter flew a serpentine course along its saw-toothed rims, while we stared like schoolboys into its awesome depths.

It's incredible! I thought excitedly.

The Black Canyon of the Gunnison was not discovered until the middle of the nineteenth century, since the seemingly impenetrable barrier of the Rocky Mountains had forced the earlier explorers and wagon trains to cross farther north in Wyoming.

Its discovery was an echo of American politics before the Civil War, when our westward expansion became a major issue in the Congress of the United States. Thomas Hart Benton was a powerful senator with thirty years in Washington, having first won his seat when Missouri was admitted to statehood in 1821. His politics were twofold, based firmly on voting for both the gold standard and every piece of legislation that favored settlement of the frontier.

John Charles Fremont had become his son-in-law, and both men were totally committed to dreams of Manifest Destiny and the concept that only railroads could bind the fledgling United States together. Benton had long argued that the most direct rights-of-way offered more promise than the proposed routes farther north through Wyoming. It was finally determined that a series of military topographic parties should explore these alternatives, and Benton cannily used his influence to secure command of the first party for his son-in-law.

Fremont's first expedition traveled the relatively known routes across Wyoming to the Pacific in 1844, circled southward into California, and returned to Saint Louis the following year. His second party attempted to prove Benton's theories that an optimal rail right-of-way traversed the Rockies farther south in Colorado. Fremont led his second party across the Kansas prairies to Bent's Fort in 1848, and the expedition nearly perished in the San Juan mountains because Fremont insisted that the route lay through the headwaters of the Rio Grande. The pitiful survivors of those early blizzards escaped back along the river and wintered at Taos.

Senator Benton stubbornly refused to admit defeat, and forced the Congress to mount a third topographic party to explore routes through Colorado. Fremont had been shaken by the fierce Colorado blizzards, and perhaps dreamed of exploiting his adventures for his own political ambitions, so their third expedition was mounted under the command of Captain John Williams Gunnison in 1853.

The Gunnison party also crossed the high-plains country to Bent's Fort, on the Arkansas in the foothills of the Rockies, and ascended the Huerfano to cross the Sangre de Cristo mountains. Circling back north through the San Luis basin, the expedition used Saguache Creek to traverse the continental divide into the headwaters of Cochetopa Creek. Gunnison and his men followed its tumbling course northward into the Tomichi bottoms, and had reached the watershed of the Gunnison itself. The country seemed relatively open, looking westward from the Cochetopa summits, and optimism over finding a rail right-of-way beyond Bent's Fort was running high when they reached the river.

Their mountain crossings had been relatively easy, and the San Luis and Tomichi basins were rich in water and game. The Gunnison is relatively placid too, in the sweeping channels and riffling shallows below its junction with the Tomichi. The party cut cottonwoods along the river and built rafts, and happily embarked on what they believed would prove an easy river trip to Utah.

There is no prelude in the terrain that suggests the presence of a formidable gorge, and the Gunnison company floated the river easily until they reached the Black Canyon.

When the party lost a raft loaded with equipment and supplies, Gunnison prudently decided to dispatch his scouts ahead to determine the character and length of the gorge. The returning scouts soon dispelled any dreams of an easy river passage farther west. The terrible precipices seemingly ended their hopes of a rail right-of-way too, but Gunnison decided to press farther west, patiently charting the unknown country he was crossing. The scouts suggested that circling past the south rim of the canyon seemed their best route, and the company crossed the scrub-oak plateaus until it reached the sluggish Uncompahgre watershed, in relatively open country.

The party constructed another flotilla of rafts when they reached the Gunnison below the Black Canyon, and passed the fifty-mile float to the Colorado without incident. Gunnison and his men rested there for several days, hunting fresh game and refitting their rafts while the scouts explored the Colorado itself. The scouts proposed using their rafts another fifty miles, to the mouth of the Dolores, and then traveling directly west past the Roan Plateau, fording the Green between its Desolation Canyon and the formidable Cataract Canyon on the Colorado. Gunnison followed their counsel, and the expedition crossed the Wasatch Range in the headwaters of the San Rafael. The terrible deserts of western Utah and Nevada still lay ahead, in a parched world where few roads exist today, when Gunnison and his party descended the Salina and made their ill-fated campsite on the Sevier.

Their campsite was attacked by hostile Indians, and Gunnison and his party were massacred. The railroad right-of-way they were seeking was never attempted.

There's the Crystal site! the pilot shouted.

The construction site lay ahead, its ugly half-completed profile already blocking the entire river. Its cylindrical siltation chambers were taking shape downstream, and its cofferdams and construction tunnels were huge scars in the river and its cliffs.

We hovered over the workings while Crandall and his engineer explained its design, and then our helicopter shadow leapfrogged its massive abutments and partially completed walls, while we flew into the doomed canyon upstream. The fifteen-mile stretch of pools and riffling shallows and rapids we would be floating that weekend were under our helicopter as we followed the gorge.

We've got some serious rapids down there! I said.

That's right! Crandall shouted above our engine. *But the river is even wilder below the Crystal site!*

It's really that bad? I yelled back.

We've had some people who tried floating through the canyon in the National Monument stretch, Crandall replied grimly, *and I never met anybody who wanted to try it again!*

The pilot circled the Morrow Point project briefly, where our party were already launching their boats, and they waved as our helicopter crossed the dam toward the reservoir at Blue Mesa. The reservoir there covers more than fourteen square miles, with almost a hundred miles of shoreline and three boat landings. Its earthwork dam has more than three million cubic yards of fill and rubble in its structure, and was completed in 1965.

Besides its popularity for boating and fishing, Blue Mesa provides more than one million acre-feet of irrigation storage, multiplying the capacity of the relatively small Taylor project completed in its headwaters during the Great Depression.

When we complete the Crystal project, Crandall explained, *it will provide a better diversion system into the Uncompahgre, and its power will make our Curecanti development capable of supplying enough kilowatts for the entire western slope of Colorado!*

It's a lot of energy, I admitted.

Blue Mesa lay glittering in the late September sun, its eastern beaches strangely turquoise with drifting algae. Fishermen were working the sheltered coves for hatchery rainbows and kokanee, and the marina at Elk Creek was swarming with boats. Country towns like Cebolla and Sapinero and Iola lie drowned in its sprawling impoundment, along with the thirty-five miles of water that once made the Gunnison the best-known trout stream in the Rocky Mountains.

Scarcely five miles of the river itself survive below Gunnison, except for the fifteen miles that are disappearing under the slowly filling depths behind the Crystal Dam, and perhaps another fifteen miles of free-flowing river lie above the town. Little of that mileage is accessible to public fishing.

Wasn't it Elk Creek where the first rainbows were planted in the Rocky Mountain states? I asked.

That's right, Crandall replied.

The pilot pulled our helicopter back into a tight climbing circle that carried us back toward our landing site at Morrow Point. The prime mule-deer mesas north of the Black Canyon flashed under our windmilling rotors, and we crossed the aquamarine depths of its canyon impoundment toward the dam itself.

Our pilot sliced over the curving structure of its rim, sliding down over the landing zone to clear its tourists, and climbed back steeply into Cimarron Canyon in a high, rotor-chattering turn. The helicopter hung at its brief apogee, before it then fluttered back almost lazily to settle in the macadam parking lot.

Pretty dramatic approach! I said laconically.

Morrow Point is a startlingly immense curve of concrete that barricades the canyon two miles north of Cimarron. Its structure is the first paraboloid thin-shell dam attempted in the United States, rising 469 feet above the river and spanning as much as 741 feet between its upper canyon walls. Its unique design is slightly more than fifty feet thick at its foundations, but only twelve feet thick at its graceful rim, and required 365,000 cubic yards of concrete.

Behind the structure itself, where the upper twenty miles of the Black Canyon have been flooded since its completion in 1969, the reservoir at Morrow Point can store another 117,000 acre-feet of irrigation capacity. Its impoundment totals more than 800 acres, although it averages between 200 and 300 feet in depth, and its steep-walled shoreline completely lacks the fertile shallows that are necessary to sustain both fish and their food-chain species. Similar biological problems will limit the fish populations behind the Crystal project too.

It hurts me to admit it, Van Gytenbeek said grudgingly, *but if any dam is beautiful, you've got to admit that a concrete thin-shell dam like Morrow Point is beautiful!*

It's a pretty exciting structure, I admitted.

But it doesn't offer much fishing, Jim Rumsey grumbled bitterly as he finished loading our supplies in his MacKenzie boat, lashing the waterproof bags and coolers under its seats, *and I'd never trade twenty miles of the Gunnison for any reservoir!*

The farmers might disagree, I said sadly.

The torrent leaving the penstock chambers under Morrow Point was turquoise and cold in its riprapped channel, tumbling past our boat landing with its fierce mixings of emerald and spume. Our flotilla had embarked there, pushing off at thirty-minute intervals, with a supper rendezvous at the beach under Moon Cliffs.

Jim Rumsey and I left our moorings last, drifting out until we were caught in a current that was surprisingly swift. Our boat accelerated in its gathering flow, while Rumsey adjusted his oarlocks and studied its rhythms in the rapids ahead.

Water slopped across our gunwales, and Rumsey skated his boat skillfully between the boulders, concentrating hard to discover the submerged hazards. There was a minor breathtaking chute tight along the cliffs, and the steep-walled gorge ahead was already shrouded in shadows. The river seemed even swifter now, and as our boat plunged and hopscotched through a steep roller-coaster slide, spray slopped over the bow and there was a frightening roar.

The river surged through a long boulder-strewn rapids, dropping into a narrow chute where the choppy waves showered us both. Rumsey clenched his teeth when the waves lifted him from his seat with their fierce back pressure on his oars.

There was a somber pyramid of granite blocking the current ahead, forcing its strength back across the river in a churning chute. *Dead Man's Rock!* Rumsey shouted. *Sit tight!*

The huge rock was freshly scarred with orange paint, and there was an ice chest in the shallows. *Look there!* I pointed.

We've lost a boat! Rumsey groaned.

The throat of the rapids was deceptively smooth, its current slicing past the boulders with a sound like tearing silk. The straining oars echoed the river's force, lifting Rumsey from his seat again while he fought for control. His technique was faultless, the boat sideslipping in the current until its bow was aimed directly at Dead Man's Rock, and skating safely away in the last moment. We plunged past the mammoth boulder and its ominous paint scar.

It's the Boutelle boat! Rumsey yelled unhappily.

Our run was still not finished, because a giant fifty-foot boulder loomed in the shadows downstream, its base alive with sucking currents that could devour a boat. Rumsey fought the current hard, straining back against the river, and backpedaling frantically to escape the chute into the quiet waters of the pool downstream.

Our entire party was moored along the rocks, and several boatmen had clambered back along the boulders to the giant rock, where the Boutelle boat was wedged in its hungry currents.

Its seats were gone, its equipment stripped free by the currents surging against its shuddering gunwales. Fishing tackle and camping gear and other duffle floated in the circling eddies downstream and a broken oar bobbed in the shallows. *They lost an oar going in!* Rumsey shook his head. *They didn't have a prayer!*

Equipment salvaged from the river was spread to dry on the rocks, and Bill Boutelle had wrapped his shivering father in a down sleeping bag from the Van Gytenbeek boat. Cooking pans and aluminum rod cases gleamed in the swift bottom currents of the pool. The crippled boat had a badly cracked frame, and the fierce currents masked the ragged holes in its submerged plywood hull.

The mishap cost most of our fishing time, since we could not fish carefully and still run the river to our campsite at twilight. Its currents were simply too treacherous. It took two hours to free the Boutelle boat, brace its badly cracked hull with salvaged thwarts and river driftwood, and patch its wounds with a plywood seat stripped from a second boat. The shattered MacKenzie could no longer carry passengers and equipment, but it seemed riverworthy enough that the younger Boutelle could travel ahead alone. His father and their salvaged cargo were transferred to other boats in the party.

It was already getting cold when we embarked again. *You look a little blue.* Rumsey searched in his duffle. *You can borrow this extra down jacket on this run.* The late sun had left the river, touching only the north canyon rim a thousand feet above its currents.

We collected lost equipment for miles. There were apples and milk cartons and cooking pots bobbing in the backwaters. Floating cushions were beached on gravel bars. Sodden sleeping bags were rescued from a silty backwater, and I spotted a shattered cooler in the shallows. Its lid was missing from its battering among the rocks, but inside were a dozen eggs still unbroken in their carton.

There was still enough fishing time to pick up several twelve- to fifteen-inch rainbows for camp meat, but the river was cooling rapidly and its fishing was slow. There was a still flat along some undercut cliffs just above our campsite, and I moved a brown trout of about two pounds there that took my marabou and twisted free.

We've still got another rapids, Rumsey warned.

We worked the last chutes in the twilight, grateful that their wild currents were free of boulders hiding in the spume, and we finally drifted in to the tiny beach where the other boats were waiting. Our cook fires were already burning, their smoke drifting high along the cliffs that towered into the twilight sky.

There were prime steaks wrapped in bacon, pot beans baked with brown sugar and diced onions, sliced zucchini cooked with tomato and cheese, hot muffins with finely chopped dill, and salads of mixed beans and fresh spinach and lettuce. *I don't understand how you managed this banquet in the bottom of the Black Canyon,* I sighed greedily, *but I'm sending my compliments to the quartermaster!*

Van Gytenbeek served the wine with a skilled wrist. *The problem we have with picking the right wines for our Gunnison navy,* he observed jokingly, *is finding vintages that travel well!*

It's a mixmaster out there, I agreed. *You could start out with a Chateau Lafitte and arrive with expensive grape juice!*

Salvaging the crippled boat had exhausted everyone, and we soon spread our bedrolls under the giant cottonwoods and spruces, talking until we fell asleep with the campfires dying slowly.

The rising moon literally exploded across the canyon rim, flooding its smooth 2,000-foot walls like giant reflectors and filling the gorge with surprising illumination. The light was so intense that we could read our watches easily at three o'clock in the morning, and it proved difficult to sleep until the moon had passed its zenith. It was almost four-thirty before I finally dozed off again.

Everybody hit the beach! Van Gytenbeek called.

His commands were drowned in a muffled chorus of catcalls and profanity from our sleeping bags. The river was shrouded in mist when our flotilla embarked after breakfast, and we startled an osprey from its fishing perch downstream. Hundreds of somber little dippers were foraging for sedge larvae in the riffles. Kingfishers darted downstream ahead of our boats, and several times we watched eagles circling patiently inside the canyon walls.

We've still got all kinds of things in here besides the trout! Rumsey explained. *We've seen things like elk and ring-tailed coati and cougar—and there's even talk of jaguars!*

I've heard rumors of bighorns too, I said.

It's possible! he agreed.

The morning character of the river was changed. Sometimes it tumbled steadily along boulder-filled riffles, or murmured softly down immense pools that offered no warning of the frightening rapids ahead. There were deep caverns scoured in its cliffs and ledges, and swift depths narrowly imprisoned between talus slides. There were happy runs that we took easily, shouting like small boys at a county carnival, and there were wild chutes like slaloms between the giant boulders that we shot with tight-lipped concentration.

Our fishing was still surprisingly poor. The chill night had left a rime of frost in the willows, and its full moon held the promise of winter. We took plenty of small rainbows, but the bigger fish eluded us. Our best trout was a three-pound rainbow that followed my streamer from a sheltering ledge and took the fly almost under the oar, jumping high when it felt the hook.

Pretty stupid fish! I laughed.

It was late afternoon when we reached a fine pool with several huge boulders in its holding currents. The river worked deep among the rocks, flowing swift and swimming-pool green. The channel wound into a quiet S-shaped bend that eddied into the sheer cliffs, scoured deep in their shadows, and disappeared suddenly. Its gentle moods held the promise of more rapids beyond.

Our next rapids is pretty tough. Rumsey confirmed my speculations. *But this is big-fish country here—we should cover this water pretty thoroughly before we go through the Chutes.*

Rumsey worked his boat expertly, holding it against the currents with the oars, while I covered each pocket. We prospected through the boulder lies carefully with our flies, and took several good trout, including a fat sixteen-inch brown. The last place was a big pocket between two mammoth boulders, and its churning depths were sheltered with a jackstraw puzzle of fallen lodgepoles.

It looks like a good hole! Rumsey suggested.

The first fly-swing worked the fluttering marabou deep across the throat between the boulders, and I stripped line teasingly until a wrenching strike pulled my rod tip into the current. The trout had broken the leader before I could strike, and its giant swirl boiled angrily back to the surface.

The big marabou was gone. *That fish was a brown as long as your boat!* I protested. *Broke a ten-pound tippet!*

Crocodile! Rumsey agreed.

The wild rapids still waited downstream, and we were the last boat in the party. The swift current gathered smoothly among the rocks, sliding along the south bank where the white water started in a surprisingly narrow channel. The first sixty yards were relatively simple and straight, with a sideslipping stroke of the oars to avoid a large sunken boulder, and then a pair of giant outcroppings divided its flow. The best route lay left of these hazards, in a strong chute that looked frightening, but was free of concealed rocks in its wild currents. Our campsite waited farther downstream.

Hang tight! Rumsey yelled.

We took the first bumpy chutes straight, our boat throwing huge roostertails of water in the troughs, and Rumsey skated us perfectly off the first sunken boulder.

But suddenly our run went sour when he tried to slide our bow back toward the second boulder, digging deep with a clockwise stroke of his starboard oar, and it struck a hidden stone.

Damn! I thought wildly. *We've bought it!*

The oar had failed to swing the boat, and we were trapped broadside in the heavy current, taking the huge boulder just above the starboard oarlock. Our gunwale shuddered and dropped, shipping water until I thought we might capsize, foundering in the flood. The hull grated sickeningly against the granite, throbbing and awash with water, and suddenly a bulging wave spun us free.

Our boat bottomed hard on another stone in the smaller channel, and its hull groaned like something hurt. The impact bounced us both from our seats, and suddenly we were sleigh-riding backward, almost completely out of control. Down the final hundred yards our stern floundered deep in the fierce current, banging across a series of concealed stones and ledges. Our boat miraculously stayed straight in its final chutes, until there was a last grating impact that stunned us both, and spun us into the campsite pool.

We drifted for several moments in relief. *Sorry about that rapids!* Rumsey shook his head. *We almost lost it back there!* We were startled by the chorus of derisive cheering on the beach.

The supper cook fire was welcome after the twilight chill on the river, and its sweet smoke drifted down the canyon. Our second campsite was in a sheltered bend, where the gorge was almost a hundred yards across, and there was a surprising grove of ponderosa pines. We laid our sleeping bags and bedrolls on several inches of pine needles and helped gather more firewood.

When our supper was finished, we sat around the campfire and talked about the history of the river and its fishing. *There's some pretty strange history on the Lake Fork too,* Van Gytenbeek laughed in the firelight, *and even the Lake Fork itself is strange!*

What's strange about it? I asked.

Everything's strange about Poker Alice country, Rumsey laughed, *and it even had Slumgullion Slide!*

It had what? I protested.

Slumgullion Slide, Van Gytenbeek confirmed. *The Lake Fork of the Gunnison starts above timberline at Sloane's Lake, but it's better known for Lake San Cristobal—which wouldn't exist without the famous Slumgullion Slide!*

How did it get its name? I asked.

It was named by the mining camps around Lake City, Rumsey explained and poured more coffee. *It was an earth slide like the one that created Quake Lake in Montana, and it was millions and millions of tons of earth and boulders and trees.*

It was triggered by an earthquake too, Van Gytenbeek continued, *but it flowed down the mountain so slowly that its firs and lodgepoles and spruce were still growing while it slipped—and the miners thought it moved like slumgullion stew!*

And it eventually dammed the Lake Fork?

That's right, Rumsey nodded.

Van Gytenbeek stoked the fire and added several logs. *And that's not the only strange thing that happened on Slumgullion Pass,* he laughed. *The strangest thing was probably Alferd Packer!*

Alferd? I grinned.

That's right! Rumsey laughed. *The judge that sentenced him told the jury that you couldn't trust a man who couldn't even spell his own name correctly!*

Sentenced him? I asked. *What for?*

Cannibalism, Rumsey smiled.

Packer was hired to guide a party of tenderfoot prospectors into the high country around Slumgullion Pass, Van Gytenbeek explained, *and when they got trapped in there by early winter blizzards—Packer simply ate them one by one!*

There were five victims of that crime, and feelings ran so high in the mining camps that Packer was taken over Cochetopa Pass to the adobe-walled jail at Saguache, in the country that Gunnison and his ill-fated party had crossed in 1853. The Packer trial attracted huge crowds to Lake City, filling the gambling hall frequented by Poker Alice, and has since passed into legend.

There were seven Democrats in the county, the prosecutor challenged Packer in the crowded courtroom, *and you ate most of them—you voracious little son of a bitch!*

Our talk of the Gunnison and its colorful history soon turned to its fishing again. The excellent rainbow fishing still echoes the first arrival of fertile eggs in the Rocky Mountains, and a California shipment that reached Denver in 1882.

Those rainbow ova had been stripped from McCloud stocks in northern California, the superb landlocked strain which displayed little migratory behavior in its native watershed. Pure strains of this remarkable subspecies have largely been lost through hatchery technology in the past seventy-five years, and our existing hatchery stocks consist primarily of hybrids that exhibit the migratory urge of their partial steelhead ancestry. The first plantings were made in Elk Creek, which joined the Gunnison near Sapinero, in the summer of 1888.

Six years after that first stocking, the fertile Gunnison was producing five-pound rainbows in consistent numbers, and a twelve-pounder was caught on a fly at Gunnison in 1897.

The river quickly became famous for its strong rainbows, and stories of its fine sport filled the pages of eastern journals like *American Turf Register* and *Forest & Stream.* The explosive fishing lasted until about the First World War, and then it suddenly began tapering off. During the early years before the rainbows were introduced, the native cutthroats in the watershed had been heavily exploited to feed the mining camps. Entire hillsides were cut for mine timbers and coke ovens and trestles, miles of river bottom were panned and dredged with wanton impact upon its water quality, and the mine tailings and seepages were toxic too. The native trout population was decimated by such pressures, from the extensive diggings at Tincup and Crested Butte in the headwaters to the historic lodes on its tributaries at Lake City. Although the impact of such mining, and the timber operations that supported the mines and smelters, is still obvious today, most biologists have concluded in recent studies that grazing and irrigation have had the principal impacts on the river since those mining years.

Livestock and irrigation have subtly triggered immense volumes of erosion in the past century, and river siltation is a problem as threatening as more obvious forms of pollution. Grazing and irrigation have raised river temperatures too, and thermal changes of a single degree can prove lethal in cold-water fisheries. Field studies in the Gunnison watershed have demonstrated worse impacts from irrigation there, finding that irrigation discharges back into the river were often as much as ten degrees warmer than the Gunnison itself. The watershed had already become too warm for its native cutthroats sixty-odd years ago, after the livestock prices of the First World War and their remarkably explosive impact on ranching operations in Colorado.

Both state and federal hatcheries attempted to restore the native cutthroat populations with transfusions of Yellowstone fingerlings in 1902, but despite stockings of more than a million tiny trout, little came of their efforts. The subtle denigration of the watershed was too well advanced to restore the fragile cutthroats.

Biologists then attempted to introduce eastern brook trout to the Gunnison and Tomichi drainages, and the *Gunnison Tribune* reported that good catches were becoming common in their headwaters in 1906. Brook trout met with limited success in the lower river, because the silts and increasing temperatures there had damaged the habitat for these introduced populations too. Despite extensive plantings that lasted until 1934, biologists found that brook trout comprised less than fifteen percent of the fish population in the tributaries, and less than five percent in the river itself.

The brown trout came to the Gunnison country when a shipment of Loch Leven yearlings arrived from Scotland and the fish were introduced into the headwaters of the river in 1893. There were less than a thousand baby trout in that stocking, and its results were virtually ignored until the *Gunnison Tribune* started reporting significant catches of brown trout in 1907.

The survival of a sizeable Loch Leven population from such a minuscule planting, limited to a single headwater tributary, soon caught the attention of local fishermen. The European species was seemingly well established as far downstream as the Black Canyon itself, and field studies conducted just before the First World War uncovered some surprising data. The river was no longer primarily a rainbow trout fishery, since the denigration caused by mining, timber operations, grazing, and irrigation had changed its character. The cunning European species was better equipped to survive those changing conditions, and had migrated downstream into the river itself. The biologists were stunned to discover that seventy-two percent of the catch in the river above Gunnison consisted of brown trout, and that the exotic species comprised almost fifty percent of the fish taken as far downstream as Sapinero. It was a remarkable display of tenacity, but the popularity of rainbows soon ended the federal propagation of brown trout in Colorado, while the state hatcheries concentrated on rainbows.

Cracker-barrel wisdom argued that the rainbows were better fish, with their bright colors and cartwheeling fight, but the local anglers failed to understand that the hatchery rainbows carried genetic flaws that would hurt their fishing. Forty years of fish culture had created a hybrid hatchery strain bred to grow quickly at less cost, but these fish were painted imitations of the wild rainbows that had originally thrived in northern California. The price unwittingly paid for such fish-hatchery philosophy was a strange new rainbow with a truncated life span, fewer eggs with reduced percentages of fertility, the tendency to attempt its egg laying in the fall instead of the spring spawning typical of wild rainbows, and a startling inability to survive the predators and stresses of a wild habitat.

These hatchery rainbows were more like poultry than wild trout, and it is no surprise that the wild brown trout that survived those original yearling plants from wild-fish parents have dominated the watershed over the years. *The world is filled with coyotes and foxes,* Van Gytenbeek laughs wryly. *It just won't work to plant stupid chickens in a world where only grouse will survive!*

Or cocker spaniels instead of coyotes, I said.

Our breakfast campfire helped to mute the morning chill until the sun spilled across the canyon floor. Several mergansers flew past, and flared in surprise when they found people on the river. Camp robbers and magpies scolded us until we broke our tents, loading our boats with fresh deer sign on the beach.

It's just impossible to imagine so much beauty, Rumsey said sadly, *particularly under three hundred feet of water.*

It's hard to figure, I admitted. *How do you weigh apples and sugar beets and melons against a trout stream?*

That's right, Rumsey nodded.

And how do you measure wild trout, Van Gytenbeek added, *against a dam that helps irrigate deserts in Colorado and California, provides more kilowatts during an energy crisis and prevents floods?*

Rumsey pushed off into the current, and we shot the long rapids below our last campsite, in a wild prelude to our final day's fishing in the gorge. The river turned abruptly against its steep cliffs downstream, and the rapids shelved off suddenly into a pool so deep that we could not detect its bottom. Cool tributary springs trickled down its cliffs through lichens and wild flowers.

We fished through its shelving throat carefully, taking a strong fifteen-inch brown. Tom and Desi Anthony had already beached two good rainbows farther downstream, and we circled out past their water, where Rumsey let his boat slide into a tumbling half-mile roller coaster under the cliffs. There was a series of swift chutes and short fast-water holes where we took several small fish, working the eddies of the heaviest currents. Still farther downstream the river worked back south, into a smooth hundred-yard flat that sparkled in the sun. Van Gytenbeek had beached his MacKenzie there, waiting lazily at the oarlocks while his wife waded out to fish the pool.

Our boat came through the rapids below in a wild hobbyhorse ride, helplessly caught in its rocking troughs until we sideslipped from its currents to a tiny beach. We sat there with our waders trailing in the river, watching the Anthony boat come leapfrogging through, and we applauded when Ben Boutelle lifted a six-pound rainbow that proved the best fish of the entire trip.

Our party gathered along the gravelly beach, talking lazily and comparing notes, and we launched our boats again to have enough light to run the famous rapids at The Falls.

We drifted the river almost lazily those last miles, perhaps unwilling to complete our trip too quickly, while we enjoyed the eagles circling between ochre-colored cliffs that towered 2,000 feet above our boats. These gentle miles soon ended in a rocky cove where the river eddied deep against a rockfall of huge boulders. Our entire party was waiting there, and in the narrow defile downstream, the roar of the river was almost deafening.

There was a half-mile portage for the passengers, over the building-size boulders and slides, along an unmarked trail fifty feet above the churning rapids. Marmots scuttled back into their burrows, and chipmunks scolded our caravan as it passed. Our trail passed the sheltering cornice of a small cave, where the bones and dried pelt of a deer lay deep in the gloom, and there were fresh cougar prints in the clay.

It took almost two hours to strip our boats and transport our equipment to the sandbars downstream. The sun had left the river, and its light was retreating up the canyon walls when the boatmen returned to the rocky moorings, and drew lots to decide who would attempt the rapids first. The river was a forbidding maelstrom.

Van Gytenbeek won! The shout came from the boulder trail upstream, *His boat is coming through first!*

Van Gytenbeek lost! his wife muttered drily.

The other boatmen were watching too, hoping to learn from his passage to help modify their own runs, and I held my breath as the Van Gytenbeek boat seemed to hang briefly in the rapids.

Rowing wildly to align his boat, Van Gytenbeek was suddenly over the brink, plunging almost vertically into the wild spume and lunging back into the chute downstream. The boat disappeared in the troughs again, seemed almost to founder briefly, and then exploded high while he fought his windmilling oars. The boat settled again, just long enough to bite the oars deep into the torrent, and its straining hull grated past a threatening boulder. The river forced him from his seat, thighs straining like a downhill racer fighting to keep his skis on the snow, and his oars bent like fishing rods. There was another huge boulder, partially hidden in the bulging currents that caught the boat, and he plunged past in a surprisingly narrow chute of angry water.

He's done it! I thought excitedly.

The river dropped more than fifty feet at The Falls, traversing the boulders in a series of churning stair steps, in a wild slalom of several hundred yards. Our party was scattered from the rocky beach downstream, where they waited with life jackets and lines, to the high trail above the worst rapids.

We sat among the boulders there, watching with a sense of dread as our boats came through empty in a nightmare of giant chutes and stones. The boats all dropped through safely, and when our last boatman had escaped its rapids, Van Gytenbeek produced a silver flask to toast our passage.

It was easier today! he beamed.

The river had seemingly spent its anger now, and the final miles were almost poetic in their gentle pools. The sun had left the river, but it was still and warm, and suddenly the fish started to cooperate. Using a large chocolate-colored stone-fly nymph, we took a dozen fine browns and rainbows, dropping our flies along the cliffs and outcroppings and ledges where the trout were lying.

There was a last chute that quickly lost its strength in the deeps downstream, the river flowed still and almost subdued until it neared the construction site. Our exit went through a freshly completed penstock tunnel, and the half-built structure of the Crystal project rose in the gathering twilight like some Eygptian ruin reflected in the river. The canyon was completely shrouded in shadows when we wrestled our boats up the rocks to our trailers. The river flowed in silence, where Van Gytenbeek stood looking back upstream.

You coming soon? I asked quietly.

Sure, he replied. *It's just hard to say goodbye.*

A PORTRAIT OF THE PERE MARQUETTE

Owls are often considered birds of ill omen and sorcery, and their cries have fascinated me since boyhood, particularly the soft, almost plaintive trilling of screech owls. Sometimes in our last moments before sleep, burrowed warmly into our sleeping bags and bedrolls, it was soothing to hear them calling in the Michigan woods. Those early memories of campsites along the Pere Marquette are filled with owls and whippoorwills in the jackpine benches beyond Waddell's Riffle and the Clay Banks, melancholy duets in the summer nights, mixed with the river sounds in the cedar deadfalls.

Some people believe that owls can foretell a death in the family, Ralph Noble once told me when we were fishing his water on the upper Pere Marquette, *but I really like hearing them!*

I've never seen one, I said.

Owls are blind during the daytime. Noble repeated the common myths. *Owls hunt at night and hibernate during the day.*

Can they see in the dark? I asked.

Sure can! he grinned.

Like most boys in those summers, I found my first owl high in the trusswork timbers of my grandfather's barn, and I believed the myths and superstitions about owls. We listened to their calling with fascination and delicate shivers of fear.

It was much later that I learned of their acute hearing, and the ability to hunt their prey almost entirely by its sounds. Their eyes have remarkable densities of light-sensitive rods and color-receiving cones, their retinal proteins triggered by minute electrical charges. Sometimes I discovered owls hunting in daylight too, and flushed them from their thickets of cedars and hemlocks, but it was many years before I learned about the delicate eyelid membranes that shield an owl's sensitive eyes from too much light.

Their comic dish-shaped faces are something more, sculptured like sophisticated parabolic microphones, the feathers adjusting to focus the sounds of a field mouse scuttling in the leaves. Their ears are surprisingly large, with right and left aural passages structured differently in size and shape, sharpening the binaural intensity of their hearing.

Owls swallow their prey whole. Once their digestive fluids have worked, the relatively indigestible bones, feathers and fur that remain are neatly compacted into egg-sized pellets and coughed up. Since a hunting owl retreats with its prey to a single feasting tree, and sits there half sleeping while it digests its kill, hundreds of regurgitated leavings are often collected under a favorite limb. There was a dense copse of cedars above the Deer Lick on the Pere Marquette where I once sought shelter from a storm, and found a feasting tree.

My God! I thought when I discovered its funeral mound of tiny skeletons and skulls. *It's an owl's feeding thicket, and those are the remains of hundreds of frogs and mice and birds!*

It was an eerie cache that remains stubbornly in the memory, along with the April grouse and red-winged blackbirds and whippoorwills that are similar echoes of the Pere Marquette.

Its character shaped my fishing skills in those boyhood summers, and we made several pilgrimages to Baldwin over the years. Baldwin has changed little from the sleepy Michigan county seat we knew then, except for its supermarkets and bowling alley, and it still has a tackle shop that sells more worms and bow-hunting equipment and minnows than serious fishing gear.

Baldwin had a surprising roster of trout-fishing characters before the Second World War. Some were refugees from its lumbercamp origins, while others found it a backwater that changed little in the bitter years of the Great Depression.

Some of these fishermen would simply disappear into the woods when we encountered them on the stream, rather than risk a conversation. The hard times had made some misanthropic and bitter, while others seemed simply to prefer river things to people. Their sole intercourse with the world of commerce had been reduced to cutting cordwood or trapping in the cedar swamps for cash. There were always stories of whiskey stills in the cedar thickets too, although I was too young to sample their wares. The river people fished and hunted deer for food. Filling out a deer permit was sometimes critical in making it through the year, and there are still men in the Michigan jackpine country who survive on fish and game. Jacklighting deer was common in the cut-over clearings along the county roads, and although it was illegal, the wardens did little to enforce the law in some cases.

These are pretty hard times, my father explained in our camp on the Little South, *and jacklighting a few deer is probably better than standing in the bread lines around Detroit.*

When the river people fished, they often fished at night with huge, crudely dressed bucktails and streamers on heavy tackle, leaving the daylight hours to the wealthy fishermen who were doctors or managed the automobile factories around River Rouge or owned the furniture plants at Grand Rapids.

Perhaps the best-known character was Harry Duffing, the colorful barber who tied trout flies in his simple shop at Baldwin when haircut customers were scarce. Duffing created the first fly-pattern to imitate the big *Hexagenia* mayflies the oldtimers stubbornly call the Michigan caddis hatch. His dressing used long-shank hooks and superb furnace hackles from tightly bound bunches strung in Hong Kong, with upright goose-quill sections tied in the elegant double-wing British style. Several slender pheasant fibers imitated the tails of these nocturnal flies, and the old barber baptized them in a solution of cleaning fluid and shaved paraffin. It was several summers of country-style haircuts and fishing talk before Duffing took me behind the curtains to see his workbench, and watch him dress one of his famous patterns at a workbench littered with goose quills and hackles and dark gray yarn.

Last season we were sitting in the bar at Government Lake, talking about these nocturnal mayflies, when one of the oldtimers on the Pere Marquette lost his patience. *Troublemakers!* the old man exploded. *You newfangled fishermen are troublemakers!*

How's that? I parried his anger.

It's all this mayfly talk about our caddis hatch! he fulminated, and finished his beer. *Caddis is goddamn caddis!*

I'm sorry, I said gently, *but they're mayflies.*

Don't care what you newfangled boys tell us! Old myths about owls and mayflies die hard. *They're goddamn caddisflies!*

No matter what entomology tells us?

Troublemakers! he grumbled.

The first time I fished the Pere Marquette country, it was not on the river itself, but on the brushy little Baldwin that rises in the cedar swamps above the village. Its narrow, willow-hung currents were difficult to fish, and I spent a lot of time retrieving my flies from the foliage in those early years. Its flow was surprisingly strong the first year, when I was fishing in rented waders that accordioned comically along both legs, but the Pere Marquette itself seemed too formidable for my boyhood wading skills.

My first experience on the river was at Bowman's Bridge. It is strange how some things persist in the memory, because I remember little about our fishing that morning, although other things are almost like yesterday in my mind. My most disturbed echo is the mixture of fascination and horror I felt while I watched a fat water snake stalking a trout from the tangled logs below the bridge.

Its strategy was a simple lesson in cunning and stealth. The snake worked patiently over the fallen cedars, sliding down the sun-bleached bark and waiting motionless when the trout seemed nervous. Each time, the trout soon forgot its apprehension and drifted back to lie lazily against the logs. It seemed to like the currents and eddies where the river welled up between two deadfalls downstream.

Suddenly the snake struck with a splash, seizing the trout's entire head with its jaws. The fish seemed helpless in its grasp, but it threshed with such panic that the snake was pulled into the river too. Writhing and rolling awkwardly, the snake and its prey were carried through the swift bend until they were lost in the riffles downstream. It was a grisly episode I have never forgotten.

The Pere Marquette is already a strong little river when it reaches Bowman's Bridge, having received the cold flowages of its three upper tributaries. Its Little South and Middle branches, like the swift little Baldwin, are well-known trout fisheries themselves. The Pere Marquette is deceptively smooth-flowing, but strong enough to have a sobering effect on the inexperienced wader. Several miles downstream, the sluggish Big South combines its swamp-dark currents to make the Pere Marquette itself a little frightening.

Twice in my boyhood I fished the lower river as far downstream as Barothy's and Timber Creek and Walhalla, searching for the first of the early-summer *Hexagenia* flies. The river seemed almost sullen and threatening there, in spite of its smooth bottom, its currents strong and smooth in the darkness. The hatches failed to come on those big-river evenings, and several times I almost lost my footing in the chest-deep water, windmilling my feet precariously along the bottom gravel while the current forced me downstream.

Once I was nearly carried into a deep tea-colored horseshoe near Walhalla Bridge, where the current dropped off swiftly between the tree-lined banks and willows. Fighting the loose sand with churning legs, I finally regained the firm gravel upstream. My legs were shaking when I reached the footpath, and I never fished there again.

The Pere Marquette is happier in its headwaters. Its beginnings lie in bogs and cedar thickets and jackpine lakes in the sandy moraines between Baldwin and Big Rapids. Its icy little Middle Branch rises in the grouse ridges that lie near Reed City, flowing toward its junction with the tea-colored Little South. Several times I explored its brushy mileage above the Forks Pool, until its marshy reaches became too deep for wading. Twice I fished its headwaters near Idlewild, taking limits of fat natives with a small wet fly fished patiently like a worm in the holes under the willows.

The Little South Branch of the Pere Marquette is completely different in character. Its bottom mileage above the Forks Pool is still and quiet-flowing under its dense canopy of trees. The Middle Branch is quite swift and clear, while the somber Little South is dark and mysterious, its color leached through the bogs and marshy ponds in its secret headwaters. We often camped along the Little South in those summers after the Second World War, in a time when the only cottages on the lower river were several miles upstream from the Forks Pool, near the county bridge on the Star Lake road. The stream had excellent early hatches in those years, and its placid currents and sheltering trees made it a difficult classroom for a neophyte.

Sometimes we traveled upstream to fish the swift mile above the

Powers Bridge with Gerry Queen, a dedicated fisherman from Detroit who often fished the Pere Marquette from Ivan's Lodge. Queen loved its simple screen-porch cottages because of their proximity to the Little South, and he knew its upper reaches better than anyone who fished the river in those years. Queen had a sense of elegance too, and refused to fish anything but the straw-colored British silk lines and Hardy silkworm-gut leaders, and a remarkable collection of fine Dickerson dry-fly rods. Queen is gone now, and no longer fishes that water on the Little South, but I remember my feelings of pride and excitement when he asked me to make his flies, using nothing but natural Andalusian dun hackles, carefully dubbed bodies of fur spun between my fingers on British working silk, and lemon woodduck feathers.

It was downstream from the Forks Pool, under the high hardwood moraine at Noble's Lodge, that I took my first fly-caught trout. The Pere Marquette is surprisingly large there, in its sweeping butter-yellow bends, and I fought its currents every summer.

The first fly-caught trout took a wet Cahill, with a technique that was perilously close to worm-fishing, since my line was merely trailing downstream in the current. The fish barely measured ten inches, but in that boyhood summer it seemed like a sailfish. It had been lying under the alders, followed the little Cahill into the sunlight, and had hooked itself. Such episodes are familiar to any trout fisherman, but that trout ended several years of fishing worms and grasshoppers, and the praise of my father and his fishing cronies was a rich climax to countless hours of apprenticeship.

That's a fine trout in your basket, they said.

We celebrated its capture on the Little South, and with that ten-inch trout in my creel, it seemed that I had finally been permitted to enter their world. The memorabilia of that world are familiar still, and I savor them happily after thirty-odd years.

There were fishing coats with woodcock feathers in their bellows pockets from bird shooting, pockets stained with paraffin and citronella, the soft wind in the pines and cedars, the rhythms of summer rain on canvas tenting, their faces in the firelight, silkworm leaders coiled and soaking between glycerin pads, creels lined with mint and freshly picked ferns, jackets bulging with fine English pipes and fishing gadgets and tobacco, bamboo rods bright with varnish and intricate silk wrappings, coffee brewed over a gravel-bar cookfire, and sour-mash whiskey from a stream-washed cup.

Their world of flies and fishing talk and hatches became mine that morning in late August, and we celebrated with my first cup of coffee, while my father and his friends toasted my minor triumph with a stronger catalyst.

The Little South was also the setting for a summer morning when we found some bait-fishermen on the water below our campsite. It was our first morning on the river that trip, and there was a man in torn working clothes fishing a nightcrawler just below our tent. His two sons were fishing worms under the willows downstream.

Who's that? my father asked.

Their battered Plymouth was parked near the bridge on the Middle Branch. *Damn!* I said. *They're fishing our water!*

Maybe we can Tom Sawyer them, my father suggested.

You really think so? I grinned and my father laughed softly. *Talk them into fishing someplace else?*

Let's give it a try, my father said.

We walked downstream along the county road to where they were fishing. *Had any luck this morning?* we asked.

Nothing! the man replied.

It's not good worm-fishing water, my father said.

No? The fisherman seemed puzzled.

You have to stand right over the trout to fish bait here, my father explained truthfully. *It spooks the fish!*

That right? He reeled in his nightcrawler.

It's pretty good dry-fly water, my father continued, *but there's better worm-fishing over at Baldwin.*

Where over at Baldwin? The fisherman waved to his boys.

Try the fish-hatchery stretch, I suggested. *There's a deep cement channel between the spillways.*

That's right! my father confirmed.

Those trout are used to people there, I continued, *and it's got some really big browns!* Our story was partially true, because we had seen such trout ourselves, and once I hooked a heavy fish in the channel that fought me more than an hour before it shook free.

We're much obliged, the man said.

Their old Plymouth rattled north into Baldwin. *It worked!* We grinned guiltily and waved. *They're going!*

It was a fine dry-fly morning. There was a sporadic hatch of caddisflies, and the trout were rising well. We both took several good fish, and were fishing the still, tree-sheltered flats below our tent when a car stopped beside the river. It was the man and his sons in their battered Plymouth.

Hey mister! yelled the boys.

Their father circled back to the trunk. *Sure want to thank you folks!* he grinned. *Can't thank you enough!*

My father looked at me strangely, and we stood there under the county road, with the smooth current sliding past our waders. *What do you think they're doing back?* I asked.

You think they're serious? my father whispered.

The young workman opened his trunk. *Yessir!* He reached inside and dragged out a thirty-inch brown. *Caught this beautiful eight-pounder right under the spillway where you told us!*

Can't thank you enough! his boys shouted.

Such memories are richly engraved in my mind, in a mixture of spring mornings bright with cowslips and pulpit flowers and violets in the sheltered places, and nights that were almost too cold for our summer sleeping bags. Twice in those boyhood years it snowed on our opening weekends, with popcorn-sized flakes that shrouded the river, and our tent sites looked like deer camps.

June weather was usually better; the forests were thick with bright young leaves and the spring spates had passed. Thunderstorms could turn the rivers milky, but in early summer their currents usually flowed clear and smooth, winding past the sandy timber-covered hills toward Lake Michigan. Columbines and summer buttercups were blooming, and in the August grasshopper season that followed, the abandoned pastures were filled with gentians and pye-weed. It was a placid time of trout-fishing summers that passed happily.

The Pere Marquette itself is a beautiful stream, cold and serpentine and swift in its hundred-mile journey toward Ludington, and its fishing taught me much in those early years.

The history of the river is surprisingly old. Its beginnings lie during French sovereignty in the old Northwest Territories, with the subsequent arrival of Jacques Marquette in 1666. The young priest left Quebec to spend two years with the mission at Trois Rivieres, studying the aboriginal languages of the Great Lakes wilderness. Marquette then traveled inland to the Ottawa mission at Sault Sainte Marie, with the remote wilderness outpost farther west at Chequamenon Bay included in his sprawling parish.

Several clashes with marauding Sioux later forced Marquette and his parishioners from Chequamenon to seek refuge at Fort Michilimackinac, across the windswept straits that separate Michigan, and their mission was relocated to Saint Ignace.

Voyagéurs and fur trappers who stopped there told Marquette exciting stories of a gargantuan south-flowing river farther west, and that the plains tribes who had told them about the river called it the Father of Waters. Marquette and his friends subsequently convinced the powerful Comte de Frontenac to dispatch him with the expedition of Louis Joliet, and left to explore the Mississippi.

Joliet had assembled a party of skilled voyagéurs, including a trapper who had accompanied Etienne Brulé into the Michigan wilderness in 1618. The expedition embarked in three freight canoes along the rocky shoreline on Lake Michigan in the spring of 1673, and followed its high cliffs south until they reached Green Bay and its sheltering peninsula.

The party decided to travel inland there, following the Winnebago deep into its Wisconsin forests. Portaging from the somber Butte des Morts country into the headwaters of the Fox, the expedition worked its way downstream to its junction with the Wisconsin watershed, thirty-odd miles below the Wisconsin Dells. Joliet and Marquette left their echoes in the Wisconsin wilderness, giving beautiful names to both rivers and places, like Fond du Lac and Prairie du Chien.

Joliet led his men down the Wisconsin to its junction with the Mississippi below Prairie du Chien, stopping to make an encampment to rest and gather provisions and hunt before traveling farther. The party left still more French echoes in places like Dubuque and La Grange and Cape Girardeau, following the immense Father of Waters past its union with both the Ohio and the Missouri.

The expedition finally reached the mouth of the Arkansas, more than a hundred miles downstream from the future site of Memphis, and Joliet and Marquette were convinced that their gargantuan discovery was unmistakably the Mississippi, the sluggish giant that reached the Gulf of Mexico near the French outposts at Mobile and Biloxi. Marquette offered a simple mass of thanksgiving, in the flood bottoms of the Arkansas there, and Joliet ordered the party back on its difficult journey to Saint Ignace.

Their company pushed hard since it was already late summer, and the nights carried a chill prelude to the coming autumn. Joliet left the river beyond Saint Louis, crossing the rich wheatgrass prairies that bordered the Illinois. Its quiet sloughs and backwaters led them across these frontier heartlands until they reached the relatively short portage to the marshy flowages of the Chicago. Joliet and his voyagéurs cheered excitedly when they finally heard the surf pounding the beaches of Lake Michigan.

Joliet and Marquette had successfully traversed two completely unexplored water routes through the American wilderness, linking their colonies at Quebec and the Gulf of Mexico. The untrammeled continent had surrendered its first secrets, and the exhausted Joliet party finally crossed the Straits of Mackinac to their mission at Saint Ignace, just ahead of the first autumn storms.

Marquette remained there, both to recuperate from the arduous expedition and to minister to his neglected parish, while completing the journals started during his travels. His accounts were subsequently published in the famous *Recueil des Voyages,* which Thevenot assembled at Quebec in 1681. It was fortunate that Marquette had meticulously recorded his observations of their journey, since the Joliet logs were lost when his freight canoe capsized in the Lachine rapids, before his party reached Quebec.

The memories of the wilderness odyssey echoed stubbornly in the thoughts of Marquette; such wilderness has its secret melodies once they are heard. The frontier priest brooded about his travels for several months before petitioning his superiors at Quebec, seeking permission to build another mission at Chicago.

Marquette was granted that permission in 1675, and impatiently waited for the winter to pass, thinking about the tribes that inhabited the fertile prairies of Illinois. His impatience smouldered through the February storms and the early thawing winds that cleared the ice from the sullen waters of the straits. Marquette could wait no longer, and started his party south in the early spring. The weather was still bitter and raw, and the cold lake was only partially ice free. It remained unusually cold that April, and the difficult work of building the mission in its harsh winds would prove tragic.

Marquette soon fell desperately ill, and his party ultimately feared for his life. Lacking medical supplies and skills at their outpost, his voyagéurs soon elected to travel back to Saint Ignace, where Marquette might find better help.

The party decided to travel the eastern shore of Lake Michigan, thinking it was the shorter alternative, but it proved a terrible mistake. The eastern beaches of the lake are steep, carved by the constant surf and their massive dunes sculptured by the prevailing winds, and it was a route that would prove a ship's graveyard in later centuries. It soon proved impossible in freight canoes.

The spring weather was still bitter and foul, and its fierce winds often forced the voyagéurs to abandon the angry waters of the lake and portage laboriously with their fallen priest along the beaches. Their progress was painfully slow, yet they had traveled more than halfway to Fort Michilimackinac when Marquette's frail health collapsed, and the priest died at the mouth of the Pere Marquette.

The river became my boyhood tutor, and it taught me about selective trout before I was twelve. It was on its headwaters that I first discovered that my father's collection of flies was not enough, that his boxes of elegant Adams spentwings and Corey calftails and Coachmen did not always catch fish. Earlier generations of trout fishermen had been spoiled by their easy sport, and when a fish refused their flies, they simply moved on to find a trout that was less picky. The trout seemed increasingly particular in my boyhood years, but I remember one morning that finally convinced me that selective feeding was a critical factor in trout fishing.

It was a hatch of small *Ephemerella* flies that forced me to stop fishing in defeat, and to collect the last of the emerging duns to discover why the trout had refused my flies. The current had literally been alive with the tiny Blue-winged Olives, and the trout took them greedily for almost an hour.

The fish refused everything in my fly boxes, and when I returned to our campsite with specimens of the hatching flies, their bright-olive bodies were a problem. I rummaged through my flytying materials in the tent, but the only solution I could find to imitate their body chroma was a frayed thread on my sleeping bag.

It'll have to do! I thought.

Several flies were tied with the specimen bottle of olive-bodied mayflies as the pattern, using dark-blue dun hackles and wings on sixteen Allcock hooks. It was a morning hatch, and the next day I was waiting after breakfast in the gravelly bend below the Forks Pool. The flies did not appear until almost eleven o'clock, perhaps because the night had been quite cold, and it took longer for the morning sun to warm the river. The dark blue-winged sailboats suddenly appeared on the water and the quiet current came alive with rising trout. My roughly dressed imitations, with the olive cotton thread scavenged from my frayed sleeping bag, took several good fish while it lasted.

It fooled them! I thought with satisfaction, and it had been an important lesson in subtle variations in color, particularly on trout that see a steady parade of fishermen.

There was another afternoon on the Pere Marquette, in the swift riffles a half mile above Noble's cottages, that compounded the earlier lessons of selectivity. There was a fine hatch of pale sulphur-colored mayflies, which the trout took greedily in the late afternoon, and then stopped when the activity ebbed. I was wading slowly back to our campsite, having failed because my flies lacked the proper pale-ginger hackles, and I was discouraged. Some really good trout had been rising during the peak of the hatch, but they had rejected every pattern I tried. I had covered fifty yards of shallows when the riffles upstream came alive with a mating swarm of mayflies. Rising and falling rhythmically over the riffle, these spinners were carrying their butter-yellow egg sacs, and when their dance was finished, the females started laying their eggs in the swift current. The fish came upstream from the deep pool below when the riffle rainbows started rising, and the trout literally went crazy in an orgy of feeding, while I frantically searched my fly boxes for imitations.

Lady Beaverkill! I thought suddenly. *It's too dark to imitate the naturals properly—but the chenille egg sac might work!*

The flies worked well enough, particularly when I dropped their yellow chenille sacs quickly over a rising trout, and the fish rose before it took the time to inspect the fly.

It was a ruse that worked almost every evening for a week, and I easily filled my basket with good fish. Fifteen-trout limits were still permitted in those years, and my creel of browns and rainbows often weighed almost ten pounds. Thirty-odd years later I am ashamed of our trout-filled summers, and the wanton baskets of fish we killed without thinking about the future.

There are memories of big trout too. Our first was a large brown we discovered working above our campsite when we returned one night from fishing the lower river. We had hiked in from the Clay Banks, hoping to find a mating swarm of big *Hexagenia* flies below the Whirlpool. There was no activity there that night, but with an irony typical of trout fishing, we found the echoes of a hatch on our tent when we came back. Its dark canvas was covered with freshly hatched *Hexagenias* that had been attracted to the Coleman lantern we had left burning. My flashlight pinpointed a mating swarm over the shallows upstream from our campsite bend, but the current was quiet.

There's nothing working! I studied the river with the flashlight. *You'd think the trout would be working!*

They've probably got indigestion, my father said.

You mean they stuffed themselves on the earlier hatch? I grinned in the darkness. *And they won't take those spinners?*

Something like that, he nodded.

We stripped down our tackle and settled into our sleeping bags, but once our camp lantern was extinguished, there was an owl calling softly and the trout had started to rise. Their feeding was tentative at first, and then we were startled by a heavy splash.

What the hell was that? I whispered.

I'm not sure, my father muttered sleepily when another spectacular splash interrupted him. *You think it's a fish?*

Some fish! I unzipped my sleeping bag.

We crawled carefully out through the tent flap, where the faint coals of our campfire still glowed, and listened to the river sounds. The trout rose greedily against the logjam behind our tent. *We were wrong about the fish!* my father whispered softly. *Some of them were still waiting for dessert!*

It was obviously a large brown trout working greedily after the smaller fish had stopped feeding, and the mating spinners had probably started falling into the current after their egg laying was completed. The fish had perhaps been interrupted when we returned to camp, and our headlights disturbed its gluttony. But once we had started to sleep, the fish drifted back out to feed.

You try him! I suggested to my father. *I'm afraid to wade that water in the dark!*

While I crouched in the willows, he crossed the current below our campsite and worked back upstream into casting position. The big trout was still rising. My father started casting, and I could hear his rod working in the darkness. When his casting sounds stopped, there was a wild splash, and his reel protested shrilly.

He's hooked? I shouted.

The reel rattled harshly as the strong fish probed angrily under the fallen cedars. *It's more like he's hooked me!* my father laughed in the darkness. *He's like a rhinoceros!*

Hold on! I yelled excitedly.

The trout writhed deep under the logjam, raking the leader along the snags, but the tippet held. Finally my father forced the fish back into open water, worked it downstream to net it in the darkness and waded toward our tent in the flashlight beam. Its spotted bulk looked almost frightening in its shining meshes, with the bushy *Hexagenia* imitation in its hook-billed jaws, and it measured twenty inches.

That's some fish! I whispered in awe.

It was several years before I took a trout that large on the Pere Marquette, although we often saw such big fish in the river. Once I frightened a huge brown from its hiding place under a fallen cedar that completely blocked the river below Noble's cottages, its bright, dime-sized spots clearly visible as it bolted past me.

My father discovered a monster fish in the Forks Pool one morning in early summer, and it was large enough to startle him momentarily. Later that season there was a twelve-pound brown taken there at night with a big streamer, and my father is still convinced after thirty-five years that he saw the fish that morning.

It looked like Moby Dick! He shook his head in awe.

Another time early in the season, when we were fishing downstream on the Whinnery riffles, I was working a polar-bear bucktail through a patient series of cross-stream casts. There was suddenly an immense swirl in the current, and a big rainbow rolled up and engulfed the teasing bucktail. It seemed almost frightening, somber and darkly sepulchral after its spawning, with its sides and gill covers still bright scarlet. The fish was a recently spawned kelt drifting back from its egg laying in the headwaters.

Damn! I thought wildly. *It's really strong!*

The struggle did not last, and my reel simply foundered under the stress, failing to handle its first head-shaking run downstream. Its death rattle was a shattered drag spring, but it probably lacked the spool capacity to fight such a trout. The great fish stopped under a cedar logjam, and the free-spooling reel was a hopeless tangle. The fish did not need another heart-stopping run to end the fight, because it simply forced under the trees and broke off.

It's gone! I groaned.

Such Pere Marquette rainbows come from the first planting of steelhead fingerlings on the river in 1885, although many fishermen seem to think these winter-run fish were part of the fisheries programs that introduced Pacific salmon into the Great Lakes.

The first steelhead were stocked from the old federal hatchery at Northville. Since our pioneers in fish culture had carelessly mixed our original landlocked and sea-run strains of rainbow in their breeding experiments, the first steelhead were not intentionally planted in the Pere Marquette watershed. Hatchery managers simply called all of these red-striped fish California trout, and the Northville stocking party did not know it was planting sea-run steelhead.

Steelhead fingerlings were commonly propagated in those years, because the strain was vigorous and displayed rapid growth. The fine landlocked subspecies, like the McCloud strain and the richly spotted Kern rainbows from northern California, were cross-bred with steelhead late in the nineteenth century. Our existing hatchery strains of rainbows are largely such genetic mixtures, and many include obvious fingerprints of cutthroat blood too.

The first consignments of fertile eggs to reach the hatcheries in Michigan and New York included varied mixtures of these parent stocks, and the subsequent behavior of the fish was unpredictable. Some fish seemed to remain where they were stocked, displaying relatively pure landlocked parentage of the McCloud or Kern rainbows, but others soon evaporated into the Great Lakes.

Fisheries experts were completely surprised over the behavior of the first rainbows placed in the Pere Marquette. The plantings seemed quite successful at first, and the small fish stocked below the Forks Pool had reached six to seven inches before the following fall. Biologists had closed that upper mileage to protect them, and their field reports glowed with optimism over the coming trout season. Michigan fishermen waited through the winter with a mixture of anticipation and curiosity. The exotic trout from California were an unknown species of the Pere Marquette, and although many fishermen had read about them in journals like *Forest & Stream,* no one really knew what kind of sport they might provide.

Both biologists and fishermen were disappointed. When the opening weekend arrived in 1886, the heavy winter snows had been purged from the cedar swamps in weeks of high water, and hordes of curious anglers found the Pere Marquette relatively low and clear. The crowds were eager to catch these new California trout, but no one caught anything but the native brook trout, and the biologists were puzzled. The river had been teeming with small rainbows in late October. It would be many years before it was fully understood that these transplanted fish were actually sea-run steelhead, and that their silvery little smolts migrated to the Great Lakes with the spring snowmelt.

The adult steelhead did not return to spawn until late October, long after the trout season had closed, and some fish arrived sporadically through the winter. There are often large steelhead runs in late February, and some years another sizeable migration occurs in early April. Spawning occurs then in the Pere Marquette, and most of the spawned-out kelts had usually returned to Lake Michigan before opening weekend, except for an occasional big female like the fish I had lost in my boyhood years. But these big rainbows were usually not found in the river during the regular trout-fishing season, and the only people who saw them there were hunters.

You summer trout-fishing guys! the oldtimers liked to chide us around Baldwin. *You summer folks catch them spotted sardines, when we got trout in the Big Pere like alligators—we see them fish during deer season and running our traplines!*

What kind of trout are they? my father asked.

Christ only knows! our tormentors laughed. *Who cares what kind of trout we see—they're alligator trout!*

And you summer people can't catch them fish! they added.

It would be another thirty years before these steelhead runs in the Great Lakes rivers were fully understood and managed effectively. Techniques for catching them consistently on flies have also been worked out in recent years, but the oldtimers who fished them still argue that fresh roe is the only bait a Michigan steelhead will strike.

The big trout we caught were usually browns, which had become established in the Pere Marquette late in the nineteenth century too, and we usually caught them at night. My first really large trout was caught on the middle reaches of the river, fishing with Maurice Houseman of Grand Rapids. We were fishing on the Green Cottage water, anticipating a twilight hatch of big *Hexagenia* drakes. It is difficult wading below its junction with the Baldwin, and I leaned into the darkening current to hold my position.

We should see some drakes soon! Houseman yelled.

The hatch was realtively sparse when it finally came, with owls and whippoorwills calling in the jackpine thickets beyond the Deer Lick, and only a few trout were working. The fish seemed small, perhaps little better than a pound, when I hooked a surprisingly strong fish along a tangle of logs.

The fish had been working cautiously. Its rise was more a quiet sucking sound than the usual greedy splash of a big brown taking these *Hexagenia* flies, particularly when they are egg-laying spinners or newly hatched duns fluttering down the current. The big trout had simply intercepted the fly with a quiet roll, although its rise was strong enough to suggest a heavy fish among the river sounds.

I've got a good fish! I shouted. *It feels pretty strong!*

Stay with him! Houseman yelled.

The fish held stubbornly in the current the first few minutes, and then it plunged downstream in a wrenching run that stripped into the backing. The trout had hooked itself hard.

It still felt powerful in the heavy flow. It ripped into a bold run that bored angrily upstream, slicing the surface with a shrill violin-string sound. Somewhere in the night upstream, the big fish jumped and fell clumsily, its splash magnified in the silence. Its strength was almost frightening, and I was worried that it might shear my tippet in the stumps and deadfalls under the opposite bank.

God! I thought anxiously. *He's really strong!*

My arms started shaking then, partly with a flush of fresh adrenalin and partly with growing fatigue. The big trout circled stubbornly just beyond my net, until finally it surrendered, threshing in the meshes as I waded ashore.

How big? Houseman shouted in the darkness.

Big enough to wear me out! I said wearily.

Since the hatch was finished, Houseman came wading upstream with his fishing light. *How about some help?* he said.

I could use it, I admitted.

His light found the big trout writhing in the net. It was a hook-jawed cockfish, its bright scarlet spots gleaming in its richly mottled flanks, and it weighed almost six pounds. It was the best fish that I took from the Pere Marquette in those boyhood years.

Those were golden summers on the rivers of Michigan. Great fishermen like George Mason and Ralph Widdicomb and Harold Smedley were along rivers like the AuSable and Pere Marquette and Manistee. Fly makers like Art Winnie and Len Halliday and Ralph Corey were producing cornucopias of trout flies through the Michigan winters, and craftsmen like Paul Young and Lyle Dickerson were milling superb bamboo rods in their Detroit workshops.

The familiar Pere Marquette Rod & Gun Club was a circle of skilled and inventive fishermen in those days. Its members included

Widdicomb, who was famous for the elegant badger spentwing that still bears his name. Vic Cramer developed unusual deer-hair flies, including a spent *Hexagenia* imitation and leaf-roller pattern, along with the woven-hair dressing of his Cramer nymphs. William Brush was a well-known automotive engineer who also patented a hook for parachute-hackle flies, which he developed on the Pere Marquette. These men fished often from the club compound, its simple buildings scattered on a tree-sheltered promontory above Waddell's Riffle.

Simmy Nolphe is probably the dean of the Pere Marquette fishermen in our time, and he lives on the fly-only water near Baldwin. Nolphe is a skilled steelhead fisherman who knows every holding-lie between the Highway Bridge and the pools below Danaher Creek. Carl Richards is another Pere Marquette regular, and joined with the equally skilled Doug Swisher to produce the books *Selective Trout* and *Fly Fishing Strategy.* Richards fishes regularly from the old Pere Marquette Rod & Gun compound, and we have shared the river there from Danaher Creek to the swift currents above the Deer Lick. Dave Borgeson is a principal architect of the Pacific salmon program in Michigan, although his secret love is probably fishing the big steelhead with flies in October, particularly in the estuary of the Pere Marquette. Borgeson was among the pioneers who worked out fly-fishing tactics on these big lake-run rainbows, proving wrong the cracker-barrel experts who insisted that these transplanted steelhead would never take flies.

The biologist was my guide the last time I fished these steelhead on the Pere Marquette. *I'll meet you at Barothy's,* Borgeson suggested. *Just bring strong tackle and your alarm clock!*

Alarm clock! I protested.

You're famous for sleeping late! Borgeson laughed. *We like to get on the river early—the first rod through the good water has the best chance of taking these steelhead this late!*

You win, I said.

April on the upper Pere Marquette can prove unpredictable, and it was snowing hard when Borgeson stood like Marley's ghost in the five o'clock darkness, pounding on my cottage door with his breath blossoming in the cold. *Reveille!* Borgeson shivered.

You're joking! I stared at the snowflakes in disbelief. *Did you remember the ice spud and tip-up flags?*

Forget the weather! Borgeson stripped his gloves and parka in front of the fireplace. *Steelheading builds character—and steelhead fishermen thrive on a little weather!*

You're nuts! I laughed. *We're going out in that?*

Steelheading builds character! he insisted.

It's crazy! I sighed.

It had stopped snowing after breakfast, but the morning still felt like duck season when we left the station wagon at the Green Cottage. *We could hike upstream and fish the Whinnery stretch,* Borgeson suggested, *but I have a hunch about the Deer Lick.*

You're the doctor, I shivered.

It seemed warmer when we had covered a hundred yards through the wintry bottoms along the river. The snowfall had completely covered the winter leaves and deadfalls, and it seemed a little like still-hunting whitetails in a fresh tracking snow. We forded the river at Shapton's Run, in the looping bends below the Whirlpool, and we stopped to watch a wild turkey scuttling ahead through the drifts and trees.

When do these steelhead start coming? I asked.

Our bright fish usually enter the river at Ludington in late October, Borgeson replied, *and those first October runs usually include some of the biggest steelhead of the season.*

Lots of fish coming in October? I interrupted.

Only a few large bellwether fish, Borgeson continued. *Our biggest runs arrive in late winter and early spring.*

Are they like the winter fish on the Pacific coast?

They're something like that, Borgeson admitted. *Perhaps more like the late-fall steelhead on the Klamath and Umpqua.*

The big runs come later? I asked.

The river was a dark necklace through the trees, winding back on itself until the high clay benches forced it back toward Lake Michigan, and we walked slowly through the snow-covered branches. *We keep getting fish sporadically all through the winter.* Borgeson held a branch until I passed along the trail. *Our first heavy run comes during the last of February, and our biggest migrations arrive before Easter—but sometimes we get a good run in late April too.*

We've got bright fish now?

You think I'd bring you out in blizzards for nothing? Borgeson grinned menacingly and laughed. *Our biologists are still tagging some bright steelhead at Ludington—so they're still coming!*

That's great! I felt less cold suddenly.

Borgeson had always believed that these Michigan steelhead could be taken with flies, in spite of the trolling and salmon-egg mythology that argued against such refinements, since he had often caught winter steelhead on the Pacific coast. Several dedicated fishermen had patiently experimented with standard steelhead patterns, and with various combinations of line densities and weighting and other equipment. The secrets were slowly ferreted out in recent years. Their consistent parade of big fly-caught steelhead, including a sixteen-pound fish taken by Simmy Nolphe on the upper Pere Marquette, was irrefutable evidence that finally led to the fly-only mileage on the watershed.

Look familiar? Borgeson asked.

It sure brings back some memories, I admitted. *We fished it every summer from the Forks Pool to Bowman's Bridge—but we never fished it when it looked like winter in the Yukon!*

It's probably better fishing these days, he said.

How's that? I asked.

It's fly-only water these days, Borgeson explained, *from the M-37 Bridge to Danaher Creek—it's got a lot of wild fish!*

No stocking of hatchery sardines?

That's right! Borgeson agreed.

We fished the riffles at Shapton's Run for almost an hour without moving a fish, until the weak April sun filtered through the trees, and we walked downstream toward the Deer Lick. It was still cold and the snow dropped in soft shards from the branches.

You sure we had to start before daylight? I asked.

You feel like we're after pike? Borgeson laughed and threw a loosely packed snowball. *Winter muskellunge maybe?*

Walleyes through the ice, I said ruefully.

Steelhead fishing and suffering are the same thing! Borgeson broke more trail through the crust that had frozen the marshy bottoms. *But getting up early wasn't as crazy as you think, because these fish lie in the deep holes at midday, particularly in bright weather—and move out into the riffles at twilight.*

You mean they spawn in the darkness?

Steelhead spawn on dark days too, Borgeson continued, *but usually they hide and work the gravel riffles at daybreak and nightfall—the early morning is probably the best time to fish them, because they won't have been bothered for hours!*

Does it hurt to fish spawning steelhead? I asked.

Not really, Borgeson replied. *The entire headwaters are closed to fishing above the M-37 Bridge—and they've got miles and miles of pea-gravel riffles where nobody bothers them.*

Are we fishing spawners? I asked.

Fish that are actually spawning seldom take the fly, Borgeson responded. *Cockfish might attack a big streamer or bucktail to defend their territory, but it's often other fish that are caught.*

Stray males and females? I asked.

Sometimes, he said.

Since the fly-only water on the upper Pere Marquette is unique among the Michigan steelhead rivers, it has proved immensely popular among knowledgeable anglers and can become crowded. Fishing it successfully involves some unusual techniques, although many of the flies popular in Michigan are standard western patterns, and would be found from San Francisco to the Aleutians.

Steelhead dressings like the Thor, Umpqua Special, Skunk, Kalama Special, Fall Favorite, Skykomish Sunrise, Brass Hat, Van Luven, Queen Bess, Yellow Comet, and Babine Special are all popular in Michigan too. Skilled fishermen like Carl Richards have experimented successfully with Atlantic salmon patterns on Michigan steelhead, and dressings like the Blue Charm, Black Fitchtail, Orange Blossom, Green Butt, Ackroyd, and Orange Charm are finding their proponents. There are also days when such bright flies seem to disturb the fish, and Michigan fishermen have started to work out fly dressings intended to imitate some of the major aquatic insects found in their rivers.

Like their winter-run cousins on the Pacific coast, the Michigan steelhead like their flies on the bottom, and successful flies are typically weighted with several turns of fuse wire under their bodies. High-density lines are sufficient to get the fly on the bottom in the shallow riffles, but some lies are too swift and deep for such tackle. Some anglers have experimented with stainless cable between their lines and leaders, while others have tried short lengths of lead-core trolling lines to sink their flies deep. Such equipment works on large rivers like the Muskegon and Manistee, but there are big steelhead in brushy pockets on the smaller Michigan rivers too. Such holes demand specially rigged tackle, since conventional steelhead methods are often unworkable in small rivers filled with deadfalls and sweepers.

Michigan fishermen have evolved a unique shot-dropper technique on such water. The secret is using a small triangle swivel, with three connections linked to a circular core. The leader itself connects the line to the first swivel, and a short tippet of six- to eight-pound test is attached to the second with the fly. The third swivel trails six inches of nylon with an overhand knot in its free end. Split shot are added to this short nylon to form a shot dropper, and a skilled steelhead fisherman can adjust the amount of weight on his dropper to suit the depth and velocity of the current he is fishing. It is not a pretty method of fishing, but it requires its own combination of subtle skills.

When it's rigged properly, Borgeson explained when we reached the swift run above the Deer Lick, *it's possible to walk the shot dropper along the bottom with the rod held high—you can actually feel the shot ticking from stone to stone.*

Skilled manipulation of the shot-dropper technique will ride the fly slightly higher in the current than the weighted nylon dropper itself. Perhaps its most ingenious feature is its ability to foul the bottom without snagging the fly too, and firm pressure will either break the dropper or strip its split shot free.

It's perfect for brushy pockets where you have to sink your fly quickly, Borgeson continued. *You can hear our steelheaders talking about favorite two-shot and three-shot riffles!*

Aren't they hard to cast? I asked.

Pretty cumbersome, he admitted, *but good roll-casting with a big rod works pretty well.*

How large can these steelhead run?

Simmy Nolphe took that sixteen-pounder here last year, Borgeson replied excitedly, *and we've seen fish over twenty!*

That's big enough! I laughed.

Snow started falling again when we walked the brushy banks along the Deer Lick stretch. The river was swift and slightly tea-colored from the marshes in its headwaters, and it flowed with a kind of sullen strength through our waders.

We've often found fish under those cedars, Borgeson pointed, *but the light is wrong to see them now.*

The snow doesn't help! I said.

The snow flurries passed and the weak April sun tried to warm the swift currents. The dark bottom showed some fingerprints of spawning activity just above the overhanging cedars, but we could see no steelhead there until the light changed.

Look there under the trees! Borgeson exclaimed.

The bottom seemed empty at first, but Borgeson pointed excitedly to the swift run across the river, and suddenly a smooth current welled up and I saw them. There were three steelhead lying there, facing into the current, fish that looked like dark-olive ghosts hovering over the bottom of winter algae.

They're big! Borgeson cautioned.

It started snowing again, and I shivered when I waded into position in the thigh-deep currents across from the fish, although not entirely from the cold. The river looped against the timbered Clay Banks upstream, and scoured back swiftly under the trees. The fresh snow cloaked the cedars, and the swirling flakes obscured the river until the fish were only half-seen shadows.

Can you still see them? Borgeson asked anxiously.

They're still there! I nodded.

It was snowing much harder when I sharply rolled the first cast upstream. Its three-shot dropper looped high and fell clumsily. Its weight settled quickly and caught briefly in the stones, until I lifted the rod and felt it pull free, ticking gently along the bottom. It took several casts to get it drifting properly, feeling the shot-dropper drag and catch in the crevices between the rocks.

Borgeson clambered up a small tree to observe the fish. *We've still got three steelhead over there,* he yelled excitedly from his perch, *and we've got another fish farther down!*

The first casts worked deep along the bottom, and I took a shuffling half step between fly-swings, covering the holding water in a series of concentric drifts. The two steelhead I could still see expressed no interest in my fly, although I covered them patiently.

We've still got others below that pair, Borgeson called. *Just stay with them and fish it through slowly!*

The fly-swing feels right! I started another cast.

The shot-dropper fell tight against a deadfall, and I stripped a little line into the drift until I felt the lead hopscotching along the stones. It grated momentarily on a gravelly shingle, drifted smoothly under the trees and there was a strong pull.

Fish! I shouted happily.

The big steelhead threshed heavily in the shallows, throwing spray with its angry convulsions, and the reel rasped in protest. The fish held stubbornly in the strongest currents. It shook its head and bulldogged deep along the bottom, and suddenly it cartwheeled under the trees and the reel was running shrilly again.

Good fish! Borgeson shouted. *Stay with him!*

How deep is that bend downstream? I yelled when the backing started to evaporate from the reel. *Might have to follow him through!*

You can wade it diagonally across the bar!

It might come to that! I said.

The big steelhead sliced past me in the shallows, its spotted back completely above the water, throwing spray into the falling snow. The fish was already thirty yards into my backing, and I picked a careful route along the willows in pursuit.

The Deer Lick is a little forbidding in its spring flow, particularly in the bend at the Anderson cottage. There is a small logjam on the opposite bank, just where the current shelves back into the bend downstream. It is deep there under the throbbing sweepers, where the strongest currents suck through the tangled roots. When a strong fish decides to leave the Deer Lick, stripping the reel well into its backing, it is a tightrope act to follow it diagonally above the shelving currents between these holes. Crossing there is the only way to follow a troublesome fish, particularly with the April currents running bank full in the willows.

He's stopped taking line! Borgeson yelled.

But he's still awfully strong! I plunged through the shallows and fought to recover some backing. *Awfully strong!*

I'm coming! Borgeson came sliding down his tree in a shower of bark and fresh snow. *Hold him out of that brush pile!*

I'm trying! I groaned.

The slender rod bucked and lunged heavily, echoing the sullen struggle of the steelhead along the logs. The straining leader hummed in the current. The jackstraw labyrinth of brush and flood debris looked threatening, but the tippet somehow survived.

He's trying it again! Borgeson warned.

Damn! I applied pressure and the rod was a tight half circle. *He's still trying to break me under those logs!*

Still think you can hold him?

My response died in my throat when the fish bored deep under the fallen trees. The rod throbbed angrily under the stress. Its pressure finally turned the fish, until several other brief runs were parried easily and the fight was almost over. The big steelhead worked splashily to avoid the net, but Borgeson captured it expertly and waded triumphantly ashore with the prize.

Good fish! Borgeson said excitedly.

Strong! I agreed. *What do you think he'll weigh?*

Nine or ten pounds! the biologist answered happily. *That's a lot of steelhead on a fly rod in that brushy water!*

Borgeson took a brace of slightly larger steelhead from the Deer Lick before we stopped for lunch. Both fish were carefully released, and we circled happily back through the river bottoms to the station wagon. The fireplace at Barothy's felt good after the icy currents of the Pere Marquette, and we drove back to the river on the Clay Banks county road after lunch. Borgeson suggested that we hike downstream on its timber ridge and then cut down the steep trail to intercept the river at its Waddell's Riffle stretch.

It's beautiful water, Borgeson explained while we walked the Clay Banks ridge with the river winding through the trees, *and we might find a few bright fish there—just coming from the lake!*

Sounds great! I struggled to keep up in my waders.

Waddell's Riffle is a beautiful half mile of gravelly shallows, its currents scouring under the cedars and willows that shelter its south banks. The cottages and outbuildings of the Pere Marquette Rod & Gun Club lie concealed in the trees there. Borgeson located a school of silvery fresh-run steelhead toward the bottom of Waddell's Riffle, and we crawled stealthily through the trees until we were perched above them in the shadows. The school of bright fish were pale olive, hovering in the smooth currents under the cedars.

Those are fresh-run fish! Borgeson whispered.

Maybe they'll take, I said excitedly.

Steelhead are seldom predictable, and we fished them patiently for almost two hours without observing any interest in the fish. We stopped to rest the school of steelhead, and sat talking while the shadows lengthened along the riffles.

Finally I tried a bright-tinseled steelhead pattern, and with its first drift through the fish, the river exploded. There was no time to respond to the fierce strike. The rod snapped into a tightly straining circle when the steelhead hooked itself, and it slashed and steeplechased upstream through the shallows. Its strength and speed were startling, and my Hardy surrendered line in a piercing wail. The fish jumped in the afternoon light and stopped.

Bright fish! I shouted.

Better watch it! Borgeson waded swiftly toward me. *There's a pretty bad deadfall under those cedars downstream!*

I'll try! I laughed.

The steelhead came back downstream swiftly. The line ripped through the water, its faint sounds something like tearing linen, and I turned awkwardly to fight its strength. The rod was seated against my waders and my left hand was working high at the stripping guide, tightening into a salt-water lock. The fish shook itself angrily, steeplechasing past the drowned deadfalls, and stopped again.

Crazy fish! Borgeson said.

The steelhead brooded momentarily and exploded again. Six jumps exploded under the overhanging cedars, and a final wild somersault carried the fish high into the trees. Cedar needles showered into the river as the steelhead tumbled clumsily back through the branches. Its sword-bright length disappeared in its awkward splash, and before I could recover, it was running again.

I told you to fight the fish! Borgeson stood laughing behind me. *Not chase him up that cedar like a coon!*

He's chasing me! I protested.

The struggle erupted in the open river, although the big hen fish threatened several times to reach the logjams in the bend downstream. It almost reached the drowned cedar twice, its spotted tail sculling weakly now, until I patiently forced it back into midstream. Finally it surrendered, its silvery length fattened on alewives and smelt, and we estimated its weight at twelve pounds.

The steelhead held tentatively in the shallows, tired from its acrobatic fight and no longer fearing us, its scarlet gill covers fluttering until their rhythms settled and grew strong. The fish still held there in the current, until suddenly it was gone.

It's still quite a river! I thought.

It is impossible to capture the Pere Marquette in words, and the memories of its fishing summers crowd the mind. There are too many echoes over too many years, from those first boyhood mornings on the Little South to the recent afternoons fishing for the giant chinook salmon that crowd its headwaters in October.

Watching their spawning rites on the Waddell's stretch was like eavesdropping on the primordial rhythms of the world. The salmon gather in restless coveys, their henfish writhing against the bottom, patiently shaping their redds in the afternoons. The cockfish aggressively defend their mates, quarrelling in great gouts of spray and roostertails of wild pursuit in the spawning shallows, and rooting with their backs showing above the water. Finally these fish will die, having completed their restless spawning in riffles filled with October leaves, drifting with the current until their flesh becomes part of the river and its fertility. Such spawning rites suggest that life still pulses in the river, its energies alive in its cold currents and the precious ova hidden in the womb of its bright gravel.

Wild turkeys are coming back along the river in recent years, scuttling through the leaves on the jackpine benches, and the ruffed grouse are drumming in steelhead time. Owls still hunt from its cedar thickets and feasting trees. Although I have learned more about owls since our first boyhood summers on the Pere Marquette, and no longer believe the myths and superstitions, something strange did happen once.

During our first summer trip north from Chicago, the automobile we had patiently nursed through the war years broke down at Muskegon, and we finally reached our campsite long after midnight. It was difficult making camp in the headlights of the Oldsmobile, and it was almost getting light when we settled into our sleeping bags. Finally I fell asleep listening to the mournful calling of owls.

The morning sun was already bright on our tent, tracing its leafy patterns on the canvas, when I finally stirred. The cooking smells of coffee and fried eggs and bacon drifted through our camp. *It's going to get pretty hot,* my father predicted. *Too hot for fishing.*

Maybe I'll go swimming at the Nobles', I said.

Makes sense! my father smiled. *They'll know what's been happening on the river this week!*

It was a half-mile hike along the county road, axle-deep in sand beyond the bridge where the Middle Branch comes welling out from its marl-bog beginnings. The road was hot in the morning sun, and coveys of red-legged grasshoppers flushed along its shoulders, settling ahead in the road. I walked slowly through the trees toward the Noble cottages, remembering the screech owls.

Good morning! I called to the college girls who were cleaning the cottages. *Where's the boss today?*

The girls looked startled. *He died last night,* they said.

THE MILL AT LONGPARISH

Dermot Wilson watched the trout dimple again, tight against the ranunculus and chara, where we sat outside his fishing hut on the Kimbridge beats. Cuckoos were calling in the copse of woods beyond the Bear and Ragged Staff. The twilight was soft and its rich shadows lengthened across the water meadows. The lights were already bright in the leaded windows of the Georgian manor house across the river, and Wilson dredged a perfectly chilled bottle of Mersault from the minnow trap he keeps in the spring.

We'll fish the beat at Longparish in the morning. Wilson unfolded his military chart of Hampshire. *It has fine fly hatches and some large fish—and I'll give you directions from Stockbridge.*

It sounds fine, I said. *Isn't Longparish the water that Dunne fished after the First World War?*

That's right! Wilson lit another Woodbine.

Dunne's work with fly-patterns and fly-dressing techniques have always fascinated me, I explained as Wilson offered me some Mersault. *I've always dreamed of fishing his water.*

Hampshire mornings are beautiful, he suggested. *You should meet me at Longparish early—and I'll bring the lunch.*

Later I returned to Salisbury, where I was staying in a seventeenth-century room at the Rose and Crown, and had dinner in the tiny second-floor restaurant called Provence. Its cuisine is well known, and its location above the market cross in old Salisbury is charming. The dinner was a really fresh Dover sole, which had actually come from that gray-walled harbor on the English Channel, and its rich wine sauce seemed complete with a delicate bottle of Vouvray. The night was particularly soft when I finished coffee and walked back through the narrow streets, with moonlight on the slender tower of the most beautiful cathedral in England.

Stockbridge still lay sleeping in its early summer mists. The old Grosvenor Hotel stood in the feeble light, its columns supporting an ugly portico leavened only by its history and traditions. The meeting rooms above the portico have sheltered the Houghton Club and its tackle rooms for almost two centuries of sport.

There was an early breakfast at the Sheriff's House in Stockbridge, where the highwayman Dick Turpin was briefly imprisoned in the eighteenth century. The beautiful little Test flows among its beds of chara and fountain moss and ranunculus below the flower gardens.

The hedgerow lanes along the river wind north from Stockbridge, past the charming villages of Leckford and Chilbolton-on-Test, where Benjamin Disraeli owned an Elizabethan manor house with a beautifully carved mantelpiece attributed to the storied Izaak Walton. The river highway crosses the Test on the masonrywork bridge at Testcombe, winds through the rich farms and chalkdowns below Wherwell, and crosses the Basingstroke motorway.

Longparish itself lies just upstream, its charming character alive with stone and half-timbered houses with sculptured thatchwork roofs. The village is sheltered between the forested Harewood ridge and the intricate labyrinth of canals and millraces and carriers between Newton Stacey and the churchyard at Hurstbourne Priors. Its fishing beats were the waters fished by Harold Plunkett Greene, the British singer who wrote of his sport in the lyric *Where the Bright Waters Meet,* which celebrated his seasons along the Test and Bourne.

Charming fishing beats and villages lie still farther upstream, under a pastoral ridge called Watership Down. Whitchurch has a delicate straw-yellow dry fly bearing its name, the handsome Whitchurch Dun that has been a favorite since Colonel Peter Hawker recorded his sport in meticulous Longparish diaries at the beginning of the nineteenth century. The Scottish poet and writer Andrew Lang, whose books included a four-volume *History of Scotland* and the graceful *Ballades in Blue China,* held a fine dry-fly beat at Whitchurch in the peaceful decades before the First World War.

Laverstoke has the ruins of a Saxon church, and the river itself is born in a vault-covered spring at Polhampton Mill. Izaak Walton lived out his twilight years at Norington Farme, and the entire Test is rich with the music of centuries.

Downstream from Chilbolton-on-Test, the river is faintly stained with silts and is often impossible to wade. The most famous waters probably lie at Houghton and Mottisfont Abbey and Kimbridge, where Dermot Wilson has a favorite beat near the inn of the Bear and Ragged Staff. The late Lord Mountbatten had a beautiful country house on the river at Broadlands, with its classical portico and columns above a putting-green meadow that reaches down to the stonework basin of the Home Pool. Mountbatten, tragically assassinated while at his country house in Ireland, lies buried along the Test at Romsey.

Although the watershed is still beautiful throughout its length, and the pastoral well-tailored landscapes of Hampshire are among the most peaceful in England, the butter-colored gravel and remarkable clarity described in the writings of Richard Durnford, Charles Kingsley, and Sir Edward Grey of Falloden are no longer found below the headwaters at Wherwell and Longparish.

The river there is still startlingly clear, flowing smoothly in its weeds and gravel. Watercress and fountain moss and stoneworts are found in great abundance there, undulating in the choreography of its currents. Its fly hatches are still profuse, although it has always lacked the storied populations of big *Ephemera* drakes so famous on the chalkstreams, and its most prolific species are relatively small. Its tiny regattas of Pale Waterys and Medium Olives in good weather are replaced by the somber Iron Blues on overcast days. Its clarity and fly hatches still match the observations recorded by J. W. Dunne is his *Sunshine and the Dry Fly* in 1924. These paragraphs introduce his historic departure from the theories of Frederic Halford:

> Many years ago I purchased, in preparation for my first visit to a chalkstream, a complete set (one dozen each of twenty-seven

patterns) of the smaller Halford trout flies. And for many years after, it used to afford me considerable satisfaction to inspect the contents of the twenty-seven nicely labelled compartments, apportioned between two fly-boxes, and to speculate upon the day when I should discover the prototype of one or another of these beautiful little flies hatching out.

The remaining five patterns had already in some measure justified their purchase. I had scooped from the current a female Welshman's Button which was quite simply pattern number 30 come to life, and a mayfly which looked like the Female Olive Spinner took the air each evening. Once in the late evening dusk, I had glimpsed drifting past the banks, a spinner remarkably like the Medium Olive. The little red-headed Black Gnat had also proved itself remarkably deadly.

And there had also been a morning when, finding a small blue-winged fly hatching in great numbers, I had put up, after some brief hesitation (for the body dressing seemed entirely different) a male Iron Blue, and had quickly annexed a brace of hefty Test trout. So I had no reason to doubt that the remaining patterns might in due course prove their worth.

But to tell the truth, I was more than a little puzzled at the number of Test flies which were not included in the Halford series. Every day, and sometimes all day long, these neglected insects were hatching out in hosts.

They were all subimagoes, sober-looking little flies with almost colorless legs and tails, with wings ranging from crinkled pewter to the pale tint of Sheffield worn thin, and with pale monochromatic bodies ranging from the palest honey to the richest amber. I could only conclude that such flies were peculiar to the Longparish parts of the Test, and that for the beautiful Olives and cream-striped Pale Waterys one had to journey downstream to Stockbridge and the Houghton Club.

However, since these latter mayflies were not to be found where I was fishing, I had to make the best of a bad job, and with the assistance of the Little Marryat and the Whitchurch Dun, did well enough on the whole.

Dermot Wilson is perhaps the best-known dry-fly fisherman in the United Kingdom, and my fishing at Longparish had been arranged through him. The beat was just below the village itself at Forton Mill. Its picturesque thatched-roof structure lies across the river, with a narrow catwalk along its intake. The millrace is the primary channel, and it has a carrier hatch which diverts the flow around the millhouse itself during spates. The carrier forms a low island across from the thatched-roof houses behind the mill. There is a charming octagonal keeper's house with a conical shingled roof. Its tackle rooms are on the second level, reached by climbing a narrow curving stair, and its windows overlook the Mill Pool.

Downstream from the pool itself, where the still currents flow through the weeds and butter-colored gravel, there was a beautiful flower garden below a white cottage. The garden reached down from the cottage to the river, past the bright roses and blue delphiniums and lilacs, and the twisted apple tree that sheltered a single white-painted bench beside the weedy shallows. It was a perfect place to sit and wait for hatches and rising fish. The skilled British angler seldom casts until he finds a trout working.

The morning had been cold and stormy, with a chill rain misting in the Hampshire hills, and there still had been no hatching flies when I joined Wilson at the keeper's house. *The fishing has been quite poor.* Wilson shook his head gloomily. *The fisherman on the upper water has already gone back to London.*

No hatches? I asked. *Not even a few Iron Blues?*

They usually like this weather, Wilson agreed, *but they've seemingly forgotten that this morning.*

The little river flowed cold and still. *When the trout decide it's too early for lunch,* I laughed and rummaged in our wicker basket, *it's time to accept their judgment and have lunch ourselves.*

Perhaps you're right, Wilson said.

The split-willow hamper was filled with roast beef and stone-milled bread and lettuce, and I sliced a fat tomato and gathered some watercress from the carrier hatch. There was a bottle of Chateau Lynch-Bages, and several bottles of English ale, along with a thermos of hot Darjeeling and a small wedge of Stilton.

You've come well prepared, I said.

Wilson spread these treasures on the table in the keeper's house and we sat watching the pool while we ate. The weather improved steadily through lunch, until the cold rain ebbed and finally stopped.

The weak sun filtered through the overcast, and we could see into the pool under the millhouse. Several good fish were holding in the smooth currents, and I studied them in the changing light.

Finally the sun broke through briefly, flooding the bottom of the pool with light. *Dermot!* I thought aloud when I saw them. *Look at those trout lying along the millrace wall!*

I wondered when you'd see those fish, he said.

There were several large trout lying there in the shadows. The fish in the tail shallows were nymphing, and they hovered just under the surface, drifting forward restlessly in the current when they took something in the flow. Their mouths would open lazily, expelling water past their gills, and flashing white each time they intercepted a hatching nymph. But tight against the millrace wall, where the watercress and elodea offered them some cover, there were several larger trout holding quietly in the current.

How large are those trout? I asked.

The smaller fish along the watercress is about three pounds. Wilson pointed to the millrace shadows. *Those others upstream are smaller, but the bottom fish is much larger.*

You're right, I thought excitedly.

We quickly cleared the table and I rigged my tackle. It was the baptism of a delicate little Howells, and I fitted it with a vintage Hardy filled with a four-weight Kingfisher silk. It was difficult to lace my wading brogues because my fingers were shaking in anticipation, but finally I shouldered into my fishing coat. It was still cold when we walked down the carrier path.

Several trout were starting to rise in the shallows below the apple-tree bench. There was a sparse hatch mixed between Pale Waterys and Medium Olives and dark little Iron Blues, but the chill wind sailboated them across the currents. Several more fish were working, but when I tried dry-fly imitations over them, the trout refused them stubbornly. The fish were still rising.

It's the weather! I thought suddenly. *The wind is blowing the flies off their usual lines of drift—and the trout are still on the nymphs because they're not affected by the wind!*

The fish rejected a pale little nymph, although several drifts along a channel of rising trout seemed perfect, but when I changed patterns and placed a dark Iron Blue imitation over a soft rise, the tippet paused and I tightened into a strong fish.

That's it! Wilson said.

Several other trout took the nymph greedily in the gravelly shallows along the garden, and the retired British colonel came down from his thatched-roof cottage to watch, settling his stiff leg across the bench under the apple tree. Three decent fish took the drifting nymph just opposite his rose trellis, and the colonel smiled. The hatch seemed to wane slightly, although I took a fine two-pound trout from a weedy channel under the willows. The wind grew cold again, and the retired soldier hobbled back through his garden to escape the chill, his rattan walking stick striking the brickwork.

Twice I missed taking fish in a weedy pocket, and when the sporadic fly hatches started again, the trout were steadily nymphing in the pool at the millhouse. Their rises were gentle porpoise rolls, their tails and dorsal fins showing in the surface film, and I worked patiently into position.

My nymph settled well above the fish, drifting back toward them in the current, and the delicate nylon darted sideways as a trout stopped the fly. It was a fat sixteen-inch fish, and I coaxed it patiently away from the others. Another trout took my nymph three casts later, but it was a strong fish of more than two pounds, and it frightened the other trout with its stubborn fight.

Several minutes passed while we rested the pool. *Look there!* Wilson pointed suddenly. *There along the wall!*

There was a soft porpoising rise along the stonework, and its disturbance ebbed and died against the watercress. The spotted dorsal fin bulged again, spreading its waves downstream.

It's the big fish! I thought.

The soft cast dropped the nymph gingerly, several inches above the trout and tight against the sheltering watercress. Its drift seemed perfect, teasing through the shadows, and I held my breath when the leader paused and I tightened.

The fish shook its head with a puzzled strength. *He's hooked,* I thought with a wild flush of excitement, *and he's hooked perfectly in the corner of his jaw.*

There was a threshing splash that engulfed the weeds, and the still currents bulged angrily. The big trout shook itself again, hanging sullenly in the flow, and then it bolted upstream to probe the swelling currents from the mill. Several times it threatened to break the fine tippet there, but each time I coaxed it free. Late in the struggle, the big trout fouled the leader in some drifting weed, but it lacked the strength to break off.

It finally surrendered and Wilson applauded its richly spotted length. *It's a beautiful trout!* he exclaimed happily. *It's the trout that we saw from the window before!*

It'll go better than four pounds! I laughed.

You're right! Wilson agreed wryly. *But catching that fish is just too unlikely—nobody will believe us!*

WHERE FLOWS THE UMPQUA

It was getting dark when we finally left Boise, looking into the dying light behind the Stinkingwater Pass. The mountains rose in layers of stark ridges surrounding Freezeout Peak and Coyote Wells, their names still bitter echoes of the frontier trappers who first explored this Oregon country. The milky currents of the Snake flowed still and deep beyond Payette, its brushy islands and shallow bars alive with twilight flocks of geese. Still farther downstream in the darkness at Farewell Bend, where the travelers on the Oregon Trail left the river to risk the difficult wagon trace to Deadman's Pass, the river was purple and mauve. There was a thin moon rising and the night seemed full of ghosts.

Still six hours of driving, Jack Hemingway said.

The highway left the river and reached into the darkness, and I poured us both some coffee when we crossed the Drinkingwater Summit. The chill wind moved restlessly in the sagebrush. We stood in the darkness beside the Peugeot, watching the headlights of the sixteen-wheel Kenworths and Peterbilts climbing steadily into the foothills that surround the arid Malheur Basin.

Beyond the outcroppings of the Stinkingwater Pass, the lights of the sawmill town of Burns looked toylike and melancholy on the horizon. Its timber comes from the Strawberry Mountains and Deschutes Plateau, and the headwaters of the John Day country.

The saline marshes south of Burns glittered in the cold moonlight, their waters a surviving echo of the brackish seas that once shrouded eastern Oregon. Other echoes are found in half-dry lakes with curious names like Mugwump and Stone Corral and Bluejoint. The narrow highway reaches west from Burns like a cartographer's grid, with virtually nothing for sixty-five miles.

Pretty empty piece of road, I said.

It's empty all right! Hemingway laughed. *Maybe we should stop and take a coffee break in Burns!*

Our thermos is getting low, I nodded.

The truckstop was brightly lighted. Its fuel pumps were surprisingly busy at midnight, and the counter stools were crowded too. Some drivers had finished and were drinking beer, while the early crews were starting breakfast so as to reach their clear-cutting sites at daybreak. The bartender was perspiring heavily, and his bulging waistline betrayed a lifetime of chicken-fried steaks and potatoes and beer. The waitress was feeding coins into the jukebox, and stood listening while Waylon Jennings' hard-driving guitar rose above the kitchen noise and laughter along the bar. She fussed with her lacquered hair while we ordered coffee, and she stopped to add another quarter to the jukebox on her way to the kitchen.

It's not exactly gourmet, Hemingway laughed infectiously, *but things will get better once we get to Steamboat—it's quiet in the cabins along the river and the food is really great!*

I've heard a lot about it, I said.

The moon was still bright beyond Steen's Mountain, its serrated snake-country ridges silhouetted in the darkness. The night was perfectly still and clear. When the waitress had filled our thermos we started west again, watching the headlights of a solitary truck on the horizon. The desert bottoms at Glass Butte were empty, and once the tractor trailer had passed, the old highway was completely dark for more than forty miles. The moon was getting low and the sagebrush was silvery with frost.

We're still about three hours out, Hemingway said.

Getting cold! I shivered and reached back for the thermos. *We've got plenty of coffee and fresh bread and cheese—we've even got some smoked oysters, but it's too cold for Chablis.*

It's never too cold for Chablis!

Hemingway had chilled a magnum of wine during dinner at Annabel's in Boise, and we carefully wrapped the bottle in a plastic bag filled with crushed ice. The map compartment of the Peugeot bulged with cassettes of Mozart and Beethoven and Bach, and their soaring music filled its multiple speakers.

How about some heat? I suggested.

You haven't heard about our mouse? Hemingway laughed.

Mouse or mousse? I grinned.

The mouse in the heating system. He ignored the question and continued. *It's been rooting around behind the instruments ever since I took delivery on the car.*

The heater's not working? I protested.

It's completely clogged, he grinned. *Smells too!*

What does our visitor eat? I asked.

Beats me! Hemingway laughed. *Some assembly plant worker probably built his leftover lunch into my Peugeot!*

Could we coax it out with some cheese?

It's a genuine French mouse. He shook his head wryly. *It'll never come out of there for a piece of cheddar—it'll probably hold out for Roquefort or Camembert or Brie!*

It's going to get pretty cold, I said.

But how many fishing trips have a French stowaway?

Yours would! I agreed.

We stopped again for coffee at Bend, where the swift Deschutes gathers itself from the lava-field seepages and plateaus, and drops into the white-water canyons between the Warm Springs reservation and its junction with the Columbia. The highway that leads south from Bend climbs steadily into the dense ponderosa forests that rise between Paulina and Packsaddle Mountain. Sawmill towns like Crescent and Gilchrist and Chemult are virtually the only habitation in the seventy-five miles of plateau country.

There was still fresh snow from the late-summer storms that blanket the high plateau surrounding Crater Lake, and there were drifts in the lodgepoles at Diamond Lake summit. It is country famous for its winter snow packs, and the highway crews had already placed the reedlike poles to help them plow the right-of-way.

Beyond the timber plateau, the Umpqua highway winds past Cinnamon Butte before it drops steeply toward Toketee and Steamboat. Its headwaters are shrouded in a mixed forest of pine and Douglas fir and cedar. Below the Toketee waterfall, the river tumbles through a steep-walled gorge of ancient lava and the highway winds high above its pools and rapids. It finally reaches the Forest Service station at Steamboat Creek, and the Steamboat Inn downstream.

There were no lights when we finally reached the inn, and found a note telling us where our beds were. Our cabins were behind the inn itself, sheltered in a stand of thick-trunked sugar pines and firs, and the tumbling river lay below in the darkness. Its music was strong, and it was almost daylight when I finally slept.

It was strangely dark the next morning, and I peered outside to check the weather when my watch read ten-thirty. The morning was clear and bright, and the sun was already strong, but the magnificent trees sheltered our cabins so completely that it still seemed early. Hemingway was already fishing the Kitchen Pool.

There are six cabins perched above the river in a gentle half circle in the trees. Their riverfront facades are connected with a curving, fir-slat deck fitted with generous railings and benches, and their split-cedar shingles were dark with moss and pine needles. The Umpqua roared its greetings a hundred feet below the deck, its depths all emerald and spume under the Glory Hole.

It's beautiful! I thought.

I walked lazily up the stonework steps, and passed under the grape arbor into the inn itself. Several backpackers and logging-rig drivers were sharing breakfast at the long table with a young poetry professor from Oregon State. Three hunters in a huge pickup with racing tires, and several rifles racked across the rear window, stopped to fill its tank. There were two deer in its truckbed, and an average trophy head was roped grotesquely across its hood, streaming blood across the brightwork like a pagan sacrifice.

Steamboat Inn leads several lives. It is the only cigarette and fuel stop in the eighty-odd miles between Crater Lake junction and Idleyld on the North Umpqua, and both travelers and logging crews stop there often. During its daytime hours, it functions as part flyfishing shrine, tackle shop, short-order kitchen, filling station, and truckstop selling cigarettes and soft drinks and beer.

Its changing cast includes its fishing regulars: a mixture of teachers, attorneys, doctors, stockbrokers and bankers, college professors, writers, book salesmen, editors, photographers, professional flytiers, artists, fishing guides, manufacturers, architects and builders, engineers, and retired soldiers who constantly return to Steamboat, sharing an ascetic love of fishing its summer-run steelhead, a species perfectly suited to contemplation and self-denial.

The Steamboat Inn is completely transformed at twilight. Its daytime chrysalis is trapped in a cocoon of beer and logging trucks and country music, but its nightly metamorphosis is total. Its doors and windows are shuttered from its daytime universe behind its bamboo blinds, and it creates its own nighttime world.

Its country music is stilled and replaced by Mozart and Beethoven and Bach, mixed with a little Chopin and Brahms. Its gargantuan table becomes a celebration of spotless linen and candlelight, and its beer bottles are eclipsed by Cabernet Sauvignon and Beaujolais and Pinot Noir. The inn is closed except to those with dinner reservations and its steelhead regulars. Its cuisine is a growing legend in the Oregon logging country. Typical fare might include vichyssoise, smoked salmon, mushroom soufflé, beef Wellington, broccoli and cauliflower, and tiny fresh peas served family style, chocolate mousse, and a richly soft California wine in a carafe.

Breakfasts are relatively unusual too. There are several kinds of omelettes, various breads baked on the premises, muffins mixed with bran and dill, perfectly cured bacon and ham, and exquisitely prepared hash-brown potatoes.

I'll try the Steamboat Special, I decided rashly.

The young blue-jeaned waitress disappeared into the kitchen. Dan Callaghan appeared on the back porch, hanging his rod in the grape arbor outside. Callaghan is among the best steelhead fishermen on the North Umpqua as well as a superb photographer.

You're finally alive! Callaghan grinned. *Hemingway told me you were still sleeping—find anything on the menu?*

Steamboat Special, I replied.

Callaghan poured himself a mug of coffee and clattered back across the room to the giant sugar-pine table, his wading calks grating on the concrete-aggregate floor. The young waitress returned with my breakfast, and I stared at a platter heaped with food. There were fried potatoes and several pieces of thick whole wheat toast, surrounding a mammoth omelette that barely held its filling of ham and tomatoes and onions, mixed with a few other vegetables.

It's awesome! I protested weakly and faltered. *How many eggs do they crack for that monster?*

Five or six! Callaghan smiled. *Steelhead Special!*

Can't they try a half-egg omelette?

You'll need it! Callaghan insisted. *The river is pretty cold and its currents are strong—and it takes hundreds and hundreds of casts to catch a summer-run steelhead!*

You mean I'll burn it off? I said.

You'll see, he smiled.

We rigged our equipment after breakfast, sorting flies from my duffle and putting up eight-weight rods and organizing other tackle into a vest designed for deep wading.

The North Umpqua is a dangerous river. Its currents are swift and deceptively clear, flowing over a bedrock of river-polished lava that is difficult to read and as treacherous as icy pavement. Even when its bottom is relatively good, in pools like Wright Creek and Kitchen, an angler is forced to wade armpit deep in a smooth current of startling power. There are many places where the river flows swiftly through narrow channels in the ledges, at depths of as much as thirty and forty feet, and other places where a smooth pool gathers itself to plunge into a reach of impassable rapids.

You really think felt-soled brogues are not enough? I asked when I pulled on my waders. *It's really that slippery?*

Callaghan found me an extra pair of wading sandals with a pattern of fresh snow-tire calks mounted in the soles. *You better use these over your wading brogues,* he warned and described their lacing system, *or you'd better tell us where to ship your effects!*

You've got my attention, I admitted.

It was starting to rain when we pulled out on the Umpqua highway and started downstream. The logging trucks roared past, heavily loaded with their mammoth trunks of sugar pine and fir chained together and en route to the sawmills in Roseburg, or racing back upriver loaded with their own rear-wheel dollies and cargo booms. The truck drivers are paid by the trip, which tempts a few foolhardy drivers to attempt more runs than are wise, and the highway patrol is always fishing sixteen-wheel rigs from the river.

It helps to be crazy! Callaghan said.

My baptism on the North Umpqua occurred at Wright Creek. Upstream the river stills itself in greeny deeps, its eddies and smooth currents reflecting a stand of towering sugar pines and firs. Huge boulders lie in its depths, their presence betrayed only by the rhythms of flow that disturb its mirrored surfaces. The steep tributary creek across from the highway was almost dry. Toward the swelling tail of the pool, the giant boulders and pumpkin-sized cobblestones on the bottom are increasingly visible, all chocolate and bronze with winter algae. There are several boulders across the pool that shelter fish, along with a dozen pockets in the tail shallows that can hold a traveling steelhead that has just ascended the rapids.

Wright Creek has a decent bottom and usually holds a few steelhead in October. Its currents swim the fly smoothly, and its seemingly gentle flow is surprisingly heavy if one wades too deeply or too close to the throat of its rapids downstream, where the flow gathers itself into a steep plunge of river that almost drowns the droning of the logging trucks on the highway.

We can spot fish from the road, Callaghan explained.

We peered stealthily through the willows into the pool, where the dim light penetrated into its secrets. The light rain had stopped and we could see the bottom clearly in several places.

Suddenly I found a steelhead hovering in the shallows. *Look there!* I pointed excitedly. *Just ahead of those stones!*

There's another beyond that fish, Callaghan said.

Well, I grinned, *they're here!*

The best holding-lies are still in shadows. Callaghan pointed. *We've probably got several more fish out there.*

Callaghan rummaged through his wading vest and passed me a perfectly dressed Cummings, an elegant steelhead pattern with its roots in the history of the Umpqua. It was misting rain again when we clambered down the steep banks from the highway, studied the holding-lies we had spotted and slipped gently into the shallows.

The river was bone chilling and I shivered slightly, half from its icy currents and half in anticipation. *You'll have to wade deep to cover the first lies.* Callaghan pointed back toward the alders. *Keep your backcast pretty high.*

There was a narrow opening where the steep path came down through the boulders and brush, and the wading-calk graffiti on the bottom cobbles and ledges clearly marked the passage of other fishermen. It was a difficult cast, lifting high through the branches and changing direction in the forward stroke, looping the unrolling line back across the flow and slightly upstream from the rocks.

Mend your line! Callaghan suggested. *Mend it!*

I lifted the rod smoothly, stripping several feet of line free of the sliding current, and looped it back upstream with a counterclockwise rolling of my wrist. The current was deceptively swift and the line quickly bellied again.

Keep mending the swing, Callaghan said, *because even a summer steelhead likes the fly slow and deep.*

I'll try it! I lifted into another cast.

We covered the boulders and pockets carefully, working down into the tail of the pool, and fishing each fly-swing out until it hung directly downstream. It held there briefly in the streaming flow, and then I worked the fly back in a rhythm of six-inch pulls, before taking a step downstream and repeating the cast. The river flowed secret and still, its smooth surface barely disturbed by the rain.

Perfect steelhead weather! Callaghan frowned when I failed to move a fish. *Let's change flies and fish through again!*

It was sound advice based on years of steelhead fishing. Callaghan selected his own variation on the Skunk, perhaps the best-known steelhead pattern to evolve on the North Umpqua. His dressing combined the scarlet tail fibers, black chenille and silver ribbing, somber throat hackles, and polar bear wing with a single turn of fluorescent green chenille at its tail.

Try this Green-Butt Skunk, he suggested.

Callaghan clipped the elegant Cummings back in his Wheatley box while I knotted the Skunk to my tippet. We worked slowly back upstream, careful not to telegraph our ripples out across the current, and trying to mute the grating of our calks on the bottom.

There's a big stone out there. Callaghan pointed across the river. *It usually has a fish or two behind it.*

I waded out into the heavy current, searching out toeholds and firm footing as the river seeped into my wading vest pockets, and I looked back to locate the casting window in the willows. The back-cast lifted high and looped the fly across the stream, dropping it behind the submerged stone. I started mending its swing in the spreading flow, and there was a strong pull that telegraphed back toward the surface in a fiercely spreading swirl.

The fish had hooked itself and bolted angrily upstream against the protesting Orvis reel. It stopped to brood behind an unseen boulder, perhaps husbanding its strengths and strategies, and then it exploded: full-length from the dark current it came, thrusting itself sword-bright from its watery scabbard and throwing spray in the soft rain.

Excalibur! I thought wildly.

The silvery steelhead spent itself mindlessly, jumping six times and holding upstream where it fought both the river and my straining tackle. It settled stubbornly along the bottom, perhaps unwilling to seek its freedom in the wild rapids downstream, remembering a swift maelstrom that had proved difficult to ascend.

Finally it surrendered, sleek and sea-polished and swimming weakly in the shallows. We admired its beauty briefly and unhooked the fly, and the silver henfish splashed free. *They're really something!* I mumbled happily and watched it holding behind my legs. *They're really something, and your Umpqua is pretty special too!*

We're lucky, Callaghan said. *She's not always generous!*

There are still many steelhead rivers on our Pacific coast, from the small spate watersheds below San Francisco to the wilderness rivers of Alaska, but most support only winter-run fish. It is the summer steelhead that capture our lyric moods.

Many fishermen still cling to the old myths that steelhead seldom take flies. Such myths die hard, and even experienced winter steelhead fishermen believe you must suffer to catch them. Steelhead on most rivers mean snowstorms and cold weather and rivers swollen bank full with winter rains, and most are still caught with hardware fished along the bottom or with pencil-sinker rigs baited with salmon roe. Winter steelhead fishing is a world of half-frozen fingers. Since the winter-run strains are more widely distributed, entering their parent rivers in late autumn and still arriving the following spring, the steelhead is usually winter's child.

It is also surrounded with a remarkable mystique, perhaps rooted in its secret migrations and coin-bright beauty and strength, and there are steelhead stories in truckstops and fishing villages and logging camps from Big Sur to the Aleutians. Claude Kreider caught something of that mystique in his little book *Steelhead,* and in these passages describing his first encounter on the Umpqua:

> Another morning we tried Rock Creek Riffle again soon after daylight, and while we raised not even a trout to our flies, we had some glorious excitement.
>
> We learned what can happen when a big steelhead goes over into the wild waters below your pool. A lusty young fellow using a short casting rod and a big spinner followed us through the riffle. Down near the tail, where the water surged through a maze of giant boulders, he hooked a good fish.
>
> "Wow, he's going over!" he yelled.

Leaping from rock to rock, sometimes wading, he followed that plunging steelhead down the river. His thumb was clamped down on his reel spool, for his stiff casting rod was jerking and whipping with each surge of the great fish. He followed it desperately, first like a mountain goat and then like a diver. I saw him wading frantically downstream and fall down, to rise dripping and shouting and still holding on.

And far downstream his great fish, which looked surely a ten-pounder, came out with a mighty leap and was gone!

Although it supports a population of winter-run steelhead, the North Umpqua is perhaps most famous for its summer fish. Unlike the smaller grilse-sized steelhead that dominate the runs in sister rivers like the Eel and Klamath and Rogue, the steelhead that return to the Umpqua during the summer are largely mature fish. Other summer steelhead rivers include the Deschutes, Stillaguamish, and Washougal, and their fish are the royalty of the Pacific watersheds.

Yet these beautiful summer-run fish are rare, and fishing them is seldom measured through success alone. The rivers that boast fine runs of summer steelhead are also celebrated in their moodiness, and of the great summer-run streams that drain into these coastal seas, the storied North Umpqua is perhaps the most ephemeral.

With its handful of sister rivers, the Umpqua is born in the remarkable lava-field aquifers that spread for hundreds and hundreds of square miles around Crater Lake. Its unique depths fill an immense volcanic caldera so large that a secondary volcano formed Wizard Island in its aquamarine waters.

The lake itself reaches more than 2,000 feet into the Stygian entrails of its plateau. Its encircling crater is the surviving echo of once-towering Mount Mazama, which erupted and collapsed violently more than 6,000 years ago. The immense forest highlands that shroud its lava spillages are famous for their winter snows, which can measure more than thirty to forty feet in depth, and their spring thaws both fill the crater and percolate deep into the sloping lava-field strata that are layered toward the rivers. Its volcanic skeleton and the labyrinth of surrounding lava form the subterranean beginnings of several famous trout streams in Oregon. Starting with the South Umpqua at Fish Mountain, their clockwise roster of flowages born in these Crater Lake aquifers includes the North Umpqua, the swift-flowing Deschutes, the fickle Williamson, the spring-fed Wood at Fort Klamath, and the famous white-water of the Rogue.

Clark Van Fleet devotes an entire chapter of his classic *Steelhead to a Fly* to the North Umpqua, and its dramatic genesis in the heart of the Cascade mountains. His description of the river and its fishing includes the following paragraphs:

> The beginnings of the average western river are pretty inconsequential: a trickle through some mountain meadow, a brook purling through a canyon strewn with boulders with an occasional cascade over some precipitous cliff, until finally a full-blown river emerges.
>
> But the North Umpqua comes in roaring; it springs from the living rock as did Minerva from the head of Jove. Presumed to be the outlet by some underground cleavage for part of the overflow of Diamond Lake, it is a river at its very source.
>
> It gathers some volume on its brawling way through the mountains to join the South Umpqua below Winchester, yet it would still be a tremendous stream without the additions brought by its few insignificant tributaries. The roar of its mighty voice fills the canyon of its passage from source to junction as it tumbles down the rough boulder-strewn cleft carved by its journey. A mile of fishing along its banks is a very real test of endurance, as you snake your way over the folds in the bedrock, scramble on jagged reefs, and cross its boulders.
>
> The steelhead to be found there are as wild and untamed as the river they ascend. When you have beached a steelhead of over ten pounds from the waters of this torrent, your pride will be fully justified.

Fly-fishing for steelhead clearly had its genesis on the swift summer-run rivers of northern California, and particularly in the sweeping bends of the Eel at Eureka. Its fishing pioneers included figures like Jim Hutchens, Henry Soule, Lloyd Silvius, Jim Pray, Sam Wells, Sumner Carson, Josh Van Zandt, and John Benn, the transplanted fly dresser who emigrated from Ireland before the Civil War.

The Rogue soon developed a similar circle of steelhead pilgrims when its summer fish proved receptive to flies, although they averaged half the size typical of the Klamath and Eel. Unlike the California rivers, their banks crippled with highways and their headwaters stripped of their life-giving timber, the Rogue was a wild river float in the Oregon solitude. Its acolytes were a happy few with a sense of adventure, and their ranks included some half-legendary steelhead pioneers like Rainbow Gibson, John Coleman, Fred Burnham, Sam Wells, Zeke Allen, Captain Laurie Mitchell, Fred Noyes, Major Lawrence Mott, Cappy Black, and the colorful Toggery Bill Isaacs, who later guided President Herbert Hoover on the Rogue.

Zane Grey was perhaps the most celebrated figure among the steelhead pioneers after the First World War. Grey first encountered these exciting sea-run rainbows in 1918, on the Stillaguamish in the mountains north of Seattle. The writer was soon obsessed with these big rainbows, joined the growing ranks on the rivers of southern Oregon, and spent his last twenty years fishing. Steelhead finally killed him, because Zane Grey suffered his fatal stroke while climbing out from the North Umpqua in 1939.

Zane Grey was a popular writer, Frank Moore observed recently at his log-framed house high above the Umpqua, *and his fishing books made him a fishing hero to many readers—but there were other men on the Umpqua and Rogue who fished rings around him!*

Grey was clearly not as popular as his books, although he was held in something approaching awe, even by fellow anglers who did not respect his fishing skills. Grey had been transformed into a celebrity, and welcomed the attention of an audience that eagerly devoured the flood of cowboy adventures that followed the publication of his *Riders of the Purple Sage* in 1912.

Other western titles that subsequently became films included *The Maverick Queen, Western Union, West of the Pecos, Robber's Roost, The Lost Wagon Train, Under the Tonto Rim,* and *Wildfire.* Grey wrote almost fifty western stories, and their immense success made him wealthy enough to stop writing popular fiction. His later books were devoted to the fishing odysseys of his twilight years.

The books that described his angling exploits included titles like *Tales of Virgin Seas, Adventures in Fishing, Tales of the Angler's El Dorado, Tales of Southern Rivers, Tales of Swordfish and Tuna, Tales of Tahitian Waters,* and the immensely popular *Tales of Fresh-Water Fishing,* which ranged from his boyhood smallmouth on the Lackawaxen in eastern Pennsylvania to billfish off the Antipodes.

His popularity soon waned along the Rogue and Umpqua, partially through his obvious vanity and largely through his practice of hiring guards and surrogate fishermen to occupy his favorite pools until he could fish them. Such selfishness soon earned Grey an army of hostile fishermen and neighbors along both rivers. It is perhaps typical that Grey seldom mentioned the North Umpqua in his writings, although it was his favorite steelhead fishery.

His arrogance and personality ultimately cost Grey the friendship of his best fishing friend, Fred Burnham, whose skills were legend along the Umpqua before the Second World War. There are two beautiful pools on its fly-only water that still bear his name, Upper Burnham and Lower Burnham, and both are still productive today. Grey sought Burnham in his early steelhead years because Burnham was the acknowledged master of the sport, and the writer envied his skills and the admiration of the fishing fraternity.

Trey Combs writes of their ill-fated friendship in *Steelhead Fly Fishing and Flies,* describing its beginnings along the Rogue and Umpqua, and its collapse on a marlin expedition off New Zealand, when Grey deliberately cost his friend a world record:

> Early in their relationship, Grey knew so little about steelheading, while Burnham was the acknowledged master of the sport. His skills were respected by Grey, and in some measure, he ultimately learned them.
>
> In the narrow confines of the steelheading hierarchy, there was no better company to keep than Burnham's, and in its limited sense, Burnham was the celebrity. Grey plainly admired Burnham, but behind their mutual respect was Grey's competitive mania. As he learned, he became an angling institution that wrote hyperbolically of his angling fortunes. Grey came to feast on the legend he himself had built, an unfortunate display of ego that would come to end his gifted relationship with Burnham.
>
> Fred Burnham married rich after graduating from the University of California and became a stockbroker, an occupation made to order for already acquired wealth. He was an outstanding athlete, possessing size and strength and coordination. He learned to present a fly with unbelieveable skill, casting an entire silk line to a desired spot while wading waist

> deep. Years after he had patiently taught Grey the intricacies of fly-fishing for steelhead, they pursued deep-sea fishing together, and did so in competition.
>
> They ultimately fished New Zealand for its trout, and in separate boats, for its billfish. There came a day when Burnham caught a marlin of record size and signalled Grey to call in the catch. Grey ignored the request.
>
> Had Burnham endangered one of Grey's many records? Whatever the reason, this unique union of angling passion born on the Rogue was permanently dissolved off New Zealand.

Similar echoes are found in the relationship between Grey and his Japanese cook during their years on the Rogue and Umpqua. Grey subjected the diminutive George Takahashi to almost constant ridicule and practical jokes and humiliations.

Grey typically took the best steelhead pools, while his servant was restricted to fishing those places that Grey usually ignored. Takahashi apparently accepted his status in silence, and fished only the pools that Grey designated. Sometimes he caught steelhead when Grey failed on the famous pools, eventually gaining a place in the hearts of the river people along the North Umpqua. Perhaps it is fitting that the river still has pools named for the little Japanese cook, the beautiful Takahashi and Lower Takahashi, while Zane Grey has no similar memorial. These lines from *Tales of Fresh-Water Fishing* offer some telling insights into their relationship:

> What a splash when he went down! It was too much for me! I jumped up out of the shade and ran to the water, thrilled beyond measure at the sight of such a wonderful fish! Then I grew horrified that Takahashi was pointing his rod straight in the direction of the fish and winding hard.
>
> "Let him run!" I shouted. "He'll break off!"
>
> George looked across at me with a broad grin, seemingly not in the least surprised.
>
> "Hold your rod up!" I yelled louder. "Let go of your reel! You can't wind him like that! Let him run!"

Despite the efforts to check him, the steelhead took more and more line. He made an angry smash at the surface, and next he leaped magnificently.

Oh, what a wonderful trout!

I saw the silver and pink glow of him, his spotted back, the great broad tail curving on itself, and the great cruel jaws. What would I have given to have had him at the end of my line? I grew increasingly incensed at Takahashi's stupidity, and in stentorian terms I started roaring.

"Hold your rod up . . . let him run!"

Perhaps the sound of my voice rather than the meaning of my words, finally penetrated his cranium. He shouted "All right!" across at me, a little grimly I thought, or perhaps a bit ironically. But I also saw that his failure to stop the steelhead had roused him.

Takahashi cannot bear advice or defeat.

"Fish no come!" he yelled piercingly. "Stick there!"

My exasperation knew no bounds, and if Takahashi had been on my side of the river, I would have committed the unpardonable sin of seizing the rod.

"Let him run then." I choked.

But even as I shouted this last despairing cry, the wild action ceased. His line hung limp in the water. His rod lost its rigidity, and the steelhead had escaped. Without so much as a word or glance in my direction, Takahashi waded out and plunged into the brush.

Grey seemingly had little respect for Takahashi in terms of his steelhead-fishing, and resented his angling success, perhaps believing that any fish taken clumsily by his diminutive Japanese cook was a trophy lost to his own skills. Sometimes Grey also expressed a grudging admiration for his stoic servant, and those feelings surfaced in his books. Courage and discipline and skill have many different yardsticks, and these brief observations from *Down the Rogue* are in that vein, although they did not occur on the Umpqua:

Reamy Falls had been the seventeenth rapid we had passed, all in only ten miles of the Rogue, and one boat lost along the way! We sat and lay around Takahashi's campfire, a completely starved, exhausted and silent group wet to the skin, and suffering from bruises and rope burns and aches!

How welcome the fire!

And the wonderful Takahashi was as cheerful and deft, as if he had not partaken of our labors!

"Hoo-ooh! All thing ready! Come get!" Takahashi sang out. "Nice hot soup and all good thing!"

The North Umpqua was already becoming famous in the years that followed the First World War. Its steep-walled canyon in the sixteen miles below Steamboat Creek was still cloaked in primeval forests. Its rocky watercourse was still unblemished except for the fishing trails that plunged steeply down to the best pools from the old highway, high above the river in the trees. The beautiful Mott Trail that leads down the south bank from Sawtooth to Wright Creek was only a rough trace in those early years. Fishing the river was a difficult challenge then, and even hiking down the steep trails was complicated with ledges and moss-covered deadfalls and boulders. Climbing back to the highway, happily tired from a long day's fishing in strong currents, with their house-sized outcroppings and slippery ledges, could seem like Homeric odysseys into the Himalayas.

It's still tough to wade and fish when you can drive along the river, Jack Hemingway observed after his daily catnap on the porch. *You like it best before you're fifty!*

Make that forty! Dan Callaghan chided us both.

The old river highway wound high along the north shoulder of the canyon, dropping back down to the river at Steamboat, where old Major Lawrence Mott retired from the First World War and started his famous steelhead camp on a beautiful site leased from the Forest Service. His charming North Umpqua Lodge soon became the Valhalla of summer steelhead fishing, and a competitive camp upstream was started by the colorful Umpqua Vic O'Byrne.

There is a photograph of old Major Mott in the Steamboat Inn, showing the portly retired soldier with a huge chinook salmon, taken with fly tackle on the Kitchen Pool in 1930.

When Major Mott died at the beginning of the Second World War, his bucolic fishing camp in the sugar pines at Steamboat was taken over by Zeke Allen, who had worked there for many seasons as the cook and chief guide. His tenure at the North Umpqua Lodge was succeeded by the proprietorship of the late Clarence Gordon, who was considered the wizard of the Umpqua through the Depression years. Gordon ultimately became as famous as the Umpqua itself.

Other storied steelhead fishermen who regularly fished and loved the Umpqua in those seasons included the ubiquitous Fred Burnham, Don Anderson, Colonel Frank Hayden, Ward Cummings, Roy Donelley, Don Harger, Charles Stevenson, Cal Bird, and Clark Van Fleet.

Cummings and Stevenson are both credited with the beautiful steelhead patterns that bear their names, and the versatile Harger apparently conceived the original dressing of the Umpqua Special. Jim Pray was the author of the Thor and Golden Demon, and although both patterns evolved on the Eel in northern California, they have since become standard dressings on the Umpqua.

However, it was Clarence Gordon who developed the Black Gordon, and apparently worked out our modern dressings for the Cummings and Umpqua Special and Skunk. When he decided to sample his first steelhead fishing, the celebrated Ray Bergman sought the tutelage of Clarence Gordon on his beloved North Umpqua. Bergman described his baptism on the Steamboat water in his classic *Trout:*

> The river is wild and beautiful and, at first sight, a little terrifying. You wonder how you are going to be able to wade it without getting into trouble. Despite this, it isn't so bad once you learn to read its bottom. Between the ledges there are often narrow strips of gravel which wander here and there, and criss-cross like downtown city streets.
>
> By walking on these, and stepping only on the reasonably flat, clean rocks or other rocks where you can see signs of previous footsteps, you can wade with fair comfort and safety. The rocks of the routes between most of the good pools are plainly outlined by the tread of many feet, and as long as you know what to look for, you will have no trouble.

> But do not try to hurry, and watch each step closely unless you have the sure-footedness of a mountain goat or Clarence Gordon. When he gets into a hard place, he simply makes a hop, skip and jump, and lands just where he wants, while you gingerly and sometimes painfully make your way after him, arriving a few minutes later.
>
> He always waits patiently, apparently, but probably in his heart wishing you would get a move on. He finds such wading so easy, it must seem ridiculous to him for other fishermen to be so slow and faltering.
>
> I once thought I was agile, and perhaps I was, from what others tell me. But Clarence Gordon on the North Umpqua—well, just ask those who have fished the river with him!

Bergman found its summer steelhead displayed a strength and moodiness worthy of their reputation. Several of its sea-armored fish were hooked and lost, and there were many hours of fruitless casting on its finest riffles and pools before the Umpqua finally surrendered a fish to his efforts. Bergman returned from the river with a mixture of awe and respect. The steelhead chapter in his *Trout* includes the capture of his first fish at Steamboat:

> Immediately after lunch I slipped down to the Mott Pool, and about halfway through I hooked a fish. The singing of the reel was music to my ears. Nothing went wrong this time, and I had the satisfaction of looking up toward the end of the fight to find Phil, Grace and Fred watching me. Phil was so anxious that I should save the fish that he took off his shoes and stockings, and with his bare feet, waded that treacherous water just so he could help land it in a difficult spot.
>
> That's sportsmanship for you.
>
> I shall never forget this spontaneous act of his as long as I live. It showed the real soul of the man, his unselfish desire to see that I got my fish. It was all very satisfying. Just one steelhead a day on the North Umpqua makes a fisherman feel like a king!

Clarence Gordon was forced to abandon his beautiful camp on the storied Kitchen Pool when the Forest Service terminated its lease, and there are many regulars still fishing the river who remember the heartbreak he suffered. Its generous dining rooms and fieldstone fireplaces and sheltering porches are gone, along with the magnificent stand of sugar pines and giant firs that surrounded the lodge and its outbuildings. There is a steel trusswork bridge that spans the river above Sawtooth, and anglers and their parties are no longer ferried across Upper Kitchen to the Gordon camp. The Forest Service cut its sheltering trees and razed its log buildings, and replaced them with a new headquarters. Gordon bitterly digested his grief and moved across the river, purchasing a smaller site on the highway above the Glory Hole, and starting the Steamboat Inn. The Forest Service headquarters is a blight, its plywood character between the obvious banality of tract housing and the outright tackiness of a trailer court, but the simple Steamboat Inn and its cabins are worthy heirs of the Umpqua tradition.

Gordon finally found that wading the river was too much, and when he retired in 1957, his operation at the Steamboat Inn passed to the ownership of Frank Moore.

Among the skilled fishermen who still work the Umpqua, it is perhaps Moore who unmistakably echoes the wading and fishing skills of Clarence Gordon. There are some knowledgeable anglers who argue that Moore is probably the best steelhead fisherman alive, since he is much younger than the earlier giants of the sport: pioneers like Enos Bradner, Mike Kennedy, Wes Drain, Frank Headrick, Harry Lemire, Karl Mausser, Ken McLeod, Al Knudsen, and photographer Ralph Wahl.

Moore has unquestionably earned his status. His casting is clean and sure, utterly free of surplus effort, and he covers water quickly with a clockwork series of skillful fly-swing mends. His knowledge of the Steamboat mileage on the North Umpqua is remarkably thorough. His strategy includes fishing each pool and taking lie rather quickly, covering its secret places and moving on, eager to fish the next steelhead pool in his private lexicon of the Umpqua.

His ability to clamber goatlike over impossible ledges and labyrinths of boulders, work through seemingly impassable jumbles of fallen trees, and cover the water without sufficient room to make a conventional cast are already legend. Umpqua lore is filled with stories of Clarence Gordon and his wading skills, but it is difficult to conceive of a stronger, more completely fearless, and agile wader than Moore. His river skills are remarkable, lying someplace between raw muscle and the cunning of a log-rolling champion, all mixed with the startling grace of Baryshnikov.

Walton was wrong! Moore insists firmly. *It's not fishing fine and far off—it's wade deep and throw long!*

Moore operated the Steamboat Inn for almost twenty years, and many of its traditions survived intact. It had always been known for its food, from its beginnings under early owners like Mott and Allen, although its cuisine was perhaps best characterized as country-style, in the volume usually found in logging camps. Its character changed under the tenure of the Moore family. Although the logging-camp portions keep spilling from the cornucopia of its tiny kitchen, the food gradually became more and more sophisticated, until its candlelight dinners offer some of the finest cuisine in Oregon.

The torch has passed into fresh hands. The young owners are Jim Van Loan and his wife Sharon, who skillfully hopscotches between its superb kitchen and her teaching duties at a regional school downstream. The character and atmosphere and cooking at the Steamboat Inn remain virtually unchanged. Its staff still consists of people devoted to steelhead fishing and fine cookery and a sense of place. Van Loan is a book publisher's salesman who tired of his rounds among the schools and bookstores and colleges on the Pacific Coast, and settled down to think and fish steelhead and operate his favorite fishing inn on the North Umpqua in 1975.

Its ambience still holds a circle of fiercely loyal patrons. Its immense twenty-foot table cut from a single sugar pine was salvaged from the original Gordon camp across the river. Photographs of its dining hall and sitting rooms and sleeping quarters are hung with pictures of its famous anglers. Bottles of wine lie in their shipping crates in the corner, decent vintages of genuine Burgundy and Beaujolais hobnobbing with fine California vineyards like Fetzer and Stag's Leap and Freemark Abbey. The fieldstone fireplace dominates one corner near the fishing tackle cabinets, and its hearth often burns with a welcome fire for anglers who have been wading armpit-deep in the Umpqua. The fly chest is a treasure of patterns dressed by skilled tiers like Joe Howells and the colorful Polly Rosborough, and the redwood ceiling is hung with a collection of old rods. The battle-scarred Winston belonged to Frank Moore, and it is suspended beside an older Powell and Edwards, both from the collection of the controversial Zane Grey.

The people who serve you are dedicated to maintaining the Steamboat Inn family atmosphere, the dinner menu tells its guests, *and you are a stranger here but once!*

The Umpqua legends continue to grow, and its fishing regulars have joined together into the Steamboaters, a happy band of anglers determined to protect their shrine from the ceaseless threats and subterfuges of the highway men and timber interests and dam builders. The proposed reservoirs and the Forest Service network of campgrounds on the primeval south bank of the river have seemingly been defeated, but the Steamboaters are still watching.

It's an endless fight. Frank Moore shook his head while we shared coffee in his kitchen high above the river. *When we win these fights it's only an armistice—but when those bastards finish a highway or build a reservoir or cut an entire forest, it's forever!*

There are fresh stories on the river each season. Perhaps the best concerns the time that Jack Hemingway promised his wife he would return early for his birthday dinner. The weather had just changed and a gentle rain drifted upstream into the mountains. The steelhead changed too, and started taking greedily. Hemingway soon forgot about everything else: his birthday and the rain and his wife.

There were steelhead everywhere, sea-bright fish freshly come from the sea, and they had arrived in a taking mood. Steelhead took his flies in Surveyor and Secret Pool and Sawtooth at the Forest Service bridge. Station and Boat Pool and Kitchen were generous too, and Hemingway beached and lost others in the wild chutes of Mott and Lower Mott and the Fighting Hole. Still more came to his flies at the Ledges and Williams Creek and Archie, and a strong fish fought him down through Upper and Lower Burnham before it pulled free.

Takahashi and Wright Creek and Big Cliffs were generous too, and Hemingway concluded his exciting day's sport at the Famous and Salmon Racks and the Honey Creek riffles, returning hours late and exhausted and drenched with the steady rain.

Puck Hemingway was furious. *Hemingtrout!* she exploded in tight-lipped anger. *You're four hours late and you're filthy wet—and for two cents I'd break your goddamned rod!* Hemingway stared at his wife in disbelief, still savoring the excitement of a remarkable day's sport on a steelhead river known for its moodiness.

Hemingway angrily stripped off his wading belt and groped through his pockets for the coins, and slapped them on the table. *Well,* he said grimly, *there's your two cents!*

His wife stalked outside, found the rod in the racks under the grape arbor, and smashed it thoroughly against the paving stones. *Hemingway!* She stood quietly holding the shattered bamboo like a broken flail. *What do you think of that?*

Hemingway started laughing uncontrollably. *Pretty thorough job,* he choked, *except that it's Frank Moore's rod!*

Other stories often involve the subterfuges and strategies that the Umpqua regulars employ to fish through the best pools first each morning. Dan Callaghan likes getting up before daylight, and is often the first angler on Wright Creek or Kitchen, but several other fishermen became determined to fish them first one week.

Their duelling soon became serious. Callaghan and his challengers were getting up earlier and earlier to reach the pools first. Alarm clocks were muffled under pillows, starting at five o'clock and reaching back deeper and deeper into the night. Callaghan was clearly winning, with his muffled alarm clock and ascetic discipline, in their competition to reach the casting ledges at Kitchen.

His challengers were getting desperate. *There's one way to get there first!* one suggested as they lingered over dinner coffee. *Let's wade out to the Kitchen ledges now!*

The waitress clearing the table was aware of their competition for the Kitchen Pool and laughingly warned Callaghan of their plans, and he gathered his tackle and hurried off into the darkness. Callaghan waded out through the familiar labyrinth of outcroppings and pulled himself out on the ledge rock to wait.

It was so dark I couldn't believe it, he said.

Callaghan sat smiling in the darkness when he heard the others coming down the Mott Trail, laughing and congratulating themselves on their cunning and craftiness. The leaves rustled under their wading brogues, and they switched off their lights when they reached the gravelly shingle that reaches down to the pool.

Might spook the fish, they agreed.

The fishermen were not familiar with the river, and had trouble crossing its current-polished lava without their flashlights. It is difficult wading in the daylight, and one fisherman slipped enough to partially fill his waders with icy water. The man stood cursing when he recovered his balance in the flow.

I didn't make a sound! Callaghan continued.

The other fisherman slipped in the lava channels too, drowning an expensive watch to keep from going down completely, and straining his wrist badly when he caught himself. The night was filled with whispered expletives. Cold and dripping and wet, both men finally crossed the waist-deep channels to the outcropping where Callaghan waited silently on the ledge, the current gurgling past his legs.

Well! they chortled smugly. *We finally got here first!*

Callaghan wordlessly lit a cigarette.

There are still many fine steelhead rivers in these Pacific mountains, but such rivers are always moody and changing, and the Umpqua is perhaps the most fickle. Its clarity is deceptive and dangerous, and its moods range from a wild cacophony of trumpets and kettle drums and cymbals to delicate passages of chamber music. But its brief passages of woodwinds and flutes and strings are deceptive too, and its still, aquamarine depths are always lost in the churning chutes and wild rapids that follow each pool on the Umpqua.

Its steelhead are often clearly visible from the highway, although there are never many in its pools. Wading is threatening in a strong current that masks its foul bottom, and there is seldom room for a proper backcast. Its sport is perpetually a challenge, and the Umpqua surrenders its fish so grudgingly that its disciples are clearly more in love with its character than its generosity.

The North Umpqua is a quality of spirit that cannot be fully understood or captured. Its shining length is scarred with volcanic outcroppings and ledges, its folded bedrock and igneous serrations polished in 1,000 centuries of snowmelt and spates. Its gorge is still cloaked in dense forests, their cathedral choirs carpeted in lichens and pine needles and fiddlebacks. The river paths are ankle-deep in leaves when the October fish are running, and other leaves drift in the current or circle lazily in the still backwaters, turning scarlet and gold in their depths.

Steelhead are lying in the silken flow, elusive shadows as brightly polished as a wedding spoon. Its summer-run fish are like rare jewels in its velvet pools, drifting like ghosts in its currents, hovering in shafts of sunlight and spume.

We are precious and we are few. Their restless liturgies are a half-remembered whisper on the wind. *We are coming home, seeking the swift riffles of our birth—catch us if you can!*

THE COHO OF KASHIAGEMIUT

Late summer rains lashed through the streets, raw and smelling faintly of winter. Floatplanes crowded the busy harbor, their tie-downs and mooring lines pulled taut by the wind, and angry waves slapped and washed in the pilings. The blaring country music at the bar in Anchorage played to a mixed audience of fishermen and pipeline workers and bush pilots.

It was raining harder when the fishermen from a salmon boat came inside, shaking the water from their foul-weather gear and complaining about the cold. Platoons of roughnecks and oil-field truckers and construction men were playing pinball.

The walls held several mounted chinook salmon over thirty-five and forty pounds, along with a solitary twelve-pound rainbow from the Tularik country on Lake Iliamna. Two caribou and a giant moose stared down at the customers along the crowded bar, and a vintage .45-70 Krag hung just below the trophies. Its military stock had been partially eaten by porcupines in a cabin beyond the Susitna. The customers wore safety helmets mixed with a few cowboy hats. The waitress had a half dozen plastic curlers in her hair, and she sat chewing gum at her bar station, listening dreamily while Gordon Lightfoot finished singing "Rainy Day People" on the jukebox. The barkeeper was a retired sergeant from Galveston, and had been stationed in the Aleutians.

Come from outside? the barkeeper asked.

Outside? I frowned and felt puzzled. *I've got an overnight to kill before I fly out to Dillingham and Aleknagik.*

Figured you was a stranger! The barkeeper washed several beer glasses and wiped them. *From the lower Forty-eight?*

Came up from Seattle this morning, I said.

That's outside! he laughed.

Alaska is changing swiftly these days, its sprawling silences interrupted by the fishing parties and oil-survey crews and modern prospectors in floatplanes and chattering helicopters. Its controversial pipeline is finally complete, its structures and right-of-way a gargantuan spaghetti-like incision reaching almost 1,000 miles into the Arctic. The pipeline sprawls from Valdez, on the ice-free waters of Prince William Sound, to the windswept tundra beyond the Brooks Range and the oil fields at Prudhoe Bay. Its construction crews and its primitive haul roads have already permitted access into a fragile wilderness, and have irrevocably damaged the fisheries in hundreds of adjacent lakes and rivers. Native Alaskans like the Aleut and Eskimo peoples have become heir to vast tracts of remaining wilderness, as well as large stipends from the government, and seem increasingly guilty of abusing their subsistence rights to the surviving populations of fish and game. The principal oil companies have committed billions on future drilling rights, and a handful of farsighted Alaskans are worried about their primeval world.

Until the Alaska Territory achieved its statehood in 1959, virtually all its lands were controlled by the federal government and its agencies. Statehood soon triggered a process of carving up its 375 million acres. The state government was permitted to select slightly more than 100 million acres, and the Alaska Native Claims Settlement Act of 1971 allowed the Eskimos, Aleuts and other native peoples to choose another 42 million acres of the Alaskan wilderness. Future development in the federally administered lands was prohibited pending the selection of approximately 80 million acres for the national park system and other agencies dedicated to their protection. The Department of the Interior finally made its recommendations for the remaining federal lands in 1973, proposing that 30 million acres become national parks, 32 million more acres be included in the network of national wildlife refuges, approximately 19 million acres become a major element of the national forests and a final million acres be designated for preservation under the Wild and Scenic Rivers Act of 1968.

These proposals erupted in a storm of controversy. Local entrepreneurs and developers were swiftly joined by several major corporations in opposing the scope of such planning. Conservation groups were equally disappointed, but argued that federal agencies had gerrymandered many scenic regions to leave key mineral rights still available for exploitation. Such opponents quickly formulated a counterproposal totaling more than 100 million acres, and these battle lines remain firmly drawn in Alaska today.

It's all going down the drain, the barkeeper said glumly, *and it's going faster than anybody really knows!*

You mean the fishing? I asked.

The fishing always goes first, the barkeeper nodded.

Who's doing it? I asked. *It's a lot of country.*

Sure it's a lot of country. He shook his head angrily. *But between the oil crews and fishing camps and the natives, it's really drying up in some places and I give it ten or fifteen years!*

It's really that bad? I asked unhappily.

It's going fast! he said.

It was still raining when the Wien 737 touched down on the gravel airstrip at Dillingham, and settled into its landing roll with a roar of its low-slung jet engines. The baggage room was crowded with fishermen and Aleuts and other passengers. George Later was waiting there, and we introduced ourselves and quickly transferred my baggage to his truck. Later served many years as the chief pilot for the Fish and Game Commission in Maine, and after his recent retirement there, Later decided to try the fishing in Alaska.

It was something I'd always wanted to try, Later explained on the washboard road to Aleknagik, *and I finally tried it!*

Most people stop with the daydreams, I said.

Later is widely acknowledged as the finest back-country pilot in Alaska these days, and his floatplane was waiting at Aleknagik. The truck was heavily loaded with baggage and supplies, and Later explained that his Cessna would exceed its allowable gross-weight payload with a passenger and his baggage added to his other cargo. The tiny floatplane lake at Dillingham is a lily-bordered postage stamp for a heavily loaded aircraft, and Later wanted a leisurely takeoff run on the river that drains the glacial lakes in the Tikchik country.

We'll need all the water we can get, he said.

We finished loading the Cessna and secured its baggage hatches, and I buckled in while Later pushed off from the beach. He clambered aboard, buckled in himself and tightened his seat belt, and punched the starter. The engine whined while the propellor started slowly, and then it caught with a steady roar.

It sounds pretty good! I said.

Later expertly jockeyed his floatplane toward midstream, steering with his water rudders and studying the gauges. Finally he seemed happy with their readings and adjusted his power settings, and he raised and locked his water-rudder ring. When he pushed the throttle smoothly into its takeoff setting, the Cessna shuddered and rolled briefly against the waves, then settled until its floats streamed and frog-walked across their rolling crests. The Cessna finally reached its flying speed and Later rocked it deftly into the air.

It was still raining slightly, and intricate patterns of moisture beaded back across the Plexiglas windshield. We climbed steadily until the overcast hung fifty feet above our floatplane, concealing the forest-covered mountains that surround the slate-colored expanse of Aleknagik. The lake and its marshy islands were under our floats, and the dark forests of lodgepole and spruce disappeared into the misting squalls. Aleknagik reached ahead into the overcast and rain, and finally we dropped down and circled the Bristol Bay Lodge, which stands in the trees above a sheltered inlet.

George Later pointed down to the main camp and its outbuildings, which include two small cabins and a smokehouse and a sauna, all clustered like a village in a fine stand of Sitka spruce. We dropped back in a tight circle, lowered the flaps and reeled up the aerial, and settled in a smooth landing off the beach. Later unhooked his water rudders and steered carefully toward the seaplane moorings below the camp, where two figures stood waiting in the rain.

Well, Later said laconically, *we're here.*

John Garry and Frank Bertaina were waiting on the rough-sawed duckboards where we secured the Cessna, and a fresh squall rattled cold rain across its wings and tail surfaces while Later fussed meticulously with his mooring lines and tie-downs.

Garry is a skilled carpenter and contractor who grew restless, and left a relatively secure life in Vermont in 1969. His wife joined his overland odyssey across the Alaskan Highway, and both decided to stay when they found work in Anchorage. Garry traveled farther west into the Tikchik country, loved the fishing and shooting he found there, and found work as a builder and guide. Garry later contracted the work on a fishing camp at the Tikchik Narrows, and during its construction he conceived the dream of building his own lodge. Such dreams are difficult in the Alaskan wilderness, because privately held acreages are scarce and building materials are costly, but Garry and his wife were determined.

Finally Garry found a small parcel of privately owned timber in the upper reaches of Aleknagik, worked more than a year with his wife to build his dream camp, and has operated it these past three seasons. His lodge is already famous for its comfort and fine cuisine, including wines and home-baked pastries and breads. Garry also believes in maintaining a series of outlying camps manned with skilled fly-fishing guides and boat equipment. Although such strategies are expensive, they provide additional mobility on both lakes and rivers once the floatplanes have landed a fishing party. Garry is also equipped with boats and camping equipment and guides to launch week-long floats on wilderness rivers like the Kisarlik and Goodnews, which reach the Bering Sea above Togiak.

Unlike many wilderness-camp operators, Garry was soon aware that the ecology of his world was surprisingly fragile, and that permitting his guests to fill their fish limits would soon destroy the fisheries on which his livelihood depended. Fish grow slowly in these northern latitudes, and the principal brood stocks in such wilderness lakes and rivers are quickly depleted with uncontrolled fishing. The emphasis at his Bristol Bay Lodge is focused on fly-fishing, and his guides are firm disciples of catch-and-release.

It's such a simple concept, Garry explains with missionarylike fervor, *but it's surprising how few people understand!*

Frank Bertaina is a retired professional athlete turned fly-fishing fanatic, using many of the same skills and cunning that baseball fans observed during his years as a relief pitcher with the Baltimore Orioles. Bertaina travels and fishes widely in operating a California-based organization for fishing travel, in partnership with Bob Nauheim, the well-known fishing writer. Like many retired athletes, Bertaina is a likeable geyser of stories about his baseball days, delivered with unique rapid-fire humor. His athletic abilities have been translated into fly-casting and fighting fish, and Bertaina is the only fisherman I know who wears a World Series baseball ring.

Well, Bertaina laughed. *You finally made it to camp—what did you think of beautiful downtown Aleknagik?*

Dillingham and Petaluma are better, I said.

John Garry grinned and introduced himself. *Bertaina's going to tell nothing but fish stories and exaggerations,* Garry explained. *We'd better get the introductions done ourselves!*

Okay, Bertaina nodded. *But we're loaded with coho!*

Fresh-run fish? I asked excitedly.

Still covered with sea lice! Bertaina rolled his eyes and spread his hands wide. *The Togiak is full of them!*

Sounds good! I said.

The Togiak is a swift river that rises behind the Tikchik country, in a barren wilderness of mountains and snowfields and lakes. It winds toward its brackish estuary through surprisingly empty landscapes, looping like a careless necklace through its scrub-willow bottoms. There are no settlements on the entire watershed, except for the Aleut fishing village at its mouth.

Its source lies between the Tikchik mountains and the Kuskokwim wilderness still farther north. Togiak Lake gathers its snowmelt beginnings and spills them into a sprawling emptiness that encompasses several hundred square miles of moraines and many-channeled flood bottoms. These headwaters are too small for floatplane operations, and the river is serpentine and utterly wild, densely concealed in willows and scrub trees and alders. Small tundra lakes and marshy bogs cover the Togiak basin, and except for its outlet at the fjordlike Togiak Lake, the river is inaccessible to floatplane parties until its junction with the swift little Kashiagemiut.

Kashiagemiut is a fine grayling and rainbow river in its own right, wading size and bone-chilling in its winding course from the mountains that conceal the Goodnews country. It joins the Togiak below a series of intricate channels, tumbling past the back-country camp that John Garry maintains on a spreading gravel bar.

Farther downstream, sheltered under a steep moraine and drying racks for salmon, the Togiak is joined by the swift Pongokepiuk in a spreading alluvial shallows. Garry maintains a second remote camp on a steep bank about ten miles below Kashiagemiut, near a series of side channels and shelving riffles that hold schools of coho, since the Togiak is perhaps the finest coho river in Alaska.

It's hot! Bertaina exclaimed. *It's really hot!*

It really is filled with bright fish, John Garry confirmed. *They're fresh run and taking well!*

How soon can we try them? I asked.

George Later thinks we can fly tomorrow, Bertaina interjected. *We'll try to fish at Kashiagemiut in the morning!*

I'm with you! I said eagerly.

The lodge was filled with the perfume of freshly baking bread, and dinner was a blood-rare roast of beef, its cuts served like flower petals on a hugh platter. There was broccoli and a freshly mixed salad, with a full-bodied Cabernet Sauvignon from California, and coffee came later with a chocolate mousse. It takes some experience with the cooking in Arctic fishing camps, from Lapland to the Labrador, to appreciate how difficult it is to provide such fare in the wilderness.

We loaded our fishing gear into the Cessna after breakfast, wrestled into our waders on the rocky beach, and climbed into the plane. It started smoothly, and George Later steered out with his rudder pedals until he started his takeoff run.

The Cessna roared smoothly across the still expanse of the lake. The mountains were still layered with clouds, although the rain had stopped long after midnight. Later lifted his floatplane into the air and wound north in a steeply climbing turn, where a series of rough-sawed peaks concealed the narrow Sunshine Valley.

It's pretty cloudy this morning, Later observed above his engine, *but the Sunshine Valley usually deserves its name.*

We flew low across the beaver ponds that stair-step along the creek above Aleknagik, startling a moose in a shallow marsh, and beyond its drainages we turned into a steep-walled corridor between the mountains. The dense overcast drifted restlessly, ragged and a little frightening, only a few feet above the Cessna.

What happens when the weather closes down? I asked. *We can't make a one-eighty in here and fly back out!*

You're right, Later smiled, *but it won't.*

Later was proved right that morning, and we threaded our way between the trees and the ragged clouds like a steamfitter in a utility tunnel. The overcast was still ominous and sullen. When the corridor between the mountains suddenly opened, like an immense theater curtain in the wilderness, the clouds were completely gone. Later pulled back into a steep climb and we turned toward the Togiak, with the Bering Sea shining in the distance.

The river was ahead across its tundra basin, and we startled huge flocks of waterfowl from a world of Arctic bogs and shallow glacier-scoured lakes. The sea was a wafer-thin slice of bright water on the horizon, interrupted by the somber outline of Walrus Island. Below our floatplane, the river ran swift and incredibly clear.

It's some country! I thought.

The remote camp at Kashiagemiut was ahead now, where the tributary creek wound in across its floodplain bottoms. George Later pulled his Cessna into a tight circle over the tents, throttled back when we turned downriver, and worked the plane toward the camp for our landing. Later set his flaps and flared, settling his floats into the swift current, and gunned the engine against the flow. The back-country camp consisted of two tension tents, and a shelter half protected its firewood. Wash racks for drying laundry had been fashioned of driftwood, and a carefully wrapped food cache was suspended from a tree.

Bus Bergman came down the cobblestone beach to meet the plane, and Later taxied into the shallows, cutting his throttle skillfully before we touched the stones. Bergman plunged into the river and wrapped an arm around the starboard wing strut.

Hello! he shouted warmly. *Been lonely out here!*

Bergman is still relatively young, but his fishing skills have been sharpened beyond his years on British Columbia steelhead rivers like the Sustut and Kispiox and Babine. The young guide explained that coho salmon were ascending the Togiak from the Bering Sea in remarkable numbers, sea bright and in a taking mood. Although there were several good places within reach of the camp at Kashiagemiut, three of the best holding-lies were within a quarter mile. We loaded our fishing equipment in a rubber life raft and forded the tributary creek, startling a school of migratory char.

Had some super fishing while you were weathered in, Bergman said, *but we've had a flotilla of Aleut boats traveling upstream, and they're netting the coho pretty hard!*

Still got some bright fish around? I asked.

We've still got salmon coming, Bergman replied, *but the Aleuts are riding upriver empty and riding low in the water coming back. They're netting a lot of fish and they're pretty hostile.*

Hurting the run badly? I asked.

Probably not yet, Bergman admitted. *They're hurting the fishing on the lower river already, and a few more seasons of netting and they might damage the entire coho population.*

It's tragic! Bertaina agreed.

We rigged our fly rods and crossed the Kashiagemiut, angling down through the channel to a driftwood backwater. Bertaina walked ahead toward the river while the young guide worked the life raft upstream. *We've got two pretty good places here,* Bertaina explained, *but the best holding water lies across the river itself.*

Bertaina worked the first holding place carefully, teasing his sinking line and baitfishlike bucktail deep among the deadfalls and broken trees. He hooked a good fish briefly, but it was gone after a short head-wrenching run. Although we both fished it carefully, there were no other taking fish in that water.

The second holding-lie was a run where the Togiak worked strong and deep along the alders, shelving off beyond some fallen logs. Bertaina missed two fish that stopped his fly-swing gently, and I took a six-pound jack coho that hit with a wrenching strike and fought hard in a series of wild cartwheels. We beached the fish in the gravelly shallows and released it.

But Bergman worked the life raft farther upstream with our equipment and waited while we finished fishing out the holding water. We fished it carefully without moving another coho. *We're wasting time,* Bertaina said finally. *We've still got some fish here, but nothing like that side channel across the river!*

Let's try it! I agreed.

Bergman walked our raft farther up the shallows, added our rods to its cargo, and we launched it into a quartering course that angled downstream with the main currents of the Togiak. The river was split into separate channels, its principal currents flowing swift and strong, and we rowed hard to reach the island. The current quickly caught the raft, and we dug wildly with the paddles to control our line of drift. Bergman deftly maneuvered the raft into the back eddies below the island, and we beached it in the dense grass.

The channel beyond the island was less than 200 feet wide, mostly waist deep and flowing smooth against the alders that covered the moraine above the opposite bank. Two coho porpoised while we rigged our equipment, and the young guide offered me a small baitfish imitation he had dressed that morning.

It might seem a little small, he said, *but they like it!*

His fly was smeltlike and dressed on a silver-plated steelhead hook with a silver tinsel body. Its mixed wing used polar bear topped with olive and pale-bluish bucktail, and a few purplish and pink hairs had been added to suggest the coloring of a tiny candlefish. It was a handsomely tied pattern designed to imitate a principal forage species in the coastal diet of the salmon.

These coho have been gorging themselves on candlefish just before they entered the river, Bergman explained, *and they sure remember what candlefish look like at this camp!*

They remember their taste too! Bertaina laughed.

How do they take this fly? I asked.

It's still a gentle, half-plucking take, Bergman replied, *and you have to get it down where they're lying.*

They take pretty softly, Bertaina agreed with the young guide, *but they'll muscle you once they're hooked!*

Bertaina worked out his shooting head expertly, accelerated its line speed with a smooth left-hand stroke and delivered a cast that dropped his fly tight against the opposite alders. He mended his line as quickly as the cast settled, and mended again as it worked deep into its swing. The line bellied around across the bottom, and when the fly-swing paused imperceptibly in its drift, he struck hard.

Coho! Bertaina yelled. *Coho!*

His reel protested shrilly as the bright salmon tail-walked down the swift-flowing shallows, stripping into his running line. Pumping and reeling hard, Bertaina forced the salmon back in spite of its sullen threshing. It shook itself angrily and made a second run upstream against the current and his straining tackle. Bertaina pumped it back hard, playing the fish with the butt of his powerful graphite rod, and it soon circled him stubbornly. The fight was over, but the coho was still strong. The fish soon weakened, rolling with increasing helplessness until he tailed it.

That's a pretty good fish! I shouted upstream. *That coho should weigh twelve or thirteen pounds!*

It's still got sea lice on it! Bertaina yelled.

Pretty fresh! I shouted back.

Bertaina released his coho in a wild splash, and I started fishing the deep run against the alders. My third fly-swing paused as it bellied back, telegraphing a faint pluck-pluck into the line, and I tightened and struck hard. The fish shook its head for several seconds before it exploded into a run that took fifty yards of backing. It stripped off more line and jumped wildly, circling toward the river itself and the heavier currents below the grassy island. Slowly I recovered line and waited patiently while the salmon bored upstream.

He'll go fourteen pounds, I thought. *Maybe fifteen!*

Bertaina was shouting again, and I turned briefly to watch his rod dancing in the sunlight. *I've got another one!* he whooped when the coho jumped twice. *We've got a double hookup!*

Both fish were landed quickly and released. It would happen several times that afternoon, hooking salmon simultaneously in the channel behind the island, and we fished it carefully from its riffling shallows to its eddying junction with the Togiak itself.

Some fish were fresh from the Bering Sea, bright coho still covered with sea lice, while others were already flushed with their spawning colors. The females were rose-colored and heavy with their ripening ova, and the cockfish were almost scarlet, rapidly developing the hookbills typical of their kind. We hooked and fought salmon for six hours, until our circling Cessna arrived above the Kashiagemiut, and we had released twenty-six fish.

Bergman loaded our life raft and steadied it in the shallows while we clambered aboard. We paddled hard into the main currents, angling downstream toward the campsite. George Later dipped his wings lazily on his downwind leg over the tents, and turned back to face the current and the wind. The Cessna touched down smoothly and settled, and Later taxied skillfully upstream toward the beach.

Later cut his throttle and the floats crunched against the gravel shallows below the camp. *How was the fishing?* he called from the cockpit of the Cessna. *You have any luck?*

It was great! I waved back.

We really caught coho today! Bertaina added. *Bergman really put us on the fish—we were really in the bucket!*

He's some coho guide! I agreed.

We shook hands with Bergman and clambered into the plane, and the engine whined and kicked over. It caught with a smooth roar and we taxied back downstream past the Aleut drying racks, where whole coho salmon hung curing in the wind. Later deftly steered the Cessna into the current with his water rudders, pushed his throttle to its full-rich setting and started into a half-mile takeoff run.

The Cessna climbed steadily past the Kashiagemiut camp, where Bus Bergman stood waving between the tents. The Togiak wound across the flood bottoms and alder thickets, where its channels hung in interlocking loops and oxbow marshes. Bitter squalls cloaked the mountains beyond the river, in the headwaters of the Kashiagemiut, and there were swans in the shallow seepage ponds. The lake at the source of the Togiak was lost in purplish storms, but our weather was clear when we climbed into the steep-walled Sunshine Valley.

There were solitary moose rooting in beaver-stick shallows, and we startled a small grizzly that was digging out ground squirrels on the barren shoulders of the pass. We circled the bear and its diggings, and the grizzly stood its ground defiantly. Finally we turned south toward our main camp at Aleknagik, while the shadow of our floatplane hopscotched across the shallow lakes and tundra.

It's some country! Bertaina said happily.

You're right! I watched the rain squalls in the trackless mountains behind the plane. *But I wonder how long it can last?*

THE PLATFORMS OF DESPAIR

It was unusually cool in northern Europe that summer. The last evening at the Frognerseter restaurant, there was a soft bluish sea fog that covered the entire fjord, muting the lights of the capital and its circling harbor. The sea fog had drifted into the city itself when I finally started back to the Bristol, its mists filling the narrow streets below the fashionable shops in the Stortingsgata. The lights along the waterfront were surprisingly yellow in the layered mists, and the shipping cranes stood like a flock of sleeping herons.

Frognerseter is a fine restaurant that stands high in the forest-covered Nordmarka hills that surround Oslo. Its excellent cuisine is well known throughout the capital. Its pickled herring and its *grav-laks,* a kind of richly cured salmon served with a dark sauce of mustard and brown sugar and dill, are worth the trip.

Sometimes I spent several hours enjoying its rich food and its unique panorama of the Oslofjord, starting with the herring and cured salmon in its dill sauce. Depending on my moods, that prelude was sometimes followed with crayfish or fresh halibut or char from Hordaland and Telemark. Desert was a simple bowl of cloudberries and sugar, with a small glass of Chateau d'Yquem.

Årøy. I thought with excitement as I sampled the wine. *You're finally getting to fish the Årøy Steeplechase.*

The Årøy has long been talked about with reverence in the salmon-fishing world, and even the legendary Charles Ritz wrote of the river with a touch of awe in his *Fly Fisher's Life.* It was a little like a dream, knowing that I would soon be fishing the Årøy Steeplechase, and with Nicholas Denissoff, the Russian exile who had held the Årøy since 1921.

It was late when I finished my dinner at Frognerseter. The headwaiter brought my change and called a taxi.

Hotel Bristol, I told the driver.

Our route wound down into the suburbs of Oslo, past the royal palace and its beautiful park, and I changed my mind about the hotel. The taxi driver dropped me at the Teatercafeen, just across the street from the National Theater. Its repertory company had just finished a performance of *Rosmersholm* and the restaurant was filling with the theater crowds. Teatercafeen has high richly decorative ceilings and tall windows hung with heavy purple draperies, like a setting in some film about Moscow or Vienna. It was already crowded with students drinking coffee, and arguing about Ibsen and Kirkegaard and Fellini. Two older men were drinking aquavit and talking politics, and a young man was arguing his theories about Edvard Munch.

The bartender warmed the glass and the cognac was soft and richly aged, and I sat enjoying its bouquet while I eavesdropped, thinking about the Årøy Steeplechase. When I finished the cognac and finally left the Teatercafeen, I walked thoughtfully back along the Karl Johannsgata toward the Hotel Bristol.

It was difficult to sleep that last night in Oslo, since my head was filled with thoughts of Denissoff and his remarkable river. I stood in the window of my room long after midnight, looking down into the foggy streets. It was almost daylight when I finally fell asleep, thinking about Charles Ritz and the Steeplechase.

You must see it! Ritz had gestured excitedly at lunch in New York, his eyes bright and his volatile eyebrows echoing his intensity. *It is like nothing else in the world—and the opportunity to fish the Årøy with Denissoff is like fishing in Valhalla!*

After breakfast I started north in a rented Volvo, winding down the Oslofjord past Sandvika, and crossing the forested hills into the Tyrifjord country. Beyond the sawmills at Hönefoss, the narrow road wound deep into the mountains that surround the Begnesdal-selva, and I stopped in the misting rain to watch its trout rising to a hatch of flies. Fagernes lies in its headwaters, and beyond the steep-walled valley at Vang, the road climbs steadily toward the Sognefjord.

Through the high barrens there, with their lakes and lonely farmsteads and waterfalls, the road finally drops down swiftly toward the Laerdal valley. Its river gathers itself in its alpine headwaters, in a plunging of wild cataracts among its mossy boulders. Its upper valley is surprisingly gentle in its moods, its currents meandering through lush hayfields and farmsteads of sod-roofed buildings. The river there is thought to offer fine trout fishing, but the Sognefjord country has several of the best salmon fisheries in the world, and a serious angler is seldom distracted by trout on salmon water.

Where the valley grows narrow, the Borgund stave church stands just above the river, its steep gables and free-standing bell tower and intricate roof frames all sheathed in shingles stained with centuries of pitch. Borgund was built in 1150, its timber framework telling us that its architects were probably Viking shipwrights. Its builders still used the dragon's-head ornaments that had earlier graced the prows of Viking longships. Columns and door frames and lintels were all richly carved with a coiling ornamentation that celebrated foliage and stags and serpents. The morning that I stopped the churchyard was empty, with no wind stirring in the birches that surround its rubble walls. Ragged clouds hung low over the valley floor, and the mood of the stave church seemed somber.

Downstream from the churchyard, the river drops into a rocky gorge where several waterfalls stop the salmon migrations upstream. I drove quickly through the winding gorge, past the timber casting platforms at Langhølen and Hunderi, where the beautiful little river flowed swift and smooth. The village of Laerdalsøyri lay ahead in the trees, and I stopped for lunch at the Lindström. Charles Ritz came walking through the flower gardens of the little Victorian hotel as I parked the Volvo across the street.

Come have lunch with us! Ritz clasped me by both shoulders. *Creusevaut is already waiting in the dining room!*

Ritz and his friend Creusevaut are both dead now, but in those first heady years of peace that followed the Second World War, Pierre Creusevaut was a world champion on the tournament-casting circuit. It was a surprising piece of luck that I had encountered them both at the Lindström, and Ritz led me upstairs to its dining room, where Creusevaut had organized a table on the balcony.

Ritz introduced us and took a wineglass from an adjacent table. *Did you arrange some fishing with Denissoff?* He filled the glass with a skilled, rolling stroke of his wrist, and passed it across the table without interrupting his barrage of talk.

Denissoff offered me three or four days.

Did he prove difficult? Ritz continued.

You predicted that! I smiled.

Creusevaut smiled with amusement, sipped his wine while Ritz accelerated his questions, and sat listening indulgently. *What did Denissoff tell you about the fishing?* Ritz continued his barrage. *Did he charge a lot of money for the entire beat?*

He told me that the fishing was excellent, I replied, *although he said the Årøy was a little low—and it wasn't cheap!*

The old robber baron! Ritz shook his head and laughed. *His fishing has been terrible this past fortnight!*

There's very little water, Creusevaut added.

Terrible or not, I accepted more wine gratefully. *You don't get the chance to fish the Steeplechase every day!*

Mais oui! Ritz agreed.

Ritz led our party to the cold table, which stood in splendor just inside the dining room doors. It held several kinds of brislings in various sauces, and several types of pickled herring. Tiny shrimps covered a huge silver bowl filled with crushed ice, and a gleaming tureen was filled with a delicate asparagus soup. There were platters of fresh sausages and fried halibut and boiled salmon netted off the mouth of the Laerdal, along with steaming bowls of new potatoes and carrots and other vegetables. Sliced cucumbers and onions stood marinating in olive oil and vinegar. Fresh fruits were artfully piled on another platter. There were cheeses and pastries and fresh berries too, along with a goat cheese from Hallingdal.

Did Denissoff ask you to bring him some wine? Ritz asked puckishly. *He's always asking his visitors to bring wine.*

Yes, I nodded. *Some salmon flies too.*

Let me guess! Ritz arched his expressive eyebrows. *Denissoff wants two cases of Piesporter Goldtröpfchen or Gewürzträminer—no that's probably wrong!* He paused thoughtfully and frowned.

You're close! I laughed. *Ockfener Bockstein!*

The old bandit hasn't changed! Ritz ordered another bottle of wine. *He still likes those German and Alsatian wines!*

Want to venture a guess about the flies? I asked.

That's really too easy! Ritz swirled the fresh wine in his glass. *Denissoff uses nothing but a 5/0 Dusty Miller!* He studied me with satisfaction and sampled the Chablis.

You're right, I admitted.

Ritz approved the bottle of wine, and the worried Norwegian steward trembled as he filled our glasses. *Ernest!* Ritz continued in a conspiratorial whisper. *You must understand about the Ockfener—you must make certain that Nicholas pays you for the wine!*

But he's wealthy! I protested.

No matter! Ritz continued emphatically, while Creusevaut sat enjoying our conversation. *That's how he stays wealthy!*

Renting his river too, Creusevaut added.

Creusevaut and Ritz left for Oslo that afternoon, and their Caravelle flight back to Orly. Ritz rummaged briefly under their luggage to display a gargantuan salmon from the Årøy.

Forty-six pounds! Ritz announced proudly.

Since there was no available space for the Volvo on the Kaupanger ferry until evening, I decided to spend the afternoon with Olav Olsen, the famous fly dresser who lives at Laerdalsøyri.

Evening comes early in the Laerdal country, and its light lingers and dwindles imperceptibly until the fjord lies silvery purple. Several cars were waiting at the ferry slips. The night ferry across the Sognefjord sounded its arrival at Laerdalsøyri, its deep-throated horn echoing along the dark, mountain-walled sea.

Gulls hovered and screamed, wheeling above our ferry while the crew loaded our cars and the freight and mail on the landing. The trip takes almost an hour, crossing the smooth expanse of the fjord to Kaupanger. The passengers walked ashore, along with several cyclists who started up the long grade toward Sogndal. The night bus to Balestrand and the Jølstradal country rumbled off the ferry, and its passengers stood waiting on the quay. Finally the car deck was cleared and I started the Volvo, turning it tightly to clear a starboard capstan. The car accelerated across the Kaupanger wharf, and I drove quickly into the forests toward Sogndal. When I reached the Danielsen pension, there was a brief message from Denissoff, instructing me to come at eleven o'clock for lunch at his fishing house.

Tomorrow is really the day! It was difficult to sleep with such anticipation. *Tomorrow we'll fish the Årøy!*

The entire fishable water on the Steeplechase measures less than a mile, although the river itself is three times that length. Its beginnings lie in the Hafslø lake, high in the mountains above the Sognefjord. Its outlet shallows are already a full-blown river, flowing swiftly over bedrock ledges, and measuring almost a hundred yards between its banks. Below those outlet ledges, the river drops into a wild series of staircase waterfalls and plunging rapids that fall 1,000 feet in less than four miles. The narrow cobblestone road winds above this torrent of tumbling water, switchbacking along the mountain until it reaches the fjord.

The Årøy Steeplechase lies just above the valley floor. Its upper beats lie at the bottom of this two-mile cataract, and their currents tumble swiftly in a final race to the sea. The river is enclosed in a sheltering little valley, embraced in its steep birch-covered hills and its mossy outcroppings of granite.

The Årven and Årøy farmsteads lie below the waterfalls that define the upper reaches of the Steeplechase, and the Denissoff fishing house stands across the river, high above the water and partially hidden in the trees. The famous casting platforms and weirs and tumbling rapids lie below the fishing house. Half-wild sheep forage on the hillsides. The masonrywork bridge that crosses to the fishing house lies between these upper beats and the Sea Pool, which flows smoothly into the tidal shallows of the fjord. There are a few other buildings, along with a small power station above the fishing house, with a turbine that extracts electricity from the river.

Its currents race past the powerhouse, dropping into a swift, sickle-shaped mile of water and timber casting platforms. The river is a little frightening in early summer, even in its fishable reaches. The wild rapids that surge under the bridge drop almost 100 feet in the last 200 yards above tidewater. Wading such currents is impossible. The fishing is limited to bank-casting and the timber frames that were constructed after the First World War, casting structures that are called the Platforms of Despair.

The currents are incredible! Charles Ritz had explained in a letter from Paris. *There are casting platforms and artificial weirs in the river, placed to create spawning and holding-lies.*

These casting platforms and spawning weirs were originally planned and constructed by Major W. J. Smith, who had served in the Somme with the British Royal Engineers during the First World War. Smith had many years of experience on the river before that conflict, and often fished with the Duke of Westminster. His river structures were built in 1919, the same year that Smith killed a giant cockfish of fifty-four pounds on the Årøy Steeplechase.

The wild torrents are the secret of the river, Ritz continued in his letter. *The flow of the river is fierce, its bottom is filled with stones the size of oranges and cannonballs and grapefruit—and over thousands and thousands of years, only the strongest and largest fish could build their redds and spawn successfully.*

Like other big-fish rivers, I thought.

The wild character of the Årøy has shaped its unique strain of giant salmon. Its fish are unusually thick-bodied and deep, and the strength and spread of their tails are remarkable.

Årøy fish average thirty-five pounds! Ritz wrote.

Bigger salmon have been surprisingly common on the Årøy over the past century. Wilfred Kennedy took a fish of sixty-eight pounds on a prawn on the Sea Pool in 1894. Johannes Årven was the riverkeeper in the first years that Nicholas Denissoff held the river, and killed a monster of almost seventy pounds while fishing the Steeplechase alone in 1921. Denissoff killed three salmon over fifty pounds with a prawn that summer, including a huge cockfish from the Tender Pool that went seventy-six pounds. That prize is still enshrined in the museum at Bergen, almost matching the world-record salmon from the Tana in Arctic Norway, but most salmon fishermen revere the sixty-eight-pound fish that Denissoff took with his Dusty Miller from the Sea Pool in 1923. That trophy salmon is widely acknowledged as the world fly record, and a mural painting of the fish was lost when the Denissoff house burned in 1969.

It's incredible fishing! Ritz liked to explain in talking of the river. *It's like the Steeplechase at Auteuil!*

Nicholas Denissoff was an affable little man of puzzling origins, and there are several intriguing stories concerning the source of his wealth. It is known that Denissoff was born in Russia in 1883, and that his family was a minor pillar of the Russian nobility.

Following the bitter insurrections of workers and soldiers at Petrograd in the winter of 1917, other workers and dissident troops embroiled Moscow in the growing civil strife. Czar Nicholas attempted to put down these rebellions with a series of vicious reprisals in the streets. His elite horse-guards brutally decimated the marching strikers, and both Moscow and Petrograd erupted into brutal riots. Two weeks later, the besieged Czar was forced to abdicate, and the fateful struggle between various political and military factions began.

Lenin, Kerensky and Kornilov all attempted to consolidate their followers in new governments, and when Lenin failed in his attempt to seize Petrograd in the summer of 1917, it briefly appeared that Kerensky and Kornilov might forge a democracy in Russia.

Their coalition proved tragically weak and vacillating in the challenging weeks that followed. Kerensky refused to control or conciliate with Lenin and his militant colleagues. Chaos plagued the fledgling Kerensky government throughout its ephemeral rule. When the war with Germany went badly, promised social reforms failed to take shape, and the Russian economy tottered at the brink of collapse, the Kerensky government was clearly doomed.

Nicholas Denissoff found himself adrift in the crosscurrents of history, and his participation in these Byzantine intrigues was extensive. He was trained in both economics and civil engineering, probably in Germany and England before the First World War, and had played a major role in the construction of the Siberian Railroad. Its trackage totalled 4,500 miles when the final roadbed was completed at Lake Baikal in 1907. Denissoff and his family also held vast tracts of timber along the entire right-of-way according to many knowledgeable Russian exiles, and Denissoff served briefly as Minister of Finance to Czar Nicholas. Kerensky also sought his counsel in the troubled summer of 1917, but it was finally obvious that Kerensky and his government would fail.

The abortive fiscal condition of the Kerensky regime caused Denissoff to resign and liquidate his family holdings, traveling to London in the late summer to explore the sale of a privately held Russian banking house. Kerensky and Kornilov quarreled bitterly while Denissoff was in London, and when Kornilov failed in his attempt to take Petrograd in September, the desperate Kerensky was forced to seek the cooperation and military support of Lenin, Stalin and Trotsky. When Lenin swiftly seized power in the bitter October Revolution, he forced the terrified Kerensky to flee, and Denissoff found himself stranded in the United Kingdom. Wild bloodshed and reprisals followed the collapse of the Kerensky coalition. When his entire family was butchered, Denissoff suddenly found himself the sole surviving partner of a private banking house in London. Most of his other friends and collegues were also killed, or simply vanished into the wastes of eastern Russia. Other stories of his wealth argue that Denissoff had anticipated the collapse of the Kerensky government from its beginnings, and had shipped a fortune in silver and family heirlooms and paintings to Zurich and Geneva. Perhaps each of these stories is true, since Denissoff held one of the most expensive fisheries in the world for almost a half century.

The source of his wealth? Charles Ritz concluded wryly over lunch at Laerdalsøyri. *Denissoff has the smell of intrigue!*

Ritz has described the Årøy Steeplechase with considerable detail in his *A Fly Fisher's Life,* particularly the excitement of his first meeting with Denissoff at Målangsfossen.

Denissoff and Popol Bernes, an old fishing comrade from Switzerland that Ritz had known for many years, had been traveling together through Arctic Norway on a holiday trip to the North Cape. Denissoff promptly invited both Ritz and Jacques Chaume, his companion that week on the Målangsfossen beat, to join them for a fortnight on the Årøy. Ritz described that week of sport in *A Fly Fisher's Life,* calling it a wild mixture of impossible hopes, an almost crazy pitch of excitement, and a time of bitter depression and despair:

> It was six-thirty when Jacques Chaume first threw his spoon into the Solkin Pool, which, with the Prawn Pool, is the best place on the river. At the fourth cast, he hooked a salmon. I went off to the platform where he was standing. Jacques was bending double and straightening up again, but could not succeed in stopping the fish, which was fighting like mad. Suddenly, his rod went straight. Broken! The nylon monofilament of .027 inches had been cut through on the rocks!

Ritz continued with a description of the tackle in the equipment room of the Årøy fishing house. The rods were immense split-cane weapons from the craftsmen at Hardy and Farlow and Sharpes, some fashioned with steel cores, and a few of these colossal rods had been made by Asbjorn Hørgård at Trondheim. Several of these rods were as much as eighteen to twenty feet in length, and weighed between fifteen and twenty-five ounces. There were a few larger rods of spliced British manufacture that were shaped of Greenheart, rods that looked more like a medieval lance than fishing tackle, and Denissoff liked fishing them with a prawn. His fly chests were filled with traditional patterns dressed on huge 5/0 and 6/0 British irons.

There was a special tool that Denissoff had developed for braiding his heavy leaders, interweaving three strands of twenty-five-pound monofilament. His reels were big Hardy Perfects, their finishes faded and worn until they gleamed like old pewter, and their spools large enough to hold 200 yards of heavy squidding line for backing. Denissoff had lost many battles over the years, and he wrapped his fly knots with heavy silk and sealed them with fine varnish. Such equipment could only be described as awesome, and in the corner of the tackle room there was a broken gaff, its handle shaped from a discarded hoe. The gaff had shattered with the threshing of a giant salmon, fracturing the riverkeeper's hip when it escaped at Solkin.

Such armaments were often found wanting on the Årøy Steeplechase, like the parade of defeated anglers that had fished its Platforms of Despair. The outbuildings behind the fishing house concealed an elephant's graveyard of smashed rods and broken tackle. Ritz writes in his *A Fly Fisher's Life* that he lost nine immense salmon during his baptism on the Årøy. This passage describes his first hookup:

> There was still a half hour of daylight. Perhaps I might have luck! And indeed, at the third attempt, I felt an appalling tug which nearly made me lose my equilibrium. I resisted the salmon with all my strength. The rod bent to its breaking point. I was trying vainly to recover line, when suddenly the rod snapped backwards, so quickly that I very nearly fell. I was broken too!
>
> Broken on a nylon monofilament of .027 inches, which had been carefully checked and tested. I was disconcerted, but had no regrets. To be soundly defeated by such a giant fish was honorable enough!

Denissoff confirmed such stories on the river during my week, including his own combat with a fish so strong that he fainted, and almost fell from the casting platform. His experience with these Årøy salmon had convinced him that the fish were unique, and those convictions have been echoed by others. Sampson Field described his adventures on the Steeplechase while we shared his beat on the Alta, and he spoke of the Årøy with a sense of awe.

The currents are literally terrifying! Field explained excitedly. *The fish can actually force you to your knees!*

Sampson Field hooked several of these monsters over the years, and many times the struggle became an ordeal. But the most frightening fish that Field saw hooked during his tenure of the Steeplechase took a big spoon off the Platform of Despair.

Field had fished through the holding currents first, and had finally surrendered the pool to Denissoff, who followed him with a heavy rod and a battered six-inch spoon. It was almost dark when the salmon stopped the fluttering lure, and it refused to move in spite of the straining rod or the tumbling rapids. Both Denissoff and Field were unable to move the fish, using all their strength until the braided leader throbbed and hummed in the current.

It can't be a salmon! Field shook his head unhappily and handed the rod to the old riverkeeper. *It's fouled on the rocks!*

Denissoff finally agreed that it was fouled and ordered the ghillie to break off the spoon while both men started back to the fishing house. Johannes Årven had fished the river since boyhood, and had killed a fish of almost seventy pounds in his youth. The keeper took the rod, walking the bank to change his position, and applied as much pressure as the straining bamboo could permit.

Hjelpe! the keeper screamed suddenly. *Hjelpe!*

Denissoff and Field came swiftly down the path, and were astonished to find the riverkeeper stumbling through the shallows, his face and arms bleeding as he fought the brush. Several times he fell among the rocks, tearing his boots and terribly scarring his legs. His hands had been badly lacerated on the line. Twice the monster salmon stopped in the churning torrents at the middle of the river, holding effortlessly against the sixteen-foot rod.

Suddenly the fish was running again, opening a terrible wound when the line burned across the riverkeeper's fingers, and the old man plunged back into the river. The lower casting platforms were ahead now, connecting the grassy banks with a marshy island where the Årøy gathers itself into the wild chute at the bridge.

It held there briefly, while the keeper fought to control the fight. The great fish shook its head in sullen anger, but the old riverkeeper refused to surrender any more line, forcing the heavy steel-core rod into a frightening circle that threatened its life.

The salmon angrily wrenched out line in spite of the riverkeeper's strength, wheeled swiftly into the heaviest rapids, and cartwheeled clumsily just above the bridge. *It was unbelieveable!* Field gestured with agitation. *I've caught several salmon over forty pounds in my life, and this fish dwarfed them—it was over seventy!*

The fish had broken the woven leader, and the steel-core bamboo was completely smashed through its butt. The men stood speechless on the casting platform, staring at the thundering chute where it had disappeared. Both Denissoff and his riverkeeper agreed that the salmon would have topped seventy pounds.

It terrified me! Field concluded sadly. *We walked back to the house without talking about the fish, sat down silently on the porch and consumed an entire bottle of Stolichnaya!*

The morning that my Årøy fishing started, I drove down past the farmstead at its mouth, where a small tree-covered island lies in the tidal flats. The fishing-house road drops down from the shoulder of the mountain to the narrow masonrywork bridge, climbing into the hayfields and birch groves beyond.

The Volvo was left in a clearing above the house, where two young ghillies were waiting to carry the wine, and I tucked the salmon flies into my shooting coat. The path wound across the meadow toward the house, where Denissoff stood waiting on the porch.

Good morning! he called affably.

Denissoff seemed surprisingly small, dressed in a rumpled suit of British barleycorn tweed. His hacking boots were wet from the fresh dew along the river, and he studied his watch with satisfaction, since I had arrived precisely on time. Although he seemed frail, Denissoff was obviously wiry and strong for his eighty-three years. His thick little beard concealed his face, although it could not hide the brightness of his eyes. His English was surprisingly fluent, with faint echoes of the London years that followed the October Revolution, and his movements were unusually agile.

He can't really be eighty-three! I thought.

We shook hands like longtime friends, although there remained a touch of formality behind his gregarious small talk, and a serving girl brought us chilled vodka and caviar. Denissoff talked excitedly about his half century on the Årøy and the celebrities who had fished the river across the years.

Before I took the lease fifty years ago, Denissoff explained, *the river was held by the Duke of Westminster.*

Didn't he fish the Alta too? I asked in surprise.

That's right! the old Russian nodded. *But he liked the Årøy for its seclusion as much as its giant fish!*

Why was that? I sampled his fresh caviar.

Coco Chanel! Denissoff laughed richly. *Coco was his lifelong mistress, and they often fished the Årøy together!*

Chanel was justly famous for her classic clothing style, perhaps the finest couturier who ever lived. She lived for many years in the Hotel Ritz, occupying a tiny suite that overlooked the Place Vendôme, where she was legendary in her own lifetime. Charles Ritz managed the hotel from his elegant apartment across the hall. British society still talks of her liaison with the Duke of Westminster, although most people remember Chanel best for her costly perfumes.

Westminster had excellent taste! I smiled.

You're right! Denissoff poured another pair of vodkas. *People in our valley tell me that he proposed marriage here.*

Proposed marriage to Coco? I asked. *What happened?*

She refused his proposal! Denissoff explained puckishly. *Coco explained that history had already seen several titled wives who had married the Dukes of Westminster, and there would probably be more—but there would be only a single Coco Chanel!*

The serving girl returned to announce lunch, and we left the scrollwork porch. We stood waiting at the table while a young English nurse helped his wife to her place, and Denissoff hovered over them protectively until they were finally seated. His wife toyed strangely with her napkin, her slender fingernails clicking a curious rhythm against an empty wineglass. Denissoff smiled when he found me watching his wife, and poured me a little Piesporter.

She's quite mad, he explained. *But she's happily mad.*

The English nurse sat impassively through lunch, while Denissoff talked expansively and poured more wine, savoring its delicate tartness. *It was difficult to find the Ockfener in Oslo,* I interjected, *but the Piesporter is fine too.*

It's quite good! Denissoff agreed.

When our lunch was finished and his wife had returned to her sitting room with the nurse, Denissoff conducted a brief tour of the house and its outbuildings. It was the main dining room that held a wall painting of the giant Denissoff salmon in the museum at Bergen, and another room was cluttered with cardboard tracings of other trophies captured over the years. There were literally stacks of these paperboard outlines that echoed fish over fifty pounds. The little workbench just inside the porch was mounted with the specially built machine that Denissoff used to braid his leaders, and the library cabinets held tray after tray of exquisite salmon flies.

You must be christened! Denissoff announced suddenly. *You cannot fish the Årøy until you have been christened!*

Christened? I asked. *What name will you give me?*

Sascha! Denissoff raised his glass.

Later we walked down from the porch to explore the casting platforms on the Steeplechase, while the young English nurse and her aging patient attempted an abortive game of belote in the parlor. Our first stop was the Platform of Despair, which lies just below the fishing house, and we walked upstream to the tumbling weir currents that frame Tender and the Home Pool. The main serpentine bridge crosses the river below the power station on the Årøy, its frightening maelstrom of currents churning through its pilings.

Sascha! Denissoff shouted a sharp warning about the rapids. *You cannot lean on the railings—they are merely for the psychology!* The wild current roared past the planking under my boots.

Thanks! I waved back weakly. *Thanks!*

Denissoff stopped at various positions on the platform to point out casting stations and holding currents among the weirs. We finally crossed the river and I sighed gratefully in relief. Solkin and Prawn were downstream along that bank, and we sat down on the ghillie's bench.

Ever lose a fisherman out there? I asked jokingly.

Never lost a fisherman, Denissoff replied with a wry smile. *But my river has drowned a few horses and pigs and cows!*

We walked slowly along the opposite bank, studying the swift lies below the groins and weirs downstream. Twice a huge salmon rolled off the lower platforms, where Denissoff and Field had lost the seventy-pound fish in earlier years. We crossed the bridge while Denissoff pointed down through the trees toward the Sea Pool.

You will like that pool, Denissoff predicted confidently.

Ritz liked it too, I nodded. *Why was that?*

My salmon are so strong that Ritz lost every fish he hooked on his first trips, Denissoff replied. *Except in the Sea Pool!*

When can we fish it? I asked. *It sounds good.*

First, Denissoff said, *we take a nap!*

It was already late afternoon when I awakened on the porch, still drowsy with the mixture of vodka and lunch and wine, and my host came down a few minutes later. Denissoff stood buttoning his tweed waistcoat, his bright eyes dancing with anticipation. The old man explained his excitement with the observation that the tide had receded while we napped, leaving the Sea Pool at its optimum flow.

The pool is quite beautiful, he said.

Denissoff was right, particularly with the shadows reaching across the water meadows and its casting platforms. The river tumbles from the birch forests below the bridge, dropping swiftly toward the salt-marsh tidewater downstream. The upper casting platform projects several yards into the current, and Denissoff explained that it fished well only when a high tide filled the lower reaches of the pool. The lower platform was yoke-shaped, reaching out through the sea-grass shallows into the principal holding-lies at low tide.

Eighty-five feet beyond the lower platform the wild currents of the Årøy Steeplechase were finally stilled, welling up smooth and silken in the afternoon light. Denissoff suggested that I rig my tackle, pointing out the primary taking places at midstream, but I wanted him to fish the Sea Pool while I watched. His ghillie readied a sixteen-foot Hardy, mounting a vintage Perfect with a mammoth agate line guard. Its woven three-strand leader was tipped with a 5/0 Dusty Miller.

Petri heil! I called from the bench.

Denissoff waved in reply and walked carefully along the casting platform, seeming almost as old as his years until he started fishing, but once his graceful Hardy was working eighty feet of fly line, his body looked lithe and surprisingly young.

Leaning back into another eighty-foot lift, Denissoff was almost like a dancer as his line unrolled into a high backcast. The old man paused while the cast straightened, and drove back into his forward stroke like an athlete throwing his javelin. His line extended smoothly, dropping the fly ninety feet across the current. Denissoff placed the rod butt between his knees, gripped its butt section just below the stripping guide, and followed the teasing fly-swing with the fierce concentration of a praying mantis. It was obvious that Denissoff understood each secret of the pool, and it took only a half dozen casts before his fly-swing stopped and he tightened into a fish.

Salmon! Denissoff cackled happily.

The heavy fish bored straight upstream, surged toward the surface and threw spray with its tail. Denissoff grunted and leaned backward into the straining sixteen-foot Hardy, its rubber butt cap firmly locked between his legs and both hands clamped around the butt guide. The fish stripped off staccato lengths of line as it probed high into the rapids, and the old Russian waited patiently.

It's a good fish! I thought.

Suddenly it tired of fighting both the river and the powerful split-cane rod, and it turned almost majestically toward the sea. Denissoff shouted gleefully when it jumped twice off his platform, writhing into its slow, pole-vaulting leaps that threshed water high on the wind. It was running again now, stripping line wildly into the fjord. When it broached far out into the tidewater, with almost a hundred yards of the backing gone, the old Russian came running along the platform. Denissoff was shouting instructions, and the young ghillie plunged across the tidal shallows to launch the lapstrake skiff that was moored in the sea grass. Denissoff clambered into the boat, and the salmon was still taking line when they pushed off, stroking hard down the still expanse of the Sognefjord.

Bon voyage! Denissoff laughed. *Bon voyage!*

The fight lasted more than an hour. Several times they worked the big fish within fifty feet of their boat, only to have it strip line again in long reel-wearing runs. Finally it simply circled the skiff, straining hard to escape and too beaten to take more line. The ghillie started rowing back slowly, half towing the weakening fish, until they reached the small tree-covered island offshore.

Denissoff fought the salmon stubbornly, remaining in the boat as the young ghillie slipped over the gunwales and walked it into the sea-grass shallows. The ghillie waded out with the gaff and waited, while Denissoff bullied the fish toward the beach. It finally surrendered, and the gaff went home in a tumultuous shower of spray. Denissoff quickly scuttled from the boat, while the huge fish came ashore fighting the gaff. The old man dispatched the fish with a stone, and they rowed back to the casting platform with the bright thirty-nine-pound henfish laid between the gunwales.

Sascha! Denissoff shouted. *Sic transit gloria!*

It was obvious that salmon fishing had lost none of its excitement for the old Russian, and his eyes glittered as the great fish was carried ashore. The old man followed the ghillie, showing no trace of fatigue from the fight. Although he held the world fly record for Atlantic salmon, and was eighty-three that summer, he still made each cast hoping for a bigger fish.

The following morning we fished the upper beats of the Steeplechase without success, working our flies through the churning salmon lies below the casting platforms. Although I was armed with a single-handed bamboo designed for fishing tarpon, when I finally hooked a fish at Solkin it proved so uncontrollable in the heavy current that I was almost relieved when the fly pulled out. We fished through the remaining lies of the Steeplechase without moving another fish, and finally drove down to the Sea Pool.

The tide had receded again, although the principal holding-lies were higher now, almost between the platforms. Denisoff pointed out the places where the currents welled up smooth and full of promise, like a cavalry officer planning his attack.

The fish are lying farther upstream with this tide, and they're farther out, he explained. *Think you can reach them?*

I'll try! I was already stripping line.

It was slightly more than ninety feet, and I loaded the powerful Young parabolic with a hard left-hand haul and shot the entire line. Each successive fly-swing worked through the holding water as I teased it with the rod-tip rhythms. Several feet were retrieved before the pickup, and I took a half step along the platform before making another duplicate cast. Covering a salmon pool properly is a mixture of precision and casting skill and patience.

Sascha! Denissoff called jokingly from the bench. *You cast quite well but my salmon are ignoring you!*

They're pretty bored! I agreed.

There was a mammoth swirl that intercepted the fly-swing in the swift currents at midstream, and my rod bent double at the wrenching strike. The fish was simply an immense weight that ignored my pressure. It hung in the strong currents, sullen with its head-shaking anger as it brooded about its mistake. It refused to surrender line, and its spade-sized tail broke the surface angrily, throwing wild roostertails of water.

We saw the great fish clearly as it porpoised less than fifty feet beyond the platform. It shook itself again, its spray carrying downstream on the wind, and the fly came free.

He's gone! I shouted unhappily.

Sixty-five pounds, Denissoff said drily. *You never really hooked him with that spaghetti rod you're fishing!*

Perhaps you're right, I said gloomily.

Later that week, Denissoff succeeded in taking a thirty-six-pound salmon in the swift currents of the Prawn Pool. It was the only fish that we landed from the Steeplechase itself, and its surprisingly brief struggle was an unusual fight.

Denissoff hooked the fish in the heavy flow just below the casting platform at the Prawn, locked the butt of his heavy Greenheart between his knees, and refused to surrender a millimeter of line. The salmon struggled and lunged against the powerful rod. It was simply a stubborn tug-of-war fight, lacking any overtones of skill or grace. The salmon fought with all its strength. It showered the old fisherman with spray, fighting in the swirling backwater under the platform. Denissoff cursed its strength in French and Russian.

Finally the fish weakened, and the young ghillie struck hard with the gaff, wrestling the salmon to the platform. *It's a fine salmon!* Denissoff sighed. *But it's only average on my river!*

Thirty-six pounds! I read on my Chatillon scale.

Our final lunch on the scrollwork porch was exquisite, sitting in the warm midday sun with the roaring of the Årøy Steeplechase in the valley below the house. Denissoff was in a typically expansive mood, touching his beard with darting strokes of his napkin, and opening several perfectly chilled bottles of Ockfener.

His wife sat silently with a gentle childlike smile, sometimes humming French nursery songs or toying absently with the tablecloth. The young English nurse sat quietly through lunch, stopping to help her patient drink some wine, and smiling faintly at Denissoff and his jokes. The cook usually prepared a cauliflower soup, or a rich consommé royale with a paper-thin slice of citrus fruit, but in honor of the first really hot afternoon of the summer, she had prepared a delicately spiced Vichyssoise.

It's delicious! I said happily.

The serving girl brought a succulent crown rack of lamb, its pink meat cooked to perfection, with tiny potatoes and vegetables and fresh mushrooms. There was a simple bean salad mixed with cucumbers before we were served the fresh fruit and Camembert. The coffee came with chocolate-covered *langues de chat,* and I declined when Denissoff offered a midday cognac with an excellent hand-rolled Habaña.

Although his boyhood Russia had been utterly destroyed in the bitter events that followed the October Revolution, there were still echoes of its world of elegant ballrooms and opera houses and glittering chandeliers in Denissoff's simple fishing house there on the Årøy.

Are you tired? Denissoff asked sleepily.

Not tired enough to join you in a nap, I parried his suggestion. *Perhaps I'll try fishing the lower water again.*

It might fish well. Denissoff nodded and studied the clock above his tackle bench. *But the tide will still be pretty high.*

Should I fish it at high tide? I asked.

You should not fish the lower platform yet, Denissoff explained. *It fishes poorly until the tide has started ebbing, and we should not disturb it before evening.*

Leaving the Volvo at the farmstead above the fjord, I walked down toward the Sea Pool. There was little current in the brackish eddies beyond the lower platform, although a single sea-bright fish rolled in its mixing tides, and it seemed like a good omen.

The wild little Årøy dropped steeply from the bridge, slowing itself quickly in the eddying current tongues and tides beyond the upper casting structure. There were no fish showing there, but I fished it carefully several times, and fought the temptation to cover the main Sea Pool itself. It took almost an hour of patient casting to convince me that my luck was still sour, although a large fish rolled once and touched the fly. It refused to come again.

Rest these fish a few minutes, I thought unhappily.

Resisting the lower platform again, in spite of the fish porpoising there steadily now, I stood watching the river in the late afternoon light. The tide had flooded high into the sea-grass border of the pool, and there was a brief flash as a fish rolled along the bottom. The fish flashed there again, catching the sunlight.

It can't be a salmon! I moved stealthily through the sea grass to get a better look. *There's too little current!*

Several fish were lying there in the shallows, slender and pewter-gray like salmon, although they seemed much smaller than the salmon we had taken. There were six fish lying together.

Sea-run trout! I thought suddenly.

Quickly rigging a lighter nylon leader and tapering it with a series of carefully seated knots to a six-pound tippet, I selected a small Watson's Fancy from my fly book. It was relatively easy to align the school of fish with an outcropping of sea grass, and I returned to the casting platform to get the proper fly-swing. The first cast dropped above the fish, and I allowed it to sink deeply before a subtle Crosfield retrieve teased the drifting fly to life.

There was a bright flash over the pale bottom, and a strong pull that telegraphed back into the rod. When I tightened, the fish stripped line from the reel in a surprising run, taking sixty yards of backing before it stopped.

Patiently I worked it back through the tidal currents, where the mingling eddies were mixing now, signaling an ebbing in the Sea Pool. The fish stripped off backing again in another wild run, jumping twice before it came back stubbornly, bulldogging over the gravel in a series of head-shaking circles.

Sea trout! I thought with excitement.

The fat sea trout finally stopped fighting, and I coaxed it carefully into the shallows along the grass. It surrendered when I seated my fingers across its gill covers, and I carried it gratefully ashore. The sea-run brown seemed huge, its coin-bright length measuring almost thirty inches, and I killed it mercifully.

The fish weighed nine pounds, and I walked back briskly toward the Årøy farmstead with its spotted tail dragging in the wild flowers. Denissoff had finished his nap when I reached the fishing house, and was sitting on the porch.

Look at the sea trout! I babbled with excitement. *You didn't tell me anything about big sea trout in the Årøy estuary.*

Denissoff looked at the fish disdainfully.

Sascha! he said with a fatherly sigh. *My river is filled with tigers and you waste our time with field mice!*

THE GHOSTS OF TREASURE CAY

It was still and cool just after daylight, and I walked the perfect chalk-colored beach at Treasure Cay, enjoying the remarkable clarity and richness of its lagoon. Schools of silvery little jacks and snappers and needlefish scattered when I approached. Stilts and oystercatchers were foraging in the sand, where the tide had left its fingerprints of shells and sand dollars and starfish. Beyond the pine-covered point, a solitary frigate bird explored the shallows of the reef. The *Miami Herald* had reported a fresh snowfall in Manhattan, with sanitation workers joining the street crews in clearing its drifts. The soft wind stirred, riffling the still surface of the bay, and moved restlessly in the pines and palmettos.

The faint wind smelled freshly of the sea, mixed with a perfume of scarlet hibiscus and flamboyan. Red-legged thrushes and yellowthroats were hunting breakfast in the hotel gardens, and a pair of bright-green hummingbirds were quarreling among the flowering vines. The sun still lingered below the horizon, but in the distance beyond Green Turtle Cay there was a single sailboat and the sun had tinted a few scraps of clouds into pink flamingos.

Should be a fine morning for bonefish, I thought.

The yacht mooring lies across a narrow part of the island, using the sheltered bay for its access. Big pleasure boats rocked lazily in the piling wash, along with a flotilla of fine sailboats and a pair of costly powerboats outfitted for billfishing. The brightwork on their decks and flying bridges and outriggers gleamed in the early sun, and I walked to meet the Preacher.

The old man was leaning back in his cane-seat chair, dozing under the white frangipani that hangs over the tackle-shop porch. *Mornin!* he grinned toothlessly. *Mornin, copm!*

Good morning, Preacher! I called from the pier.

Preacher was not a large man, although everything about his face and character and body seemed to spell size. His stomach and his good humor seemed to spill over in their free generosity. His voice was surprisingly lyrical and soft, almost a singsong whisper as the old man worked his boat pole and searched the tidal flats for bonefish. There was a wild half-rumbling quality to his laughter, which always ended in a choking, high-pitched giggle. The other guides often joked about his fierce temper. Several teeth were missing, and several others had gold fillings that flashed in the bright sunlight on the Bahamas bonefish flats. His hands and leathery ears and happy grin were huge, like the chest and stomach that bulged in his faded shirt. His dungarees were cutoffs amputated just at his knees, beltless and rolled over under his spreading girth. His calves were hard and knobby, and his big pigeon-toed feet splayed across the planking.

Sorry I'm late! I lowered my gear to the boat.

Dass awright, copm! the Preacher shook his head. *Dem bonefish is spose to wait—and dem fish is waitin awright!*

Should we fish the creeks? I asked.

Dass right, copm! he agreed.

The Bahamas were discovered on a soft October night in 1492, when a seaman on the *Pinta* named Rodrigo de Triaña first sighted a silvery beach in the moonlight. Like many thinkers before that time, his expedition commander Christopher Columbus had become convinced that our world was spherical. But unlike the more competent astronomers of his century, who calculated its circumference with remarkable accuracy, Columbus thought it was slightly less than twenty percent of its actual size. His error helped Columbus to enlist the support of King Ferdinand and Queen Isabella for his three-ship expedition. Columbus planned to reach the fabled wealth of the Orient, sailing westward rather than traveling the arduous trade routes across Asia Minor, or attempting to circle the entire continent of Africa.

Rodrigo de Triaña had actually sighted San Salvador, merely one of many outlying islands in the Bahamas, although Columbus and his company still believed they had reached the threshold of the Orient. Their ships wandered these subtropical seas, looking for the half-legendary cities of jewels and precious metals and jade built in the centuries after Kublai Khan, and finding only more Caribbean islands. Columbus added Rum Cay and Long Island to his ship's charts before sailing back toward Cuba, partially aware that he had stumbled across the peripheral landfalls of the New World.

Juan Ponce de Leon followed Columbus into the Bahamas in 1513, exploring Rum Cay, Mayaguana, Samana Cay, San Salvador, and Elbow Cay. Although their expedition had sought the capture of slaves at Bimini, Ponce de Leon and his party failed to locate that island, and passed northward to strike the coast of Florida.

Ponce de Leon was completely unaware that he had landed on the American continent, believing that Florida was merely another island larger than the others he had explored above Puerto Rico. His route back to its colonial harbor at San Juan, and the sheltered anchorage under the mammoth walls of its Morro fortifications, carried Ponce de Leon past the shallow reefs of the Bahamas Banks. His meticulous ship's logs described these treacherous island waters as *bajamar,* the Spanish term describing shallow seas, and maritime history has proved the shallow Bahama passages remarkably perilous.

Perhaps the first cartographic references to the Bahamas appear in a chart prepared by Juan de Costa in 1500. His remarkably accurate map included Exuma, Rum Cay, Long Island, Caicos, Crooked Island, San Salvador, and Great Abaco and its beautiful Treasure Cay.

Vague references to these islands are also found in the charts prepared by Pieter Martyr in 1511, and twelve of them are precisely drawn in the famous Turin folio of maps prepared a dozen years later. The hazardous coral reefs and limestone outcroppings in these subtropical Bahama passages were more quickly known to the Spanish mariners who sailed these waters than to the cartographers in the institutes of Italy and Portugal and Spain.

Throughout the sixteenth century, navigators returning to Portugal and Spain from ports in the Caribbean were terrified of the storms and shallows in the Bahamas. Seventeen ships from a single Spanish fleet foundered among the outlying islands, and were lost in a wild storm off Abaco in 1595.

Britain claimed the Bahamas in 1629, when Charles I granted proprietory rights to both these subtropical islands and the relatively unmapped territories in the Carolinas. However, the king was captured and executed before his royal grants became established, although the proprietory rights were renewed with the restoration of the throne. The earlier French attempts to colonize the Bahamas had proved abortive, and little remains of their tenure on Abaco.

Like the colonial settlers in Massachusetts, the first British settlers in the Bahamas were Puritans in search of religious freedom. William Sayle was their leader in Bermuda, and after several disputes in that colony, Sayle returned to England seeking help in 1647. His stories of persecution in Bermuda bore fruit. Sayle reached the Bahamas with a party of seventy settlers the following year. Sixty more Puritan immigrants arrived in 1649, along with food and clothing and other supplies donated in the Massachusetts colony. It was a hard existence in those first years, hunting whales and cutting braziletto scrub for dye wood, and these Puritans in the Bahamas had almost decided to give up when a treasure ship was salvaged off Abaco in 1657.

When Britain completed its first census in the Bahamas fourteen years later, almost 1,100 people were recorded. Perhaps half of that population were slaves, and that mixture forms the principal ethnic structure of the Bahamas in our time. The American Revolution triggered a wave of refugees who had remained loyal to King George III, and these fresh immigrants trebled the population in the Bahamas in the five years that followed the surrender of Cornwallis at Yorktown in 1781. These colonial refugees from the American territories totaled almost 8,000, including a fresh influx of slaves, and brought plantation life and cotton to the Bahamas.

Treasure Cay was a part of these changes in the late eighteenth century. Its charming little hotel is sited on a slender beach-pine peninsula in the Abacos, where hundreds of colonial refugees settled on Man-of-War Cay in the winter of 1782. There is a fine candy-striped lighthouse rising 100 feet above the harbor at Hope Town, which is located on Elbow Cay.

Marsh Harbour is a settlement of several hundred people on Great Abaco, and like Treasure Cay farther north on the island, it has regular air service from both Miami and Nassau. Abaco had few inhabitants in the early years of the Puritan settlements on New Providence and Eleuthera, and its existing population is largely rooted in the migrations of the loyalist refugees and their slaves, who fled the mainland after Yorktown. The highly skilled carpenters and shipwrights on Man-of-War Cay, as well as the lobster fishermen and guides, are all descended from these immigrations in 1782.

The Preacher started his outboard, maneuvered his skiff skillfully through the sailboat moorings, and we skimmed out the channel at full throttle toward the tidal creeks. Coming around the rocky point, we startled a somber heron and several egrets from the shallows, our wake spreading deep into the mangroves. There was a large bow wave ahead of our boat where we flushed a sand shark from a muddy backwater, and we watched it undulate slowly into deeper water.

Dat shark be bad lazy, copm! the Preacher grinned.

The old man cut his outboard and drifted toward a limestone outcropping in the brackish flat, lifting his pole rhythmically to handle the boat. The limestone was scoured and undercut over centuries of September storms, and a good fish flashed in its shadows. Picking up my fly line and accelerating its speed with an urgent left-hand haul, I dropped a pink bucktail shrimp over the swirl. It disappeared in a slashing strike.

Dass a dommed cuda! the old man cursed. *Cuda, copm!*

The silvery barracuda made a strong run across the shallow flat and threshed wildly. *Preacher,* I said, *you're right!*

Dommed ole cuda! he grumbled.

The slender fish fought bravely for its size, making a half dozen runs that reached into my backing. It was surprisingly strong, but its razor teeth somehow failed to sever my tippet, and I finally forced it back toward the gunwale of our boat. The Preacher struck skillfully with his gaff, and wrestled the struggling barracuda aboard. His brass priest mercifully dispatched the fish, but it smashed a gill cover and blood splattered across the lapstrake hull. The barracuda shuddered as its eyes glazed and dimmed.

Get dat bastard fore he gets me! the Preacher said.

Makes pretty good sense! I agreed. *Barracuda can cut you pretty good if you're not careful with them!*

Dat cuda done bleed everplace! the old man growled.

Better clean that off, I suggested.

Copm! The old man shook his head. *We swab down dat gurry fore it go bad sticky and smell sour!*

You eat barracuda at Treasure Cay? I asked.

The Preacher carefully wiped the duckboards and hull, and washed the bilge with several fruit cans of sea water. *Some folk dey tells dem cudas bad poison.* He grinned and his teeth flashed in the sun. *Some folk tells de spots is de poison too!*

Some places, I nodded, *the barracuda are poison!*

Dass right enough, copm! the Preacher agreed. *But our Abaco folk dey eats dem cudas regular—spots and stripes too!*

They must be okay, I laughed.

We searched all morning for bonefish, finding only two small schools that scattered like quail, long before we could cover them with a fly. We caught several more barracuda, and lost several flies to the teeth of others we hooked. Back in the mangrove shallows, we took a few snappers that darted out from the roots.

Finally the wind came up behind the island, cool and smelling of the Gulf Stream, and when the tide began gathering imperceptibly in the creek we decided to quit. The Preacher started rowing back toward the yacht channel while I took down my tackle and stowed my other gear in the duffle. There were laughing gulls beyond the tidal flats, and in the freshwater lagoon beyond the point we watched a kestrel hunting its breakfast in the shallows.

Copm? the other guides called laughingly when we cut the motor and coasted toward the dock. *Hab some luck?*

Not much, I said ruefully. *Caught some barracuda.*

Copm! they laughed. *Everymon cotch cuda!*

The Preacher grinned toothlessly and fussed with the mooring lines. *Dass awright!* his eyes twinkled with suppressed laughter. *Copm gonna cotch a boatful ob bonefish tomorra!*

Where can we find a boatful of bonefish? I asked.

Copm, he said quietly, *behind dis here cay we got de biggest bonefish flats in dese here parts—call dat place de Marls!*

Lots of bonefish on that side? I asked.

Copm! the others agreed. *Marls got plenty bonefish!*

Okay! I said. *Meet you after breakfast!*

The Preacher was waiting behind the boathouse when I walked down through the palm trees, and I helped him load a cooler of fruit and sandwiches and beer into his vintage Plymouth. It was a strange palette of color, its original lacquer scoured over years of traveling the coral-dust tracks of Abaco. The windshield was badly shattered, its glass terribly pitted with blowing sand, and it was virtually impossible to drive into a setting sun. The fabric was badly stained, and rusting springs protruded through the seats. The Preacher crawled across the front seat, because the driver's door was loosely wired shut with a coathanger.

Copm! the Preacher grinned. *We got a good mornin!*

Chalk-colored dust billowed out behind the Plymouth when we left the pavement beyond the hotel, and the old man careened along the back roads of the island, fishtailing through axle-deep places in the sand. We surprised a small herd of wild pigs that was rooting along the twin-rut trace, and they bolted into the palmettos.

Copm, we sprise dem wild pigs! The Preacher flashed his gold-filled teeth. *We cotch dem wild pigs pretty good!*

You have lots of wild pigs on Abaco? I asked.

Copm, he grinned, *we got plenty pigs!*

The trace wound through the palmettos toward an overgrown inlet among the mangroves. Half concealed in marsh grass, the weathered pier provided a mooring for two small boats. Rainwater glistened under the duckboards, and the Preacher spent several minutes with a bailing can while I transferred our gear from the Plymouth.

Copm, we ready! he said finally.

The small freshwater creek was overgrown and mysterious. The labyrinths of mangrove roots rose from the dark water, mahogany colored and encrusted with tiny mussels. Bitterns and cattle egrets and terns watched our passage toward the estuary. The Preacher dipped his paddle into the still, tea-colored creek, stroking deep and slow until he raised the dripping blade while we drifted toward the sea.

Baitfish darted ahead of our boat. Baby jacks and mangrove snappers bolted into the shadows, and swamp cuckoos were trilling in the brush. The tiny creek finally widened into its marshy estuary, where a huge flock of spoonbills roosted in a thicket.

So this is the Marls, I thought.

The tidal estuary spread into an immense chalk-soft flat, reaching to the horizon except for a few mangrove shoals and tidal bars. The Marls stretch along the entire western shore of Abaco, spreading hundreds of miles along its completely undeveloped coastline. These huge flats lie seventy-five miles across the channel to Grand Bahama and its famous bonefish club at Deep Water Cay.

Both islands are prime spawning and feeding grounds for some of the largest bonefish in the Caribbean. Fish of six to twelve pounds are relatively common there, and even bigger fly-caught bonefish are taken each season. Sometimes these trophy fish cruise in small schools, but the really large fish always forage alone, solitary shadows that drift like ghosts over the pale bottom.

Copm! the Preacher said. *Marls got plenty bone!*

We hooked a good fish almost immediately, but its swift flight quickly stitched my fly line through the mangrove roots, breaking the tippet. Several small bonefish came restlessly across the flats, tailing and stirring up blossoms of muddy water. My pink shrimp imitation dropped ahead of the school, and I let it settle while they approached, starting a slow-stripping retrieve. We held our breath when a pewter-colored shadow darted forward and seized the fly.

Bonefish! I said happily.

The Preacher giggled with excitement and planted his push pole in the marl to steady the skiff. The fish was small, perhaps two or three pounds, but its reel music was sweet when it burned a hundred yards of backing from my old Hardy. Pumping and reeling steadily, we worked the fish back toward the waiting net. When it finally saw us silhouetted against the sky, it bolted again and I raised my arms high to hold the line free of the water. It was a circling run almost as long as the first, and the backing audibly sliced the surface.

Bone! the Preacher sang softly. *You ole bone!*

Finally the old man netted the fish, unhooked the pink shrimp-fly and released it with a giggle. The Preacher clearly loved his bonefish and their crystalline feeding shallows. Several times I found him daydreaming, watching an osprey stalking baitfish in the mangroves, or the interlocking circles of a frigate bird.

Bone, you ole bone! His singsong was deep and scarcely audible. *Where you hidin youself dis morning, you ole bone?*

These liturgies and incantations were mixed with the sucking rhythms of his boat pole in the bottom marl.

Bone! he repeated. *You ole bone!*

We explored the shallows along a small mangrove-covered island, and I watched a pair of stripe-headed tanagers quarreling over a possible nesting site. Stilts and skimmers were feeding in its gentle wash, and a solitary godwit competed for food with a flock of sandpipers on the tiny beach. The boat was drifting when the Preacher suddenly whistled a warning and pointed.

Bone! the old man whispered. *Big bone!*

Two large shadows ghosted through the pale-bottom shallows to starboard, and I stripped line while they came within range. *Dass some big bonefish!* the Preacher added. *Dem bone comin, copm!*

They're big! I thought excitedly.

My fly line worked back and forth quickly, accelerating until it had the velocity for a left-hand stroke, and I dropped the pink shrimp far ahead of their foraging. Both shadows turned suddenly and disappeared when I delivered the cast.

Damn! I muttered to myself. *You spooked them!*

The Preacher stood on his toes, shielding his eyes from the sun while he searched the flats. *Copm!* he whistled through his teeth. *Copm, dem bone ain't spooked—dey comin back, copm!*

You're right! I exhaled.

The fly rolled out with the working line and settled in front of the fish. Swirls and brief boils of discolored water betrayed their passage beyond the boat, and for several heart-stopping seconds I lost them in the light, but I started my retrieve.

There was no warning flash or rolling take in the surface. The reel started screaming shrilly before I knew a fish was hooked, and its run stripped my backing until it threatened to reach the bare spindle. With 200 yards of backing gone, I strained to hold the rod as high as possible, hoping to keep the running line free of the bottom. Twice it raked through the marl, or caught briefly on a small mangrove shoot, but the nylon tippet miraculously survived. The fish was still hooked and circling fast. Several times I patiently worked to recover backing, only to lose it when the bonefish spotted us, and stripped out line in a run that made the Saint Aidan sing.

Bonefish music! I thought.

Finally the big bonefish circled the boat, still too strong for the waiting net, and the Preacher giggled boyishly when he ducked under the straining fly line. The old man laughed and slapped his thigh when the fish circled back and forced him to duck again. The struggle was almost finished, and he readied his boat net. Its linen meshes blossomed like a parachute in the tidal wash, and the old man stood waiting like a fat grinning heron.

The fish shook itself weakly now, and bored away from the net, but its explosive strength was gone. Its run was less than twenty-five yards and I turned it easily. The fight was over, and the old man scooped it into his long-handled net with a surprisingly quick stroke. We stood like a pair of schoolboys, admiring its slender olive-mottled length in the meshes.

Copm, dass a big bone! the Preacher said. *Big bone!*

You're right, I said. *What will he go?*

Copm, we got big bone on dese marls, the old man replied. *Dat bone go maybe twelve pound—dass my guess, copm!*

Good fish, Preacher! We shook hands. *Thank you!*

Copm, dass my pleasure! he said.

Filled with excitement over the twelve-pound bonefish, we decided to stop fishing and started back. It was still too shallow for the outboard, and the old man worked his boat pole across the flats, humming to himself with the rhythms of his sixty-five years. It was getting hot, and the sun beat straight down into the turquoise shallows. Spoonbills were still roosting in the mangroves, and we almost passed over a small stingray. It bolted off in a churning flood of dirty water, its rubbery wings undulating powerfully along the bottom. Our passage across the marl shallows was lyrical and slow, its pace measured in the lazy boat-pole cadences of the Preacher.

We had almost reached the swimming-pool green depths of the channel when I turned to ask the old man something, but he was lost in memories, listening to the secret music in his mind.

Ole bone? he sang softly. *Where you hidin dis time, bone?*

OKLAHOMA SUNSHINE

The jukebox was a shrill dirge of cowboy guitars when George Kelly walked into the Silver Dollar at Jackson Hole, his infectious grin barely concealed in the reddish labyrinth of his beard. Kelly waved to the bartender and waitresses. The tiny bandstand stood silent, its electric guitars and trap drums catching reflections in their chrome-plated fittings. The country music trio was from Chugwater, in the foothills sixty miles north of Cheyenne. Its singers had joined the cowboys and truck drivers and hunting guides at the bar, while the drummer wandered off with his girl friend.

The guitars swelled and filled the crowded saloon, and a barmaid stood dreamily listening to the jukebox, absently rinsing dirty glasses in the sink. Stacks of mugs and cocktail glasses and bottles stood glittering along the mirrors and beer signs. The drummer's girl wandered over to the jukebox and fed it several quarters.

Kelly lit his cigarette skillfully, using a single hand and cupping the match without looking, like a solitary rider with his other hand on the reins. His darkly tanned features and faded stovepipe jeans and Frye boots blended perfectly with the cowboys and elk outfitters and truckers that lined the circular bar. The hunting guide at the pay telephone cut himself some fresh chewing tobacco, straining to hear his party over the shrill music:

> *New York woman trying to make me love her;*
> *A sad-eyed girl with rollers in her hair;*
> *Down the hall, somebody's cooking cabbage;*
> *Kids are running up and down the stairs.*

Kelly settled lazily across an empty stool, and the other guides laconically acknowledged his arrival. It was still snowing heavily, and the patrons in the Silver Dollar were wearing old sheepskin jackets and goose-down vests. The bartender drew four mugs of draft beer, holding them all expertly with a single hand while he worked the beer tap. The jukebox was still playing loudly when several young cowboys settled their checks.

Why does old Waylon Jennings always sing like he's horny? George Kelly laughed. *Horny and a little hung over?*

Don't know, I smiled, *but you're right!*

Two exhausted truck drivers came inside, leaving their huge trailer-rigs at the filling station down the street, and stood shaking the fresh snow from their caps and parkas and logging boots. We sat drinking Coors and watching the snow falling softly into the street. Its feathery popcorn-sized flakes muted the street lights and the garish bright-colored signs that advertised souvenirs and tribal jewelry and float trips on the Snake. The fresh snow had already covered the jeeps and rifle-hung pickups and campers parked outside.

> *Then I'll be standing in that Oklahoma sunshine;*
> *Just got off the bus from another world;*
> *Kissing mom, shaking hands with papa and;*
> *Drying the tears of an Oklahoma girl.*

The driving four-four music ebbed and stopped, and the bartender served us another round. There was laughter when a truck driver spilled a pitcher of beer, and a rattle of coins in the pay telephone when the young hunting guide finished his call. The shrill threnody of glasses being stacked was mixed with scraps of talk, and a fresh explosion of laughter when a truck driver finished telling a story. The solitary young cowboy worked several coins from his jeans pocket, slipped them into the brightly lighted machine, and stood pushing its selection buttons awkwardly. Its sorting mechanisms traveled soundlessly behind its glass case, and Waylon Jennings filled the room again.

Oklahoma Sunshine! Kelly sat staring gloomily into the blizzard. *You have any trouble coming over Teton Pass?*

Got across just ahead of the storm, I replied

Good weather for the elk hunters! Kelly signaled the bartender. *It takes a little squaw-winter snow to push the elk out of the high country—it should clear up before tomorrow night!*

Strange weather for fishing, I nodded.

Kelly's taking you out fishing? The young cowboy laughed. *Some people are for sure crazy!*

George Kelly grinned and waited for their laughter to wane. *Takes a little September snow to make the fish forget about summer, and it gets the big fish moving—particularly the browns!*

You talking about the Yellowstone?

It's pretty good, Kelly admitted, *and the Madison has a pretty good run of browns in the fall too, but it's not the only water—I've got some other hole cards!*

Jackson Hole has long been famous for its great fly dressers and big-game outfitters and fishing guides, dating back to half-legendary flytiers like Roy Donnelly and Don Martinez who came in the summers, and fishing outfitters like the late Bob Carmichael. Such men are gone now, like the postage-stamp fishing shop where Carmichael held court thirty years ago at Moose Crossing, but they have been steadily replaced by a fresh generation of skilled fishermen.

These younger men include several anglers with superb fly-dressing and river skills on the swift channels of the Snake. Their roster includes Dan Abrams, Jay Buchner, Jack Dennis, Paul Bruuns, and Vern Bressler. Some are not just boatmen and skilled big-water fishermen, but are equally skilled in both fly hatches and their ability to engage in the chess-playing problems of the spring creeks, where the cutthroats can be as difficult as the chalkstream fish of England—and George Kelly is among the best.

We first met briefly years ago at the Red Onion in Aspen, during its October lull between the flood of summer people and the explosive crowds of ski season. It is a brief respite when Aspen seemingly belongs to its residents, mixed with a few hunters and serious fishermen working the Frying Pan and Roaring Fork. Kelly had been fishing the Frying Pan that afternoon, talked about my book *Matching the Hatch* with a surprising mixture of knowledge and detail, and mentioned a fine hatch of tiny mayflies he had observed that week at Ruedi. We talked fishing for fifteen minutes, since the Onion is no place for serious conversations, but his knowledge of fishing and fly hatches was impressive.

Several years later I discovered that Kelly had spent his boyhood on the same Michigan rivers where I first learned about trout fishing, and had subsequently added studies in fisheries biology at Ann Arbor. *You decided that you didn't want to work in biology?* I asked Kelly one afternoon on the river. *Why was that?*

Politics! Kelly replied softly. *It didn't take long to discover that biology didn't have much part in fisheries work—it's ninety-nine percent politics and one percent biology!*

That's true, I agreed unhappily.

Kelly spent several years working at various jobs in the Colorado ski country, including regular ski-patrol work at both Aspen and Vail. During those days, there was a winter trek through the high country between those famous ski towns that had heads shaking in admiration in the saloons. Kelly has always preferred back-country skiing, detested the crowds and lift-lines of the downhill slopes, and soon committed himself almost completely to winter camping and cross-country trips. Kelly often skis into back country, exploring the headwaters shared by the Yellowstone and Snake in the remote Two-Ocean Pass drainages. Such wilderness skills are unusual, since few outfitters would attempt the arctic problems of the high country in winter.

Kelly is laconic about such ability, and is usually less talkative than the taciturn ranchers and cowboys who inhabit his chosen world, but his silence conceals both education and experience. *What makes you risk the high country in winter?* I asked.

I like it, he replied simply.

Three years ago, when I had stopped to fish with René Harrop on the Henry's Fork in eastern Idaho, we found the river virtually empty of fishermen. Harrop is perhaps the finest fly dresser in the region, and is among the best fishermen on one of the most difficult rivers in the world. Its fish are so selective and shy that it challenges everyone who fishes there. The river is a favorite among the guides themselves, and when we walked downstream through the Harriman Ranch, it was no surprise when we found George Kelly.

Kelly! Harrop shouted.

Kelly was clean shaven that summer, and was crouched low in the meadow, working on a bank feeder. *We didn't know you without the beard!* We shook hands when he circled back from the bank. *We stopped off to fish the last day of the season—you come over the pass?*

Came over to tell the river goodbye, Kelly smiled.

Since there were still a few weeks of fishing left in Wyoming, Kelly invited me to float the Snake in Jackson Hole. It was a fine October morning when we launched our boats at Schwabacher's landing, with a fresh snowfall on the mountains and a bright flotilla of cottonwood leaves in the current.

We pushed off and started our float. *No matter how many times I see them,* Kelly skillfully worked the boat and looked across at the Tetons, *I never get tired of those mountains.*

They're unique, I agreed softly.

It was during our lunch, sitting on a gravel bar in the warm October sun, that we talked about the problems of guiding fishermen on these big western rivers.

It's too much water for most fishermen, Kelly explained. *They're used to fishing small streams, and the fish are in the obvious places they can read—under the bushes and logs, and behind boulders and rocks and ledges that break the current—but out here you're looking at water a hundred yards wide and there isn't a clue!*

There's a lot of water, I admitted ruefully, *and they're not able to cover it steelhead style?*

It's the only way sometimes, Kelly nodded. *Cover the entire river with fly-swings until you find the fish.*

But you can teach them that, I interrupted.

That's right, Kelly continued, *but the casting is different too, particularly when you're floating a big river—it's a quick pickup and cast to get your fly into the next spot.*

And the current gives you only one shot! I agreed.

There's mobility too, Kelly said. *We've got thousands of miles of water out here, but when a fisherman comes out to fish with us, he still thinks like he does at home.*

How's that? I asked.

Most people fish a pretty small region, Kelly explained, *and when they come out here, the distances seem vast to them.*

You mean they want to fish one or two streams?

That's right, Kelly interjected, *and they've got reservations to stay someplace and feel tied to it the whole trip.*

You mean travel back each night?

Driving back and forth is just part of the problem. Kelly poured another round of coffee. *You know how this fishing goes in the fall—the rivers are moody and the weather can go sour, and you have to cover some country sometimes.*

The fly hatches are pretty moody too.

That's right, he agreed excitedly. *For really great fishing you've got to fish like gypsies—travel to the river that's really hot, cadge meals when the hatches stop and the fish aren't eating and sleep anywhere you can!*

But that's not easy, I said.

It takes a camper, Kelly grinned, *and the accommodations and food aren't always that great—you're getting a little spoiled with your gourmet cooking and wine lists anyway!*

You mean it's time for bologna and beer?

It's time you got back to basic things! Kelly teased while we loaded the boats. *Fishing isn't Camembert and Chablis!*

Bologna and beer is too basic! I protested.

We agreed to meet again the following season just to test his theories and spend a few weeks like fly-fishing gypsies. The October sun was still warm when we discovered a still flat alive with cutthroats taking *Tricorythodes* spinners, and we stopped to fish them while it lasted, taking several good fish between us. Big nymphs and muddlers produced their share of cutthroats during the remaining float, and we explored the braided channels back and forth across the valley floor, with the serrated ramparts of the Tetons silhouetted in the afternoon light. It was a golden twilight among the cottonwoods when we finished, and it was suddenly quite cold when we reached Moose Crossing.

> *Standing in that Oklahoma sunshine;*
> *A dream that I have dreamed so many times;*
> *A blue-eyed girl with golden hair still loves me;*
> *When I go back to Oklahoma in my mind.*

Another winter passed before we talked again, and I found Kelly having dinner at the Totem in West Yellowstone, fishing the fine late spring hatches on the Firehole and Henry's Fork. Kelly was meeting two fishermen the following day, when the daily flight arrived from Denver and Salt Lake, for a week-long guide trip in Idaho and Montana. Some of the rivers are still swollen with melting snow, but the Firehole and Henry's Fork and Big Hole are consistently fishable after May, along with the famous spring creeks south of Livingston.

How's it going? I asked.

Pretty good. Kelly seemed tired but happy. *Guiding is always a tough haul and it's difficult to handle people you don't really know, because guiding is a little like a week-long marriage. But when you've got people who can fish, it comes together!*

That's a problem everywhere! I laughed wryly. *The weak link is usually the fisherman paying the bills!*

Exactly! Kelly agreed quietly.

We spoke again briefly along the Henry's Fork the following week, just before a superb spinner fall of large *Ephemera* flies in the still waters on the Harriman Ranch. Both fly hatches and fishing had been excellent, and we agreed to meet in early October, planning a leisurely circle through the entire Yellowstone country.

There were early September storms in the northern Rockies that year, and six inches of snow covered Sun Valley during a birthday party for Jack Hemingway in the Trail Creek Cabin, where his father had once hosted a boisterous celebration for the late Gary Cooper.

The bleak landscape surrounding the Craters of the Moon seemed almost forbidding under the overcast, and a chill wind seared the empty bunchgrass barrens beyond Arco, with their solitary buttes and cinder cones on the horizon. The weather thickened through the afternoon, and the bitter wind stripped the cottonwoods and aspens in the foothills that rise toward the Teton Pass.

It's almost winter here! I thought.

It did not start snowing until I had crossed the summit and had started into the steep grades toward Jackson Hole, where I met Kelly in the Silver Dollar. It had stopped snowing, but it was still overcast when we met for breakfast at the Wort Hotel, and the clouds drifted in the trees just above the town. *It's still pretty cold!* Kelly admitted ruefully. *Hope it's got the browns moving on the Green!*

You mean a spawning run from Flaming Gorge?

That's our hole card. Kelly attacked his pancakes. *When the Fontenelle reservoir finally went into operation, its cold tailwaters transformed a hundred miles of desert squawfish water into some of the best brown-trout water in the Rockies.*

What happened when Flaming Gorge was completed?

It was only the beginning, Kelly explained. *It created an inland sea with enough depth to support trout and with an alkalinity as rich as our best fisheries, but the river was silty and warm.*

Like it was in frontier times? I asked.

It was a dry-bottom river in the summers then, Kelly confirmed over coffee. *That's why the frontier scouts crossed it between Commissary Ridge and the Big Sandy—it still had enough water to get them across the Bridger Basin and was easy to ford.*

Fontenelle changed all that?

It's cold tailwaters could support trout, Kelly nodded, *and its silts precipitated out into Fontenelle itself.*

How much new water did it create?

It's a trout fishery all the way to Flaming Gorge, Kelly replied. *It's got trout where there were only long-nose suckers in frontier times, and it's got some of the biggest browns in Wyoming.*

Why isn't it fished more? I asked.

It's pretty big water and it's not perfect, Kelly explained while we settled our breakfast check. *It's got some quicksand and a smooth bottom without much cover for fish or fly life. Its changes in discharge from the reservoir are always a problem too, and winterkill out there is always troublesome.*

But tailwater discharges have a pretty uniform temperature, I interjected. *The fish should winter better.*

It gets fifty below, Kelly observed drily.

We started south along the Snake after breakfast, winding along the smooth hills that enclose its fertile bottoms, and I was wondering what the country looked like when John Colter first crossed it in 1807. Colter had accompanied Lewis and Clark in their earlier expedition to the Pacific, and returned to the northern Rockies to trap and explore fresh beaver grounds for Manuel Lisa, the fur trader who established a stockade on the lower Yellowstone.

Jackson Hole itself is christened after David Jackson, the scout who first crossed the drainage traveling to Oregon with William Price Hunt in 1811. Jackson returned to work his traplines in western Wyoming, working for the celebrated Andrew Henry and William Ashley, who organized the first trapper's rendezvous on the little Henry's Fork of the Green in the summer of 1825.

George Kelly shifted gears in his camper where the highway leaves the Snake in its steep-walled canyon, climbing east into the mountains that conceal the swift riffles of the Hoback, which tumbles cold and turquoise toward the Pacific.

It's a pretty river, I said. *How's the fishing?*

It's fished pretty hard and it scours out badly in the spring, Kelly responded, *but it's got some good cutthroats.*

Where did it get its name? I asked.

John Hoback was a frontier trapper from Kentucky. Kelly shifted back again on the steep switchbacks. *Hoback came into this country with two partners in 1811, and they were all killed by a war party the following year in southern Idaho.*

It was pretty hard country then, I observed.

Still is, Kelly said.

Cattle had drifted south with the storms until they were bunched along the highway at Bondurant, where we crossed the Hoback Rim. The Herefords stood quietly along the fences, their breath blossoming in the morning cold. We crossed the saddle between Bondurant and Pinedale, where the serpentine headwaters of the Hoback wind through the coyote willows, dropping down into the Green River country.

The October storms were bright on the Wind River mountains, which dominate the eastern horizon across the hundred miles between Union Pass farther north, and the sagebrush barrens on the South Pass, in the threshold of the Sweetwater.

South Pass is perhaps the most famous crossing in the entire Rocky Mountain chain, its barren shoulders rising only 7,550 feet, in a traverse that became the fulcrum of the Oregon and Mormon trails. The mountains farther north include Gannett Peak, which rises 13,804 feet above the Wyoming countryside, and the spectacular Fremont Peak, first climbed by the vainglorious John Charles Fremont in 1842. These wilderness ranges dominate the remote drainages that give birth to the Colorado, the Snake and the storied Columbia itself.

Squalls scattered fresh snow across the highway where we turned south into the sprawling half-desert basin of the Green. *The Bridger Basin is really hard country.* Kelly squinted toward the horizon. *It's named for a real frontiersman from the fur-trapping days—Jim Bridger built his trading post out there.*

What's it like out there today? I asked.

It's a pretty old-fashioned world between here and Flaming Gorge. Kelly avoided a jackrabbit in the road. *It's still open range, pretty much like it was when they first explored it.*

Where was the Green River trapper's rendezvous?

It was held on those benches over there. Kelly pointed across the river bottoms. *It was later the site of Fort Bonneville in the years after the Sublette brothers, who were part of the first expedition of the Rocky Mountain Fur Company in 1824.*

Who was Bonneville? I asked.

Bonneville still has the smell of plotting about him. Kelly grinned knowingly. *Because he left the army to start this fur-trading post on the Wyoming frontier. But he spent more money than he made, and his trappers spent most of their time exploring.*

Captain William Bonneville hired the half-legendary Joseph Reddeford Walker as his primary scout, and recruited a company of more than a hundred frontiersmen to travel into the northern Rockies in 1832. His party ascended the Wind watershed, past the site of the trappers' rendezvous on the Popo Agie, and crossed over the mountains into the headwaters of the Green. Bonneville later established his trading post, a full-fledged fortification with stockades and extensive breastworks on the Green, and hosted its trapper's rendezvous in 1833.

Bonneville later spent an unsuccessful season trapping with Walker and his men in southern Idaho and western Montana. The party subsequently returned to his stockade in Wyoming, and promptly outfitted another expedition to California.

It's a pretty strange story, Kelly continued. *Bonneville had built a military-type fortification that controlled the existing routes into Utah and Oregon and California—and then spent two years exploring alternative routes to the Pacific Coast!*

Sounds like they didn't do much trapping either!

That's pretty curious too, Kelly laughed, *and when Bonneville got back to Washington, President Andrew Jackson promptly gave him back his regular commission in the army!*

Bonneville does have the smell of intrigue!

Seems like it! Kelly agreed. *It makes you believe we were already thinking about control of Oregon and California—and twenty years later old Bonneville was given command of the Oregon Territory when it was finally surrendered by the British there.*

Funny how things work out! I grinned.

Our route reached farther south into the windswept country of the Bridger Basin, and the mountains between these sagebrush flats and the drainages of the Snake were somber on the horizon. Fresh squalls covered the Absaroka ridge behind Big Piney. We stopped in the empty windswept street at La Barge for fuel and provisions, since it was the final outpost in the eighty miles across the Bridger Basin to Rock Springs, where the outlaw who called himself Butch Cassidy acquired his alias while working in a slaughterhouse. It started snowing again and pale storms worked along the Commissary hills beyond the town. The street in front of the saloon was filled with four-wheel-drive pickups, their truck bodies set high on their frames above wide racing tires. The pickups were fitted with two-way radios and rifle-filled gun racks across their cabs, and there were freshly killed mule deer in several truckbeds, lying in their blood and hair.

We crossed the dusty street to the saloon. Kelly purchased extra six-packs and we sat over several rounds of Irish coffee. The bitter wind ripped along the street, scattering dust and gravel along the board sidewalk, and rolling several thistles across the road. The mixture of whisky and coffee tasted good. The jukebox started playing while we sat watching the wintry squall spend itself in the street and move east into the bottoms along the river:

I'd love to leave this God-forsaken city;
But I can't go no matter how I try;
But once again I'll be in Oklahoma,
Tonight when I lay down and close my eyes.

The highway is poor beyond La Barge, dropping south along the sagebrush benches past immigrant trail sites like Names Hill, where the pioneers carved their fingerprints in the soft prairie sandstone bluffs, and the crossing of the old Mormon Ferry. It is a particularly barren country, frightening to travelers more comfortable with trees and a landscape offering more sense of shelter than a world defined only by its horizons. The cold October wind still seared the bunchgrass and hawksbeard bottoms along the river, and its ragged winter-looking squalls still hung in the Absaroka hills.

The Oregon wagon trains called those hills the Commissary Ridge. Kelly gestured toward the western foothills on the horizon. *When they finally crossed these alkali flats from the South Pass and forded the Green, their scouts and hunters pushed out on point, well ahead of their wagons, to kill elk and antelope and deer.*

Kelly left the old highway at twilight, passing the site of the Emigrant Springs, and wound back through the grassy benches to the cottonwoods that lined the river downstream from the Fontenelle Dam. It was still raw and windy, in spite of the sheltering bluffs that anchor the earthworks that contain the reservoir, and we had decided not to start fishing when we saw several huge brown trout jump full-length like migrating salmon below the dam.

See that one! Kelly laughed. *Get your heart started?*

It was getting colder when we wrestled into our waders and thermal underwear, and finally waded out into the icy shallows a few hundred yards below the spillway.

The wind whistled and grew across the river, stripping the last brittle leaves from the cottonwoods under the bluffs below the dam, and after twenty minutes I was chipping ice from the guides and immersing the reel in the river to keep it unfrozen. We fished down the big flats and channels downstream, covering the water carefully with Muddlers and marabous like feather dusters. Several times we watched big browns porpoise or break water, falling back clumsily into the riffling currents, but we failed to interest a fish and our fingers were almost frostbitten when we reached the camper.

Had enough? Kelly grinned with chattering teeth.

While I tied more big bucktails and streamers, weighting their long-shanked Limerick hooks with fuse wire, and setting the tightly wrapped lead in lacquer, Kelly prepared our dinner expertly. His menu combined rare roast beef with mixed vegetables and salad, and a superb Stag's Leap Cabernet Sauvignon from northern California. We ate ravenously and finished with ripe pears and cheese, and a perfect pot of coffee.

Civilization comes pretty slowly. Kelly sipped the last of the wine. *But we're doing better than the wagon trains!*

Kelly, I admitted, *you do pretty good work!*

You get the dishes! Kelly smiled.

It snowed heavily during the night, and my wading brogues outside the camper were frozen solid in the morning. Our sleeping-bag warmth was tempting, and when I finally unzipped and clambered out, I stood shivering in the cold. It took a fifteen-minute bath in the river to thaw out my wading brogues, and I anchored them with a stick in the shallows. Breakfast was a perfunctory menu of coffee and fried eggs and toast, and we started walking south along the high chalk-colored bluffs above the river.

It was colder and clearing now, with a pale teal-wing sky behind the Absaroka hills. The river was warmer than the faint morning wind, and except for our chilled feet and half-frozen fingers, it seemed like a better day for fishing.

What are we looking for? I asked. *It's all pretty big water down there, and it's a little hard to read it.*

These browns behave a little like salmon.

You mean they're lying in spawning currents? I interrupted him. *Down toward the shallow tails of the pools?*

That's right, Kelly nodded.

Okay! I stared out across the sweeping bends between the sandstone bluffs downstream. *How do we find them?*

It's pretty easy, Kelly explained. *The river bottom is coated with chocolate-colored algae, and when these big trout start spawning, they sweep the gravel clean. We just hunt for the yellow circles they make in the tail shallows.*

Like those down there? I asked.

Kelly found a rocky path that dropped steeply through the sandstone outcroppings to the river, scattering loose gravel under our boots and brogues. *There's one good thing about the cold,* I laughed and shivered uncontrollably. *It's too cold for rattlesnakes!*

The river was cold and surprisingly swift, and it took both effort and concentration to ford its shallows below the spawning redds. When we had crossed, we circled back upstream along the willow-covered island to fish back through where we had seen evidence of nest building. We both fished patiently with several fly-patterns, stopping often to thaw our aching toes, but we caught nothing.

We hopscotched downstream along the river, climbing back on the chalky bluffs to locate other spawning sites, and we fished through several carefully. We took a few two-pound fish there, but moved nothing really large that morning, although we saw some giant fish with the restlessness of spawning salmon.

There were several frontier graves on the high bluffs, and a steep wagon track cut down toward the water, where several islands split the river into several shallow channels. Sheltering cottonwoods lay in the bottoms beyond, offering perfect campsites with plenty of firewood and forage for livestock since frontier times. The wagon trail climbed back into the barren hills.

It's pretty wonderful to still see it after almost a hundred and fifty years. Kelly pointed to the wagon tracks cut into the sandstone bluffs and stitched into the parched bunchgrass flats. *You can still see where the wagons crossed the river here, before turning south toward Utah or west toward Oregon.*

We fished on the Green three days, walking its bluffs and trying the several riffling shallows where we had located fish. I took a henfish of about four pounds in the great flat below the Fontenelle tailrace, but we failed to capture a really large brown until the last morning, when I heard Kelly shouting downstream.

When I reached the pool, circling out through the cottonwoods at a dogtrot and taking the steep path back to the river, Kelly was leaning back into a strong fish with a desperate bend in his tackle. *It's been like this ever since I yelled!* Kelly explained and tried vainly to recover line. *It's a really strong fish!*

How big do you think? I asked.

Don't know, Kelly grunted as the wrenching fish took back two or three feet of backing, *but it's a war!*

Don't force him, I said, *we've got three weeks!*

We've got until sunset! Kelly laughed grimly. *It's too cold out here after the sun goes down!*

Kelly fought the trout more than an hour before it showed its first symptoms of tiring, and we could see its spotted flanks flashing gold in the depths of the swift, tea-colored river. It was another thirty minutes before it surrendered enough that he could force it into the gravelly shallows. Kelly turned it expertly in the last moments, turning its hook-billed head toward the shallows, and the great fish weakly beached itself with its hunchbacked silhouette rising from the water. *It's huge!* I gasped in excitement. *It's really huge!*

It's better than thirty inches! Kelly grinned happily.

Twelve or thirteen pounds! I guessed.

Kelly risked frostbite in his scarlet fingers as he cradled the huge brown trout in the quiet currents along the bank, holding its great head into the flow, and rocking it gently to work the water past its fluttering gills. Its gasping gill rhythms were weak and erratic at first, and then relaxed and steadied and grew stronger. Its muscled length rippled with brief spasms that gradually became stronger too, until the great trout finally wrenched free.

Congratulations! I said excitedly.

We waded back upstream along the rocky bars, where the river scoured and shelved off into its tea-colored channels, and started a big fire at the camper. Kelly stripped off his waders and zipped into a sleeping bag, wrapping his numb fingers in its warmth. *River's really cold this morning.* His teeth chattering turned it into a brittle stammering. *Can't even feel my fingers and toes!*

Your fingers look like fresh hamburger, I agreed.

Hot coffee fortified with two fingers of sour-mash whiskey soon restored his circulation, and we sat around the fire talking about the strong cockfish and the impact of these tailwaters and reservoirs on a river that only supported coarse fish in frontier times.

The weather grew steadily worse, colder with a bitterly rising wind that smelled of winter, and we retreated into the camper when we had drowned the fire. Dark ink-colored clouds gathered along the foothills, and our camper shuddered in the wintry gusts.

Try another river! Kelly suggested.

The snow had stopped after midnight, and we started north from Jackson Hole after breakfast. The dust of fresh snow still held in the meadows above the town, but the morning was windless and clear, and the snow would be gone before noon. The towering rock shards build gradually northward, each saw-toothed summit surpassing the last like an orchestra in shattered glacier-stripped granite, until the entire range has its climax of trumpets and kettle drums in the improbable serrations that surround the Grand Teton itself.

The mountains completely dominate their world, literally exploding from the pastoral basin at Jackson Hole, and their ramparts filled the morning as we drove toward the Yellowstone country. We circled the still lake beyond Moran Junction, crossed the lodgepole flats in the headwaters of the Snake, and climbed into the plateaus beyond through the startling crevasse of the Lewis Canyon.

The river spills across its lacework waterfalls from Lewis Lake, which lay still and mirror perfect in the morning. Several fishermen from Nebraska were cleaning an early catch of lake trout at the boat landing when we backed the trailer down its ramp.

Feels like a pretty good morning, Kelly predicted.

The boat-trailer rack levered our boat into the shallows, its pulley-rig squealing in the cold, and there was still fresh snow in the lodgepoles. We started across the still surface of the lake; its silence was suddenly ruptured with the wild, half-mocking laughter of a solitary loon.

Kelly rowed into the tule-filled lagoon across the lake. *You'll like the Shoshone Channel,* he said.

The flowage is imperceptible in its lower lagoons, particularly in late fall, where it connects Shoshone and Lewis lakes in the southern plateaus of the Yellowstone. The spawning grounds there are limited to a brief half-mile reach of riffles just below Shoshone itself, and the entire Shoshone Channel is a warped hourglass drainage consisting of two beautiful fountain-moss lagoons, with a narrow cliff-lined gorge at its waist. Its emerald depths are lined with deadfalls, and reflect primeval stands of Englemann spruce and fir.

The morning was still except for the somnolent rhythms of the oarlocks and oars. *It's perfect,* I said softly. *It's really beautiful when you get away from the roads and campgrounds.*

Wait until you see the Aquarium, Kelly predicted.

Neither lake held fish when John Colter and James Bridger first explored the Yellowstone early in the nineteenth century, perhaps because their basins were formed by a combination of earthquakes and lava flowages after the Pleistocene millenniums that distributed the trout and grayling populations on our continent. Before the First World War, both lakes were first stocked with togue from Maine and beautiful Loch Leven browns from the Howietoun hatcheries of Sir Ramsey Gibson Maitland in Scotland. These Scottish brown trout are strongly mottled, lacking the reddish-orange spotting typical of other brown trout strains. Few pure stocks of these Scottish fish remain, although they were once widely distributed in our western mountains, because the Loch Leven subspecies freely crossbreeds with other brown trout after they are planted. The red-spotted strains are apparently genetically dominant, and the populations in most of our western rivers are mixtures of brown trout stocks from Europe.

Although both lake trout and browns are fall spawners, there is happily no redd-building competition between them. Brown trout are riverine spawners that must have currents to saturate their nests with dissolved oxygen, while the more primitive lake trout are reef spawners in the lakes themselves. Since the surprisingly few tributary creeks feeding both lakes are reduced to trickles in autumn, and the outlet of Lewis Lake consists of a series of bedrock shallows that cannot provide spawning gravel, the primary spawning areas for the remarkable Loch Leven populations of both lakes are limited to the brief gravel flowages between the lakes.

The persistent brown trout found their spawning grounds and have thrived without subsequent plantings. Unlike other fisheries in the Yellowstone, there are no restrictions of fishing methods on either Lewis or Shoshone lakes, except for the limit of two fish per day. The south entrance highway passes Lewis Lake, en route to popular Old Faithful and the heart-stopping beauty of the Yellowstone Canyon, and its campground shores are heavily fished. Trolling is also popular with visitors who are not serious trout fishermen and are more familiar with the fishing methods of lesser altitudes in the Middle West. Shoshone is more remote, with only forest trails that reach its crystalline depths, and its axe-shaped waters measure almost eight miles from its ranger station to its headwaters under the Pitchstone Plateau. Lewis is almost three miles in diameter. Their scope and fertility are such that with a steady harvest throughout the summer months, and the relatively limited spawning grounds available to the population of both lakes, their trout are plentiful and average fourteen to sixteen inches. However, there are problems on the horizon, since the entire brood-stock populations of both fisheries are concentrated in the lagoons and flowages at Shoshone Channel in October.

George Kelly rowed steadily across the still lagoon, while I rigged both rods and trailed a big marabou a few yards behind the boat. We had covered only thirty-odd yards when there was a heavy strike, and a big fish hooked itself briefly before pulling free. *You'd better stay on your horse,* Kelly laughed. *That was a good fish!*

It ambushed us! I agreed.

We reached the south shoreline and I started casting to the submerged deadfalls and boulders. There was a fat two-pounder almost immediately, but we took nothing in the next 200 yards except for a solitary monster that followed the marabou almost back to our boat. It refused to inspect the fly again. It had been lurking like a muskelunge in a tangle of fallen trees, and its shadow behind my retrieve was so stealthy that I was fascinated, like watching the lazy undulations of a hooded cobra, and I completely missed its strike when it finally came.

There was another party fishing the lower water just below its hourglass narrows. *They've been working this over with spinners!* Kelly said angrily. *Let's go through and try the upper lagoon!*

They just released a three-pounder, I said.

That's what they're doing! Kelly said in disgust. *There are lots of three-pounders around in the fall, and they're getting ready to start spawning in a few weeks. They're starting to feel aggressive and show their spawning territoriality, and when they're in that kind of mood they're suckers for hardware!*

But they're letting fish go, I said.

The limit is still two fish, Kelly explained bitterly, *and without any restrictions on method, those hardware-throwing bastards can come in here when all of the big browns in both lakes are vulnerable!*

You mean they're culling fish to kill two big ones? I was stunned when I finally understood. *That's terrible!*

That's right! Kelly growled unhappily. *They'll hook twenty or thirty on hardware until they get a couple of five- or six-pounders to take home —and those other big fish will probably die too!*

Can't it be stopped? I asked.

The Yellowstone regulations are the problem! Kelly shook his head. *The two-fish limit is working pretty well, and we don't need any restrictions on fishing methods through the summer months, but when the prime brood fish in both lakes are gathering here to spawn, it's possible to damage the fisheries pretty quickly!*

You think it should be fly-only and no-kill fishing?

That's the best method we have, Kelly agreed grimly, *but only here in the Shoshone Channel itself—and only in the fall!*

It's not too late to change the regulations, I suggested.

Maybe not, Kelly said grudgingly.

I missed a heavy strike in the ledge-rock narrows, and then we took a brace of butter-fat browns along the fallen trees upstream. Two other fishermen were working the riffles beyond the upper lagoon, and Kelly worked our boat into a quiet backwater.

They're welcome to that stretch, he grinned wryly.

Why is that? I asked.

Their boat is over there in the reeds, Kelly explained puckishly, *and this is grizzly country in here!*

Lots of grizzlies? I asked warily.

You know about bears! Kelly laughed. *When you've got only one grizzly around, you've already got one grizzly too many!*

Amen! I agreed.

The sun was getting high while I changed reels. The Aquarium is a smooth-flowing lagoon that shelves off from the chara and potamogeton and elodea shallows upstream. The deeper currents reflected the beautiful Englemann spruce forests, their depths richly aquamarine with the bright beds of fontinalis weed on the bottom. It was surprisingly warm and we stripped off our parkas. Fall spawners jumped occasionally like salmon, ripening and impatient for their mating time. There was still no wind on the water in early afternoon, and in the emerald channels there were darker shapes above the moss and algae.

What are those darker weeds? I asked.

You mean those dark shapes on the fountain moss? Kelly responded slyly. *Those are trout—that's why it's called the Aquarium!*

My God! I gasped when one moved. *You're right!*

The Aquarium is quite deep, and we needed the sinking weight-forward line on the other reel. Fishing patiently down the almost imperceptible currents, we covered the lagoon in a series of eighty-foot casts and slow hand-twist retrieves, working big nymphs and bucktails back along the bottom. We took a half dozen fish between three and five pounds. There were still bigger trout lying deep along the moss, and when I finally hooked a strong seven-pound henfish, it was followed by two curious monsters that dwarfed it. Both fish drifted back into the shadows and refused to come back when we tried them.

Well, Kelly smiled, *seven pounds isn't bad!*

It grew colder when the sun left the water, and there were threatening clouds on the horizon when we reached the boat landing. Our feet ached from the icy shallows while we wrestled with the trailer and its pulley crank. There was a cold moon rising above the trees when we finished securing our equipment, and started north to spend the night in the campground at West Thumb on Yellowstone Lake. The camper radio was suddenly alive with our friend Waylon Jennings:

> *New York woman trying to make me love her;*
> *A sad-eyed girl with rollers in her hair;*
> *Down the hall, somebody's cooking cabbage;*
> *Kids are running up and down the stairs.*

There was frost in the high meadows along the lake after breakfast, and the high summits of the wild Absaroka mountains were twenty miles across the crystalline stillness of its northern outlet. We passed the old Fishing Bridge, where the summer people have caught countless numbers of Yellowstone cutthroats in the past century. Since these smooth-flowing outlet currents are perhaps the most important spawning areas for the entire lake, which totals almost 140 square miles and lies at 7,731 feet, the waters at Fishing Bridge have been closed to fishing. Visitors are currently limited to watching the hundreds of large trout holding in its currents, spawning in their brightly colored mating rites in early summer, holding like pale ghosts over its straw-yellow gravel and rising softly to midges hatching from the lake itself.

The first miles downstream from Fishing Bridge are closed to fishing too, primarily to protect the cutthroat fry hatched there until they migrate out into the depths of the lake, and the principal fishery in these headwaters lies at Buffalo Ford.

It's been pretty good all summer, Kelly explained. *We could check it out this morning and still catch some evening fishing on Slough Creek or the Lamar—and we could make Chico Hot Springs later.*

Sounds like good strategy, I agreed.

Buffalo Ford is a famous stretch of the Yellowstone, lying between Fishing Bridge and the remarkable buffalo-grass meadows of the Hayden Basin below the Mud Volcano. The heavy fishing pressure in these accessible miles of water had seriously decimated its fine cutthroat fishery since midcentury. Few large trout were being reported when it was finally decided to close the Fishing Bridge entirely, and radically change the regulations farther downstream. The biologists decided to close the Hayden mileage too, protecting the baby cutthroats hatched there in a handful of prime spawning tributaries. The mileage between these pea-gravel preserves was designated fly-only water, and the fish legally caught may not be killed. The principal access to this stretch lies in the old picnic grounds at Buffalo Ford, and these changed regulations have worked a miracle.

Five years ago, Kelly explained when we left the Fishing Bridge, *it was really a good day when you could catch a half dozen cutthroats on the Yellowstone here.*

What's the fishing like these days?

Terrific! Kelly pulled our camper into the picnic grounds. *The fish are getting harder to fool when they've been hoodwinked a few times, but a good fisherman prepared to match the hatches can usually catch fifteen or twenty a day.*

How large are these fish? I asked.

Ten-inch cutthroats were good fish here five years back, Kelly replied, *but an average fish today is eighteen or twenty!*

But the fish were like that in frontier days, I said in disbelief. *The military journals of General William Emerson Strong described fishing like that a century ago!*

The new regulations have brought it back!

Fly-only regulations can be pretty unpopular, I said, *and the no-kill rules just add heat to those arguments.*

That's probably right, Kelly admitted, *but the Yellowstone field biologists were alarmed by the declining fisheries, and even the game-management people were getting worried.*

Why were the other biologists alarmed? I asked.

Park visitors were killing so many fish that the forage populations needed to sustain fish-eating species like otters and pelicans and ospreys were threatened, Kelly continued, *and even the bears were getting hungry—but our bears are another problem!*

What else happened? I asked.

The park biologists finally convinced the Congress about their no-kill policy when the park visitors were killing several thousand fish a month, Kelly explained grimly, *and throwing away more than a thousand of them in the campground trash!*

No wonder they were angry! I said.

We fished the smooth currents at Buffalo Ford for several hours, working on the shelving breaks beyond its lodgepole islands. Several times I took large cutthroats on nymphs and wet flies, and there were so many fish in these waist-deep flats that we often looked down to find them around our ankles in the flow.

Have you got fish holding around your legs? I called.

Three! Kelly laughed across the smooth riffles. *It's getting like that all the time these days!*

You mean the no-kill regulations have saved so many fish that our legs are like stones breaking the current?

Any old ankle in a storm! Kelly laughed again.

During lunch on the gravelly beach, we discovered several good cutthroats working softly in the shallows where two channels came together, their sipping rises barely disturbing the surface. The feeding activity was both steady and almost imperceptible.

Since there had been no swarming mayflies in the morning, and we could see nothing on the current, it seemed logical that the trout were taking *Diptera* pupae drifting from the still water upstream. Tiny spent mayflies or midge pupae are usually the catalysts for such steady feeding rhythms, and I decided to try a tiny pupal imitation in the film. The lowest fish was holding behind a chalk-colored stone, pushing its spotted nose into the film steadily, and my black seal-fur pupa dropped softly just above its station. The cutthroat drifted back under the tiny pupa and inhaled it with a quiet dimple.

It was a brightly colored two-pounder, slightly under the average weight at Buffalo Ford, its gill covers scarlet and its sparse spotting distributed densely toward its tail. We took turns on the platoon of cutthroats lying there, taking more than a dozen that size before the feeding stopped, and our best fish was better than twenty inches. The fishing was so good that we stayed until late afternoon, and there was no time to explore Slough Creek and the Lamar. The lodgepole shadows were getting long when we crossed Dunraven Pass, and the setting sun glittered in the fresh snowfields on Mount Washburn. There were elk bugling in the timbered ridges when we stopped in the Yankee Jim Canyon on the Yellowstone, and when we left the highway it was already getting dark. The massive Absarokas were bright in the moonlight across the river, and we climbed steadily toward the lights where the steaming Chico Hot Springs waited in the mountains behind Emigrant. Its superb restaurant was still open when we finally arrived, and in the saloon several cowboys were playing pool and feeding the jukebox:

I'd love to leave this God-forsaken city;
But I can't go no matter how I try;
But once again, I'll be in Oklahoma;
Tonight when I lay down and close my eyes.

Chico Hot Springs has sheltered travelers since the Yellowstone trains ascended the Yellowstone watershed en route to the park headquarters at Mammoth. The resort has evolved through several stages since its nineteenth-century genesis, when its waters were celebrated for their healing powers and church revivals and backcountry baptisms.

It was later a casino and society bordello with shipments of fine first-growth wines and champagnes and barrels of Chincoteague oysters chilled with crushed ice. Its brief career at baccarat and spinning roulette wheels and flashing cards, with the red-plush rooms and candelabra and mirrors of its *maison de rendezvous* quarters in the upper floors, was filled with controversy and tumult. Those glittering days were ended, and the string quartet music fell silent, when the resort passed into receivership again. The doldrums that followed were only partially ended when the Chico Hot

Springs endured another cycle of religious retreats and revivals.

The current proprietors are restoring its elegance patiently, and started that renaissance with a startlingly good cuisine and wine cellar unmatched in many cities. The hot springs still bubble from their fissures in the earth, and these days it is possible to find a Porsche or Rolls-Royce or Lamborghini gleaming between the line of jeeps and pickups parked outside. Sometimes there is even an aircraft in its parking lot, when loyal patrons fly in to dinner and land their Pipers and Cessnas on the county highway.

We walked through the dining room to the tiny bar and waited for a table. *It's really a nice place.* Kelly sipped his whiskey carefully. *It's probably the best food in Montana.*

The menu included fresh oysters and escargots and smoked salmon with capers, and its list of choice meats included such elegant alternatives as crown rack of lamb, immense cuts of rare roast beef and a superbly prepared beef Wellington.

It seems a little strange to find such cooking in ranching country, Kelly grinned, *but we're coming around too!*

You've got my vote! I said.

There was a spell of unusually warm weather in the week that followed, and the fishing on the Yellowstone itself was slow. We floated the river from Emigrant to the old highway bridge above Livingston, where the sweeping valley narrows between the mountains. The steep mountains behind Pray and Piney Fork still held somber clouds in the mornings, but there was no prelude suggesting rain, and the nights were surprisingly warm. It was hot on the river at midday, and we stripped down to our fishing vests and stopped often to wade the flats, more for their cool temperatures than their fishing.

The trout think it's still summer, Kelly grumbled.

Our last float started in the sweeping bends at Mallard's Rest, on a morning bright with the rich chroma of cottonwoods and aspens under the slate-colored escarpment of the Absarokas. The riffles glittered in the sun, and the hayfields along the river were stacked with a harvest of golden bales, like miniature pueblos and cliff dwellings and castles. Several cinnamon teal exploded in a shallow backwater, and the hard-frost nights had already started the greenhead mallards migrating toward the Missouri Breaks.

The hot weather had forced the trout back into their summer pools and chutes, and in the first few miles of river, we took only small hatchery rainbows and whitefish. *Pretty morning,* I suggested, *but I don't think the fish have noticed yet!*

It's going to get hot again, Kelly said.

We stopped fishing after a few miles, committing ourselves to the river for the simple pleasures of drifting its serpentine channels and riffling currents. Its music was muted in the fall, drifting with yellow leaves and its snowmelt spent months before, and its channels were an arboretum of bright-leafed cottonwoods and aspens.

We beached our river boat on a shelving gravel bar alive with the fallen confetti of cottonwoods and sumac. *Smell that October perfume,* I sighed happily. *It's not such a bad life out here!*

You've got that right! Kelly grinned.

Kelly stopped again in the labyrinth of gravel-bar channels along the Dana Ranch, where the sagebrush benches and ancient flood channels and alluvial cottonwood bottoms give birth to the famous Nelson Spring Creek. There are many spring creeks in Montana, from the Poindexter water on the Beaverhead to the famous artesian springs at Lewiston, and they rise in geyser basins and alluvial bottoms and sedge bogs. Such streams are not unlike the storied chalkstreams in Wiltshire and Hampshire, where dry-fly fishing was born a century ago, and the rich little spring creek on the Nelson place is among the finest.

Several deer were grazing below its loading pens, and there were cattle grazing in the straw-colored meadows, where the bottoms reached down toward the cottonwoods that lined the Yellowstone. The corrugated roofs of the ranch and its outbuildings were half concealed in the trees beyond the irrigation trestle. Beyond the ranch the foothills were still deep in shadows, but across the river and its cottonwood bottoms, the afternoon sun was warm on the pale hawksbeard benches and the high smoke-colored mountains beyond.

The spring creeks just above Livingston are among the principal spawning grounds on the entire middle Yellowstone, and since the ranchers on the opposite bank have foolishly constructed barriers that keep the river trout from ascending their creeks, the little Nelson Spring Creek has improved steadily through its incubation and hatching of their wild offspring.

Actual oviposition starts taking place in the late fall and early winter, but the big browns start arriving in the deep pools below the creek in the last weeks of September.

We prospected the first pools in the river below its colder mouth with big nymphs and bucktails for trophy-size fish. Such fall spawners are known for their moodiness. They were uncooperative after lunch, and we covered the pools carefully without moving anything over fifteen or sixteen inches. *Let's try the creek too,* Kelly suggested.

The Nelson Spring Creek tumbles directly into the Yellowstone when its early-summer snowmelt is running, but in the fall when the smaller channels of the Yellowstone are almost dry, its flowages are still running in the rocky bed of the river. Its weedy currents are springhead cold and clear, and slide swiftly a full 200 yards down the empty skeleton of the Yellowstone channel. Since this final reach lies outside the ranch property itself, it has become a favorite with knowledgeable guides who float in hot weather.

It was too bright and there were no hatches, although an occasional trout took something softly. Some were fat whitefish that nosed the fly and were not hooked, but a few were good browns too, and I was broken twice when they bolted and stitched my tippet in the weeds. The spring creeks are patient work.

Kelly hiked back downstream along the lower stretch, leaving me the better water at the boundary fence, where I found a brace of good fish smutting. They were difficult and refused an entire fly box of tiny patterns fished in the film. Finally I tried a twenty-eight Griffith's Gnat. The first trout sipped it without hesitation, but the tiny hook pulled out when I felt its strength. It was several minutes before the other fish started working again.

It bulged and took the tiny midge imitation too, and when I tightened it exploded upstream into the swift currents. It stopped and drifted back past me in the clear shallows, puzzled and shaking its head, with its bright-poppy markings and butter-yellow belly.

It's bigger than I thought! I stammered to myself. *It's better than twenty inches!*

The big trout saw me then, and bolted sharply back upstream into the hole under the boundary fence, slicing the leader shrilly through the current like a guitar string. The fish bulldogged stubbornly on the bottom for several minutes, rolling and flashing there, before it moved upstream and scattered a school of whitefish like frightened quail.

The fragile tippet hummed steadily in the flow, and the sullen fight lasted almost thirty minutes. Suddenly the fish shuddered and shook itself angrily on the bottom, forcing the struggle deep along the elodea. The leader caught its leafy stems twice and slipped free, but when it touched the weeds again the tiny hook pulled out. It had been a great fish hooked on cobweb tackle, and I walked happily downstream in the lengthening shadows, singing softly to myself:

> *But when the cold wind blows in this big city;*
> *A part of me flies home to where it's warm;*
> *New York woman thinks that I'm still with her;*
> *Just because I'm sleeping in her arms.*

Two weeks passed quickly before we explored another spring creek at Livingston, with its swans quarreling in the nesting lagoons above its startling Greek revival house, and after lunch we found an excellent hatch of pale little mayflies below the cattle gate. It was a cool afternoon with a fine haze of clouds, but its chill wind held the promise of more bad weather.

We took several good rainbows there, mixed with a few surprisingly large cutthroats, while the yellow-bodied flies were hatching. There were two strong fish that jumped wildly in the willow-hung channel below the tractor bridge, and a huge rainbow that engulfed the fly and quickly shook itself free in the riffles upstream.

He's still feeding! I thought excitedly.

It took several minutes before the fish settled again, working in the calm rhythms of a trout preoccupied with feeding. Its huge dorsal showed as the fish bulged to the fluttering hatch.

Finally it drifted back, inspecting the pale dry-fly briefly in its bobbing course along the watercress, and impulsively took it again. It darted downstream like a salmon and exploded in a series of clumsy cartwheels, before racing back suddenly to jump again and shower me with water. It bolted into the riffles upstream until it deftly sliced the leader into the watercress and was gone.

There were several other good fish still working tight along the watercress downstream when the hatch seemed over, and although they were no equals for the big rainbow, some were coaxed into taking a fly before a bitter squall surprised us.

Kelly came downstream through its popcorn-fall of snowflakes. *It's winter again!* he laughed and wiped the snow from his beard. *Let's get across the pass before the rangers close it tight!*

Where should we try fishing now?

Between Old Faithful and its other geysers, Kelly said thoughtfully. *The Firehole will stay warm in spite of the weather—maybe we should try looking at Mule Shoe or Ojo Caliente.*

Let's try it tomorrow, I said.

It was snowing hard when we reached the Yankee Jim Canyon, and decided to have dinner and spend the night at Gardiner, which was the original entrance to the Yellowstone. There was still snow in the high Gibbon meadows when we crossed through the park in the morning. It was still cold when we reached the Firehole, with its geyser steam pluming high into an ink-colored sky, and elk were trumpeting their shrill challenges in the trees beyond the Nez Percé meadows.

It's pretty arctic! Kelly admitted.

The Firehole is beautiful! I shivered and tried to string the rod. *But I get mixed feelings when my fingers won't work!*

It's a pretty strange valley, Kelly nodded. *Can you imagine what John Colter thought when he discovered a valley filled with hot springs and geysers when he wintered here alone in 1807?*

Didn't people call it Colter's Hell?

That's right! Kelly continued. *When Colter told people about a river with spouting steam and springs hot enough to cook its trout, nobody really believed him.*

Bridger told some Firehole stories too? I asked.

Bridger liked tall stories. Kelly grinned wryly, *and he told anyone who would listen about a stream that flowed downhill so fast that it got boiling hot from the friction!*

No wonder people laughed!

The Yellowstone is virtually empty of people in late October, and the vast cotton-grass basin was filled with hundreds and hundreds of buffalo. *Look at them out there!* We sat watching their awesome breath blossom like hot springs in the cold. *They're so beautiful that they're worth the entire trip!*

The smooth currents in the Mule Shoe water slide over ledge rock of chalky outcroppings and seepage crusts, wind back sharply toward the highway under a slope of tall ponderosas and hot-spring seepages, and work downstream along the pale bluffs. Immense billows of steam rose and eddied in the wind, tumbling from the smoking potholes and caverns, and obscuring the entire river in places.

There is a gravel stopping place a hundred feet above the water, where it was possible to observe the primary holding currents in the 300 yards of the Firehole without leaving our camper. We sat with binoculars and studied the river for rises.

Nothing going on, Kelly grunted.

I don't see anything either, I said unhappily, *but sometimes the fish are working in the lodgepole bend below Sentinel Creek—particularly when there's nothing going on elsewhere.*

Let's take a look there, Kelly agreed.

We circled back through the geysers downstream, where the steam drifted in churning clouds across the highway. *Our time's gone pretty quickly,* Kelly said when we crossed the Nez Percé bridge, where Chief Joseph and his warriors had camped during their heroic retreat late in the Nez Percé War. *It's been a good trip!*

It didn't last long enough, I said. *It looks like our weather is getting better again.*

We should try it again next year, Kelly suggested. *We could take our time and cover the country farther west, hit the Big Hole and Jefferson and Ruby, and maybe try the alligator-sized browns on the Missouri below the reservoir at Canyon Ferry.*

Sounds pretty good, I smiled.

Sometime we should float the New Fork in Wyoming, Kelly continued, *and the headwaters of the Teton in Idaho—and you've never tried the big cutthroats at Henry's Lake.*

Cancel my plane seat! I said jokingly.

Kelly turned off into the Fountain Flats along the Firehole. It is popular dry-fly water in the summer months, perhaps too crowded for pleasant fishing, but it holds large trout and boasts excellent fly hatches. Kelly reached for the binoculars, and between the windy gusts that blew angrily across the flats, we located a surprising hatch and rise of trout in the lodgepole bend upstream.

Look at the fish work! he said.

We called it right! I rigged my tackle excitedly. *Let's get the show on the road—what are they taking?*

Pseudocloeon flies, Kelly guessed.

You're probably right, I grinned happily. *But that means we need bright-green spinners—got any polywings in your vest?*

You get your gear, Kelly said. *I'll tie some.*

Kelly dressed a half dozen quickly on minute twenty-six hooks and we shared them before he trotted upstream. The trout were working in steady overlapping dimples along the grassy banks and in the silken channels in the elodea and chara. It was the last afternoon of our three-week expedition, and we both took a number of good browns and rainbows in the still currents.

The wind dropped down when the river was carpeted with tiny bright-green spinners, and the sun was lost in the swirling clouds that drifted low across the basin at Sentinel Creek. It was strangely warm and still for almost an hour. The gunmetal escarpment of the Pitchstone ridge disappeared in a series of gathering squalls, and the still surface of the river seemed like polished Sheffield, until the storms finally reached us and broke. The wind struck while I was attempting to leave the river, scattering pebbles against the camper. It lashed the river into whitecaps and erased the mountains in its angry clouds, and it was suddenly bitter cold. Thick snow filled the bottoms when I finally reached the road, clinging to the hawkweed and wheatgrass, and when the raw wind dropped I heard Kelly whistling:

Then I'll be standing in that Oklahoma sunshine;
Just got off the bus from another world;
Kissing mom, shaking hands with papa and;
Drying the tears of an Oklahoma girl.

DEATH OF A RIVERKEEPER

It was still and bitter cold at daylight. Snow held in the sheltered places in the mountains, and puffins and razorbills were nesting in the volcanic cliffs above the sea. Clouds hung over the strange indigo-colored glaciers at Thorisjökull. Hot springs in the headwaters of the river were shrouded in steam, belching and breathing from ragged potholes and fissures. Their mists smelled of sulphur bubbling deep in the molten entrails of the earth, and their acrid steam drifted high in the lingering darkness like a primordial encampment of cookfires.

Coarse grass covered the burial mound of a dead chieftain below a solitary farmstead. Tiny wild flowers and lichens grew profusely from its ancient stonework. Hekla stood silhouetted miles across its treeless moors, its brooding profile drifting with fog from the snowfields of Vatnajökull.

There was still no trace of wind, and from the rough circle of stones in the dry lake bottom beyond Thingvellir, two ravens croaked and rose flapping in the early sun.

Fourteen years have passed since that first trip to Reykjavik and its salmon fisheries. Greenland lay partially hidden in clouds long after daylight, its uncharted snowfields and glaciers and bleak mountains filling the morning below our Britannia. Harsh crags and escarpments were fleetingly visible through the patchwork clouds, and were lost when the weather closed again. The bitter coastal currents and estuaries were filled with drifting icebergs.

The turboprop engines whined for several hours. Our flight had crossed the bright spiderwebs of lighted cities and towns beyond New York. Boston and Montreal were sprawling patterns of lighted streets and buildings and bridges. The towns and fishing villages grew faint and widely spaced in the Maritime Provinces, until finally the dark landscape of the Labrador was below, its vast lakes and forests and coastal mountains lying in the moonlight. Our route crossed the Labrador coasts beyond Goose Bay. The cabin lights were finally dimmed and the passengers slept fitfully.

The sunrise came early, its palette bright above the layered clouds that covered the straits at Angmagssalik. Fifty miles off the peninsula at Snaefjellsnes, the coastal seas glittered coldly in the morning light. The weather was better. There was a fine haze that veiled the early sun, and the smooth seas were wrinkled with the toylike wakes of fishing boats.

Iceland is quite beautiful. The voice was both startling and sepulchral. *Once you can accept its emptiness.*

The old woman in the window seat was returning to Reykjavik after eighty-one years in America. The morning sunlight filled the starboard portholes, and the old woman was fully awake long before I opened my eyes. She introduced herself and we sat talking while the crew prepared breakfast. Her voice was both solemn and shrill, and she looked tired except for her fierce eyes.

You're returning to Reykjavik? I asked.

I'm finally going home, she said quietly. *I'm old and I've outlived all my children—I'm going home to die.* The old woman spoke almost casually, her frail hands working restlessly at her sleeves. The stewardess came back along the cabin and stopped to adjust her blankets. The wrinkled old woman looked up and smiled.

Does that sound strange? she asked.

Breakfast service was starting and the stewardess worked back toward the galley. *It must sound strange,* the old woman continued, *because you're still too young to understand such things.*

That's probably true, I said.

You'll understand once you've seen my country, she mumbled thoughtfully. *We're a simple people of farmers and fisherfolk and shepherds who lead hard lives—we live alone in remote places and death is no stranger.*

You've really missed your country, I said.

All my life, she nodded.

The stewardess returned with our breakfast trays from the galley, and helped the old woman strip the vinyl package from her tableware. When the girl returned to the galley, the woman tried her omelette briefly and spoke again in her brittle voice. *You're right about missing my country.* She stared absently past her porthole. *Fjarlaegdin gerir fjöllin bla.*

What does it mean? I asked.

It's an old proverb about homesickness, she explained. *We're seafaring people and travelers and we're always homesick for our country.* The old woman carefully buttered her breakfast roll. *The proverb means a mountain seems more blue from far away.*

It's a beautiful proverb, I said.

Happy relatives surrounded the old woman once the stewardesses had helped her through customs at Keflavik. My luggage was already there, but it took some time before my fishing equipment arrived on the conveyor. When I wrestled a suitcase and rod duffle toward the customs inspectors, the old woman waved from her wheelchair.

Good fishing! she wished shrilly.

Her country is a unique little world of fire and ice. It rises without warning from the subarctic waters between Greenland and the Shetland Islands, and its barren coastlines belong less to the earth than to its bone-chilling seas.

Its topography of glaciers and lava fields and volcanoes is merely the outcroppings of a vast mountain submerged in the North Atlantic. Iceland consists of approximately 39,758 square miles, and its interior is largely uninhabited. Its mountains are perhaps the highest of the volcanic growths and fissures that scar a gargantuan, barely healed wound that lies the length of its ocean floor, reaching from the Arctic seas to Tristan de Cunha.

Medieval theology concluded that Hekla, perhaps the best-known volcano in Iceland, was literally the fiery portal to Hades. Jules Verne placed his story *A Journey to the Center of the Earth* in western Iceland, and his characters entered the netherworld through a fissure in the Snaefjellsnes crater.

Its several volcanoes are still alive, although many have been seemingly asleep under the largest glaciers in Europe. Their silence has been short-lived. Startled herring fishermen watched in utter terror in 1963, when the coastal seas behind their fishing boats began to boil and suddenly erupted in explosions of steam and fire. Spouting lava soon belched from the smoke and falling ashes, and the sudden birth of a volcanic island called Surtsey had changed the charts of the Atlantic, echoing the primordial birth of the world.

Hekla concluded its centuries of silence in 1970, with an eruption in the spring storms that startled the entire country. Three years later, on a chill night in late January, two fishermen in the Westmann Islands were walking off the effects of an all-night party in the sheep meadows above the harbor. The entire island started to rumble, and before their frightened blood-shot eyes, the gentle ridge beyond their fishing village was torn apart in a series of wrenching explosions.

Searing geysers were shooting flame and showering molten lava into the moonlight, and the two fisherman ran drunkenly back toward the village. The Heimaney eruption lasted several weeks, and it almost destroyed the most important fishing center in the country, crushing its outbuildings and smothering everything under its falling volcanic ash. The older wood-frame structures were cremated and entombed. Spilling lava threatened to eradicate the steep-walled harbor below the village, but its ominous flowages finally stopped in a ragged breakwater with sulphurous fumes still rising from its smoking fissures. The volcanic eruptions had completely subsided in six months, and the hardy fisherfolk came back to salvage their possessions and dwellings and shops from their death shroud of bitter ashes. The fishing village of Heimaney had narrowly escaped the entombment that had sealed the fate of Pompei.

It is remarkable that no one was killed in the Heimaney eruption. The country and its people have not always been so fortunate. The terrible eruption of Laki on the southwest slopes of the Vatnajökull glaciers was the worst in their long history. It occurred in 1783, and its fumaroles and exploding vents and fissures spewed more lava and volcanic ash than any other eruption in the world. Its toxic fumes and smothering shrouds of ashes decimated crops and livestock throughout Iceland, and stained the pristine snowfields of Greenland and the Labrador farther west. Although there were no casualties in the Laki eruption itself, more than a fifth of the population starved in the terrible months that followed.

Since its harbor sheltered perhaps the finest fleet of modern fishing vessels, and its fish-processing plants were among the best in Europe, the Heimaney disaster had a serious impact on the country and its fragile economy—and the social and economic echoes of the eruption are still obvious today.

Like other remote populations, and rather like all people who live in the grinding isolation of sheep camps and high-plains farms and ships, the people of Iceland are fiercely preoccupied with their loneliness and sense of place. Such preoccupation sometimes surfaces in the mixture of myths and half-comic illusions and ancient truths that shape their character.

Such brooding introspection is both unique and more commonplace than the people of Iceland can accept or understand. Their barren little island is not unique in its isolation. Yet there are rhythms in the blood of these fair-skinned people that are startling, and those threnodic melodies were already forged in the singular literature of their Sagas, the beautiful vellum manuscripts prepared in the twelfth century.

Such ancient writings have often echoed the principal traits in the character of the people that produced them. Many scholars have observed, perhaps beginning with Charlemagne and his Carolingian renaissance, that Odysseus typified the psyche of classical times. Shakespeare obviously excelled in capturing both the spirit of his contemporaries and the timeless fingerprints of the human condition. Goethe and Wagner unmistakably displayed the disparate faces of cruelty and sentiment found in the German mind, and poets like Whitman and Sandburg and Frost have remarkably American voices. Iceland and the richly complex character of its people are captured in the storied Egil's Saga.

It is clearly a masterpiece in the tradition of Beowulf, and is the twelfth-century biography of Egil Skallagrimsson, an ancient warrior and poet buried at Borgarnes. Its hero was restlessly volatile, fierce and independent and hopelessly stubborn, filled with a sense of righteous vengeance, eager for enterprise and action, embittered in his ancient feuds and grudges, utterly fearless and proud, quarrelsome and irreverent and foolishly quick to argue, and the willing prisoner of his appetite for food and drink and ribaldry.

Skallagrimsson was also a skilled settler who chose and worked his farmstead prudently and prospered. His Saga portrays a devoted friend and fiercely combative comrade-at-arms, mixed with a loving father whose grief at the death of his sons drives him to the threshold of madness. His sanity is ultimately protected by his poetry, and its sad music both purges his grief and demonic anger and forges his place in our history.

No other personage in the medieval literature of Iceland so completely captures the puzzle of its character, and the seemingly incompatible traits that form the paradox of its people. Skallagrimsson embodies the conflicting skills of farming, shephered, seamanship, warfare, patriarchal wisdom, and poetry in a single protagonist who actually existed, and the rich calligraphy of his Saga contains such lines as these amid its bitter feuds and hardships:

Neither gleams the gold in me
Nor gaudy letters shine;
My beauty is all held within myself,
For learning makes me fine.

During the twelfth century, the making of books throughout Europe literally depended on livestock and animal hides. The artisans who made the medieval Sagas used calfskins. The rich literary period that flowered between the twelfth and fourteenth centuries in Iceland suggests large herds of cattle and prosperity, since a large supply of calfskins was needed to produce the remarkable vellum found in the surviving manuscripts at Reykjavik.

The hides were first shaved with scraping tools and sharp knives. Great patience and skill were required to prepare them, since the skins were stripped completely free of hair and flesh, without scarifying or cutting the delicate calfskin itself. Such flaws were common in medieval manuscripts, and the calligraphers often concealed them with ornamental designs or leapfrogged them in the middle of a word. When a fresh hide had been completely shaved, it was carefully scraped and cleaned and pulled. It was stretched on a sturdy frame, pulled and carefully kneaded like bread and then painstakingly stretched again. The pulling tool was called a *brak,* and it was typically a circular or horseshoe-shaped die of horn. The fresh calfskin was twisted tightly until it could be pulled back and forth through the *brak* until it became soft and pliable. Patient craftsmanship with such simple tools created a fine parchment, its texture and character and color not unlike the finest grades of paper, but these medieval calfskins were stronger and richly soft.

The calfskins were finally trimmed into single pages, and in the largest folios there were pages consisting of a single parchment hide with its irregular borders trimmed. Folding an entire skin into two leaves formed a folio size, while cutting a single calfskin into paired sheets created a four-leaf fold called a quarto. Folded skins were finally arranged in sections of eight leaves, like the quires or signatures in more modern books. Before the calligraphers lettered and illuminated these freshly prepared skins, both columns and lines were carefully defined with a stylus.

It is unlikely that a country as sparsely populated as twelfth-century Iceland, lying just beyond the cartographic knowledge of European scholars, could have produced the number of scribes and artisans found in the British Isles. Yet literacy and the ability to write were surprisingly widespread throughout medieval Iceland. Some calligraphers and scribes were obviously more skilled than their colleagues. The richly illuminated pages of the famous *Flateyjarbók* manuscripts were copied by priests for a wealthy landowner in northern Iceland, and their exceptional skills at calligraphy and ornamentation are still visible in Reykjavik today.

The scribes made their inks from boiling the juices of the bearberry plant. Its pigments are dark and glossy and remarkably durable. Such properties have proved important, since these ancient manuscripts have survived striking ordeals and odysseys.

Their pens were surprisingly crude, commonly fashioned of the primary wing-feather quills of upland geese and swans, although sometimes other birds were used. *With this quill pen I am well pleased,* confirms an ancient passage, *though it is from a raven's wing.*

The production of these manuscripts itself was obviously difficult and expensive. The exquisite *Flateyjarbók* contains 225 parchment leaves, requiring the skins of more than 100 calves. Both the painstaking preparation of so many calfskins and the elegant lettering and illumination of the leaves themselves unmistakably demonstrate the time and patience and art involved in creating the Sagas. This passage from *Eirik's Saga* describes the ill-fated colony in Newfoundland:

The ships cast anchor there and waited, and after three days the scouts came running back to the shore: one was carrying some grapes, and the other had some wild wheat. They both told Karlsefni that they thought they had found good earth. Both were taken back on board, and the expedition sailed on until it reached a fjord. The ships were steered into it. Near its mouth lay an island, where there flowed strong currents, and they named it Straumey.

There were so many birds there, it was impossible to walk between their eggs. The party named the place Straumfjard, and unloaded their ships and settled into their camp. They had brought livestock and they searched for food. There were mountains and the country was beautiful, and they spent much time exploring it. Tall grass was everywhere.

Such ancient manuscripts give tiny Iceland and its people a remarkable sense of continuity and history. Since their language is virtually unchanged after more than 1,000 years, schoolchildren can read these medieval manuscripts as easily as our children read the King James Bible.

It has been argued that the people who live in the farmsteads and fishing villages and remote sheepfolds of Iceland are often the most acutely conscious of its traditions. Among such reclusive people are typically found its most striking characters. The sheepherders and farmers are less touched by urban life, and each valley has its people worth meeting. Deeply rooted in their ancient stories, and often surprisingly versed in poetry and their own literature and the classics, such country people are also remarkably current in their knowledge of the world.

Hospitality is the unwritten rule on these remote farmsteads, and entire families are eager to debate and wrangle over world affairs with outsiders. Some speak several languages well. Their arguments are often sharp and challenging. During past centuries, these people were passionately involved in life, and it has always been unthinkable not to receive a traveler and offer shelter without charge.

The sense of history is strong in these households. Such involvement is more easily understood when we see that virtually each settlement has visible echoes of some event in the Sagas, or the violence that has scarred later centuries. There is a charming story which perfectly illustrates the role that the ancient manuscripts still play on the modern farmsteads. A traveler passing through a back-country region once stopped at a solitary sheepfold, where he overheard the sheepmen discussing a death in the district. One deplored the fact that death had come tragically at an early age, and the other speculated on the remarkable gifts and skills that had been unhappily lost to their country. The stranger finally succumbed to his curiosity, but when he asked the shepherds who had died, he was told that they had been talking about Skarphedin Njalsson, a character in the thirteenth-century masterpiece Njal's Saga.

Fisherfolk in the coastal villages display similar character throughout the country. These seafarers are part of the oldest traditions of their population, working on modern trawlers fitted with the most sophisticated fishing and navigation equipment available. The coastal seas are unusually fertile off Iceland, with their singular alchemy of Arctic currents and hydrothermal seepages and the ebbing flowages of the Gulf Stream. Marine life thrives there, including the finest surviving populations of Atlantic salmon, since these sea-bright fish are protected from coastal harvest. Using their modern equipment, the skilled fishermen of Iceland harvest six times the tonnages of other species per capita than the commercial fishermen of any other country.

The fishermen of the capital are typical, and the coastal fisheries account for more than ninety percent of the domestic economy and virtually all of the foreign exchange. Reykjavik harbor is larger than the other fishing ports, with its bobbing masts and brightly painted hulls and throbbing engines. The chill wind smells of herring and kelp fields and salt water. The stonework quays glisten in the summer rain, and coveys of fish trucks gather for the cargo carried below the blood-spattered decks of the trawlers. The work continues busily until long after nightfall, with burly crewmen in boots and bright-yellow slickers working under the floodlights, covered with blood and fish slime and glittering scales.

Like all seaport towns across the world, Reykjavik has its share of drinking and entertainment on its waterfront, although there are no taxi dancers or prostitutes. There are bars that cater to fishermen, while their officers and shipowners gravitate to the tiny cocktail loft above the Naust, a superb little restaurant fitted like the hold of a sailing ship. Singing is a skill highly prized in Iceland too, and voices are often raised into the early morning hours, lubricated by whisky and other spirits and a local beer so weak that only a skilled chemist could detect its alcohol.

Yet the fishermen and sailors in Reykjavik and the other coastal villages are unusual. Bookstores are as important in their lives, and in the life of the entire country, as the restaurants and dance halls and waterfront bars. These seafaring men are voracious readers, and form a surprisingly large percentage of the customers who purchase a remarkable 500,000 books each year. Such sales total more than twice the population of the country. Sixty publishing houses exist to serve a market of fewer than 60,000 families, and the population of Iceland reads and publishes and writes many more books per capita than any other country in the world.

Literature is startlingly alive among these people. Simple farmers and fisherfolk can recite whole collections of poetry, often using bars and restaurants for their spontaneous performances, and some are combatively eager to argue recent trends in literature and its sister arts. Such fishermen and farmers often have extensive libraries, including many volumes in both English and Latin.

General R. N. Stewart is well known throughout the country for his little book *The Rivers of Iceland,* and its chapters are charmingly based upon almost forty years on its salmon fisheries. Stewart wrote engagingly of seventeen rivers, including such famous streams as the Viddidalsá, Midfjardará and Vatnsdalsá, which are consistently among the most productive waters in the country. His simple prose also tells warmly of his encounter with a remarkably literate shepherd in the beautiful little valley at Borg:

> I think our main attraction was that we had some whisky, but he was always interesting late in the evening, having a fund of stories and folklore which were great fun to hear. During one of his first visits, he asked if we were scholars. Perhaps we had both rather boasted of our education in the United Kingdom, with the result that our guest insisted on speaking in Latin. I hope we bluffed him into thinking that we understood him; as he persisted in the practice I believe we must have done, but never again have we laid claim to any education.

Since the country has virtually no poverty, and few families of extensive wealth, its people have evolved a relatively small society that is remarkably free of class distinctions. Each citizen seemingly feels as secure as his neighbors, and is both strikingly and combatively conscious of his worth.

These people are largely the children or grandchildren of simple farmers and fisherfolk and sailors, and since there is free mobility between all walks of life, little feeling of inferiority exists in the so-called working class of Iceland.

Fishermen and skilled workers and farmers are often better paid than teachers and professionals and public officials, but educated people are still deeply respected. Although their compensation is often less generous, such people are the acknowledged keepers of a flame that can be traced to the myths and warriors of the ninth century. Sigurdur Magnusson, a well-known writer in Reykjavik, made the following observation in *Atlantica:*

> The man of action and enterprise is still highly esteemed, but the character closest to the heart of everyone in Iceland is the creative spirit: the poet, the painter and sculptor, the composer, and the scholar.

However, in spite of its modern society and its ancient respect for learning, the population of Iceland remains surprisingly committed to the myths and superstitions and folklore of its beginnings. Pagan beliefs still lurk behind a facade of Protestant culture. Ancestor worship is almost Oriental in its widespread intensity, and the ancient gods and spirits of nature found in Scandinavian mythology are quite alive in Iceland.

Spirits are as real to many people as their neighbors. Seers and palm-readers and psychics prosper, along with mediums who focus on the interpretation of dreams. Most valleys in the country have enchanted places, and their role in the daily lives of the people is sometimes surprising: in recent months the population of a community in northern Iceland stopped the construction of a highway because its citizens sought to protect an enchanted ravine.

Yet it should be understood that in less than three generations, these remarkable people have transformed themselves from an almost medieval society into a contemporary welfare state with obvious echoes of Sweden and Norway. It is difficult to comprehend the social and psychological impacts of such rapid growth and change. Sigurdur Magnusson also offered these perceptions in *Atlantica:*

> Our people are a rather quarrelsome lot. They love heated argument and verbal fencing, and in this respect they resemble their Irish cousins. They like to think of themselves as a rational people, but in actual fact they tend to be much more emotional than rational. They approach most issues emotionally, even though they will always try to make their emotions seem rational in any discussion. One noteworthy thing about them is that they have never produced any original or profound thinker. Philosophy is almost nonexistent, while poetry thrives.

Since the worship of nature is deeply rooted in these people, both salmon and their tumbling rivers figure strongly in their poetry and myths. The country has sixty-odd salmon fisheries, and several of its rivers are among the finest in the world.

Although the Atlantic salmon is threatened with extinction almost everywhere in its range, the fertile rivers of Iceland are still virtually untouched. The threat to the species has evolved from the combination of modern fisheries technology, the effects of pollution and changing land use and dams and the discovery of large marine feeding-grounds off Sukkertoppen in western Greenland. Denigration of the parent rivers has existed since medieval times, and was accelerated explosively after the Industrial Revolution.

Since the Second World War, the development of drift-net systems created the first fisheries technology capable of harvesting vast tonnages of salmon on the open seas. Such nets were impossible before the invention of synthetic materials like nylon and polyacrylonitrile fibers and dacron. Suddenly net fibers of remarkable strength were available, and those fibers lasted much longer than mesh structures of cotton or linen. Drift-net systems as extensive as thirty-five miles were possible, set like vast, invisible curtains across the feeding routes of the salmon. Sonar has been employed to locate the migrating schools. The flotation devices supporting these mesh barriers included signal floats fitted with tiny electronic devices that could tell a factory ship that its drift nets had intercepted a school of fish, and precisely where its meshes were filling along its thirty-odd miles of length. The factory ship itself was fitted with cooling rooms and freezers sophisticated enough to get fish as delicate as Atlantic salmon back to the shops and delicatessens and restaurants of Europe.

Drift-net technology soon spread across the coastal waters of northern Europe, decimating salmon populations from Portugal to the Arctic forests of Lapland. Other marine fisheries harvested vast tonnages of salmon spawned in rivers from Maine to the subarctic barrens at Ungava Bay. The storied salmon fisheries of the British Isles suffered an almost mortal blow when the effects of serious droughts, a fresh infestation of the salmon disease that had crippled European rivers a century ago, overfishing in estuaries and coastal waters, and the drift-net fishery off Greenland were all combined in recent years. Spain and France are virtually finished as salmon-producing countries. Baltic fisheries are almost totally based on the planting of hatchery smolts to sustain the commercial fleets, and salmon have been extinct in Switzerland and Germany since the First World War. The famous salmon rivers of Norway have been largely stripped of their giant fish through extensive netting from Oslo to Hammarfest in less than a dozen years.

Catches in the Maritime Provinces of Canada also plummeted, and even the wilderness fisheries in Quebec, Newfoundland, and the Labrador were badly hurt. Government attempts to restore several salmon rivers in Maine displayed limited success before these efforts were checkmated in the waters off Greenland, with Danish fishing boats making the largest harvests; several million dollars had merely supplied smoked fish for the Copenhagen markets.

The salmon rivers of Iceland have escaped a similar fate. The state of its fisheries is the product of an intriguing combination of ecology and legislation and self-interest. Both its rivers and its coastal seas are remarkably fertile, and that unusual fertility comes from its volcanic roots and hydrothermal discharges, combined with the rich nutrients carried north in the Gulf Stream.

These coastal feeding grounds are so richly populated with forage species that few salmon apparently migrate beyond the waters of Iceland itself. Large schools of salmon simply circle its coastlines, riding the marine currents while they fatten themselves on silvery armadas of pilchard and tiny crustaceans and capelin.

The farmers of the country own the fishing rights on their salmon rivers, and those rights must be rented in the European tradition. The rural interests of Iceland have largely dominated its parliament since its founding at Thingvellir in 930, and to protect their remarkable fisheries, the farmers pressed for legislation that declared the salmon the property of the parent rivers that spawned them. These fisheries laws, which were written almost fifty years ago, banned all commercial harvesting of salmon from coastal waters. Commercial traps were also banned from the rivers themselves, except for hereditary netting rights in the milky glacier-silt flowages of the Hvitá and Olfusá. Since its half-comic codfish wars with British fishing boats and frigates, Iceland has extended its coastal juridiction to 200 miles, and this combination of factors promises to protect the best salmon fisheries left in the world.

Salmon fishermen are almost as migratory as the silvery, sea-armored fish that possess them, and restlessly search their shrinking range for salmon rivers that offer fine sport. It was the salmon fishing that first carried me to Reykjavik, after more familiar rivers had experienced a shocking decline. Like other salmon fishermen, who had fished rivers like the Spey and Restigouche and Laerdal, I had turned to explore the storied rivers of Iceland.

Fishermen dominate its population, and the citizens of the capital catch halibut and mackerel and codfish from its piers and breakwaters. Fishing tackle is a common bond throughout the country, and the young customs inspector smiled when he studied my baggage cart piled with baggage and salmon-fishing equipment.

Flugustengur? the inspector asked.

It was a little like Norwegian and I nodded. *That's right,* I said. *They're bamboo fly rods in a canvas carrier.*

Salmon fisherman? he asked.

Yes, I replied. *I've taken a week's fishing at Husavik.*

The Laxá in Pingeyjarsysla? the inspector said.

How did you know? I brightened.

It's the best river there. The customs inspector slipped the butter-colored Garrison back into its aluminum tube. *You'll proabably fish with the best riverkeeper in Iceland—he's a retired teacher who lives at Neskirkju and a fine poet too.*

What is his name? I asked.

Steingrimur Baldvinsson, the inspector said.

The chill morning stirred, and the sullen roaring of the waterfalls at Gullfoss thundered into their gaping earthquake fissure.

Postpile cliffs are lost in drifting spray, where the entire river plunges into a gorge as somber as a freshly dug grave.

Somewhere in the treeless hills a solitary sheepdog was barking, and the pale morning light filled the moors. The wind stirred again, sifting a fresh snowfall in the empty chocolate-colored pass at Kaldidalur. The wind grew stronger in its brooding cornices, and the dust of snow scattered across its barren deserts. The wintry gusts were bitter now, and soot-colored clouds obscured the morning sky. The harsh wind rattled stones along the pass, showering bright snow plumes against a darkening sky, and scuttling a flock of ptarmigan toward shelter in the craters and potholes.

The bright colors along the morning horizon were gone, and it was starting to rain when we loaded our equipment into the airport bus. Keflavik is like military airfields across the world, and its characterless structures rival the drab collage of Bentwaters and Furstenfeldbrück and Tachikawa.

The airport highway crosses a disappointing landscape of lava fields and cooling fissures and cinder cones. Its utter lack of character is the principal reason for building the airfield there during the Second World War, when the convoys sailing to Russia were battered in fierce battles with submarine wolf packs. The emptiness of these lava-field barrens offered excellent instrument approaches to its runways when instrument-landing techniques were still primitive, and bad weather was frequent throughout the year.

There are no trees to relieve its emptiness, and the half-wild sheep huddled in the rain are the only signs of life. The sea lies beyond the highway, and a small flotilla of fishing boats from Vogar and Njardvikur was working its leaden swells. The pitiful cairns of stone beside the highway served in the old days to mark the route in winter, when it was a mere pony trace in the snow.

Reykjavik lies ahead across the water, with its fishing-port suburbs at Kopavogur and Hafnarfjordur. Its bright skyline is surrounded by somber foothills and mountains and craters, and beyond the capital lie the softly folded summits of Esja.

The capital itself has filled its peninsula with houses and office buildings and apartments. It has its roots in the ninth century, when the Viking chieftain Ingolfur Arnarsson came ashore and decided to build his turf-walled longhouse there. Such dwelling forms had their origins in Norway, roughly boat-shaped in plan with longitudinal walls of stonework banked with turf insulation. Simple timber trusswork spanned their living spaces in the smaller houses, with rows of poles supporting the roofs of larger farmsteads. Stave planking defined the interior walls and shaped the roof, which was sheathed in thick layers of sod. The cookfire was in a central pit directly below the smoke vent at the ridge beam. Primitive dwellings of this character were common in the Scandinavian countries.

The first farmstead at Reykjavik stood between the rocky cover that sheltered the longboats and the freshwater pond and boiling springs that still form the Tjarnargata gardens. Its site is still echoed in the streets there. Adalstraeti is the ancient pathway leading from the turf house to the boat landing. Sudurstraeti and Tungata were the pony trace leading toward the south and the footpath that crossed the house meadows. Austurvollur is the tiny square beside the Althing, the parliament building of Iceland, and its name simply tells us that it was once a field lying east of Arnarsson's farmstead site. Reykjavik itself is named for the smoking hot springs above its sheltering harbor, and the ancient farmstead settled by Ingolfur Arnarsson has grown into a modern city of 100,000 people.

Its starkly concrete houses and high-rise apartments and hospitals are surprising. Boulevards and parkways are lined with graceful street lamps, and there are clusters of neighborhood shops. The houses are typically white, their corrugated roofs painted the red and bright blue and green found throughout Scandinavia, and the older houses are sometimes sheltered with a few carefully cultivated trees. Such bright roofs in these bleak latitudes suggest that these people are attempting to preserve a sense of warmth and shelter, and that behind their doors is a world of food and family life.

Reykjavik is entirely heated with boiling water from the famous hydrothermal springs at Reykir, transported sixteen miles into the city through a pair of earth-covered aqueducts. The hot water for the capital is transported from hot springs too. Reykjavik is virtually free of pollution, except for its relatively light traffic and its fishmeal factory.

It smells, its people joke when an offshore wind fills the waterfront with its odors, *but it smells like money!*

Like its sister capitals in Scandinavia, Reykjavik is quite modern and carefully planned and clean. Its older buildings include the parliament and fisheries bank and the stolid offices of *Morgunbladid,* the principal newspaper in Iceland. There is a strikingly modern cathedral, its intricately carved bell tower rising above its neighbors in the old quarter of the city, and its partially completed nave is still hidden in its cocoon of scaffolding. Its streets and character are a pleasant surprise to travelers from England and the United States.

Hafnarstraeti, Laekjargata and Austurstraeti are the principal thoroughfares above the harbor and the focus of life in the capital. The Loftleidir and Saga are large and comfortable hotels, although many seasoned visitors still like the solemn Borg in Parliament Square for its echoes of the past. The Holt and Esja are smaller hotels, but both are modern and have excellent restaurants. Hafnarstraeti has fine shops like Rammargerdin and Islenskur Heimilisidnadur, with richly stocked shelves of jewelry and handmade woolens and handicrafts typical of the country. It also shelters several fine bookstores with large selections of titles in English. Some visitors like the restaurant called Odal in the Austurvollur, but most agree that the most pleasant dining in Reykjavik is found at Naust.

After several hours of sleep, I met with Sigurdur Magnusson over lunch at the Loftleidir. Magnusson is an immensely knowledgeable writer well known in London and Reykjavik and New York, where he worked in both journalism and public relations. His skills helped me confront the native foods in the sprawling buffet tables, and he ordered a bottle of Piesporter.

There are no rules for the cold table, Magnusson explained, *except that you choose anything you like, and you go back as often as you want and you clean your plate each time.*

Where do you usually start? I asked.

We usually start with the herring. There were a dozen kinds, pickled in various sauces in earthenware crocks. *We usually eat the herring with some rugbraud and sweet butter.*

Are these large shrimps?

Those are tiny lobsters called smàhumar, Magnusson said, *and you should try the dried halibut in butter sauce—it's a special delicacy we call riklingur.*

We circled the buffet tables indecisively.

Ptarmigan in the dark berry sauce is excellent too, he suggested, *and try a little hangikjot.*

What is hangikjot? I asked.

It's smoked lamb, Magnusson replied wryly. *It's probably our favorite dish—except for cauliflower and potatoes.*

We filled our plates with herring and ptarmigan and halibut and smoked lamb, and returned to our window table. The young wine steward carefully served the Piesporter.

The herring is excellent, I said.

You like it? Magnusson laughed. *We've got other things like hákarl and svidásulta too—if you really feel sporting!*

What are they? I asked warily.

Hákarl is a river-cured shark's meat, he replied. *It's sliced into thin strips and buried in river gravel.*

Buried? I asked. *Buried how long?*

Magnusson laughed. *It's usually several weeks.*

Several weeks? I said weakly. *It's raw?*

Raw! Magnusson laughed heartily.

Doesn't it smell a little?

It smells, Magnusson admitted waggishly. *We won't be disappointed if you don't try the hákarl today!*

I'm afraid to ask about the svidásulta! I said.

Boiled sheep's heads, Magnusson continued with mock solemnity, *preserved in a marinade of sour whey.*

What about the eyes? I asked gingerly.

We eat svidásulta, he laughed, *eyes and all!*

I'll stick with the herring, I said.

Magnusson is a writer in a tiny nation of poets and writers, and our talk soon turned to the touch of the poet in its entire population. He spoke warmly of the simple rhythms of life in the fishing villages and farms, and the deeply rooted sense of place that the people had for their country. Magnusson believed that the past was quite alive in his people, and finally I told him about the old woman on the flight coming in from New York.

She seemed utterly at peace with herself, I explained, *and told me that she was coming home to die with her people—and everything she said had a kind of poetry.*

We are still simple fishermen and country folk, Magnusson nodded when I finished. *No matter what we are doing or where we are living, and it is both our failing and our strength—but we live close to the earth and the sea, and that sustains us.*

But she was so matter-of-fact about dying!

Cities isolate people from the ancient truths and cycles of life, Magnusson continued. *They can't watch the wind on the moors, watch their crops growing in earth they have tilled, butcher their animals for meat or really smell the changing seasons of the year—and it's possible to forget the old truths that all life is sustained by death, and that the ritual of death always completes it.*

That's probably true, I said.

Magnusson described his life on the country farmsteads, talking about cutting the hayfields long after midnight, and the white-painted farm buildings with their bright blood-colored roofs. The sitting rooms and kitchens and sleeping quarters are spotless, and he remembers his mother polishing table glasses in the light of her sun-filled curtains, like a figure in a painting by Vermeer.

Fishing boots and shoes are left at the threshold, like the clogs left on the woven matting outside a Japanese tea house, and heavy knitted socks are common footwear. Most farms have telephones and electricity now, but some country exchanges accept calls only a few hours a day, and candles and oil lamps are common. The plumbing is simple but adequate, although bathtubs are rare. Fine books and original oil landscapes and music boxes are found in virtually every farmhouse. Vintage clocks and intricately carved snuff boxes and harmoniums are typical too, and sometimes there is a fine violin. Particularly old and prosperous farmsteads boast a piano, and several centuries can be studied in their leather-bound family Bibles.

Simple gardens and livestock and hayfields provide the staples for their families. Life is difficult in a country where the cattle and sheep must winter in barns. Their forage must be harvested from the river meadows and stored in the brief summer. The winter's food for the families must also be gathered then, and the climate can turn hostile in any season.

The country diet is probably too limited, Magnusson admitted unhappily. *Meat and potatoes can mean a lot of heart trouble.*

And few telephones and doctors, I added.

That's often true, he agreed. *Last winter I lost an old friend who died of exposure during a blizzard, trying to collect his flocks only three hundred meters from his dooryard.*

Tell me about funerals on the farmsteads, I said.

Country funerals are typical, Magnusson replied, *but they would probably seem strange in Europe or America—our dead are simply kept in the farmhouses and are seldom embalmed before burial.*

Aren't the children frightened? I asked.

Not really, he said thoughtfully. *The period of mourning in the farmhouse is called the Husvedja—it's an ancient custom in the countryside that goes back to our beginnings.*

How old is the Husvedja? I asked.

Its roots lie back beyond the twelfth century, he replied, *and it probably is part of our Viking heritage. Everyone in the valley comes to visit the dead.*

It seems barbaric, I responded.

Perhaps it comes from barbaric times, Magnusson nodded, *when the dead were placed on funeral pyres and chieftains were set adrift in burning longboats under full sail. But now it seems almost like the dead are merely sleeping, and members of the family sometimes stop their work to talk with them and kiss them.*

Children too? I asked.

Country people have little fear of death, he said.

It's remarkable, I said.

Our farmers are pretty remarkable people, Magnusson agreed thoughtfully. *Many of them participate in the local councils, work skillfully and hard on their lands, are passionately interested in politics, read widely in several subjects and languages, know the local fauna and plant species and birds, and are often writers and poets too.*

Like the riverkeeper on the Laxá in Pingeyjarsysla, I interrupted. *Steingrimur Baldvinsson.*

Steingrimur is a perfect example, he said.

We lingered over coffee and cognac, talking about fishing and the riverkeeper on the Laxá who was also famous for his poetry. Magnusson pointed out that Baldvinsson liked to structure his work with familiar images of fishing and country things, using these commonplace echoes as metaphors for life itself, much like the poetry of Robert Frost. Reciting effortlessly from memory, Magnusson offered several passages to buttress his thesis about Baldvinsson and his work:

Wearing green and gold-embroidered shoes,
Spring walks through our wintry valley.
Pale hope, shining with bright and joyful eyes,
Walks hand in hand with springtime.
Winter senses death in its first thawing snows,
Retreats and flees our world,
Hiding in the hills.

There were somber examples of his verses too, and Magnusson spoke of the poems Baldvinsson had written about his stepmother's death. The strong contrapuntal themes of sorrow and happiness were obvious in his work; melancholy echoed his winters when sunlight appeared briefly in his arctic latitudes, and the circling of the seasons became important symbols of his world. Some of his poetry has an almost mystical perspective of the seasons, like these final lines about the death of summer:

Cold raindrops touch my flowing river,
And the shining blackness of the roof slates
Will answer like the footsteps of
Some dark ceremony: and
I listen—but who is there?

Baldvinsson had a remarkable escape from death in the wintry moors of Pingeyjarsysla, and that encounter became the source of one of his best poems. It describes falling through a false snow bridge that concealed a dark pothole in the lava fields at Neskirkju. Baldvinsson was walking home from teaching school when a bitter February storm caught him without warning, and he spent almost five days in the darkness of that cold prison. Expecting death from hunger and exposure, the young poet suffered a terrible test of his strength and spirit. His fierce intensity is found in these lines:

Feel a thick and closing darkness,
Breathing slowly tightens.
But life still glows outside this gloom;
It once was mine,

It is certain that many people
Forget life's shining happy gift of light;
Until that fading sun, few seemingly stop to
Write eulogies in cold earth.

I thought that I had understood
How winter twilight is filled with dark foreboding;
Yet there was no secret warning in my heart,
Such fearful music in the wind.

How could any mortal really know
Such terror cloaks our wintry twilights;
Darkness holds such bitter darkness,
And such deathly silences.

Baldvinsson obviously took great pleasure in both his river and his salmon-fishing skills, and both were sometimes important images in his poetry. There are many references to the river and its fishing in many poems across the years. It is a richly fertile river, its flowing weeds and fountain mosses a legacy of the hot-spring basins in its headwaters. Its principal wellsprings lie in the crystalline lagoons in the highlands of Myvatn, where hundreds of thousands of waterfowl find shelter among the drowned cinder cones and lava chimneys. Its fertile bottom is richly layered with marl, and the river that spills from the broken ledges at its outlet winds almost like an English chalkstream through its Arctic valley. The serpentine river and its muses obviously filled his heart:

Here where the Laxá flows,
Softly playing the tunes of her lyre,
It becomes almost easy to forget my sorrows,
Coming to know I can never
Feel loneliness.

Our discussions returned to the surprising literary tradition that exists in modern Iceland, and the remarkable number of poets and writers there. The writer Halldor Laxness, whose books *Salka Valka* and *The Fish Can Sing* have earned him the Nobel Prize, is a remarkable figure in such a small population. Magnusson argued that the country has a unique cultural heritage that favors writers and poets, mixing its singularly unbroken literary history with isolation in its northern seas, and a bitter climate to temper its people.

Our winters have played an important role, Magnusson insisted. *Our isolation has protected and purified our language, and the length of our winters has given us the opportunity to dream and think richly and sharpen our feeling for words.*

Like their neighbors from Copenhagen to Helsinki, the people of Iceland revel in their fleeting summers after the winter nights. Sunbathers emerge from their winter cocoons at the most ephemeral opportunity, and during those few summer weeks when the sun never sets, it is possible to schedule a round of golf after midnight. Most people prefer sunbathing or swimming in the public baths or feeding the ducks with their children in the Tjarnargardur gardens. Some prefer to putter in their vegetable gardens, or spend their summer weekends in the huts and simple summer houses outside Reykjavik. Still others like the hardier life of fishing and pony-trekking and camping in the mountains. There is a seemingly pathological fear of flabby muscles, and many of these people drive themselves in strenuous summer leisure. Winter is the time for more contemplative moods.

We sleep and read books and eat in winter, Magnusson laughed. *But serious literature takes time, and our country is blessed with winters that seem like centuries!*

How many poets and writers do you have?

It's really impossible to tell, he replied slowly, *because we have poets and writers in every valley in the country—we have so many that they hold poetry matches.*

Poetry contests? I suggested.

Not contests or competetions, he said. *Poetry matches!*

What are they like? I asked.

Magnusson explained that the fishing villages and remote valleys hold extemporaneous competitions between local poets in the schools and community halls. Large audiences gather to hear their favorites recite their published work, as well as compose humorous verses and sardonic exchanges of wit. Success is ultimately measured in laughter and applause, and the serious poets of Iceland are still remarkably close to their ancient roles as minstrels and jesters.

Except for wrestling and chess, Magnusson concluded, *poetry is probably our national sport—and it's probably safe to admit that we have better poets and chess players than athletes.*

The weather grew steadily worse in the mountains. Rain squalls misted through the highlands, until huge flocks of geese along the Grimsavatn rose flapping toward the bottoms at Hvitabakki.

There were early summer campers in the scrub-birch thickets at Thingvellir, where the swift Oxnará tumbles through its earthquake fault. The rising wind snapped their bright-orange

tents like sails in their rigging, and their tethered ponies stirred restlessly at the scent of an arctic fox. The wind was stronger now, blowing chocolate-colored pebbles in the roads, and moaning through the strange, serrated fissures along the river bottoms.

The huge lake at Thingvellir had been smooth and smoke-colored at daylight, but the wind had stirred it into angry whitecaps under these sullen clouds. Waves broke fiercely on its rocky beaches. The wind still grew and howled past the sod-roofed farmhouses, rattling talcum-fine sleet across their windows. It billowed clouds of volcanic ash through the horse farms above the capital, and the driving rain filled the streets. The fierce squalls worked down the darkening fjord, driving their leaden swells into the breakwaters.

Magnusson had arranged a half-day ticket of salmon fishing on the tiny Elidaá, the swift little river that supplies potable water to Reykjavik and its suburbs. It rises in the foothills behind the capital, its headwaters a series of lagoons and shallow lakes and waterfalls in colonies of brightly painted cottages. Magnusson himself has a small summer house there, with a tiny vegetable and flower garden. Below the municipal reservoir, where the salmon smolts are released to wax fat on midge pupae and to suffuse their senses with the olfactory fingerprints of the Elidaá, the river actually winds through parts of the capital. Its serpentine pools and musical riffles flow through several clusters of high-rise apartments, and it passes a huge power station just before it spills into the tidal flats. Its fertility has been jealously protected from the rapid growth of Reykjavik, and it consistently surrenders 1,500 to 2,000 rod-caught salmon each season, in fishing beats that total less than five miles.

Ingolfur Arnarsson and his son Asgeir Ingolfsson were my hosts on the little river that afternoon. Arnarsson is a seasoned fisherman with a sparse shock of white hair, his spare features brought alive by his osprey-sharp eyes. Ingolfsson is a writer, and has done translations and contributed to *Morgunbladid* and television programs in Reykjavik. His skills on a salmon river are polished, fishing more delicate tackle than anyone else in Iceland, and he is remarkably knowledgeable about the salmon.

We met over breakfast and sat talking about the country and its salmon fisheries. *There are more than sixty salmon rivers in Iceland,* Arnarsson explained over coffee, *but there are only a few that regularly produce more than two thousand fish each season.*

Which are the best? I asked.

Several rivers near Reykjavik are good, Ingolfsson replied. *Particularly the Laxá at Kjos, and its sister Laxá in the Leirasveit valley farther along the coast. Both are small but quite productive.*

What about the northern rivers? I interrupted.

Those rivers are often excellent and have later runs of salmon, Arnarsson answered. *The seas are colder on the north coasts, but they have some excellent salmon fisheries, particularly rivers like the Viddidalsá and Midfjardará and Vatnsdalsá.*

What about the Hrutafjardará in the Hunafloi?

You've been reading the book written by General Stewart, Ingolfsson smiled. *Hrutafjardará was his favorite years ago.*

That's right, I said.

It's still a pretty good river, Ingolfsson continued, *but it's not in a class with the Midfjardará these days.*

Stewart also wrote about Laxadalur, I said.

That was on the Laxá in Dölum. Ingolfsson shook his head in agreement. *It is excellent sometimes, although it's a spate river and its salmon runs depend on its summer rainfall.*

General Stewart fished the Straumfjardará, too, I said. *What is its fishery like these days?*

It's a pretty small river on the Snaefjellsnes coast, Arnarsson explained. *Its fish are small too, but it fishes well.*

Haffjardará is the river there! Ingolfsson added.

That's right! Arnarsson agreed quickly. *It's a fine salmon river with two shallow lagoons in its headwaters, and those lakes are perfect nursery grounds for its baby salmon.*

They probably protect the spawned-out kelts in the winter too, I interjected. *Wintering the kelts is important.*

That's right, Ingolfsson agreed. *The entire river is owned by a single family, and it's been carefully looked after for fifty or sixty years—the river holds some really big fish.*

How large do its salmon run? I asked.

Most will run between eight and twelve pounds, Ingolfsson replied, *but there are some twenty-five-pounders.*

But we like the Borgafjordur rivers best, Arnarsson said.

Where is Borgafjordur? I asked.

It's the district at Borgarnes, Ingolfsson answered. *Its drainage basin has four of the best salmon rivers in Iceland.*

Borgarnes is a simple fishing village on the rocky headland in the tidal reaches of the Hvitá. It is the principal town in the most fertile valley in Iceland, and its sheltering amphitheater of mountains and glaciers spawn more than a dozen salmon fisheries. Four are among the most productive salmon rivers in the world: the pastoral Langá and its waterfall at tidewater, the rocky Thverá that rises in the barren central highlands, the moody Grimsá and its waterfalls, and the smooth-flowing Nordurá in the shadow of the Baula volcano, still regarded the Queen of Rivers among many of the anglers in Iceland.

Which are the best? I asked.

That's impossible to measure, Ingolfsson parried. *The best ones all produce two to three thousand salmon each summer, and each river is beautiful in its own right—but they're all completely different.*

Nordurá is a pretty early river, Arnarsson explained. *Its fish are already running before the middle of June.*

But its fish are getting stale in August, Ingolfsson said.

The other rivers fish well later? I asked.

That's right. Ingolfsson poured the last of the coffee. *The others are better in July and early August.*

Big fish too? I asked.

Six to twelve pounds mostly, Arnarsson replied. *Except for the Thverá and Grimsá—both rivers have fish over twenty pounds.*

The Grimsá has a few fish over thirty, Ingolfsson added.

That's a big salmon anywhere, I said.

Thirty pounds is a giant in Iceland, Ingolfsson said.

What about the Laxá at Husavik?

The Laxá in Pingeyjarsysla is probably our most famous river, Arnarsson said excitedly, *because it was fished by famous British fishermen like Ackroyd and Crosfield a century ago. It's in a class by itself, although it's an unusually moody river and surrenders its salmon grudgingly—but it has the biggest fish in Iceland.*

How big are they? I asked eagerly.

Laxá salmon will average twelve or thirteen pounds, Ingolfsson answered. *It produced our national-record too—a salmon of forty pounds caught by Jakob Hafstein in 1942.*

I can't wait to fish it! I said excitedly.

We drove out through the high-rise suburbs north of the capital, past the simple monument to the sturdy little ponies of Iceland and their primary role in the settlement of the country. It seemed improbable that a salmon fishery could survive among the row houses and apartment towers and stores that surround its tiny meadows completely.

When we registered for our fishing ticket, and reached our afternoon beat on the Elidaá itself, it seemed even less possible. The little river is scarcely twenty to thirty feet wide. Its salmon beats are on the lower river, starting with the first small pools above tidewater, and total only five miles of stream.

It seems completely impossible, I thought aloud, *that such a tiny stream could produce fifteen hundred to two thousand salmon a year.*

It's heavily stocked with smolts, Arnarsson explained.

We've had some problems too, Ingolfsson admitted. *Our worst pollution comes from a riding stable on the river.*

Well, I laughed, *coliforms are coliforms.*

You're right, Arnarsson nodded.

We sprawled in the warm grass along the river, enjoying a picnic lunch with a bottle of wine chilled in its riffles upstream, and waiting for our afternoon beats. The fishery laws in Iceland prescribe a limit of eight hours' fishing each day, and on most rivers in midsummer, the morning beats run from seven until one o'clock, while the afternoon fishing starts at four and lasts until ten. Since it does not really get dark from late May until late August in these latitudes, it is usually bright enough for color photography at curfew.

It's almost four o'clock, Arnarsson said.

They walked with me along the rented beats before the fishing started that afternoon, pointing out the best pools and holding places and taking-lies. There are no large pools typical of salmon fishing on a full-blown river, since the little Elidaá is more like a meadow trout stream. It offers a series of undercut banks and rocky little pools in its meandering coarse-grass channel. Swift runs spill across its lava outcroppings and ledges. Its serpentine bends sheltered deep holes that all held fish. There was one lava shelf so deeply undercut and cantilevered over its eddying currents that it was virtually a submerged cave, with almost as much volume of flow under its banks as the tiny pool itself. There were even fertile beds of aquatic weeds in the still pools and shallow flats, and in all of the likely holding-lies and currents, salmon were rolling and flashing.

It's full of fish! I thought.

Several times I rolled a salmon, hitching a small double-hook Fitchtail in a smooth-flowing lie, but I could not coax the fish into taking the fly. Salmon porpoised and jumped everywhere, falling back clumsily into the tiny pools or almost beaching themselves on the grassy banks, flopping until they regained the river. Several others flashed and boiled under my hitching fly, sometimes engulfing its skimming wake in a rolling black-spotted wallowing, but the salmon were not actually taking it. Ingolfsson hooked a small fish downstream.

It took a small Silver Grey! he shouted.

There was a small Silver Grey in my fly book and I tried it. Three casts later, there was a strong pull and a fish was hooked briefly before the fly pulled out. Another fish took and sheared free when it sliced the tippet across an abrasive outcropping.

Desperate rummaging through my bulging vest failed to locate a second Silver Grey, but I found several sparse Silver Rats dressed on size-ten doubles. There was a smoothly bulging current against the trailing grass, and a salmon flashed along the bottom before I could finish clinch-knotting the Silver Rat to my tippet. The second cast dropped tight against the grass, and I mended the line to slow the fly-swing where the fish had shown itself. There was another flash that boiled up into the currents and a strong pull.

He took it! I thought happily.

It was not a large fish, but six or seven pounds is a handsome salmon on such a tiny river, and it fought gamely. Twice it cartwheeled across the entire pool, and finally it hopscotched wildly downstream, scattering fish with its struggles. It surrendered in a foam-flecked backwater and I laid it gently in the wild flowers.

Congratulations! Ingolfsson called.

Fishing packets and trawlers still rocked clumsily at their moorings in the morning. The weather was getting better. Rolling swells still rose and spilled over the breakwaters. The cold wind was still singing in the ship rigging, and the fishing boats were draped with their folded nets and trawl floats. Gulls and terns swarmed about their masts and followed the boats offshore, foraging shrilly in the wakes of the successful trawlers. Mergansers and mallards huddled inside the quays and jetties, riding out the dying echoes of the storm.

Beyond the rooftops of the city, the ancient folds and shattered crusts of the lava fields were a spectrum of subtle colors. Their dark, heat-polished outcroppings still glistened with rain. The rich palette of chocolate and rust-colored oranges and tarnished yellows were frozen in flowages that had congealed centuries before. Lichens and wild flowers had filled the fissures and healed their wounds. From the twin-engine Fokker flying to Husavik, the abrasive spillages and broken skeletons of these lava fields are softer, like giant stone flowers pressed between the pages of a farmstead Bible.

Hot springs seethed and gurgled in the foothills too, their seepages and lagoons forming intricate little atolls, encrusted with pale, minuscule escarpments of crystalline rime. Phytoplankton created potholes of startling colors. Shallow pools glittered like shattered mirrors in the early morning light. Broken shards of reflections were pink and bright emerald and azure between fissures breathing smoke and steam. Bleached growths like cauliflowers and chalk-colored sponges were shiny with hot foam at Geysir, after its towering explosion of boiling water and steam was spent. Its smoking vent still gurgled with tiny waves and spume that spread rhythmically across its shallows.

Coarse-maned ponies huddled together against the wind, their warm breath billowing like hot springs in the cold. Gyrfalcons were circling along the precipices at Esja, plummeting down past the cliffs and riding the growing thermals back along the rock chimneys. The somber postpile cliffs at Svartifoss were alive with nesting sea birds, and the feathers and pale droppings of thousands and thousands of guillemots and thick-billed murres and puffins stained the coast for miles. The graceful sea bridge at Dyrhola was the sanctuary for a lone sea eagle, its pale almond eyes malevolent and afire.

Our sturdy twin-engine Fokker taxied out past the corrugated hangars and outbuildings at Reykjavik, and its landing gear trundled noisily toward the takeoff threshold. It paused there for its engine checks while a brightly painted Apache settled into its landing roll, and the pilot completed his checklist as the small plane came back along the apron. The Reykjavik tower cleared our departure.

The shrill turbine whine filled the narrow cabin, and we rotated and climbed out steeply past the cathedral and its scaffolding, turning toward Akureyri on the northern coast. The first officer adjusted the engine settings to a shrill purr, and we circled almost lazily above the brightly painted rooftops of Reykjavik.

The crowded piers and jetties of the harbor were under the plane, and the morning horizon was still somber and dark. The mountains were brooding beside a pewter-polished sea, and the snowfields beyond the whaling station in Kvalfjordur were shrouded in mists. The fjord there is remarkably deep, having the bathography to handle a carrier of the *Enterprise* class, and its seemingly peaceful mountains and empty stone beaches have witnessed more desperate times. There are still concrete ruins from the Second World War, when immense convoys of freighters and fighting ships rested and refitted there on the bitter voyages between our eastern ports and Murmansk. There is still a naval fuel dump there, with corrugated military huts and grass-covered ordnance magazines and storage tanks. Those were desperate years, when the German wolf packs left the horizons filled with burning and sinking ships, and the parties that echoed through these remote farmsteads had a wild threnody that tried to forget those cruel seas.

The Åkranes ferry was returning to its moorings in the Myrargata, trailing scraps of smoke across the pale harbor. The wind had dropped down and the rain had stopped. The weather was getting better offshore, and the faint sun glittered weakly beyond Borgarnes. It was already bright over the peninsula at Snaefjellsnes, and in the distance the mountains seemed strangely blue.

Beyond the sprawling basin at Thingvellir, the interior is an empty world extensively scarred by centuries of fire and ice. There are lava barrens of fissures and volcanic craters and fumeroles, mixed with sprawling deserts of pumice and fire-blackened moors and volcanic ash. These interior regions have often been compared to the moon, like the lava fields east of Sun Valley, or the spectacular Valley of Ten Thousand Smokes in Alaska.

Such lunar metaphors are perhaps too timid to describe the vast lava outcroppings at Askju or the emptiness of the Oddadhraun, which cover hundreds of square miles, although the astronauts who actually explored the moon first trained in these lava barrens.

It is difficult to imagine eruptions of such violence and scope. The first recorded eruption of Hekla occurred in 1104, and eradicated an entire settlement at Thjorsadalur. Hekla has erupted sixteen times since that disaster, causing widespread damage throughout the country. During its spectacular eruption in 1947, Hekla spewed an immense column of fire and acrid smoke and ash that rose more than 100,000 feet. Its spilling lava spread across more than thirty square miles, and its eruptions occurred sporadically for more than a year. Several minor craters and fissures surrounding Hekla have also produced some impressive fireworks, with perhaps the most famous eruption offering a grim portent of the First World War.

The bitter heritage of Hekla begins in *The Book of Wonders,* which was compiled at the monastery of Clairvaux in the twelfth century. It reported that the terrible eruptions that had destroyed Pompei and decimated Sicily were mere cookfires when compared with the inferno called Hekla. Herbert of Clairvaux was apparently its author, but its knowledge of Hekla undoubtedly came from the archbishop of Lund, who had been born in Iceland and lived at Clairvaux.

The literature of Iceland itself is strangely silent about Hekla and its sister volcanoes, although there were many eruptions during the centuries that witnessed the flowering of the Sagas. Their explosive impact of medieval life in Iceland was perhaps accepted stoically, simply as unmistakable evidence of the hostility and fury of their world. Such impassive acceptance of adversity is typical of its population, and the character of the Vikings who settled there.

The manuscripts of medieval Europe were curiously preoccupied with Iceland and its improbable wonders. Its strange mixture of glaciers and volcanoes struck a responsive chord of medieval superstition. Caspar Peucer was a physician at Wittenberg and the son-in-law of the celebrated Philip Melancthon, and his writings further embellished the growing mythology that surrounded the country:

> Out of the bottomless pits of Hekla, or rather from the caverns of Hades itself, rise countless cries and loud wailings, so that lamentations can be heard for miles and miles.
>
> Coal-black ravens and vultures hover around the mountain and have their nests there. Hekla is clearly the Gate of Hell, for the people know from long experience that whenever terrible battles are fought, or there is bloody carnage somewhere on

the globe, there is heard from inside the volcano the most fearful howlings and despair, weepings and gnashing of teeth.

The sixty-minute flight between Reykjavik and Akureyri crosses several important landmarks in Iceland. Thingvellir is a sprawling caldera, its bottoms partially submerged in a huge lake not unlike Taupo in New Zealand. The cold depths of the lake sustain a unique subspecies of char. Its encircling mountains also shelter Reykir, the smoking hot springs that heat the capital, and the earthquake fissures of the Oxnará. Its cliffs include a spectacular rift with nearly perfect acoustics, where the summer tribal conclaves of ancient Iceland finally evolved into the Althing, the parliament these Viking settlers forged there early in the tenth century.

Thorisjökull and its sister Langjökull lie behind a range of treeless foothills and a small pumice desert. The glaciers are a strange palette of indigo and swimming-pool green and turquoise under their snowfields, their shimmering ice exposed in shelving cornices and brittle ramparts and battlements. Between these glaciers lies the empty lava-field pass at Kaldidalur, where the bitter winds are harshly cold even in midsummer.

Beyond these glaciers lies the thermal basin at Hveravellir, and the hot springs and geysers that sheltered several outlaw bands during the eighteenth century. Perhaps the most famous of these brigands was Eyvind Jonsson, whose story inspired the playwright Johann Sigurdjonsson to compose his drama *Eyvind of the Hills* in 1912. Its success soon made Jonsson an almost legendary figure, fully the equal of the ancient folk heroes described in the *Saga of Gisli* and *Grettir the Strong.* Such themes of outlawry and the brigand hero are common in the literature of Iceland, and Hveravellir has become a shrine.

The rugged mountains beyond Vatnsdalsá are a somber plateau of bitter-chocolate basalt, its cirques deeply scoured by ancient glaciers into a series of radial valleys that drain like fingers toward the shallow fjord at Akureyri.

Our final approach into its airstrip dropped past these snowfield cornices, slicing and crabbing in the crosswinds along the pinnacles and saw-toothed ridge at Hraundranji. The steep escarpment was behind as we settled into the smooth air over the fjord, and our pilot pulled the Fokker back into a tight turn. The tidal shallows flashed under the plane and its tires protested our landing.

Akureyri is the so-called northern capital of Iceland, and many travelers consider it the most beautiful city in the country. It is a center of both education and commercial activity, and an important port working the extensive fishing grounds along its Arctic coasts. It has about 10,000 citizens who are intensely proud of their northern city on the Eyjafjordur. Akureyri boasts four hotels, public swimming pools and saunas, botanic gardens that are the pride of its population, museums of surprising diversity and scope, winter sports, and an improbable golf course where it is possible to play all night just a few miles from the Arctic Circle. The city lies along its coastal beaches, its church towers sharply etched against the mountains, and the sun was bright on the green hills of Skogur.

Our odyssey was still not finished. There was still a fifty-mile journey to the river at Husavik, and a choice between three hours of jeep roads through the coastal mountains or twenty minutes in a small twin-engine Cessna. *It's almost the same price as hiring a jeep,* the charter pilot explained, *and it's hours faster!*

How can we tell them we're coming? I asked.

We simply make a low pass over the farm, the young pilot laughed, *and waggle our wings—we contact them like that all the time!*

Well, I decided suddenly, *let's fly.*

It was raining again, and the ragged overcast hung just above the coastal mountains. The pilot slipped the Cessna between the clouds and the glacier-polished saddle of the pass, sliding past its snowfields on the wind. Mountain farmsteads flashed past the hopscotching shadow of the plane and children waved from the hayfields. We followed the narrow highway through its narrow valley, completing the bad-weather route between the fjord and the river valleys beyond. The overcast was still ragged and low, scudding past the Plexiglas canopy of the plane. Fine patterns of rain beaded across the windshield. We crossed a braided glacier-melt river at less than 500 feet, and another river lay ahead on the horizon.

Laxá! the pilot yelled. *That's your river!*

The other rivers had flowed milky and shallow, the riffling melt of glacier silts in the interior. The beautiful Laxá in Pingeyjarsysla tumbled swift and clear over its lava outcroppings and black volcanic sands. We crossed a farmstead and small church along the river, and the pilot circled back into a second pass. *Husavik?* I pointed to the village on the coast.

That's right! the young pilot nodded.

The young pilot throttled back and started letting the Cessna settle into its downwind pass, setting its flaps and pulling back into his final approach. The Husavik airstrip was only 3,000 feet of wine-colored gravel crushed from the lava outcroppings and cinder cones in the coastal moors. Orange-painted petrol drums marked the boundaries of the strip, and the simple communications hut is seldom manned except when the weekly Fokker arrives from Reykjavik.

Our Cessna fishtailed and crabbed slightly, fighting the crosswinds on its final approach. *Look over there!* the young pilot pointed. *The farmers are already coming to get you!*

The farmers had obviously understood our low-altitude pass over Neskirkju, because an old Russian jeep was coming swiftly along the cinder highway toward the airstrip.

The farmers own the fishing rights on the salmon rivers. Although there was no feudal tradition to create the heritage of fishing rights, as existed to evolve that concept in central Europe, British fishermen who traveled to fish its salmon rivers after the middle of the nineteenth century established the precedent in Iceland. Such fishing rights must be leased, like those on the classic salmon rivers of Europe, and each fisherman is rotated twice daily to fish specific beats. Fisheries laws established a fixed number of anglers who can fish each river daily, and its beats are specific stretches of river which are clearly marked and assigned to each fisherman.

Our engines stopped and I popped the starboard hatch as the Russian jeep arrived on the airstrip. *Heimir Sigurdsson!* the chief ghillie introduced himself warmly. *Welcome to Pingeyjarsysla!*

Vurli Hermodsson! the young ghillie added.

The pilot unlocked the baggage compartments in the fuselage and engine nacelles, and we wrestled my luggage and equipment to the jeep. The brisk wind billowed dust along the runway, smelling of the Arctic seas offshore, and rattled fine gravel across the tail empennage of the Cessna. There was still snow in the mountains across the fjord, and a pair of whooping swans flew downstream.

It's an unusual summer, Sigurdsson said.

What's unusual? I asked.

So much snow in summer on the Viknafjöll. The old ghillie pointed to the coastal mountains. *The fish are running late too.*

But they're coming well now, added the young ghillie.

Sigurdsson drove us downstream past the sprawling Laxamyri

farm, and wound out across the barren cliffs to the waterfalls at Aedarfossen. The harsh wind rattled stones against the jeep. The river tumbles down through a broken lava field softened by thickets of scrub birches, and suddenly it spills over a fifty-foot volcanic fault in a series of wild chutes and broken waterfalls. Below these waterfalls, the river winds in a gentle sickle-shaped course across its somber lava beaches to the sea. Its brief estuary is a bitter-chocolate channel that suddenly drops off into pelagic depths just beyond its mouth, and sea fog obscured the Arctic islands offshore.

What's this place? I asked the ghillies.

We want to show you something. Sigurdsson grinned and clambered out of the jeep. *Come see our surprise!*

We walked from the jeep toward the cliffs, ducking our heads into the chill wind off the fjord. *Look down there!* Hermodsson pointed into the swift currents fifty feet below. *Look where I'm pointing just above those boulders under the falls!*

Where? I asked excitedly.

Just ahead of those boulders! they repeated together.

The tumbling rapids concealed almost everything on the bottom, but suddenly I understood that the river was relatively shallow, and that its dark bedrock made it seem deeper. The gray shapes were a big school of salmon. There were thirty or forty fish under the falls, lying close together and shifting restlessly in the flow.

Yes! I said happily. *I see them!*

Steingrimur Baldvinsson was waiting at his Neskirkju farmstead when we arrived, and he invited us to share afternoon tea with him in the sitting room. The old riverkeeper followed us inside, poured the tea from a table filled with cakes and other pastries, and welcomed me to his salmon river.

Baldvinsson wore a simple work shirt and baggy wool trousers and sturdy English brogues, and an old soft-wool sweater with an ancient Pingeyjarsysla pattern. Its intricate triangles used six natural colors of uncarded wool from the half-wild sheep in the hills. Several buttons were missing and its elbows were worn.

It's my fishing pullover, Baldvinsson apologized. *My wife hates it, but I won't let her mend anything—it would mean bad luck!*

His round face was full and somber, and when he laughed it became almost jolly, yet his laughter was always betrayed by the fierce intensity in his pale-gray eyes.

Like farmers throughout the world, Baldvinsson had learned to live with exposure to the sun and wind, and had a faintly pale hat line just above his eyebrows. His white hair had thinned back to expose a huge milky-white forehead. Baldvinsson simply brushed his hair back around his head like a silvery helmet, although he often worked his fingers through it restlessly while speaking, and it was usually a wild tangle utterly unlike the dignity and discipline he displayed.

The farmhouse was simple too, its white-painted walls and bright-red corrugated roof surprising in the hayfields and lava barrens, and beyond it was the river flowing against the Neshvammur hills.

There were windows crowded with plants and flowers, and heavy pieces of faded furniture with antimacassars covering the worn arms and backs. The German piano played by his married daughter stood along the sitting-room wall. Old prints and paintings hung everywhere, mostly etchings of eighteenth-century life in Iceland, and rough palette-knife landscapes of Pingeyjarsysla. There were flowers in the sheltered dooryard, and a phalanx of muddy boots guarded its stone sill. The chill wind eddied restlessly in the filmy, lacework curtains like the curtains in the Wyeth paintings of Pennsylvania and Maine.

Where are the fishing beats? I asked.

Baldvinsson offered us more cake and whipped-cream crêpes and rich cookies. *Our river is divided into seven beats.* The old man poured more and handed me the small map on the beat card. *The beats have been divided according to their productivity and the character of their pools and access—not merely the length of water.*

The first beat on the card was a single pool at the boundary of the Neskirkju water. *That means Grastraumar is the best,* I interrupted. *It's the only pool in the first beat.*

That's right. Baldvinsson smiled like a country teacher with a promising pupil. *Grastraumar is a beat in itself!*

What about the second beat? I asked.

Vitadsgafi and Presthylur are both slow-flowing boat pools, the old keeper replied. *Thvottastrengur is bank-fishing.*

You will like the Vitadsgafi, Sigurdsson predicted.

Beat three is all bank-fishing water, Baldvinsson continued. *It has fine pools like the Kirkjuholmakvisl and Skriduflud—both are beautiful pools and I believe you'll like them.*

Skriduflud is my favorite, Sigurdsson added.

Kirkjuholmakvisl takes its name from the tiny clapboard church at Neskirkju, with its simple wooden belfry and a small churchyard surrounded by a wall of mossy stones. The pool is a hundred yards of silken currents, lying behind the church where the Laxá divides around a grassy little island of harebells and buttercups.

Beat four is farther downstream, Baldvinsson said. *It includes Oddahylur and Eyjarhylur and the island pools at Straumeyjar.*

It's pretty moody water, Sigurdsson confessed wryly.

We drive downriver to fish beat five. Baldvinsson ignored his head ghillie with twinkling eyes and continued his description of the river. *It has two pools called Tjarnarholmi and Simastrengur.*

Every river in the country has a pool called Simastrengur, I said. *What does the name mean?*

It's simple enough, Sigurdsson laughed. *It's named for the telephone lines there—it means the Telephone Current.*

Thvottastrengur is the Clotheslíne Current, the keeper added.

Their names sound better in your language! I said.

Beat six is still farther downstream, the old riverkeeper explained, *just above the Nupafossen bridge. Its pools are the Fossbrun, which fishes from both banks, and the Hofdahylur.*

Hofdahylur is the famous pool? I interrupted. *Isn't it the pool where Jakob Hafstein took his record cockfish?*

That's right, Sigurdsson nodded.

Beat seven is below the Nupafoss bridge. Baldvinsson poured fresh coffee and offered us more pastries. *It reaches from the Laxatangi to Breidengi and Straumall—both are rather moody pools too, but when they're right, both pools fish well.*

How do your weekly catches run? I asked.

Our fishermen average seventy-five to a hundred salmon each week, the old keeper replied, *with seven rods fishing.*

And the fish themselves? I asked.

Our salmon average twelve or thirteen pounds, he said.

They're pretty large for Iceland.

You've learned a little of our language, Baldvinsson said. *Have you fished salmon in Iceland before?*

I've learned a little Norwegian, I confessed.

We're always a little surprised when anyone attempts a bit of our language, Baldvinsson explained. *It's a difficult language that many people compare with German, but some of our grammar can make German seem as simple as kindergarten.*

Some people tell us they try, Sigurdsson said, *because they want to attempt reading our Sagas in the original language.*

We find that strange, Baldvinsson smiled puckishly. *Because our ancient stories are really quite incomprehensible in any of the translations—and pretty obscure in our language too!*

Well, I suggested, *some people are never content with being baffled in their own language.*

Our grammar is really a nightmare, Sigurdsson laughed.

It's really gender that is the nightmare, the riverkeeper added. *Our men are masculine and our women are feminine, and that seems straightforward enough, but all logic stops there!*

It's complete chaos! Sigurdsson agreed. *Chocolate bars are neuter, pork chops and sausages and bacon are masculine, and soft drinks are feminine—because of the shape of Coca-cola bottles!*

Children are always neuter in our language. Baldvinsson was laughing at my confusion. *But codfish are masculine!*

Forget it! I said helplessly.

The afternoon fishing beats started at four o'clock, and we agreed to meet at the fishing house in the meadows below Neskirkju. Sigurdsson drove me over to their *Veidihus* quarters and helped me settle my luggage and fishing gear into my room. While I sorted through my fishing equipment, Sigurdsson sat talking about the valley and its salmon fishing, and particularly about the old riverkeeper.

It soon became obvious that Sigurdsson and the entire population of Pingeyjarsysla viewed the old riverkeeper with a remarkable mixture of awe and affection and respect.

When I mentioned his poetry and writing, the head ghillie spoke engagingly about Baldvinsson's work, but it was unmistakably the old riverkeeper's counsel and cautious judgment and wisdom that commanded the most respect from his neighbors. When I talked about the somber poetry I had heard in Reykjavik, and suggested that Baldvinsson seemed serious and dour, Sigurdsson countered with these brief lines:

I merely hear a
Second mocking tune in things,
So smile—my Mona Lisa!

The weather had turned bright and still in late afternoon, and the old keeper arrived in his battered Russian jeep at four o'clock.

The beats were decided with a dice cup, and I rolled a combination of sixes that started my fishing at the famous Grastraumar. We loaded my fishing duffle in the back and fitted my rods in the roof clips, and started down through the sun-ripe hayfields, where an immense flock of long-haired sheep were foraging in the coarse grass.

The sheep are a good sign, Baldvinsson observed.

Grastraumar is a curious pool. It is less a salmon pool in the classic sense than an hourglass narrows above a shallow lagoon filled with nesting swans. The river tumbles down a series of ledges from the Boat Pool at Holmavadstifla, where its swift currents divide around a rocky outcropping, and then glides into the weedy channels at Hrutaholmi. Its currents gather and quicken there, echoing some imperceptible change in its bathography, and it slides into the strong flow that has shaped the broken throat of the pool.

Its upper reaches are constrained between outcroppings of rust-colored lava, with submerged ledges breaking the smooth flow on the steep banks of the Neskirkju side. Salmon hold in the shallows above these ledges and deep along the sheltering ledges themselves. Holding places are also found farther downstream, where the smooth currents of Grastraumar reach out into the waterfowl flats of the Mori lagoons, with their flocks of eiders and buffleheads and swans.

These seemingly still shallows can hold salmon over the gravel-bottom channel almost 300 yards into these Mori lagoons, and although a fisherman unfamiliar with the Neskirkju water might have little faith in such slack currents, fishing them will quickly demonstrate that the lower reaches of Grastraumar can hold taking salmon much farther downstream than he suspects.

Start just above the ledges, Baldvinsson said.

The old riverkeeper had suggested that I start fishing much farther upstream than I might have guessed, and when I asked about salmon holding in such quiet places, Baldvinsson told me that several bathtub-shaped pockets in the bedrock sometimes sheltered fish. It was obvious that a fisherman who had learned to read salmon rivers in Canada, Norway, and the United Kingdom might have trouble in Iceland.

The currents were surprisingly weedy and quite warm, since the Laxá is born in the marl shallows at Myvatn, perhaps the most fertile lake in the country. Both its marl bottoms and the spectacular hydrothermal basin surrounding the lake are its secret, and the wellspring of the river's fertility too. Its baby salmon grow quickly on a rich diet of *Anisomera* midges, creating bigger smolts than its sister watersheds, and when its silvery smolts reach salt water they forage more greedily and wax fat on their marine diet. The result is a unique strain of strong-bodied fish that ascend a series of high waterfalls coming home, and typically spend two to three years feeding in the coastal seas off Iceland. The Laxá fish boast the highest average weight in the country, although it is strange to find them in a weedy British chalkstream displaced into these Artic latitudes.

Fountain mosses flowed back and forth in the current, and I fished just beyond the weeds. I fished through the upper lies woodenly, although the anticipation of exploring an unfamiliar river is always exciting. It did not really seem like a salmon pool. Each cast dropped softly across the holding water, the line bellying in the subtle currents until I mended its lazy swing, and I patiently fished it through before taking a step and casting again.

Salmon fishing demands a mixture of patience and discipline and hope, and with sufficient skill it will cover a pool with a series of concentric fly-swings. Each cast comes closer and closer to every fish in its depths, teasing its curiosity until the fly-swing that covers its holding-lie with an enticing presentation. Patience and discipline and skill will cover every fish in the pool, but casual casting is likely to miss several possible salmon, and no other method can adequately cover pools that are difficult to read.

You should change tactics now, Baldvinsson called when I reached the narrows and its submerged ledges. *The salmon lie deeper now, just outside those currents—perhaps a sinking-tip line?*

I've got one on the spare reel in my back pocket, I said.

Baldvinsson fished the extra reel from my fishing coat, and I changed lines and waded back into position. Although I fished down the ledges carefully, there was no sign of a salmon anywhere, and I worked on through with a sense of growing disappointment. When I had passed the ledge-rock narrows, and the currents eddied far out into the Mori lagoons, the old riverkeeper came down the steep path.

The bottom is almost black, the old man explained, *and it's not as deep out there as it looks—you need a floating line again.*

Casting patiently and mending each fly-swing, I fished very slowly down the long waist-deep flowage into the lagoons themselves. It was surprising how well these seemingly placid currents could sustain the proper fly speed. There was nothing down the full 200 yards, not even a teasing swirl or faint pull at the fly. I stopped fishing a moment and stood watching a regatta of swans downstream.

Fish another fifty meters! the keeper called.

The currents seemed too sluggish and pondlike farther downstream, and I started fishing with little faith. The dozen casts that followed found nothing, and fatigue began to fill my mind as the excitement of a strange river started to wane. But the cast that followed triggered a huge swirl under the teasing fly-swing, and since it had seemed like a particularly good fish, I waited before casting again.

The fly dropped softly across the smooth current, working back as the mending line teased the fly past the place where the salmon rolled before. Suddenly I felt its weight before its heavy swirl echoed back to the surface, and the reel was protesting shrilly before I could respond. The backing dwindled quickly, and when the salmon jumped back upstream, I was surprised to discover it had circled back through the Mori shallows. The line was hung with weeds and fountain moss, and when the fish jumped again it was suddenly free.

He's gone! I shouted sadly.

Come back and have some coffee! Baldvinsson suggested. *We'll rest the pool awhile and fish through it again!*

Good thinking! I laughed. *My feet are frozen!*

We sat drinking coffee and listening to the ducks and swans feeding and quarreling in the Mori lagoons. Getting the riverkeeper to discuss his poetry proved difficult, but Baldvinsson spoke freely and intelligently about the Sagas.

The old riverkeeper believed that these ancient manuscripts were not only our source of knowledge about life in medieval Iceland, but also the sole written record of the Teutonic peoples before their subsequent conversion to Christianity.

The parchment folios created by the medieval calligraphers in Iceland were also the principal source of our knowledge of Norse mythology, and made German romantic literature possible. Richard Wagner used themes from the Sagas extensively, particularly in operas like *Das Rheingold,* its fiery sister work *Die Walküre,* the heroic opera *Siegfried,* and the stormy *Die Götterdämmerung* that concluded the tetralogy he completed after the middle of the nineteenth century.

There are a few other sources too, particularly the half-mystical chronicles which describe the explorations of early Celtic priests to several islands in these stormy northern seas. These manuscripts tell us about voyages as early as the sixth-century odysseys of Saint Brendan in his frail skin-covered curraghs. The following passage from the faded manuscript *Navigatio Sancti Brendani* seemingly describes their discovery of Hekla:

> Another morning, there came into view a large and lofty mountain in the stormy ocean, not far distant, toward the north, with misty clouds round about and smoke billowing from its summits; then suddenly, the wind drove the boats rapidly toward the rock-bound island until it almost touched the shores. The cliffs were so high they could scarcely see the tops, and were black as coal and sheer as a wall.
>
> Afterwards a favorable wind caught their boats and drove them back south; and as they looked back, they saw the peak of the mountain unclouded, and shooting flames up into the sky and drawing them back again, so that the whole mountain was like a burning pyre.

The medieval manuscripts confirm that Celtic priests followed the routes of Saint Brendan to Iceland. Such religious colonies apparently existed before the first Viking settlers arrived in 860, when a longboat sailing to the Faroe Islands was lost and blown off course in a fierce storm. The evidence that these hermit priests existed is primarily literary in character, and the Sagas tell us that these Celtic exiles later fled the country, leaving behind their liturgical bells, manuscripts and croziers.

Such Celtic manuscripts have apparently been lost, but several ornaments and objects of jewelry and coins found in the Viking burial cairns of Iceland are unmistakably like objects excavated from ancient sites in the British Isles. During some highway construction at Thingvellir, workers discovered a small Celtic crozier of bronze. It had been embellished with richly zoomorphic images, and such imagery was common in early Irish religious art. Tiny bells were also important in Celtic liturgy. The delicate bell attributed to Saint Patrick still survives, and three similar bells have been recovered from the tenth-century burial sites at Kornsá and Biskupstungur in Iceland, as well as a particularly rich boat grave in Patreksfjord.

Since its medieval manuscripts fully describe the first settlement of the country, along with the ancient journals of the Celtic pilgrims, it is clear that little Iceland is the only country in Europe that can actually trace its entire history. It is also remarkable that its entire evolution has occurred within the fabric of a single language and literature.

Several other early manuscripts, like the singular *Voyage of Mael Duin* and its sister *Voyage of Bran* in the eighth century, also describe explorations in the waters off Iceland. Bede mentions Celtic religious hermits there in his classic *Historia Ecclesiastica Gentis Anglorum* in those same years, and Dicuil also discusses them in his *Liber de Mensura Ornis Terrae* in 925. The famous *Life of Saint Columba* also describes three epic voyages led by a bold clergyman called Cormac into these hostile northern latitudes.

They must have been remarkable priests, Baldvinsson concluded, *daring our seas in boats covered with hides!*

Shall I fish through Grastraumar again? I asked.

We still have time, the keeper said.

It was still surprisingly warm and bright, and Baldvinsson lay in the warm grass, staring absently into the twilight beyond Grimsey. The river felt cold when I slipped into the waist-deep flats and stripped line to cast. The first fly-swings worked back across the glassy flow, and arctic terns scolded me shrilly. The patient series of casts explored the first hundred yards of the Mori shallows without moving a salmon, and I stopped fishing.

We've still got fifteen minutes, the keeper called.

Downstream in the waterfowl shallows, the twilight on the still lagoon was purple and gold. Each cast worked back smoothly before I took a step and repeated its swing. There was no sign of salmon, and I had virtually given up when the fly simply stopped in the smooth current. It was like being snagged, except that there was nothing in those gravelly shallows to foul the fly-swing, and when I tightened, the fish wrenched itself and shook its head.

Salmon! I shouted.

The fish hung there briefly in the current, perhaps deciding on its tactics, and then bolted past me and exploded into the twilight. It showered the river with water and its splash seemed loud in the evening stillness. The delicate Hardy shrieked in a shrill ratchet song that surrendered line into the silty lagoons, and when it threshed and cruised along the shallows, frightened ducks rose in a clamor of wingbeats and splashes. Arctic terns screamed and circled. The salmon spent itself in the still Mori flats, collecting moss on the leader until its head was completely shrouded with vegetation.

It can't see anything now! I worked the big henfish back and finally tailed it in the shallows. *It's mine!*

Twelve pounds! the keeper guessed.

Baldvinsson stopped at the fishing house to celebrate my first salmon from the Laxá, and we toasted the fish in pot-still whisky. The old riverkeeper sat drinking and talking about his country, mentioning the Roman coins discovered in its burial mounds.

The first coin was minted during the reign of Diocletian, and the second coin discovered in Iceland was from Aurelian's time. Probus was the emperor when the third coin was minted in Rome, and the last Roman coin unearthed in Iceland was found at the farmstead site near Skaholt. Historians have dated its minting to the brief six-month reign of Marcus Claudius Tacitus late in the third century.

These few coins have precipitated two disparate theories of history in Iceland: some experts believe these coins were probably stolen during the Viking raids in ancient Britain, while others argue that they arrived in Iceland with Roman seafarers themselves.

Perhaps the most puzzling fact about these coins is that all four were minted of copper, and each was struck in a surprisingly brief period of less than fifty years. Coin hoards excavated from Viking sites in other countries suggest that these warriors were interested only in gold and silver, and historians argue that a typical raiding party would not have bothered to carry worthless coppers back to Iceland. Since the coins were minted across forty-odd years, some historians suggest that all four might have traveled to Iceland in a single purse. Their skein of logic strongly points to the presence of Roman visitors in Iceland as early as the fourth century.

Roman sea power had reached its apogee in that period, and a warship's reaching Iceland was clearly possible. It is curious that it was Viking military pressures on the periphery of the Roman Empire that were the catalyst for that naval growth. Viking raids on the coastal settlements of northern Europe had forced Diocletian to mount a powerful fleet on the seacoasts of Gaul.

These Roman forces were under the command of Carausius,

and history tells us that Carausius was powerful enough that his ships defected to Britain and proclaimed him emperor in 287. Since his coastal sanctuary was constantly harassed by the Viking expedition, and many of those raids were launched from Iceland, it certainly seems possible that Carausius used his formidable sea power to patrol the North Atlantic, and to pursue Viking longships back to their bases.

Baldvinsson also spoke of the Sagas, and their stories of the exploration and settlement of America. *The recent discovery of the Viking settlement in northern Newfoundland,* the keeper said, *and carbon-dating of its artifacts centuries before Columbus was no surprise to anyone in Iceland—it has always been in our Sagas!*

Viking navigators had established settlements on the bitter fjords of eastern Greenland in 985, and these colonies maintained that foothold for almost five centuries. It was a longship commanded by Bjarni Herjolfsson that was forced beyond Greenland, according to the famous *Groenlendinga Saga,* drifting helplessly in storms and sea fogs. When the bad weather finally lifted, their ship found itself hundreds of miles farther west, lying off a coast of dense forests. Herjolfsson decided against landing there, despite the protests of his thirsty men, and sailed back toward Greenland. Three days later, the party sighted another landfall that was still not Greenland, but was obviously a large forest-covered island. Herjolfsson landed to secure water and fresh provisions, and pushed on toward Greenland, where Herjolfsson was finally reunited with his family. Herjolfsson and his crew survived their adventure in 986.

Leifur Eiriksson sailed regularly between the settlements on the Greenland coasts, the colony at Breidafjord in western Iceland, and Trondheim in Norway. His exceptional seamanship and experience made Eiriksson the logical choice to attempt retracing the Herjolfsson expedition to the country beyond Greenland.

Eiriksson embarked with his longship and a crew of thirty-five seamen late in the tenth century. His party sailed west until it found the first landfall Herjolfsson had described in their conversations at Breidafjord. Eiriksson sailed south along the forested coasts of the Labrador and explored the waters off Newfoundland. It is not clear how much farther south Eiriksson sailed, but the calfskin folios of the *Groenlendinga Saga* tell us that the party wintered on a fertile coastline that was surprisingly mild:

> They went ashore and looked about them. The weather was fine. There was some dew on the grass, and the first thing they did was to get some on their hands and put it to their lips, and to them it seemed the sweetest thing they ever tasted.
>
> Finally they went back to their longship, and sailed into a sound that lay between the island and the headland jutting out toward the north.
>
> They steered a westerly course around the headland. There were extensive shallows there, and at low tide their ship was left high and dry, with the sea almost out of sight. But they were so impatient to land that they could not bear to wait for the rising tides to refloat the ship; they ran ashore to a place where a river flowed out of a lake.
>
> As soon as the tide had refloated their ship, they took a boat and rowed out, and brought it up the river to the lake and they anchored. They carried their hammocks ashore and put up wattle huts, but when they decided to winter there, they built large houses and a compound.
>
> There was no lack of salmon in the river or the lake, bigger salmon than they had ever seen. The country seemed so kind that no winter fodder was needed for livestock. There was never any frost all winter, and the grass hardly withered.

Eiriksson and his party had reached America a full five centuries before Columbus and Vespucci. Their ship's logs and stories finally prompted Thorfinn Karlsefni to mount a full-blown settlement expedition from Greenland. The beautifully illustrated parchments of the *Eirik's Saga* tell us that his party embarked from Brattahild in two longships carrying 160 settlers and crew members. Karlsefni took his wife Gudrid on their voyage, and the manuscript describes their settlement on the northern coasts of Newfoundland.

Sigurdur Stefansson prepared a chart in 1590, which placed the site of the Promontorium Winlandiae, the storied Vinland christened by Leifur Eiriksson himself, at virtually the precise latitudes where modern archeologists are steadily excavating what is unmistakably a Viking settlement dating to the tenth century.

But the story of Gudrid is stranger still, the old riverkeeper continued, *because she finally died in Europe.*

How did that happen? I asked.

Baldvinsson explained that Gudrid had spent three years in the New World with her husband. During that time she bore Karlsefni a son whom they christened Snorri Thorfinnsson. The *Eirik's Saga* records a second settlement established in the more fertile latitudes farther south, and that it was later abandoned after several attacks by hostile bands of natives. Gudrid and her seafaring husband eventually returned to their birthplace in Iceland, bringing with them the first European child born in America. Gudrid subsequently became a nun after her husband's death, and still later made the long pilgrimage to Rome, where she remained until her death. Her surprising odysseys undoubtedly made Gudrid the best-traveled woman of medieval times.

Gudrid could have told them some remarkable tales in Rome, Baldvinsson observed drily, *but I'm sure nobody asked!*

Flocks of fat half-grown eiders, still in their brown-mottled baby feathers, flew downstream just after daylight. Swans were foraging in the reeds above the fishing house at Mori, and the mating sounds of snipe echoed in the moors. Two woodcock fluttered up from the bracken, startled into their whistling flight by a flock of long-haired sheep. Their erratic flight ended on the island at Kirkjuholmakvisl.

Arctic terns screamed in protest upstream, working their bright choreography in a mating swarm of sedges. Several goats were grazing on the wild-flower roofs of an abandoned turf farm, and the snowfields on the Viknafjöll were covered with clouds.

Fishing boats were tightly moored along the breakwater at Husavik, where the somber fisheries bank dominates a skyline of small, bright-roofed houses. Two tiny snowfields held stubbornly in the barren mountain behind the village. The Hvitserkur shoals rose from the swells offshore, like a pale beast grazing in the kelp shallows. Lichens and bleached scurvy grass and sandworts cling stubbornly to the skerries where the herring boats were working.

There was a crisp north wind coming off the Skalfandi, and several flocks of geese flew upstream in ragged skeins over the lava fields and farms, bound for the highlands beyond Myvatn. Baldvinsson arrived at the fishing house during breakfast and was excited at our prospects. *The weather has changed!* the old keeper explained. *Vitadsgafi is always good in such winds, and we have Presthylur and Thvottastrengur this morning too!*

Let's see, I suggested.

The regatta of swans seemed strangely foreign in the morning sun, and the ponies seemed restless in the bottoms at Mori, where the children were gathering ptarmigan berries.

Vitadsgafi is a smooth-flowing boat pool, its currents almost imperceptible on windless days. Plover and jacksnipe flushed ahead of our jeep. The deeply rutted tracks wound back downstream through the sheep meadows, where the river bends north against the wind-polished Neshvammur hills. The bottom there is coal-black sand, with thick beds of weeds in its backwaters, and the pool seems sepulchral and deep. There are no visible echoes of the taking-lie in Vitadsgafi, except for a subtle bulge in its placid flow. Some salmon fishermen dislike boat-fishing pools, but the silken currents at Vitadsgafi have proved themselves among the best taking-lies on the entire Laxá flowages.

Cast against the weeds. The old keeper pointed.

Baldvinsson gently held the boat steady in the current while I stood and prepared to cast. There are only about thirty casts of holding water at Vitadsgafi in its typical levels of flow, and the keeper rowed softly while I fished it through. His oarlock rhythms were patterned to match my casting, letting the boat drift down with such precise control that each successive cast placed my fly two feet farther downstream. We moved nothing at the Vitadsgafi.

Presthylur is a series of gravelly channels in the weeds. Its holding-lies are surprisingly far from the fence-stile where the skiff is moored. Its weedy channels remind a well-traveled fisherman of Hampshire chalkstreams like the Itchen and Test. The salmon pool itself lies below a quiet backwater, where cool springs trickle down through the wild flowers, and the Mori shallows contribute drifting beds of moss to its gentle currents. During unusually warm weather, the channels at Presthylur gather the cool discharges of the springs farther upstream, and the salmon gather there too. The bottom is a coarse rubble of rust-colored stones. Presthylur has been a puzzle over several years since that first week of fishing, although I have often rolled salmon there and lost fish after hooking them briefly.

It has never been particularly kind to me over the years, but the pool has a solid reputation among anglers who fish at Neskirkju.

Baldvinsson shook his head unhappily when we fished through without moving a salmon. *It's finished here,* the keeper said. *Perhaps the Thvottastrengur will go better.* We rowed ashore and moored the skiff and took the jeep downstream.

Thvottastrengur lies below a half-mile lagoon that is filled with nesting goldeneyes. The pool was difficult to read with a light, riffling wind. Its best taking places are found in a spreading silk-smooth channel in the weeds, just above its broken tail shallows. The pool is fished from a rocky path along the weeds, and there are worn places in the grass above the best salmon lies, about a hundred yards above the serrated lava outcroppings that define its tail.

The pool lies under its sheltering hills, and figures extensively in the writings of Jakob Hafstein. His beautiful book *Laxá i Adaldal* was published in 1965, and is the definitive book on the river and its fishing. Like the Swedish book about the river, titled *Lax i Laxá* and written by Gösta Unefaldt, it is ample testimony to the stature of the river and its fishing. Hafstein described his experiences at Thvottastrengur in these translations:

> Thvottastrengur is an exceptional fishing place. It has hillocks and cooling faults in the shallows, and is a perfect pool for fishing small flies. I have many happy memories of this pool, and I pitched my tent there during many a summer.
>
> Once a large salmon was lying there in a cooling fault, a fish so large that it startled me when it jumped and I first saw it there. It only jumped two or three times each day, and always showing between seven and eight each evening.
>
> I tried for it day after day, displaying the contents of four fly boxes without luck. The contest was concluded when it took a small trout fly when I was fishing for sea trout. It just lay in the current as long as it liked, as if nothing had really happened, until it tore free.
>
> On that same trip, I took a twenty-nine-pound henfish on a small salmon fly. It took just above the lie of the larger cock, so I thought I had been given another chance. It took more

than an hour to grass it, and I never saw the fish until it was landed. It was a disappointment.

Arnold Gingrich also wrote about the river in his charming book *The Well-Tempered Angler,* and observed that although the country has more than sixty salmon rivers, its beautiful Laxá in Pingeyjarsysla is unique because its fish are twice the average weight typical of most other salmon fisheries in Iceland.

Since Laxá simply means salmon river, the name is always used in concert with its district or some important landmark in its watershed. The river at Husavik is usually mentioned with its Pingeyjarsysla district, or with the Adaldal valley at Neskirkju, to distinguish it from several other Laxá watersheds throughout the country. Gingrich was right in his perceptive observations in *The Well-Tempered Angler:* the Laxá in Pingeyjarsysla is unique.

Its fine sport has attracted a parade of famous anglers. Its long tradition had its beginnings with legendary British salmon experts like Charles Ackroyd and Ernest Crosfield, who traveled to fish the Laxá from Edinburgh and Aberdeen in the nineteenth century. Their first expeditions used the small steamers that offered fortnightly service between Scotland and Seydisfjordur on the eastern coasts of Iceland. It was a difficult journey overland from those mountainous eastern fjords to the gentle valley between Husavik and Myvatn.

Ackroyd and his fishing colleagues later traveled directly to Husavik in his steam yacht, with his own Scottish ghillies and boatmen aboard, and they lived at various farmsteads along the river. Ackroyd was a superb fisherman, with years of experience along the classic Dee and Spey in the Scottish highlands, and the famous fly-pattern that bears his name was first dressed by George Blacklaws in 1875. The fishing skills of Ackroyd and Crosfield, and the Scottish ghillies and boatmen who accompanied them, were so completely absorbed by the farmers that the Laxá still has the finest ghillies in Iceland.

Ernest Crosfield was perhaps the most subtle and creative salmon fisherman of his generation. His technique for stillwater salmon has become known as the Crosfield Pull throughout the salmon-fishing world. It has joined the older techniques as the primary tactic for coaxing salmon in quiet waters. The Laxá ghillies are firm exponents of pulling the swinging fly, shortening the line to increase its fly speed and bring it alive in their smooth currents. Both the old riverkeeper and his ghillies were fierce disciples of the Crosfield technique, although they seemed unaware of its origins.

Crosfield was also a superb fly dresser who developed several fine salmon patterns. His elegant style displayed the slim bodies and sparse throat hackles and wings typical of more modern flies, and both his proportions and his tiny heads had a remarkable impact on modern salmon flies. His original patterns included the Black Silk and Crosfield, and he is widely accepted as the author of the contemporary dressing for the storied Blue Charm, perhaps the finest salmon pattern ever conceived.

General R. N. Stewart confirms the presence of these legendary nineteenth-century anglers on the Laxá in his book *The Rivers of Iceland,* and mentions their regular trips to fish in Pingeyjarsysla. His observations on those years are worth remembering:

> There seems to be the widespread notion that salmon fishing in Iceland is something recently discovered. This is quite untrue. Far back in the last century, there were a number of British anglers who had been to Iceland for its salmon fishing, and one of those early visitors was Ackroyd, who travelled to the Laxamyri on the north coast. This was quite an expedition, as he took boats and ghillies with him.

Bing Crosby and Lee Wulff have traveled to fish the Laxá in Pingeyjarsysla too. Its sport still triggers a summer migration of salmon fishermen from Europe and the United States. Such migratory anglers are constantly finding other fishermen in hotels and restaurants and airports, bound for the fertile rivers of Iceland. Fishermen are seemingly as migratory as the fish themselves.

Knowledgeable anglers have sometimes compared the Laxá and its ecology with the Yellowstone and its origins in the large hydrothermal basins surrounding Yellowstone Lake. Similar geology and hot-spring discharges and rich marl deposits in the depths of Myvatn lake have all combined to shape the remarkable fertility of the Laxá. Yet the Yellowstone is a much larger river, and the Laxá is more like the famous Firehole, a smaller Wyoming trout stream that rises in the extensive geyser fields that include Old Faithful.

Fishing on the Laxá below the lake is limited to brown trout, because the salmon cannot ascend past the waterfalls in the gorge at Laxarvirkjun. The trout fishing on its upper ticket water is quite good, offering some of the best sport in Europe.

There are few salmon-taking places on the beats below the Laxarvirkjun waterfalls, and except for nightcrawlers and ironmongery, few salmon are caught there. Sudureyrihylur is considered the first fly water of any quality, and the major fishery really starts in the brief mileage above the beats at Neskirkju. The famous pools really begin at the Holmavad farmstead, where the salmon hold restlessly in the gathering currents below a stone-walled sheepfold.

Benedikt Kristjansson is the riverkeeper there. His handsome aquiline features and osprey eyes are familiar throughout the valley, and like his better-known neighbor Baldvinsson, Kristjansson's simple farm at the threshold of the lava fields might have prospered better had he spent less time fishing the river and its salmon.

There is some outstanding water below the famous Neskirkju water too, particularly the beats upstream from the river's mouth. Downstream from the bridge at Nupafoss, the river winds north along the foot of its rolling hills. It spills through the masonrywork abutments of a ruined bridge near the airport, and there is a famous pool there too. Below the Husavik road, the sprawling white house and outbuildings of the Laxamyri farmstead lie above the river. Jon Thorbergsson was its riverkeeper well into his eighties, and remembered the Ackroyd parties with their sleek yacht moored off the lava-field estuary.

Laxamyri has several excellent pools, as well as a tributary that receives a good run of grilse in early September. The first pool in the Laxamyri water is the Bakkastrengur, and many fishermen believe that the Heidarenhylur just above the Myrarvatn stillwater is the best pool on the river. It is pleasant to fish and its salmon hold surprisingly close to its grassy banks. Jakob Hafstein loved fishing the Laxamyri beats at the farmstead above the sea, and these paragraphs translated from *Laxá i Aldadal* clearly demonstrate his feelings:

> It is good to live at Laxamyri. It takes only a quarter of an hour to walk from the farm to the waterfalls at Aedarfossen, but the beauty of the wonderful islands in the river, with their growth and bird life, constantly keeps one stopping to admire the surroundings.

Directly opposite are the mountains of Kinnarfjöll and Nattfararvikur. The still of these calm evenings and quiet mornings on these waters is majestic. It is best to proceed slowly, and try fishing at Mjosund, at the uppermost island. The casts must reach between thirty and forty meters to cover the salmon there. The salmon often take quietly, stopping the fly, but show a good fight being fresh from the sea.

At the falls, the river branches around numerous isles and outcroppings. The Kistuvisl channel to the south has the most water. The best-known fishing place lies below the north waterfall, but its fish are mostly taken with the worm.

Baldvinsson fought his old Russian jeep through the hummocks of coarse grass, and stopped with a shudder of its worn clutch to silence its sputtering engine. We stood above the Thvottastrengur while he explained its holding channels and the taking-lies along its ledges in the tail shallows. The old riverkeeper concluded his observations and pointed to the bulging flow below the weeds, where the current echoed a smooth outcropping in the lava.

It's the best place, he explained.

We fished the pool carefully. Once a salmon rolled and pulled at the fly, but it was merely curious and was not hooked. Two other fish jumped in the tail shallows, rolling like salmon that had just arrived in the pool, but neither responded to my casting. Finally I had covered the best holding-lies and had worked down to the swift pockets against the grassy banks downstream. There was nothing, and I had fished through my morning beat.

Baldvinsson frowned when I stopped fishing. *There is nobody on the beat at Breidengi this morning,* he said thoughtfully. *We deserve a fish after such hard work!*

We walked slowly back toward his jeep, fatigue and dour moods mixed with hunger, and drove down through the lava fields to try the Breidengi water before lunch. The narrow road to the farmstead at Breidengi crosses the river at the Nupafossar waterfall. Beyond the tiny farmhouse, Baldvinsson turned into the freshly cut hayfields toward the river. Nupabreidan lies there between soft grassy banks, its brief taking-lie a telltale bulge in its flow.

Sometimes the fish turn and come to the fly like sharks, Baldvinsson explained, *and it's not easy to watch them follow and wait until you feel their strength—not when you see their fins!*

Baldvinsson muttered something and shook his head when I fished it through without moving a salmon. The old man pointed farther downstream, and we walked through the water meadows and wild flowers to the last holding-lie at Straumall.

What do you call this casting method? he asked.

It's called the double haul, I replied. *It's a technique developed by tournament casters to get more distance with a single-handed rod, and it simply builds more line velocity with the left-hand pulls—until you can shoot the entire line at the final stroke.*

Too much work for an old man, Baldvinsson smiled. *I'll stay with the bigger two-handed rods!*

There were several mallards nesting in the marshy bottoms, and the brown-mottled hens protested as we passed. One female scuttled ahead in the coarse-grass path, trailing its wing to coax us away from its nest. The river flows smoothly at Straumall, sliding into a narrows where it deepens and gathers speed. I fished its holding water carefully, working the fly-swing back until it almost touched our bank, and then I took a step downstream and cast again.

It is a basic salmon-fishing technique that covers the water in a series of concentric fly-swings, and with enough patience and discipline and skill, an angler also covers every fish lying in the pool. Deep in its quickening currents, there was a strong pull that spelled salmon, but the fish was gone when I tightened.

It's not my morning, I thought.

It was already one o'clock and my morning beat was finished. *It's hopeless!* The old riverkeeper shook his head.

We walked silently back through the hayfields toward his jeep, lost in dour thoughts about our luck, and drove back along the valley in a misting rain. *They tell me that you're a poet,* I said tentatively, *and that you write sometimes about the river.*

That's right, the keeper said.

I'd like to talk about your poetry sometime, I suggested abruptly. *Could I see some of your work?*

The riverkeeper drove silently through the rain, and the wipers beat their rhythms on the windshield. *Our fishing should go better this evening,* he said when we reached the farmstead.

The weather is changing, I agreed awkwardly.

The tiny church at Neskirkju is a simple wood-frame building. Its brightly painted roof has a small belfry above its dark-blue entrance, its bell from an earlier turf-walled church on the site. The church stands inside a stone-walled churchyard, its closure embracing the gravestones like an old sheepfold on the gentle slope that reaches toward the river at Kirkjuhol makvisl.

Several scrub-birch trees surround the church, although only those along its south facade are more than waist high. The trees are sheltered there from the winds off the Arctic seas, and get more exposure to the fleeting warmth of their northern summers. There are graves from the fifteenth century, mixed with freshly worked plots of more recent vintage, where the brittle soil has settled.

There were bright flowers in the churchyard too. Its old graves were thickly grown with lichens and snow buttercups and harebells. Two ravens settled on the churchyard wall, their coal-black wings flapping clumsily in the chill wind off the fjord, and walked croaking and foraging among the gravestones.

Baldvinsson arrived at the fishing house a few minutes early, and his ghillies soon followed in their vehicles, gathering in the kitchen over coffee. The riverkeeper sat quietly, his handsome face looking both gentle and stern, its solemnity betrayed by the scarcely concealed softness and twinkle in his pale eyes. He was wearing a simple denim work shirt buttoned to the collar. His worn trousers were stuffed into riding boots and a soft, intricately patterned cardigan sheltered him from the chill weather. His silver hair plumed back around his balding forehead like the helmets in Renaissance paintings.

We'll change our luck tonight, he predicted happily. *You've been fishing hard and my river is playing tricks.*

You're right about the tricks, I said.

The ghillies gathered outside, helping the other fishermen with their equipment, and we started to the river. We passed the farmhouse and the Russian jeep whined down the steep cattle lane behind the old churchyard, its gearbox protesting shrilly. Two ravens rose awkwardly into the wind, working their somber wings in solemn cadences, and dropped back into the moors along the river. *Some people believe that ravens are bad omens,* the keeper observed quietly.

I've heard that, I nodded.

But once in the winter, the old man continued, *when a snow bridge collapsed and I fell into a fissure in the lava fields, a raven came and kept me awake in the freezing cold until I could shout to the men who were out searching.*

You must think ravens are lucky omens, I suggested. *Didn't you write a poem about that time?*

That's right, Baldvinsson said.

Our evening beat reached from the classic Kirkjuholmakvisl to the shallow, broken-ledge pool at the Skriduflud. Its fine reputation is richly deserved among the fishermen who know the river well, and the Kirkjuholmakvisl is its best-known pool.

Its fishing starts where the river divides past a grassy, keystone-shaped island, shelving off in a strong fountain-moss current past the tiny churchyard. The river is puzzling there and difficult to read. Its primary flowages seem to lie in the wide stretch of broken water beyond the island, where its tumbling currents reflect the steep green hillsides and earthquake faults.

The salmon choose another route altogether, refusing to ascend the obvious currents outside the island, and circle its flower-covered banks in a seemingly minor channel instead of migrating directly upstream. It is a surprising pattern in their behavior, rooted in subtle differences in the hydrology and character of the river.

It is the churchyard itself that gives the Kirkjuholmakvisl its name, and the character of the pool is also deceptive. It begins in a series of potholes and bathtub-sized hollows and fissures in its rust-colored bottom. These invisible folds and cooling faults and sinks in the bedrock lava conceal fish in hidden cushions of flow, and its salmon can lie almost anywhere from the grassy island to the path at a fisherman's feet. The entire throat of the pool must be patiently explored in a series of fly-swings.

Sixty yards below the boat mooring, where a skiff is kept for crossing to the island itself, the channel narrows and shelves off in surprisingly deep water. The winds from the fjord are usually upstream, and it is a challenging cast to drop the fly tight against the wild-flower banks more than ninety feet away. The holding water there lies from the island bank, where reeds and coarse grasses trail in the smooth current, into the dark throat of the pool itself. The casts must drop along the flowers, where the fish lie like trout in the bank shadows, and fish through an entire fly-swing until it bellies deep on a sinking line into the bottom currents under the casting path.

Baldvinsson loved the pool, and its character and images are both found in some of his best-known poetry. It often proved generous from the fishing records at Neskirkju, even surrendering the best salmon of the entire summer in several years, but its true puzzles were perhaps the property of its keeper in these lines:

When a flyfisher is skilled,
Working gently with his slender rod,
Our lyric Kirkjuholmakvisl has a
Secret music that will prove itself
The best of pools.

Kirkjuholmakvisl is not the most productive pool among our evening water, since Skriduflud produces better annual catches, and is second only to Grastraumar. However, fishing-log records are not the best yardsticks of sport, and the Kirkjuholmakvisl has a special poetry. Its unique character is most obvious on its bright summer mornings with a cool wind burnishing its dancing currents, and shining in a shower of silver rain, and its subtle character includes grace notes and surprises that cannot be captured in mere catch figures.

Start fishing just below the boat, the keeper said. *Cast as far as you can and fish through carefully!*

I fished patiently over the potholes and fissures in its throat without moving a fish. Its middle currents flowed dark over its bitter-chocolate bottom, mutely jealous of its secrets. Tight against the wild flowers across its flow, I thought I moved a salmon in the shadows, but it was only a current echoing the flowing weeds.

Kirkjuholmi is a deep and seemingly still current lying directly downstream against a fence-stile, and I fished it through with a growing sense of failure. It has a minor holding-lie in its swiftly flowing shallows, where the current slides and quickens into the main channel beyond the island. Fish sometimes stop there, lying just along an outcropping that breaks the flow. *Perhaps you can reach that current just off the lava.* Baldvinsson pointed across the river.

It's a pretty long cast, I hedged.

The fly line worked out rhythmically into the bright sunlight, gathering speed and lengthening. It rolled out sharply in a tight loop that dropped the fly above the outcropping. *Not many fishermen can cover that place,* Baldvinsson observed approvingly. *It's not bothered often and we might find a salmon there.*

The cast worked across in a teasing fly-swing, swimming back under the surface against the looping belly of the line, and there was a lazy swirl behind the fly. *Salmon!* I said excitedly.

The fly was still working across the currents, teasing with a subtle rhythm of the rod. There was another rolling boil behind the fly, and then I felt weight and tightened. The shallows exploded as the fish felt the pressure of my straining tackle, throwing a roostertail of spray as it stripped line downstream into the rapids.

He was following the fly! the keeper laughed.

The salmon jumped wildly in the rapids, pirouetting twice in showering water that carried on the wind. It stopped running and bolted back upstream. Its second run passed me and it flashed over the emerald moss on the bottom. The reel was running shrilly again, and the salmon was rolling and head-shaking angrily, until it jumped again off the fence-stile at Kirkjuholmi. It wrenched still farther upstream, stripping out backing in great rasping lengths of line, and circling the grassy island into the Kirkjuholmakvisl. It threshed there briefly and sulked while I came running, trying desperately to regain control. The fish suddenly turned without warning and bolted back. The line went slack and I was reeling frantically, but the salmon had pulled free.

Our fish are strong. Baldvinsson shook his head. *Perhaps you should fish one of my two-handed rods.*

The rod didn't cost me that fish, I said unhappily.

Perhaps not, the keeper said.

Skriduflud was the bottom pool of our evening beat, although we both felt discouraged enough to stop fishing before we reached its glassy holding-lies. It has a brief salmon pocket in the currents at its throat, where the flow circles past a grassy promontory toward the worn casting path. Its opposite bank lies under the beautiful Neshvammur hills, which rise several hundred feet above the water. Although the broken currents that form the spine of the pool sometimes surrender a fish, the best taking water lies just above the ledges that contain its smooth flowages.

Like the Thvottastrengur farther upstream, Skriduflud has a series of small pockets in its bedrock lava, spreading into a broad, fan-shaped shallows that also hold fish. Black volcanic aggregates lie under the glassy currents, making the pool seem much deeper than it actually is, and trailing weeds line its taking channel.

It's a fine pool, the keeper said hopefully.

There was no sign of salmon, not even a fish jumping or porpoising restlessly. Several times the fly-swing fouled in drifting weeds. The river seemed almost lifeless. There were still a few casts left to cover the tail shallows. The pale weight-forward taper worked back and forth in the deepening twilight, and I dropped the sparse little Blue Charm across the current just above the ledges.

It started back into its bellying fly-swing, settling into the silken holding-lie. The children were herding dairy cattle behind the pool, working them past the fence-stile to the farmhouse above the river bottoms. I had turned to watch the children, letting the fly-swing come too far into the shallows. There was a gentle pull, and thinking that it had touched the bottom or intercepted some drifting weed, I started to retrieve line. It tightened stubbornly and the tail shallows erupted in the gathering twilight.

Salmon! I shouted in disbelief.

The children left their cattle and came running back across the moors. The old riverkeeper shouted with joy when the fish jumped six times in the darkness, leapfrogging and pole-vaulting wildly across the pool. It stubbornly took line until it hung past midstream, shaking its head while I tried to coax it back. The salmon jumped again and I lowered the rod.

There were seemingly no more runs, and the fight was going better. Suddenly it exploded into another wild, bulldogging run that reached across the entire river, throwing spray in the darkness and threatening to carry the fight into the rapids downstream.

Backing line still evaporated from the reel, until the fish was running against a dwindling spool and almost a hundred yards hung throbbing in the current. The salmon was beyond control now, and I held the rod high above my head, hoping to keep some line free of the strong currents. The fish jumped again and fell with a heavy splash, and suddenly the fight went completely sour. The salmon was still there, because its angry rolling telegraphed back through the line. The nylon was intercepting drifting weed until it hung taut, straining and shuddering under its accumulating weight, although I could still feel the struggling fish in spite of its burden.

It's fouled! I said helplessly.

Baldvinsson sent his grandson downstream to bring the boat moored at Sandeyrarpollur. *The boy can row us out across the pool,* the old keeper explained, *until we can pick up your line and try to work it free from the other side.*

The boy was already running through the moors and had passed the Oddahylur when the old riverkeeper followed, dogtrotting laboriously in the darkness. The horizon was surprisingly bright with a setting sun, and the old man was silhouetted against its light.

Take it slowly! I shouted downstream after him. *The salmon isn't going anyplace—and neither is the fisherman!*

Baldvinsson laughed and stopped running, while his young grandson wrestled the boat into the water. The surprisingly warm wind eddied along the river. Several upland geese passed overhead in the darkness, and I looked up when I heard their chanting cries. The fouled salmon struggled briefly on the bottom.

He's still there! I thought unhappily.

The old riverkeeper stood looking downstream into the dying light beyond the fjord. His grandson had already slipped the boat into the eddies along the casting path and was towing it steadily upstream, leaning hard into its anchor line. The boy had reached the shallows at Oddahylur, and the boat grated in the bottom gravel while he worked it patiently upstream.

The old riverkeeper was still standing in the moors downstream, looking back into the brightly gilded light, when suddenly he had fallen heavily. *What happened?* I thought wildly.

The old keeper fought back to his knees in the wild flowers, struggling to regain his feet. *Maybe he's all right!* I thought anxiously. *Maybe he's just slipped in the wet grass!*

Baldvinsson was still on his knees at Sandeyrarpollur, but he finally reached his feet and wobbled a step forward. The old man stood there for several moments, staring downstream into the twilight, and seemed to stumble. He fell backward slowly then, twisting like a broken doll in a clumsy spiral. His knees buckled and collapsed, and the old keeper fell hard on his back in the grass.

Steingrimur! I shouted and pointed downstream.

The children stared into the twilight, and suddenly they understood that their grandfather had collapsed beside the river. The boy quickly heaved the boat ashore, and the children were running down through the moors.

I broke the fish off and laid my rod in the hummocks, and then I was running too. *Cover him!* I was stripping my parka and sweaters, and threw them to the children. *Cover him with these!*

The old man was still alive, lying in the harebells and snow buttercups, and there was spittle on his face. His mouth was slack and I worked his tongue free of his throat with my forceps. His pale eyes rolled slowly and flickered, focusing on mine briefly before they stared mindlessly again. Their pupils seemed huge and more spittle seeped from his mouth. His face was blotchy and white, and the old keeper was breathing weakly, rasping and shuddering deep in his broken chest. He tried to speak, but his wet lips failed to shape the words, and a huge bubble formed slowly and broke.

There was a strange rattling in his throat. His pale eyes focused momentarily again, and his mouth worked like a gasping fish, but his face held a strange contentment. Finally he clenched his fingers and stiffened, shuddering in a series of fluttering spasms until his chest relaxed in a gravelly sigh.

The old riverkeeper was dead.

The children helped to carry him across the moors to his jeep. The little girls struggled with one leg and his grandson lifted the other, while I hooked my arms under his shoulders. The smallest girl supported his head until we reached the jeep. The other girls cradled his rolling head in their skirts, and the old riverkeeper's boots wobbled limply beyond the tailgate. The sweaters and parka still covered his body. There were no tears, and the children stared and said nothing as we drove slowly back to the farmhouse. The jeep climbed past the churchyard, its gearbox straining with a strange growling, and we stopped in the dooryard. The children sat quietly.

You all right? I asked.

The children nodded blankly and climbed down. The old riverkeeper had not moved, and his pale eyes stared into the twilight. We were lifting him across the tailgate when his daughter came out. *We've been expecting something like this.* She sighed and stood looking at her father sadly. *It's been coming for years.*

I'm really sorry, I shook my head lamely.

He's collapsed like this before, she explained. *He's had a long history of heart trouble—is he really gone this time?*

Yes, I said quietly. *I'm afraid he's dead.*

It's no surprise, she said.

It happened on the river at Skriduflud, I stammered clumsily. *There was nothing anyone could do when we got there—it seemed like his heart and a stroke together.*

It's not your fault, she said softly. *The doctor warned us.*

Nothing seemed to work, I continued awkwardly again. *It's terrible to die over a salmon—and it was a fish of mine!*

His daughter nodded wordlessly and smiled. *My father wanted to die along his river,* she replied gently. *It's strange how often he talked about dying in the meadows there—and how terrible it would seem to waste away in the hospital at Husavik.*

It did not make me feel better.

The young woman went inside to call her mother, and the old woman came outside wrapped in a heavy shawl. The old woman stared woodenly at her dead husband.

Steingrimur! she whimpered faintly. *Steingrimur!*

He's gone, her daughter sighed.

We stood looking at the dead riverkeeper. Finally his daughter and her children helped me carry him through the narrow hallway into the back bedroom, while his widow carried his head gently. The old woman was crying softly now, and the tears streaked her tired face as she shuffled beside me, reaching to open the bedroom door. The brass bedstead was covered with a flower-patterned quilt over its feather ticking, and we lowered his body gently.

Steingrimur! the old woman stroked his silvery hair.

The farm people work late through the Arctic summer nights, and they gathered slowly from the stables and hayfields and barns. Children waited silently in the sitting rooms and halls. The young woman came out of the bedroom and called me back into the house.

Don't leave, she said.

There's nothing more I can do, I explained, *and I feel like an awkward stranger in your house tonight.*

But you brought my father home. She stopped me gently.

Her mother came out too, smiled faintly and said something to her daughter. *What's the matter?* I asked.

Could you help us with his riding boots?

The riverkeeper looked strange, limply sprawled across the

faded quilting. The women had closed his eyes and lighted candles. There was a dark serge suit hanging on the armoire, with a pale blue shirt and a wine-colored tie with a sparse yellow pattern. There was a strong odor of moth crystals in the room.

The old keeper had seemed more at home in the wild flowers beside the river. His feet were damp with perspiration, and his boots came off stubbornly. There was mud on his rumpled trousers, and shirt, and there was coarse grass tangled in his cardigan and hair. The women were washing his pale face, and his eyes worked open again, staring milky and glazed like a freshly killed salmon.

His feet were cold and chalk-colored when I stripped off his wet socks and laid them on the chair, staring at the dull veins under his skim-milk skin. *He's really dead,* I thought sadly.

Several farmworkers and young boys arrived from the potato fields and pastures, leaving their boots and tools in the dooryard, and stood drinking coffee in the sitting rooms. The children sat quietly in the corners. The women sat talking softly while the widow fussed with the worn antimacassars, and her daughter was busily serving coffee and sugar biscuits and cakes.

The sun was getting bright again, after the brief twilight of the Arctic night, and several jeeps arrived from Husavik. Several young people arrived on ponies. The ghillies stood waiting in the dooryard for Heimir Sigurdsson to arrive from his farmstead at Gardi. There was nothing more I could help with, and when I started outside the women followed and we shook hands tearfully. The widow said something I could not understand, and I nodded awkwardly when she kissed me for bringing her husband back from the river. There were more jeeps coming along the Myvatn road when I finally reached the fishing house. It was four o'clock in the morning, and the bright sun glittered on the Mori shallows. The people of Pingeyjarsysla had already begun their ancient farewell to the dead.

The sharp wind gathered itself at daylight and stirred across the moors, driving several ponies into the sheltered bottoms and lava fields beyond Grastraumar. Farmers were busily working in the hay meadows to take advantage of the dry weather. The dooryard of the keeper's house had been crowded with jeeps and tethered ponies and trucks since his death.

Carpenters were painting and repairing the Neskirkju church when the gravediggers arrived with their tools.

The morning of the funeral was clear and cold. The farmstead was crowded with cars and cattle trucks and jeeps, and the freshly cut hayfield below the house was filled with grazing ponies. The people from the ancient farmstead at Holmavadi, which lies at the edge of the lava fields above Grastraumar, came on a hay wagon pulled by their Russian tractor.

The early sun was bright on the river. Flocks of young eiders flew swiftly downstream beyond the little churchyard, and the nesting swans were quarreling at the Mori lagoons. The fat eiders still wore their brown-mottled baby feathers.

The snow still held after two weeks in the mountains across from Neskirkju, particularly in the dark amphitheater on the Viknafjöll, and many people remarked that it was unusual in late July. Several farmers had gathered at the stables, away from the women and children, and stood in the sheepfold passing a bottle of aquavit while they talked of fishing and the riverkeeper and their crops.

Several hundred people had come. Two extra flights had arrived at the gravel airstrip at Husavik, and people had been arriving for days. Some families had pitched their bright-orange tents in the lava fields and moors along the river. The funeral crowds engulfed the tiny churchyard at Neskirkju, talking and rebuilding old friendships and sharing gossip as they gathered among the mossy gravestones.

There was little room in the tiny twelve-pew church itself, except for the family and its closest relatives, and most of the population of the entire country shares a few distant cousins. Some of the mourners were well known, and there was a television crew from Reykjavik. Finally the churchyard itself was filled, and the congregation spilled down the grassy slopes toward Kirkjuholmakvisl. The doors and windows of the church were left open, permitting the people outside to follow the burial services.

The church was spare and simple. Its ceiling is a barrel vault of pale-blue wainscoting, hung with a single brasswork chandelier from Copenhagen. There is a miniature choir loft above the entrance, reached by a steeply narrow staircase, and the sanctuary has a circular balustrade of wood. There are several portraits of past clergymen hung in the vestry. The worn hymnals and old *sálmaboks* were racked behind the straight-backed pews. The strong blue-and-white flag of Iceland hung beside a primitive folk-painting of Christ, done by a farmer in the early nineteenth century, which depicts the teaching of children among the lava fields typical of Pingeyjarsysla.

The crowds fell silent when the clergymen and the ghillies, who were serving as pallbearers, carried the coffin outside into the bright sunlight. The family and its close relatives and friends followed behind the pallbearers.

We could hear the river in the stillness. Several buffleheads passed overhead, and we listened to their swift wingbeats. The footsteps of the tiny procession seemed surprisingly loud in the crushed lava of the dooryard. The church doors scraped on the stone sill and their hinges creaked as the pallbearers started into the foyer. One ghillie stumbled beside the coffin and caught himself. The cortege disappeared inside the tiny church, and great flocks of finches chirped past, settling into the hayfields below the cemetery.

The coffin had been milled and carpentered in the ancient shape, tapering gracefully from its head and shoulders to its foot. It was painted white and had an intricately fitted cover. It seemed pale and small in the sanctuary of the tiny church. Since there are no forests in Iceland, it had been built in the woodworker's shop of a dense Karelian pine from Finland. The young pallbearers straightened the blue-and-white flag that covered the coffin, and the ancient farewell to the dead had ended.

There were several clergymen, including the white-haired preacher from the Neskirkju parish. The first minister to offer a prayer was a young nephew of the riverkeeper, whose own parish was on the Straumfjardará in western Iceland. The second minister delivered a brief invocation welcoming the congregation to Neskirkju. There were three poems written for the funeral, and they were read by the poets themselves. Another prayer was offered before a poem was sung by a young farm wife from Akureyri, her remarkably clear and bell-like voice filling the church.

There were two complete eulogies, in a rather unusual departure from custom. The first eulogy was spoken by Jakob Hafstein, the landscape painter who also wrote and illustrated the fishing book *Laxá i Adaldal,* and had been a friend of the riverkeeper over many years. The second was given by Karl Kristjansson, a boyhood companion from Pingeyjarsysla who had been elected to the parliament in Reykjavik.

Hafstein is a short, thick-set man with wavy hair and a large sloping forehead above his heavy-lidded eyes. His jocular face seems haunted by its dour moods, and it seems more jovial than its owner, but Hafstein is a serious man with a strong vein of piety and stiffness mixed with sentimentality. His eulogy for the dead riverkeeper started with a fragment of Baldvinsson's poetry:

Hér vida laxar horplusátt
Harmi er létt ad gleyma
Eg hef, finnst mér aldrei att
Annars stadar heima.

Under the steep walls of the Hvammsheidi, sheltered beneath the wonderful Neshvammur hills, the setting where he first listened to the enchanting lyre music of his river, on the pool he loved best, rod in hand and guiding another fisherman from another country—our friend and riverkeeper fell to the earth and embarked on his final sleep.

There beside his river at Skriduflud, Steingrimur Baldvinsson of Arnesi crossed that other river between life and death. He was the many-sided farmer that lived among you here, but he was not a simple man: familiar poet writing of country things, unsurpassed master of humor and spontaneous poems, teacher of many winters in this valley. This strong and gentle man has left us in this quiet way, and his death makes me remember these lines too:

Here in the slopes of the heath
I walked my first tiny steps
When these dancing nights of springtime
First spoke softly to me.

It has been almost a year since I sat with Steingrimur along the Laxá at Kirkjuholmakvisl, just below the church where we are sitting. We had talked less often these past few years, accepting the fateful currents in our lives, but missing the music of the river. Its lyric songs brought our minds together, slowly and without speaking, through its beauty and its solemn passages. We watched its currents slide past, their fingerprints never changing and forever fresh. Men have always watched its mysteries.

Steingrimur loved this place at Neskirkju. He loved everything about its world, and particularly his river with the Kirkjuholmakvisl at its heart. He worshiped and honored its banks in these heaths and moors of Adaldal.

Would he have chosen another place to die?

Anyone who knew our riverkeeper would doubt that, since the river was his world, and he tells us that in death in the verses I spoke first. It was his fiefdom, and along its grassy banks he had become its king, no less than the greatest of our Viking chieftains in the old sagas.

And there Steingrimur lived and died.

Our country farmer at Neskirkju was undoubtedly our finest child of nature, and the best admirer and skilled observer of its character that I have known. He loved the rhythms of the earth, and he felt and understood them well. He loved our tiny country to the core of his heart, and that love for our country was fiercely held.

Steingrimur was gentle too, and was often completely lost in his thoughts. Some people found him withdrawn and reserved, but such moods could change quickly, and he could be warm and outgoing too. Baldvinsson was a farmer of Iceland in our ancient tradition, his remarkable strength and self-sufficient character mixed with love for art and language. There was an unusual softness too, as well as a fierce temper, which he always sought to control in a gentle manner.

Our riverkeeper particularly loved the spring. He loved its soft evening light and its fresh rebirth of growing things more than anything. Steingrimur rejoiced with spring, glowed and reveled in it like a child. It filled his poetry and his thoughts, and he often walked his river then, enjoying its moors and grassy hollows and heaths. He loved its beautiful hillsides filled with sheep, and its lava fields and grassy islands too. Listen to these lines written there:

> *Laxá in a sun-filled summer night,*
> *Mirrors echoing both earth and sky:*
> *What perfect beauty lies between its hills!*
> *Its bright palette fills my eyes*
> *With the dying light of these rich days!*
> *Our river reflects a many-colored*
> *Spectacle of the world.*

Steingrimur also loved its fishing, but he loved its beautiful salmon more. His discerning eyes could find them in its weedy pools, resting and strongly seeking its currents, struggling to climb its waterfalls and rapids, and he understood the poetry of their journey home.

For many years, Steingrimur was a teacher in this valley, greatly loved and respected. Yet his most powerful lesson took place outside his classrooms there.

It came in the lava fields, where he was walking home after a long day's teaching. The snow collapsed and he fell into a fissure in the lava, and was not found until four days later. But our riverkeeper possessed such strength and warmth of spirit that his life's flame did not flicker. His gentle soul and spiritual force were a lesson for everyone in his valley: that strength and love can duel with death itself.

Steingrimur was often asked to discharge ceremonial duties in Pingeyjarsysla. Such gifted people are often called in such matters. Their days can become crowded with such duties, leaving them less time for friends and families and crops. But such gifts are also responsibilities.

Steingrimur was also the finest fly-fisher in this valley, and from my boyhood years along the Laxá, he was always generous with his knowledge and skills.

Our friend was also a well-known poet, who was constantly willing to share his spiritual wealth, as well as his rich feeling for our language. Poetic language was perhaps the single thing in life that Steingrimur admired most.

Steingrimur was also a gracious host, along with his loving wife, to friends and strangers alike. When I was a mere youth learning to fish his river, he accepted me with open arms, and his heartiness and generosity were a prelude to the affection, trust and friendship to come.

There is sorrow in Adaldal today.

Its beautiful river valley finds itself poorer today than it was last week, because its famous riverkeeper, Steingrimur Baldvinsson, is lying in this church. May our Good Lord watch over this river valley and give his comfort to the widow, Sigridur Pettursdottir, the children and grandchildren, and the entire family. May the Good Lord also comfort the people of Pingeyjarsysla in this time of loss.

Nafni pínu lengi, lengi
Lydir velja heidursess!

The congregation sang a hymn after the Hafstein eulogy, an old melody that every mourner in the churchyard could join, and another clergyman offered a long prayer. The old silver-haired politician rose slowly to deliver his eulogy for the riverkeeper.

Karl Kristjansson was a childhood friend of the river poet, and had spent his adult life in politics. His career had included several local offices in the Pingeyjarsysla district, including three terms as the mayor of Husavik, and had finally carried him to leadership in the parliament at Reykjavik. His seat in the *Althing* there was obviously a source of great dignity and pride. Both Kristjansson and the dead riverkeeper had been founders of a liberal political movement with its roots in the fishing villages and farms along the northern coasts of the country.

The old politician is a somber little man, his blue eyes deeply set behind his steel-rimmed glasses. His bulldog features are weathered from the early years of pitchforks and herring boats and tractors in Pingeyjarsysla, and his white hair is a fierce tangle that seems like a haycock after an early snowfall. Kristjansson stood silently at the lectern, and finally his deep voice filled the church:

Skilled herdsman and farmer, teacher, expert fisherman, and a well-known poet and writer, Steingrimur Baldvinsson lies here in his flag-covered coffin at Neskirkju, where he spent much of his life. Steingrimur will soon sleep in its churchyard, in the arms of our native soil.

We have lost an important and intelligent man, perhaps a pillar in his beloved Pingeyjarsysla over these many years, and now he is gone to join our ancestors.

It is impossible to ask him, as our people have so many times past, for his poetic words or courtly eloquence when the people of these valleys needed to express themselves at meetings and important occasions.

There will be no fresh poems to help us find some happiness and grasp the meaning in our lives. Without this old friend of many seasons, our valley here at Neskirkju seems as empty as it might if God chose to erase his river, and that emptiness touches everyone today.

We would like him back.

But death refuses to excuse anyone, no matter what his importance in our lives, or how much he is loved. We all live in the power of death. Such knowledge is our only certainty. Steingrimur himself put it well in these lines of poetry, strangely written only a few weeks ago about the meadows where he died. It is a prophetic death-poem:

> *Like the salmon*
> *Struggles against my line in this deep pool,*
> *I feel my strength is ebbing now;*
> *No matter how we struggle, we cannot win:*
> *Death never loses a fish.*

The tiny church fell silent after the poem, and we could hear the scuttling and cooing of pigeons under its eaves. Kristjansson continued his eulogy with a brief retelling of the poet's life, and a tracing of his family origins.

Kristjansson spoke of his mother's death in their boyhood years, and the remarkable role the poet's stepmother had played in his youth and early manhood. His stepmother figured in one of his best-known poems, and the old politician quoted a few of its verses. The poet's older brother had been Adálsteinn Baldvinsson, the famous scholar who lived and worked at Árbot. Through his dead mother's family, the poet was also related to Ásgrimur Jónsson, the best-known modern landscape painter in Iceland.

The old speaker observed that the painter's strong brushwork, which echoes the somber moors and bitter lava outcroppings and forbidding mountains, held images not unlike those found in Baldvinsson's poetry. Kristjansson concluded his eulogy with the observation that each of the sister arts is rooted in these soils of tradition and family ties and courage, and added that both salmon fishing and poetry were consistent with the keeper's character.

The eulogies were finished, and the principal clergyman of Pingeyjarsysla offered his final prayer. The entire congregation joined in a last hymn. Their voices soared in the tiny church and its funeral services were over.

The young pallbearers stood awkwardly in the sanctuary, waiting to lift the coffin from its rude catafalque. The flag slipped from its fitted lid, and a small girl rose swiftly and caught it. The ghillies carried the coffin slowly along the aisle, under the brasswork chandelier and past the simple straight-backed pews. The coffin looked surprisingly small in the sunlight.

It was strangely bright in the churchyard. The midday sun glittered on the snowfields in the mountains. The cool wind stirred across the moors, blowing the pale hair of the women and lifting the corners of the flag. Its colors seemed startlingly intense over the chalk-white millwork of the coffin. Cattle looked up as the cortege walked slowly through the churchyard, watched the procession briefly and went back to their grazing. The cool wind stirred again, riffling the still flats along the Thvottastrengur. The young ghillies reached the freshly dug grave, stumbling and shuffling a little among the hummocks and headstones, and two arctic terns scolded them shrilly when they stopped. The burial party ignored the fluttering terns and lowered the coffin to the rough-sawed timbers that bridged the grave. Heavy ropes were looped under the coffin.

The clergyman from Neskirkju offered his graveside prayer. The entire congregation drew close to the grave, gathering among the old headstones and outside the mossy walls of the churchyard. The young farm wife from Akureyri sang a burial prayer from a *sálmabok* written in the seventeenth century:

Lonely flower in the lava fields,
Beautiful and growing in its morning hours,
And is suddenly cut with a scythe,
Losing its leaves and its bright colors:
So human life is ended.

Her soft voice wavered emotionally and fell silent. The clergymen lifted the blue-and-white flag from the coffin, folded it carefully and gave it to the family.

The wind seemed colder as it stirred again through the churchyard. The rough jute ropes strained against the soft-pine corners of the coffin as the timbers were pulled free. The young minister from the parish at Straumfjardará stooped to take a handful of reddish soil from the fresh mound beside the grave.

The ghillies lowered the coffin carefully, and it grated at the bottom like a boat reaching a gravelly shore. The jute ropes rasped and rattled against the coffin when the ghillies stripped them back. The coffin rested safely in the grave. The preacher scattered the handful of lava across the coffin, and it left a harsh, rust-colored stain across its white lid.

The churchyard service was finished too. The family walked sadly back into the tiny church to sing psalms and pray with close relatives and friends. Their halting voices began softly, singing the seventeenth-century hymns of Hallgrimur Petursson, until their voices slowly gathered strength and soared.

It was getting much colder, and fine clouds had started to shroud a feathery, half-rippled sky. Terns screamed above the swift shallows, competing with a choreography of swifts in a swarm of hatching flies. Goats and sheep were foraging in the lava-field pastures. Young boys and white-haired girls were returning to work the freshly cut hay fields. Dry weather is too precious to waste in northern Iceland, even during a state funeral for an important poet, and there was a soft threnody of tractors in the distance. Swans were rooting in the weedy lagoons above the farmstead, where the river stilled its swift currents in the silty backwaters, and the sharp clamor of their quarreling came faintly on the wind.

The churchyard emptied slowly after the funeral. Small groups of friends and salmon fishermen and neighbors stopped to visit together, sharing a mixture of gossip and small talk and sorrow. The people were starting back to the towns and fishing villages and farms of Pingeyjarsysla, and above the psalm singing in the tiny church, they could hear the bitter rhythms of gravelly soil being shoveled into the grave.

Special acknowledgments must be rendered to several airlines for their cooperation in travel arrangements for promotional considerations. Such carriers include the Scandinavian Airline System for its role in several magazine assignments in Norway, Loftleidir for its extensive courtesies over many years of salmon fishing in Iceland, Aer Lingus for its generous help in fishing both Ireland and England, Western Airlines in cooperation with Fishing International and the Bristol Bay Lodge in Alaska, and Braniff International for its skill and support over the past twenty years.

Permission to reprint or modify material written in recent years by the author has been equally generous, and the following publishers are entitled to these acknowledgments: the story called "Thoughts in Coltsfoot Time" appeared under that title in slightly different form in *Fly Fisherman,* volume 7, number 5, May 1976; the article entitled "A Tale of Two Hemingways" was published under that title in a much abbreviated version in *Sports Afield,* volume 175, number 5, May 1976; and similar material simply called "Silver Creek" was published in the *Nature Conservancy News,* volume 26, number 2, Spring 1977; the essay titled "The Trout of the Shamrocks" was extensively changed and retitled "The Maigue River—

the Angler's Eden" in *Sports Afield,* volume 180, number 2, August 1978; the piece titled "The Fly Book" was published earlier in *The Flyfisher,* volume 10, number 3, Summer 1977; several articles have used material on the Henry's Fork of the Snake in eastern Idaho, and "The River of Humility" includes some anecdotal material found in "The Best Dry-Fly Stream in the West" from *Sports Afield,* volume 173, number 3, May 1975, and additional content found in "The Puzzle of the Henry's Fork" in *Fly Fisherman,* volume 10, number 3, March 1979; the article on Alaskan salmon titled "Coho of Kashiagemiut" first appeared in the *Fishing Annual,* volume 1, number 2, Spring 1977; the essay titled "Farewell My Lovely" was published in slightly abridged form under the title "Farewell, My Lovely Gunnison" in *Sports Afield,* volume 177, number 4, April 1977; the chapter called "A Portrait of the Pere Marquette" contains some material published in another article "New Techniques on Fly-Fishing Big Steelhead" in *Sports Afield,* volume 172, number 4, October 1974; the long story titled "Where Flows the Umpqua" first was printed in *Fly Fisherman,* volume 10, number 2, January 1979; the relatively long Norwegian essay titled "The Platforms of Despair" was also first published in *Fly Fisherman,* volume 8, number 3, March 1977; some material found in "Oklahoma Sunshine" first appeared in "The Kingdom of the Trout Is Crowned by the Tetons" in *Sports Afield,* volume 176, number 2, August 1976; and the bonefishing story titled "The Ghosts of Treasure Cay" first appeared under the title "Preacher's Promise" in *Fly Fisherman,* volume 9, number 4, April 1978. All of these stories have been revised and modified, and several pieces have been extensively rewritten for this collection.